A Hoarse Half-human Cheer

an entertainment

X. J. Kennedy

CURTIS BROWN UNLIMITED

ISBN-10: 0692270736
ISBN-13: 978-0692270738

Seraphs and saints with one great voice
Welcomed that soul that knew not fear.
Amazed to find it could rejoice,
Hell raised a hoarse half-human cheer.
— *John Davidson, "A Ballad of Hell"*

Thanks

Thanks to Graham Greene for calling some of his novels entertainments— pot-boiling thrillers which, however complex, he didn't want mistaken for more serious efforts. Not that I have any fiction more ambitious than this, but in following Greene's example I hope to suggest that this isn't a somber literary novel but, perhaps, a diverting read.

Thanks to Gerald Sullivan for scrutinizing my manuscript and its church lore; to Matt Kennedy for refining basketball scenes and for plot-strengthening; to Anthony Palisi, who shared recollections; to Nicole Gabriella Scipione, author of a film script for my children's book *The Owlstone Crown*, who believed I could tell a story; to mystery writer and mortician Tim Cockey, from whose *Murder in the Hearse Degree* I first learned of exploding corpses; to Don and Val Gallie for background information about Secaucus; to friend and writer Howard R. Webber for computer assistance and encouragement; to two late friends for inspiration: George R. Fox, author of *Inside Man*, and James F. Powers, who showed priests to be human; to literary agent Mitchell Waters for his trust, patience, and knowing advice; and not least to Dorothy M. Kennedy, who bore with me and this book and found constructive fault with it.

One

Slowly and carefully, Moon's grandmother dragged the tortoise-shell comb down through the pale yellow hair of the corpse. She inspected her work, licked an index finger, and pasted a wayward curl into place. "Poor cutie. She *would* have to fall for a louse. Just like me and H. G. Wells."

Leaning his chair against a wall in the mortuary basement, Moon Gogarty nearly toppled over. "Gran, you're kidding. You actually knew Wells? H. G. Wells? That wrote *The War of the Worlds*?"

"Did I know him? I sure did. For one night."

Moon stared at his grandmother as though he had never seen her before. "Good gosh, Gran. How did it happen?"

"Oh, I was a little fool, that's all. Wells was one of the events in the Morristown Lyceum Lecture Series. Somebody gave me their ticket. What did I know about him? Nothing, but they told me he was a celebrity. So I went, and I fell for the rat. Must have been his English accent. I hadn't ever heard one before. After his talk I went up and asked him to sign my program. Next thing I knew we were up in his hotel room, him pouring gin down me and working my stockings off."

"What was he like?"

"None of your business."

"I mean——as a person?"

"Mousy little middle-aged man with a shaving brush mustache. Awful blabbermouth. First thing when he woke up in the morning, he started yakking about the future, how all the countries in the world were going to combine into one. But I could tell there wasn't any future for him and me."

"When did all this happen?"

"Back before the big war."

She always called it the big war, Moon reflected. The war with the Kaiser. As if the war with Hitler and Japan hadn't counted.

In the basement the scent of formaldehyde clung to the air. His grandmother kept working the comb. "Poor kid," she muttered. "Lookit here, that tree branch went right through her skull. Too bad. Too bad she took a joy ride with that no-good Randy Harrigan."

Moon stared at the slender girl on the table. Loretta Snow, his date for the junior prom last year. An hour ago he had received a shock. At six o'clock as usual, bringing his grandmother her supper in a paper bag, he had stepped into the cold concrete grooming room to find Loretta stretched out naked, tubes stuck in her jugular vein to replace her blood with embalming fluid, her face locked in a terrified mask. Her forehead looked like snow crust that a footstep had cracked. For an instant his gaze had taken in her puny breasts, the soles of her feet all callused from going barefoot, the matted thicket of her pubic hair. Trembling, he had shut his eyes.

Oh, there had been a time when he would have given anything to see Loretta bare. Lying beside him on the river bank that night, when she had been warm and alive. But tonight he hadn't wanted to look anymore. He had fled the room, waited an hour, and returned when Loretta had been dressed, wearing the frilly blue gown she had worn to the prom.

His grandmother had worked magic. The terrified eyes had been closed, the twisted lips forced shut. Cotton wadding had given the girl a sickly smile. Her forehead had been rebuilt with wax and plastered with pancake makeup and now his grandmother was combing the girl's yellow hair down across the reconstruction. Four gallons of dyed embalming fluid pumped into the carotid artery had given Loretta an unnaturally healthy glow. In life, her skin had reminded him of vanilla ice cream.

"Why is she so pink?" he wanted to know.

"This new mixture. We switched to a different formula after Mrs. Spritzer blew up."

"Blew up?"

"In the cemetery. Blasted a hole in her mausoleum and took off the iron door. They found it six yards away, bent out of shape."

"Mrs. Spritzer did all that?"

"Big stout woman. When they were hauling her out of here, I said to myself, something isn't right. Why, she was gurgling like a tea kettle."

"I didn't know corpses could blow up."

"Only happens when the mortician did a lousy job, or when somebody didn't get embalmed at all. There's a lot of force bottled up in a person. Believe me, James, every dead body is an atom bomb waiting to go off."

Moon felt his stomach trying to gallop into his throat.

His grandmother wiped her lips on a paper napkin and said, "You know Harrigan, do you?"

"Sure. He went to Dover High. He was in our class of '46 till he dropped out."

"What do you bet he was driving drunk," she said. "And what makes me mad, they aren't going to do a blessed thing to him. The cops didn't even arrest him. There was a hearing in front of a police judge and they called it an accident. I think he must of had somebody in back of him paying off the cops."

"Matter of fact," Moon said, "I ran into Harrigan yesterday. When I went to Saint Cash's to sign up for classes."

"Don't tell me a dumb bozo like him is going to go there too."

"Nope. He's got a job driving for the college president. He was wearing a chauffeur's suit, sitting in a 1940 Caddy."

"Holy Mary and Joseph! A Catholic school hired a bum like him?"

"Saint Cash's is hiring anybody these days. They've expanded fast. A year ago they had only a handful of students. Now this fall they'll have over four thousand."

"Where did they get all those from?"

"Ex-GIs coming home with the GI Bill. Government's going to pay their tuition, give 'em money to live on besides. And Monsignor O'Malley, he's the president, wants to make Saint Cassian of Imola's the biggest Catholic college in the world."

"Well I just hope Harrigan don't crash the president into a tree like he did to poor Loretta here. You talk to him?"

Moon fell silent. In his mind's eye he could still see Harrigan's ugly face, Harrigan snarling his best Edward G. Robinson gangster snarl, "Listen, punk, you tell anybody about that girl got killed, it's curtains for you, understand?"

His grandmother set down her comb. "My Lord, James Gogarty, you'd better keep away from that rat. They say he pals around with gangsters. God knows I don't want to see you here, be working on you."

"Don't worry, Gran, I'll watch out."

"Ah, James, the world is full of rascals like Harrigan. I hate to see you leave home and go out in it."

"Well I have to go sometime. Been shaving since I was twelve. I'm six inches longer than my bed."

"But, dear saints, you're still a green kid. I hope and pray it will make a man of you, this Cash College."

That night, in his outgrown bed, Moon fell into a troubled sleep. A bug-eyed Martian was slithering over the Pulaski Skyway, coming across the New Jersey meadows, the way Orson Welles had reported on his broadcast of *The War of the Worlds*. Its suction-cupped tentacles held Loretta Snow all dressed for the prom, her lips parted in a scream. He wanted to run after it, snatch Loretta away, but bullets were whining past his ears. Randy Harrigan, driving hearse number two, was bearing down on him. All of a sudden Mrs. Spritzer blew up with a roar, flinging pieces of herself like shrapnel far and wide.

Two

In the college chapel, Douglas Knox had just whipped through a nine-minute Mass. At seven-thirty in the morning there hadn't been any worshipers except the nuns who taught at the prep school, the school kids compelled to attend, and Sir Terwilliger Feeley, the senile old papal knight. Knox closed the little gold door of the tabernacle, genuflected, dipped fingers into the bowl of holy water, divested himself in the sacristy, and wearing his workaday black suit and black biretta stepped out into the warm September sun.

He was heading for the priests' refectory when the two mugs ambushed him.

His early warning system hadn't kicked in. Even so, before the sapper landed he heard it whistling down on him. He ducked and it missed his head, but caught him on the right shoulder. Thrown off balance, he sprawled on his back on the sidewalk watching the first guy, big heavy character, aim a kick at his crotch with the pointed toe of a boot.

That was the guy's mistake. Knox grabbed hold of the boot and gave a heave and let his assailant's weight propel him into space. The guy crunched down on the sidewalk with a grunt of surprise. Knox scrambled to his feet. The second assailant, taller and thinner, hadn't expected his partner to crash-land, but now he collected his wits and swung at Knox's chest with a fist cased in brass knuckles. This second guy was dumber than the first. Knox tensed, swung his left forearm across his chest and stopped the guy's fist in midair. At the same time he blocked the punch, he drove his left into his opponent's midsection and gave a loud "HAI!" as the blow struck home. The guy went "Oof!" and looked surprised. He lurched backward, but came on again. This time Knox placed his open palms on the guy's shoulders, swung his right leg back, clamped hard on the shoulders and drew the guy's upper body forward, and with another "HAI!" slammed his right knee into the guy's groin. The guy pitched face-down onto the walk. He didn't get up until his partner scrambled over and hauled him to his feet. The big one with the boots had a Guinness belly and a face as wide as from Dublin to Dingle. Knox didn't think he'd seen him before. The lanky one had his face concealed in a black silk stocking, no eyes, just dark dents.

"You working for somebody?" Knox inquired.

The big guy said under his breath, "Next time, padre." The pair of them staggered off.

Knox let them go. Lucky for him they'd been so over-confident that they hadn't been packing. He stood there watching their retreating backs, working his sore shoulder. He must have taken a bruise where the sapper struck, but thank God, his shoulder blade wasn't broken. He brushed dust from his coat, rummaged the grass, retrieved his steel-rimmed glasses.

Stiffly, throwing glances around him as he walked but spotting no further trouble, he got to his office in the new gym building and unlocked the door that said DIRECTOR OF ATHLETICS. Hell's bells. The doorknob came off in his hand. Damned builders. The whole gym had been a fast and sloppy job. Not bothering to flick on the lights, Knox went into the inner office, slumped into his swivel chair, yanked off his Roman collar, and hoisted the half-gallon bottle of John Jamison out of a desk drawer meant for hanging-files. He was nursing a shot and smoking a Gauloise Disque Bleu when Tim Walsh stopped by.

Walsh said, "I saw your door was open. Starting early this morning, huh?"

"Join me?"

"A light one. Not like what you're having." Walsh accepted an inch and said, "Here goes the good of my morning run."

They sipped in friendly silence. Walsh had on a flannel workout suit. He was tall, built thick like a football player. Broad, open face with a permanent half-smile. He was six years younger than Knox, but they'd met back in Darlington Seminary when Knox had begun his studies. Nowadays on Saturday nights, they heard each other's confessions.

Walsh said, "You still smoking those frog coffin nails?"

"Yeah. After a Gauloise, an American cigarette is nothing but sucking wind. Want one?"

"I'll settle for the booze. Pretty good stuff you pour, for a Calvinist."

"That was my grandfather. Born in Scotland, but he converted when he came over here. Fell in with bad Irish company."

"How come you opened shop so early?"

Knox told him.

Walsh gave a low whistle. "Jesus Mary and Joseph."

"All they wanted to do," Knox said, "was throw a scare in me. You don't come at a man with nothing but a sapper if you mean to kill him. You only want to give him a souvenir."

"Know why they went for you?"

"Got a pretty good notion. Yesterday I went to the gym to coach practice and there, big as life, was Cosimo di Montecassino. Game fixer. They say he works for a bird called Ricky Peru. You heard of him? Boss of the North Jersey mob. Anyway I went up to Cosimo and told him if he ever set foot on this campus again I'd shove his necktie down his throat and pull it out his ass. Laughed in my face, the bastard, but he beat it. Then I told the players anybody ever talk with him or any other stranger wearing sharkskin shoes and a diamond stickpin, they're off the team."

Walsh sipped thoughtfully. "OK, I can see why that might annoy the mob. But they resent you bad enough to beat you up? I think the mob avoids publicity. Likes to operate on the Q-T. You know, Doug, you're kind of a celebrity around here. Anything happens to you, it would get in the papers."

"Everybody gets in the papers, eventually," Knox said. "At least on the obit page. Come to think of it, Peru has another reason to have it in for me. When I heard he was putting up money to restore the chapel, I went to the Monsignor and told him we shouldn't take handouts from crooks."

"And what did the Monsignor say?"

"Said it was all rumors. Mr. Peruccese was an upright Catholic businessman."

"How would Peru find out you had his number?"

Knox sat upright. "Hey, that's it. I remember. When I had that talk with the Monsignor, Glauco Vastasi the business manager was in his office."

"You figure Vastasi is in with the mob?"

"Could be. He's Italian."

"Not all Italians are Mafia, Doug. The Holy Father isn't."

"Yeah. Although I hear he rides around in a bullet-proof Rolls."

"So what now? You going to notify the campus cops?"

"Campus *cop*, you mean. The only one there is is old Pat Callahan and that poor son of a bitch couldn't pour piss out of a cowhide boot with complete directions on the heel."

"How about the Dedwood cops? The state police?"

"What could they do? I just have to wait for the bastards to try again. And hope to catch one of 'em."

"But now they're wise to you. They know you can defend yourself. Next time they'll come with artillery."

"So I've got to be ready, that's all."

"Look, Doug, you can't keep your guard up for twenty-four hours a day. If the Newark mob has it in for you, you're up against an army. Why don't you tell the Monsignor about this attack on you. Let him move you out to Darlington for a few months. Duck whoever is after you."

"Go into hiding? Now, at the start of the season? In a pig's ass, Timmy. You know, ever since Spunky Ford got the D.T.'s and I had to take over the coaching, we've had new talent come along that needs cultivating. We've got the strongest squad this place has ever seen. Like this black kid, Pohl. He's a miracle. OK, so Holy Cross might give us trouble—Doggie Julian's a better coach than me— but Loyola, Fordham, and Simeon Stylites ought to be pushovers. Holy Sepulcher will be a tough nut to crack, but we can beat them. I want to stay here and do the job. Right now, I'm kind of necessary."

"Yeah, Doug, but how useful can you be if you're six feet under?"

"Not if I see them coming."

"Good thing you know karate. Zen monk gave you lessons, did he?"

"Not a monk. A local aviation mechanic, black belt, master at *isshinryu*. That's karate Okinawan style. Learned a few tricks from him while I was chaplain at Sasebo after the war ended. Helped pass the time."

"Some guys would have passed the time with a mama-san."

"Never tried it myself."

"You were married once. You're a delayed vocation."

"That's right."

"What happened?"

"She died."

"Sorry, Doug," Walsh said gently. "I didn't mean to stir that up."

"It was a long time ago. We had two good years together. Before we found out she had cancer. Want another shot?"

"No thanks. You won't go see the Monsignor again? Tell him what happened this morning?"

"Naw, he's got plenty of problems on his mind."

Walsh sighed. "Don't I know it. We're in a state of emergency. Not enough classrooms. Staff shortages. My department is so hard up for instructors I had to hire a woman."

"No crap. Don't we have a rule against woman teachers?"

"It's a whole new game."

"Who is she?"

"Name's Aisling. Wife of your pal Vastasi the business manager. She has a master's in biology. Not that it matters, but she's one terrific-looking dish."

"She ought to be. Aisling. You don't say 'azeling,' it's 'ashling.' In Gaelic that means a vision."

"Since when do you know Gaelic?"

"Had an aunt by that name. She was no vision, though, she was a sight. So can your Aisling handle a room full of ex-Marines?"

"She's a pretty tough cookie. Used to be a nurse lieutenant in the WAVES."

"Vastasi have to twist your arm to get her hired?"

"Well, give him credit. He knows an agency that recruits teachers. They've found us a lot of professors from Europe, displaced persons. Not that they'll teach what they know. There's a guy, law degree from Utrecht, going to teach accounting. Another from the University of Krakow is teaching public speaking."

Knox laughed. "I've met the guy. Little fat kielbasa sausage. Can hardly talk English. We really need guys like that?"

"Doug, somebody's got to give these courses. The Monsignor has insisted we take in every qualified veteran. Qualified means he can walk and talk and has the GI Bill. But can these troops crack a book anymore? What do you bet some of them haven't read anything but pass-around fuck stories for the last five years?"

"Like 'The Green Door.' Well that's your problem, you faculty. Educate 'em. All I do is run basketball."

"But I don't like it, Doug. Only last year Saint Cash's was an honest little place that got a few boys ready for the sem. Now overnight we're a huge degree mill with four thousand five hundred ex-GIs, all of 'em expecting to become business administrators."

"So they can make up for lost time. Earn big bucks and drive Caddys."

"Yeah. Should be a wild scene when all of them graduate. Ought to be enough of 'em to administrate every business east of the Mississippi."

Knox sipped the last of his drink. "Anyhow the college is up to its ass in tuition money."

"Sure. But all the gold in the Vatican couldn't make us respectable overnight. So long, Doug. I have to go run the bio department."

Walsh left. Knox put away the bottle, buttoned his collar back on, switched on the office lights. A skinny blonde with freckles plunked down her purse on the desk in the outer office.

"Morning, Maureen," Knox called.

Maureen stuck her head in. "Why, Father, on the job already? This isn't like you, you'll forgive me saying."

"Had a seven-thirty in the chapel. Couldn't go back to sleep. You're early yourself."

"Father, there's a thing you ought to see. Something peculiar. It came yesterday just before quitting time. It didn't come by campus mail, somebody stuck it under the door. Wait a second, I'll get it for you."

She returned holding an envelope with Knox's name pasted on it in letters of different sizes, cut out of headlines from a newspaper.

Knox tore it open. Inside, the message was formed of whole words, clipped out and pasted. QUIT BASKETBALL COACH JOB OR DIE.

Maureen was curious. "What's it say, Father?"

"Just a love note from some admirer. Maureen, honey, I think I'll go over to the refectory and grab me some bacon and eggs."

Three

Where a sign proclaimed in gold letters COLLEGE OF ST. CASSIAN OF IMOLA, the cab hauling Moon and his baggage up from Dedwood station turned in and crunched along a winding gravel drive. On the flat top of the hill it halted in front of a twin-winged Victorian stone mansion.

"Here you are, pal," said the driver. "The house that menstruation built."

Moon didn't wait to ask what that meant. He jumped out, clutching his bulging suitcases. "Where's Temporary Shelter Thirteen?"

The driver frowned at his tip. "Beats me. One of them Quonset huts maybe."

Abandoned, Moon stood cringing under a cold steady rain. Down below, across the road, lay the old campus, four seasoned red brick buildings and a small squat chapel with rose windows. On the hilltop around him, a new campus had started to bloom. There was a brand new gymnasium, a windowless concrete box. The mansion, now surrounded by sheet-metal Quonset huts, looked like a weary old battleship ringed by a convoy of submarines.

As Moon tried to get his bearings, a long black Cadillac sped up the road, scattering gravel. Its driver wore a chauffeur's cap. Randy Harrigan. The car stopped beside him and Harrigan rolled down the window. He craned his head out and glared at Moon.

"You here again, punk? Don't forget what I told you. About watching your big mouth."

The rain was forming a pool around Moon's feet. "Randy," he pleaded, "where's Temporary Shelter Thirteen?"

"Up your ass." Harrigan cranked the window shut and sped away.

At last Moon found his home-to-be. A large tin can balanced on cement blocks, a ventilator pipe thrusting out of its corrugated roof. The front door was ajar. He kicked it open all the way and struggled in and dropped his bags. The heavier bag hit the floor with a crackle of fracturing swing band records. He stood there wiping the rain off his glasses.

"H-h-hullo," a voice stammered. "You must be M-M-M-Mister J-J-James G-G-Gogarty?"

The owner of the voice, like Moon, was a kid just out of high school. He was bespectacled too, with lenses like glass doorknobs. His black oiled hair was parted in the middle. His case of acne had run amok.

"They call me Moon. And you?"

"K-K-K-Konny. That's K-K-K-Konstantinos for short."

Holy Pete, Moon thought. To talk with this kid you'll need time on your hands.

In the middle of the room a kerosene burner was blasting, stuffing the hut full of heat. From the only armchair, a second kid languidly got to his feet. A delicate boy. Pale skin. Wearing light blue bathing trunks.

"Excuse my get-up," he said, thrusting out a limp hand. "Or should I say get-down? It's really warm in here. You may have heard of me. Francis Percival Crews Numeral Three. Grandson of Francis Percival Crews, President

Harding's Assistant Undersecretary of the Treasury. Moon, huh. That's a funny name. Why do people call you that?"

Moon sighed. "Somebody in high school said I looked like Moon Mullins in the funnypapers. And it stuck."

"Oh. And did you know our fellow tenant is the son of a priest?"

"It's tr-true," Konny said. "M-m-m-m-my d-d-dad is Greek Orthodox. In our ch-church p-p-priests can m-m-marry."

Crews sank back in his armchair as if he owned the place. "Now don't think that all this space is just for the three of us. There's one more roommate coming. Konny and I got here first, so we took the back room, away from the heater. But if you want, I'll get Konny to move. Wouldn't you rather come on back with me where it's comfortable?"

"I like it warm," Moon said.

"As you wish." Crews looked disappointed.

"Where's the bathroom?"

"No such luxury. You want to take a shower you go over to Prep School, across the road."

"And if you have to take a crap?"

"Same place. I advise you to get an empty apple-juice bottle for when you want to make wee-wee. You can dump it outside under the bush."

Moon's jaw dropped. "We're supposed to live like this?"

Crews shrugged. "Oh, we simply don't rate. There are only four of us boarders, you know, not counting the lucky fellows on the basketball team. They live over in the mansion with marble bathtubs and Oriental rugs, eating T-bone steak. We have to take our meals at the Prep. And share the bathrooms over there with the altar boys."

"No fooling," Moon said. Saint Cash's wasn't conforming to his dream of a college. "Why did you guys come here anyway?"

"Ch-ch-cheapest pl-pl-place," Konny said. "And my d-d-dad was b-b-bugging me to make a suck—suck—suck—"

"Spit it out," Crews urged.

"Suck—suck—"

"Easy, now."

"CESS of myself!"

"As for me, to come here was inevitable," Crews said. "I went to St. Cassian's Prep. I was valedictorian, so I got a full scholarship to the college. And I'm going to be college valedictorian, too, if you don't watch out."

"Go ahead and be it," Moon said with a shrug. Something told him that this was going to be a long four years.

"Maybe I'll go into the priesthood," Crews said. "Wouldn't I look neat in a chasuble? Except, I don't know. Priests always have such an awful wine breath. So what are you majoring in?"

"Pre-med," Moon said.

"What fun. Be a doctor, you'll get to examine people in the altogether, won't you? You hoping to see some pussies that way?"

Moon thought of Loretta. He didn't want to remember her lying naked on the table. Trying to sound casual, he said, "Oh, I've seen some already. I'm an apprentice mortician."

"A *what?*"

"An undertaker. But you understand, I don't plan to do that for a career. I had to be designated an apprentice mortician so I'd be legal. So I could go into the laying-out room sometimes."

"Sounds juicy. Me, I'm in communications. You'll hear me every night on WDED."

Konny offered sticks of Orbit chewing gum, a wartime brand Moon hadn't seen since V-J Day.

"You still chewing this stuff?" Moon said.

"Yeah. I h-h-hoarded t-t-too much of it. Here, k-k-keep the p-p-pack."

Crews said airily, "I'll bet, Moon Gogarty, you don't know a blessed thing about this college. The Cassian Fathers run it. They're a teaching order, almost as smart as the Jesuits. Do you know about Saint Cassian of Imola? How he was martyred? He was a schoolmaster back in Roman times. His students hated him, so they stabbed him to death with their pens. Any questions?"

Moon thought. "About the mansion. The cab driver that brought me here said menstruation built it."

Crews gave a whinnying laugh. "That's right. It was built by a patent medicine king. He made a fortune out of Feeley's Formula for Female Difficulties. Millions of women bought a bottle every month. Oftener. It was practically pure alcohol, they say."

There was a sudden bang as the door flew wide. In barged a short heavy-set man with brush-cut hair and a black glove on his right hand. His GI trenchcoat dribbled water. He flung a dufflebag down on the floor and stood glowering.

"Jesus Christmas!" he bellowed. "It's raining like a tall cow peeing on a tin roof! Who the hell are you? My room-mates? You squirts look like you only just been hatched."

They introduced themselves, Crews standing up.

The newcomer slumped into the armchair. "Roscoe Beckett," he said, lighting a White Owl cigar with a Zippo lighter. "Call me Sarge. That's what I used to be. Would have made master sergeant if the bastards hadn't kept busting me. Godamighty, how can you stand it in here? This place is hotter than a whore's dream." He reached over and switched off the oil-burner.

"Oh dear," said Crews. "It's going to get chilly."

"Well for Chrissake put some pants on," the Sarge ordered. "What are you anyhow, a frigging queer?"

"Don't you wish it," Crews shot back, in a whisper the Sarge didn't hear. He scampered off to the back room.

"So how old are you?" the Sarge asked Moon.

"Sixteen. But I'll be seventeen in October."

"Huh. Hell of a chance I've got, going to school with high school kids. You twerps will learn circles around me. I been holding a Browning rifle for so long I dunno if I can still hold a pencil. And to graduate they say we got to take twenty-two goddam credits of Scholastic philosophy! So where's my bunk?"

"There's only one left," Moon said. "In the front room."

"Where's the kitchen? Where's the john?"

"There aren't any."

"Come off it."

"You've got to go across the road."

"Holy fucking saints. This looks rougher than the infantry."

Crews came back in a T-shirt and denim pants.

The Sarge blew a smoke ring. "So what's going to happen around here?"

"T-t-tomorrow morning is c-c-convocation," Konny said.

"That's right," Crews chimed in. "President Malachi O'Malley is going to talk. He's the cat's pyjamas. Youngest monsignor in America, and youngest college president."

"Yeah?" said the Sarge. "And I'm the oldest college freshman."

"How old is that?" Moon asked.

"Thirty-six. I was in a long time. Would have stayed in, too, if they hadn't bounced me for disability."

"What happened?"

"This," said the Sarge, yanking off his black glove. Strapped to his right arm was a mechanical hand. It reminded Moon of a steel claw in a coin-operated machine that fished for prizes. The Sarge clenched and unclenched it while his roommates gaped.

"Lost my meat-hook at Anzio," the Sarge said. "Eight-inch shell."

"Germans?" Moon asked.

"Naw. Our own guns."

"That's sh-sh-shitty," Konny said.

"That's war," the Sarge said. "Shit is all it is, mostly."

Crews coughed. "Sergeant Beckett, do you really have to smoke in here?"

"Damn right I do."

"It bothers my allergies."

The Sarge blew another smoke ring. "Well," he said, "your mother-fucking allergies had better get used to it."

Four

Glauco Vastasi, business manager of the College of St. Cassian of Imola, eased back in his swivel chair, his lizard-skin shoes parked atop his wide mahogany desk. In a voice all smiles he crooned into his phone, "Morning, Father Knox. This is your pal Glauco over in the mansion."

Knox gave a snort. "What do you want?"

"Father, it's not what *I* want, it's what *you* want to do. And I know you want to please a very important man, big friend of the college. All you gotta do is set aside a couple of box seats for basketball season."

"Plated in gold? With diamond ashtrays? And who would this king of the monkeys be?"

"I think you heard of him, Father. Newark businessman, gives a lot to charity. Ricco Peruccese."

The phone let out a squawk. "Ricky Peru? I've heard of him, all right. Biggest crook in the state. I just caught one of his weasels sneaking around our gym trying to bribe my boys to throw games."

Vastasi's feet dropped from the desk and hit the floor. "That don't make no sense, Father. Mr. Peruccese couldn't have had anything to do with it."

"No? And right after that, a couple of his thugs tried to do a number on me."

Vestasi did his best to sound innocent. "Father, you don't mean this. Thugs?"

"Yeah. But I did a number on them. Don't tell me they weren't Peru's soldiers."

"That's crazy, Father, you don't mind me saying so. Mr. Peruccese would never stoop—"

"No? I hear he stoops lower than a garter snake's belly. I hear he runs gambling around here, the whores, the loan business. And I think those guys trying to beat me up, that was no coincidence."

"I don't know nothing about none of that, Father. All I know is Mr. Peruccese gave fifty thousand bucks to fix up the chapel. Out of the goodness of his heart. We didn't even ask him for it."

"Big deal. He's trying to buy us."

"Father, you got Mr. Peruccese all wrong. He's a God-fearing guy, devouter than Saint Francis. Nobody's ever proved anything against him. He's had a bad press is all."

"Press? I'd like to press him through a juice-squeezer."

"Listen, Father. Maybe Mr. Peruccese would donate you new uniforms for the team. You want me to, I could drop him a hint—"

"Just drop this whole thing. You tell that son of a bitch go take a leap at a rolling doughnut. Those box seats aren't for sale. They're going to go to people who deserve them."

The phone banged silent.

Vastasi swore. Getting tickets out of Knox was going to be harder than he had expected.

The intercom crackled to life. His receptionist said, "Your wife is here, Mr. Vastasi."

Two seconds later Aisling Weinstein flounced into the inner office holding a bundle in a pink blanket. A wide-eyed infant, mouth plugged with a pacifier.

"Hi, lover, it's me." She planted her short-skirted bottom on Vastasi's desk in the middle of a stack of purchase orders.

Vastasi glared up at her. A bosom that her blouse could barely contain. Tiny sparks dancing in large green eyes. Long auburn hair drawn back in a braid, long white legs in black net stockings.

She pursed her lips and made kissing noises. A wave of violet scent rolled down over him. Facing him, the green-eyed baby stared, lower lip trembling, working up to a bawl.

Vastasi said, "Listen, cunt, I told you never to come in here during business hours. What are you after? Money?"

Rocking the baby in her arms, Aisling sprawled across the desk languidly. "Just imagine I'm Dorothy Lamour in a sarong. Even though I'm nursing. As a matter of fact, lover, I *could* use a few bucks. That crib for Kiki Sue you borrowed from the convent? It was so old the bottom fell out. I gotta go down to Bamberger's and buy one that'll stay together."

"Put it on my charge account. I don't like you handling cash. You run through it like it was water."

Aisling drew herself and the baby upright, her eyes flashing down at him. "That's not fair, Glauco Vastasi, and you know it. I'm the cheapest mistress a man could possibly have. And Kiki Sue is supposed to be *your* child, remember? You'd better treat her right!"

"Keep your voice down! You want the whole goddam world to know?"

"Tough if they did. Gimme your Bamberger's card."

Vastasi fished in his wallet. "Only a crib, you understand. No dresses or jewelry, you hear?"

Aisling hiked up her skirt, revealing white hairless thighs. She tucked the charge card under a garter. "Thanks, Fat Daddy. Just a crib, I'll buy. And maybe some black opera stockings. One of mine is missing. You didn't pinch it to sniff, by any chance, did you, love?"

"Come off it."

"You be home for supper?"

"Aw no, I won't be. I was going to call you. I got to see my wife and kids tonight. It's been so long now, the old lady might sue for divorce. You can get by without me for one night, can't you? Stay home and keep your nose clean. No visitors."

"It'll be hard to do without you, lover, but I'll try. Hey, when you see your wife kiss her for me, will you? Give her a good hot meat injection. She's probably spoiling for it."

After Aisling and her child had left, Vastasi sat there like a man in a trance. He didn't look forward to a night with his wife. Having Aisling for a mistress, pretending they were married, keeping her in a house on campus was like keeping a pet whirlwind. But what the hell. In bed she was sensational.

Miss Prowdy, the gray and withered bookkeeper, minced in with some figures that didn't look right to her. Hadn't the college received more than just a dozen crates of surplus Army compasses? That's what Vastasi had told her to put down in her book, but the government had sent her paperwork for a dozen dozen.

"Sure, sure," Vastasi told her, "make it a gross. I didn't remember right. I got too much stuff on my mind." He waved her away.

What did Miss Prowdy's books matter? They were only for display. The real books Vastasi kept in a dime-store notebook locked in his bottom drawer.

Next came a phonecall from an agitated curate in Chatham. Christ, it was one of those days.

"Mr. Vastasi? I've got a serious problem here. You know all those Navy life rafts you've stored in our church basement? Well they're inflating. Blowing up like balloons. I'm worried they're going to push the windows out. I tell you, this situation is desperate. Can't you send a truck over here and take the things away?"

"Now, Father, calm yourself. It must be the hot weather we've been having. All you got to do is let a little air out of them. They got valves, you know."

"What? You expect me to go around and let air out of hundreds and hundreds of the things? When I agreed to store them for you I didn't know they'd be any trouble. How soon can I get rid of them?"

"In a few days, Father, in a few days. Just hang on for a little while. Right now, I don't have any room for those rafts here."

"Well what am I supposed to do? These things are getting bigger by the hour."

"Look, why don't you call your CYO and Knights of Columbus people? Tell 'em you got an emergency, come over and help you do a little valve-squeezing. They'll do it, right? Father, you'll get your reward in Heaven. Oh, by the way, did you get that check I sent for your Rosary Society?"

The priest soothed, Vastasi told his secretary to put him through to Washington, to the Dominican Embassy. He plunged into animated talk with the Dominican purchasing agent, learned that the deal was clinched. Next week he could ship the life rafts to Ciudad Trujillo.

"Gracias, Señor Ramirez," Vastasi said. "You're getting a real bargain, you know. Only reason I can give you them rafts so cheap is the war is over."

His next visitor was a gangling teen-ager in a chauffeur's black suit that looked too tight for him.

"About time you got here," Vastasi said.

Randy Harrigan stood in front of the desk, shifting from foot to foot. Vastasi didn't invite him to sit down. "What you want to see me for?"

"You know why. I send you on a simple assignment and you fuck up. Father Knox went to work on you buggers, threw you all over the place."

"Who told you that?"

"Benny. He reports to me."

Harrigan looked sullen. "How were we supposed to know the guy did karate? Nobody told us nothing."

"Did he see you? Recognize you?"

"Naaaa, I wore a stocking over my head. A black silk one I pinched off of the girl friend."

A black silk stocking. It struck a faint gong in Vastasi's memory. Could it be—? Naw, that was impossible.

"The trouble is," Vastasi said slowly, "now you've put him on his guard. Next time we try to teach him a lesson, he'll be ready for us."

Harrigan drew himself up with pride. "Any time you want me to whack him just say the word."

"Next time I'll call somebody knows what he's doing. You know, Harrigan, if you're ever going to get anyplace in this organization you got to move a lot faster. When you jump a guy you got to sap his head first."

"That's what we did. It didn't work."

"Another thing. You been sending Knox letters telling him he should quit being coach?"

Harrigan's jaw dropped. "Huh?"

"One letter, anyway. Made of words cut out of a newspaper. That your idea?"

"No sir, I don't know nothing about it. I never sent nobody a letter in my life."

For a moment Vastasi sat back musing. He had heard about the threatening letter only this morning, when Knox's Maureen and his own receptionist Patty had discussed it in hushed but audible voices. If a dumb bastard like Harrigan hadn't sent Knox the letter, who had? Some nut, probably.

He fixed Harrigan with a stare. "Now listen to me, you punk. Keep an eye on Knox. Follow him around, but don't let him know you're watching him. Any time he does something funny, like he's talking to the cops, you let me know. And today I want you to do another thing."

"Like what?"

"Take the van and go over to Saint Whatever-it-is's in Chatham. Priest there's got a basement full of life rafts. Pick 'em up, take 'em down to the Trading Company."

"Aw, that's a goon job. Why don't you get the janitor? This afternoon I got to take the Monsignor over to the Chancery in Paterson to see the Archy."

"Then pick up the stuff after you get back. Who you working for, anyhow, the Monsignor or us?"

"Well it's got to look like I'm working for him, don't it?"

"You better not forget your number one job, you squirt. Remember who your friends are. Didn't we get you off of that rap in Morris County? When you got that girl killed? You didn't get the screwing you deserved. Now get out of here."

Harrigan got.

Then came the last phone call in the world Vastasi wanted. It didn't come in on his regulation black phone, but on the red, white, and blue phone he kept hidden in a desk drawer. A private line nobody could listen in to.

He took a deep breath. "Hello, Uncle Ricky, what's on your mind? You and Tessie, you in good shape these days?"

"Cut the bull," Ricco Peruccese said. "I hear you sent two swat men to rough up the sports priest. I hear he beat the bejesus out of them."

"No, no, Uncle Ricky, he only got away is all. Our boys scared him, they really did."

"Nephew, you are one dumb dodo. What in the fuck did you pull a stunt like that for?"

"He insulted you, Uncle Ricky. I heard him talking to the Monsignor. Called you a crook. And you know, he threw Cosimo out of the gym. I figured you'd want to teach him a lesson, so I—"

"Don't ever make a move like that without you talk to me first. That was stupid. D-U-M-B. To go for him right there on the campus. You could attract attention. We don't want no heat, we got more important things going on."

"All right, all right, Uncle Ricky. But I still think Knox is dangerous. He's making it hard to work with the basketball players, you know? Also, he's smart. He could catch wise to things."

"So I leave him to you, nephew. Just keep an eye on him."

"That's what I'm doing. I got a man assigned to follow him."

"OK, make sure Knox stays sidelined. He starts nosing around, let me know, I'll take care of him. Ram a piece of pipe up his ass. And Glauco, did you get those box seats for me?"

"I'm working on it, Uncle Ricky. Don't you worry, by game time you and Tessie will be right there front and center."

"We better be. How's the war surplus business?"

Vastasi brightened. This was his chance to redeem himself. "Good news, Uncle Ricky. The Dominicans are taking the life rafts for forty grand." Vastasi made a mental note to hold back five grand for himself.

"Is that enough? Peron wouldn't pay more?"

"Naw. I tried him. Besides, the Dominicans are easy to deal with. With Peron, you always got red tape. Trujillo is our best customer. I figure he's planning to invade Haiti, take over the whole island. And he's going to buy them Browning automatic rifles from us, too. Eighty cases."

"How many will that leave us?"

"Twenty, thirty. But maybe we can sell 'em to the Haitians, the rich ones that got their own army. We'll tell 'em about Trujillo planning to invade. They'll need guns to fight back."

Peru chuckled. "Yeah. I like that. We sell to both sides. Let 'em shoot it out."

"I go to Washington again this week, I'll say the college needs more rifles for the drill team. And I'll drop by the Haitian embassy."

"Don't be easy on them. Get the same price we get from Trujillo."

"Sure, sure, Uncle Ricky. Ain't it beautiful? The government gives us all this stuff for nothing, and we turn around and sell it for big bucks. Another thing—the teacher recruiters are bringing in the hay also."

"Yeah? That employment agency of yours—that shit is worth bothering with?"

"Is it ever. All it takes is we plant two guys down on the pier in New York, meet the ocean liners coming in full of displaced persons. Plenty of professors out of work in their old country. We meet 'em right there on the dock, sign 'em up to teach business courses, science, any goddam thing. They give us their first month's pay and twenty per cent every month after."

"That's a deep cut. These smart guys don't know no better?"

"Well what are they going to do? They land in this country, they're hard up, need a job, they don't know shit about how to get one. And there's somebody on the pier steps up and hands it to them."

"How many of these guys you sign?"

"Thirty so far. College pays 'em a grand a month, so right away that's thirty thou for us."

"Not bad."

"And that ain't all. I got Lew the Shark working on a student loan program. The college has four and a half thousand vets, lot of 'em married with kids. The government don't cover all their bills. We got a whole slew of customers ripe for picking."

"All right, I like it. Keep me posted, nephew. Sometimes I think your head ain't fat all the way through."

Five

The idyll had begun in terror. Flying to Iwo Jima on a mission to evacuate the wounded, she had heard a burst like hail. Bullets were striking the fuselage, making loud twangs. A Japanese Zero had spotted them and they were getting strafed. Their bulky old Douglas DC3, converted to a transport, was a flying target. It didn't have any hospital markings. From the ground came the low bang of antiaircraft fire. Then there was a colossal boom. The plane staggered as if kicked by a giant.

"Left engine's hit!" somebody yelled.

The Zero, seeing them stricken, had turned tail and gone. Slowly losing altitude, they had managed to stay airborne for another twenty minutes, then pancaked down in the Philippine Sea. She could still hear the splash, feel the jolt as the big plane hit the water, see the five of them crowding frantically into the one inflatable boat, the slim wiry pilot and the big Texan co-pilot taking charge, the two hospital corpsmen paddling, and she, WAVE Lieutenant Aisling Weinstein in the stern, riding serenely over the water like Cleopatra on her barge.

They had come down a few hundred yards from a white sand beach on a ring-shaped atoll that had palm trees and in its center a broad lagoon. Kikisu, the atoll was called, though it didn't appear on any map. They had learned its name from two fishermen who had stopped by in a tiny sailing sloop and paid them a visit. Bronzed, friendly guys, white-toothed grins. Didn't speak any language they knew, but led them to a bubbling spring, showed them how to catch fish, even gave them a line with a hook on the end of it. The co-pilot had had a lighter that still worked and they had built fires of driftwood to roast little pink-fleshed fish that tasted like cashews.

For a month she had reigned over the atoll, the men vying to bring her the most succulent cracked coconuts. The tension of their brush with death had snapped, and so had military discipline. Except that at first she had followed the chain of command, taking on the pilot, next the co-pilot, then the enlisted men. Skinny-dipping in the lagoon, guys swimming up from behind, fondling her with warm hands, planting long kisses on her neck and shoulders. Sprawling on the coral sand under palm fronds that stirred in the breeze, laced up with one good-looking man while another with upright cock awaited his turn. What the hell, maybe they'd never be rescued, maybe the Japs would find them. They might as well make hay. It had been the happiest month of her life. When at last their bonfire had attracted a passing reconnaissance plane, she had almost wanted to cry.

Two weeks later, a missed period. Who was the father? Could have been anybody. She had decided to have the baby, name it after the atoll. Medical discharge with combat bonus and pension for service-related disability.

In the next room, Kiki Sue was bawling. No going back to sleep now. Aisling shoved aside her memories. She thrust one long white leg out from under the covers, followed it with the other, and went to the crib. Randy Harrigan grunted and rolled over, hugging his pillow tight.

Cradling the child in her arms, saying, "Aw what's the matter, honeybun," she planted her bare bottom in the rocking chair, brushed a loose strand of reddish brown hair out of her eyes, grasped one purple-veined nipple between two fingers. The baby's head, zeroing in on food, wobbled from side to side. The chair rocked to and fro, emitting squeaks. The baby chomped hungrily.

In bed, Harrigan growled, "Your baby's worse than a goddam alarm clock."

"You ought to thank God I have a baby, creep. If somebody didn't wake you up you'd sleep till noon. Anyhow, I thought you wanted to get up by six-thirty."

"Don't rush me, honey. I rouse slow."

Kiki Sue sated, Aisling placed her on the changing table, making clucks and coos. She opened the safety pins of a soiled diaper, set it aside to be rinsed, swabbed the little bottom with oiled cotton, pinned a fresh diaper into place, snapped on rubber pants. Then she nuzzled the child, murmuring pleasantries, and lay back down on top of the covers like a Goya nude, the baby face up in her arms.

Harrigan needed talking to, or else he'd go back to snoring. "Saw a friend of yours yesterday," she said. "One of your buddies from Dover. Signed him up at registration. He's going to be in my class."

Harrigan snorted. "Not pretty-boy Gogarty."

"The same. He's cute."

"You think anything is cute that has balls." Harrigan sat upright, reached for a pack of Luckies, shook one free, poked it between thin lips. "Gogarty's a little piss-ass son of a bitch," he said.

"What do you have against him?"

"Knew the bastard in high school. Used to suck up to all the teachers. They made a pet of him. Want a drag?"

"Want one of my own, creep. But not now. Never smoke when I'm holding Kiki Sue, might get ash in her eyes."

Harrigan lay back, making the end of his cigarette glow red. Like the child in Aisling's arms, he felt satisfied. His right hand stole out and cupped her pubic zone. "So when can I come over again?"

"Not till I ask you. Vastasi sleeps here most nights."

"Where's he go the other nights?"

"What do you care? Sometimes he sees his wife, sometimes he's away on business. So why do you have to start work so early today?"

"Got to polish the Monsignor's car, run some errands. Would you believe it, I gotta drive all the way down to Manasquan for crabmeat. What they sell in the fish market ain't fresh enough. Tonight the Monsignor's throwing a little dinner party for Ricky Peru."

"Oh yeah. He's Glauco's uncle."

"Don't blab it around, but he's boss of the Newark mob. I don't think the Monsignor knows that. All he knows is Peru gives the college plenty of dough."

"That's nice. Maybe if I gave him a little nookie he'd lay a few bucks on me."

Harrigan inched close. "Yeah? I bet Peru couldn't give you a thing like this." He drew her hand over on top of him.

"I've had worse," Aisling said. "But, kid, the trouble with you is you're green. Don't know any techniques. Obviously you've never screwed anything but high school girls before. O Mother Mary, deliver me! Nymphomania is a terrible cross to bear!"

"Aisling, you're really something, you know it? What did you say you're teaching them GIs? Biology?"

"That's right."

Harrigan snorted. "The birds and the bees, that what it's about?"

"And more. You wouldn't understand."

"Sheeee-it."

"Too bad you dropped out of school. Maybe now you wouldn't be a lousy crabmeat-fetcher."

"School wasn't getting me noplace," Harrigan said. "And I don't just drive the Monsignor's car, you know. That's only part-time. I've got other, more important interests."

"Like pussy."

"Like a whole nother career."

"You better get out of here. Glauco was over in Orange seeing his wife last night, but pretty soon he'll be dropping by for breakfast. And I've got to get me ready for opening convocation."

"How bout a little blow job before I go? You can forget about Glauco for a few minutes. And your goddam kid."

Aisling's fist slammed into his jaw.

"OW!" he said. "Whad you do that for?"

"Don't damn Kiki Sue. And besides, I'm still mad at you for swiping one of my good stockings."

"So what if I did? I brought it back, didn't I?"

"Yeah, with a run in it. What did you do, you pervert, chew on it?"

"Naaa, pulled it over my head when—oh, never mind."

"Go on, get out of here. And take that cigarette butt with you. Be a hell of a thing if Glauco found it in the ashtray. By the way, who's Loretta? You kept talking in your sleep about some Loretta."

Harrigan scowled. "Just a babe I knew in high school. What's the matter, honey, you jealous? She ain't even alive anymore."

Six

Knox had to line up with the procession waiting to march into the gym. The generous donors, businessmen the college wanted to flatter, fell into place ahead of him. He found himself standing behind a short, swarthy, balding guy in a blue silk suit with a violet shirt and a red tie emblazoned with gold unicorns.

The guy turned around and peered at Knox through bifocals that made his eyes bulge like a frog's. His head sprouted out of his body with no neck in between. The white line of an ancient scar zigzagged across his forehead as if someone had tried to jimmy off his scalp.

He stuck out a hand weighted with gold rings. "Father Knox, that right? I'm Ricco Peruccese."

Knox let the hand dangle. "Oh yeah. Ricky Peru. I've heard of you."

Peru buried his hand in his pocket. For an instant Knox expected him to bring it back out with a gun, but instead he cracked a smile. Gold front tooth, a tiny diamond in it.

"You and me, Father, we're old buddies. Didn't we march together in the Holy Name parade in Union City last Saint Paddy's Day?"

"We could have," Knox said.

"Going to have a great team this year?"

"Might."

"That colored boy, what's his name, Pohl, he going to develop?"

"He ought to."

Peru's grin persisted. "You always this talkative in the morning, Padre? You know, why I'm here is I gave this college a sweet piece of change. I'm big on good causes. Your department, now, I bet you got a few needs?"

"Sure. But if we need anything we'll just add another game to the schedule."

"Chickenfeed, Father. Maybe I could come up with some real dough for you. Like, say, some athlete scholarships. Certain boys you want to bring here, give 'em new cars."

"Mr. Peruccese," Knox said evenly, "there are plenty of people ready to hand me money—ticket scalpers, talent scouts, people looking for favors—but I don't like taking their dough. Some of it might have dirt on it."

Peru's laugh came out a croak. "That's funny, Padre, real funny. You're a card."

Knox was about to say he didn't like finding Cosimo di Montecassino in the gym and he didn't like mugs in stocking masks trying to beat him up. See how Peru took that. But just then a blast of music shot out of the gym. The procession lurched and stepped off, with the college president, Monsignor O'Malley, in his scarlet cape leading the way.

Tense with anticipation, Moon had got up with the sun. The first day of his college career! He'd found the Sarge up already ("Never sleep late—if I do I keep dreaming I'm back on Anzio") and they had brewed instant coffee on the Sarge's illegal hot plate using tinfoil G. Washington Aces.

Then he and the Sarge, Konny and Crews had wedged their way into the Prep School bathroom. All the preppies were brushing their teeth. Moon had asked a kid what time was breakfast—"Jeepers, mister, you new here? Not till eight o'clock. They starve us till after Holy Communion."

By and by the shower stalls had emptied and they were able to take their turns. Moon noticed Konny keeping his arms in front of him, trying to hide a tattoo on his chest. A mean-eyed American eagle, just a body that didn't have any wings. "H-Hurt like hell g-g-getting it," Konny had admitted, "so I never went b-b-back for the rest of it."

Breakfast in the school cafeteria. Lumpy oatmeal, toast, orange Kool-Aid, no coffee, milk. "Growing boys shouldn't drink coffee," the nun on the serving line had explained. The Sarge, maneuvering jelly onto his toast with his mechanical claw, wouldn't let Moon help him. Crews pointed out which nun was which. Sour-looking Sister Mary Immaculata was the one to blame for breakfast. Moon found himself staring at Sister Margaret Rose, the youngest nun, a beauty—white hands, smooth round face, the only features that her cowl and habit left exposed. Instantly, Moon's thumb had drawn an imaginary circle around her face, a secret ritual he always performed when he first saw a woman he would willingly fuck. Then a pang of guilt had darted through him. For Christ's sake, she was a nun! Down, boy.

The four roommates had spooned oatmeal in silence. Withered old Sister Dionysia, the Prep School principal, paused at their table and beamed down at them. "Are you enjoying everything, dears? Have a blessed day."

They hiked to the new gymnasium. This morning the hilltop campus had been transformed into one vast traffic snarl. The solitary campus cop was waving the commuter students into freshly created parking lots. Thousands of cars, their drivers honking and shouting, forced their way in onto acres of lawn, jostling for space and shredding the grass with their tires.

"Migod," said the Sarge, "what a shit pie. That cop could fuck up a two-car funeral."

At the gym Moon and his roommates claimed seats in the sixth row. After a long wait they watched the academic procession file in, while the Prep School band struggled through "Holy God, We Praise Thy Name" and the "Academic Festival Overture." On the heels of President O'Malley and his vice-president, the Right Reverend Augustine Hoar, came a couple of tottering octogenarians. The old man wore a get-up like that of some European count, a glossy black uniform with braided cuffs and a stripe running down the side of his trousers. He kept tripping over a sword in a golden scabbard. His companion wore a flowing white dress and a round-brimmed bonnet like a golden halo. Both had to be helped up onto the stage, where they dithered and doddered until persuaded to sit down in their chairs.

"See those two old coots?" said Crews. "Sir Terwilliger Feeley and Dame Millicent. He's a papal knight of the Order of Saint Gregory the Great and his wife is a papal dame. Like I said, they gave the college their eighty-acre estate, with their old family mansion for an admin building. They get to keep living in it till they die. Shouldn't be too long now."

"How do you get to be a papal knight?" Moon wanted to know. For answer Crews pinched two fingers together as if counting cash.

The other generous donors came strutting in, trailed by members of the administration. Father Douglas Knox entered with loping stride, mouth fixed in a scowl, and claimed his chair on stage.

At the end of the line marched the faculty, trooping into rows of metal folding chairs on the main floor. Knox recognized them all. First came the teaching priests: Father Methodus Sargasso, the fat little professor of logic; Father Boniface Scully, professor of anatomy, a gray, shrunken death's head of a man; kindly old Father Samaritan Goodminton, professor of ethics; lean, ascetic Father Jasper Fry, professor of theology; Father Hoke Jim Honeycrutch from Georgia, visiting professor of business administration; young Father Timothy Walsh, assistant professor and department chairman of biology; and Brother Dermot Drumgoole, a gray-haired monk in an olive-green robe tied with a rope, instructor in apologetics.

Then the laymen entered, capped and gowned, most of them newcomers whose names Knox didn't know. First came department heads: Praxiteles Moss, Feeley Professor of Ancient History; Dr. Maximo Bopp, doctor of veterinary medicine, professor of history; Michael O. "Mickey" Spillane, Joyce Kilmer Professor of English; S. Blowden Lowndes, sitter in the endowed Chair of the Sacred Blood, professor of advertising; slim, debonair Booker T. Cook, the token Negro, professor of marketing; and Bonzo G. Hookey, professor of education, a withered veteran of nine school systems. Then followed a long line of displaced persons, among them Raoul Pigout, instructor in French and Wladislaw Wyszynski, instructor in voice and diction. Bringing up the rear came the lay members of the philosophy department, young men given jobs after their expulsion from the seminary for drinking or sodomy.

In the faculty parade, the center of all eyes was a cream-skinned, red-haired young woman with full lips, who wore her mortarboard cocked at a jaunty angle. Moon recognized her at once. She was the same stunning professor who had signed him up for classes. To get a clearer view, he took out his handkerchief and polished his glasses. His thumb revolved, drawing a double circle around her face. As a candidate to be fucked she deserved high priority.

The Sarge gave a low whistle. "I seen that babe before. I could hunker down with her anytime."

"Better not go near her," Crews put in. "She's married to Mister Vastasi the business manager. He's one tough customer."

Moon's heart leaped. "Oh boy! I'm going to have her for biology!"

"Lucky bastard," the Sarge said. "Think I'll switch to pre-med like you."

The student body remained on its feet until all the procession was in. Most had no choice, for there were not enough seats. Veterans in GI jackets lined the walls. In the packed gym, which still smelled of varnish, each man had to struggle for his share of oxygen.

"Be seated," commanded the Reverend Vice President, and those who could do so, did.

The president began his welcome. This was the first day of a glorious new era. St. Cassian of Imola's would soon become the largest Catholic college east of the Mississippi. Already, more than four thousand five hundred veterans had enrolled in this freshman class. Obviously, there would be growing pains, little inconveniences which he knew the students would endure. The president congratulated them on their wisdom in choosing a Catholic college. St. Cassian's would provide them not only with business skills, but with a firm grounding in ethics and morality.

As the president orated on and on, Moon withdrew into his favorite world of dreams. No longer was he a helpless freshman in a sweltering college gym, he was Glenn Miller up on a bandstand, gazing out over an adoring crowd while his band swung powerfully, driving through "Little Brown Jug." He took a solo on his imaginary trombone, to a thunder of applause. Titsy teen-age girls in tight sweaters jitterbugged past, throwing him screw-me smiles.

On stage in his hard metal chair, Douglas Knox shifted from one buttock to the other. He felt himself on display. Monsignor O'Malley introduced the dignitaries on stage in order of their generosity. After Sir Terwilliger and Dame Millicent, the next most prominent donor was Mr. Ricco Peruccese, chairman of the Latin American Trading Corporation. This worthy had offered to provide the college chapel with a much-needed restoration. The Peruccese Rose Window would be dedicated next spring by the Governor of New Jersey. Peru took his time getting to his feet. He reminded Knox of Mark Twain's celebrated jumping frog of Calaveras County, loaded with so much buckshot that it could hardly move. He shuffled forward to let the President pump his hand.

Knox squirmed in his chair, crossing and re-crossing his legs. What in hell was the Monsignor doing, buttering up this crook? Peru, face dripping with smiles, went back to his seat. Knox noticed that, unlike his own, it had been favored with a cushion.

Packed thick with bodies, the balcony looked in danger of collapse. Today was the first real test of the new gym's hurry-up construction. Knox scanned the walls, looking for indications of strain—plaster cracking, anything out of line. So far, OK. But he was worried. When basketball season started, the building would have to hold hundreds of tons of crowd.

His gaze dropped to the seated faculty, passed along male faces. Bored laymen, bunch of paycheck cashers. But on the far right of front row sat the most appetizing woman Knox had ever seen. Cream-colored skin, long auburn-red hair, moist lips, breasts that looked hand-sized even through her academic gown. Not a movie-star type, maybe a few pounds too heavy, and yet she fitted Aquinas's definition of beauty. She had all three elements: wholeness, harmony, and radiance. She sat at ease, one bare foot with red-nailed toes creeping out from under her academic gown. Must have kicked off her shoes. White teeth flashing now, turning to share a laugh with the guy next to her. He knew who she must be. Vastasi's wife, the new biology teacher. Lord, what would she be like to be married to? Knock that off, he told himself. Don't ever think in that direction. How could a priest live with a woman? Sorry, God, I can't do nine o'clock Mass, Johnny has an earache and I've got to take him to the pediatrician.

All of a sudden the Monsignor was pronouncing his name, his title—Director of Athletics and Acting Coach of Basketball. Knox stood up, strode to the microphone, and glared out over the crowd.

"Some of you are here to learn," he began, "and some of you have come to watch the games."

An approving roar.

"I think there's going to be plenty to satisfy you both," Knox went on. "In the past, Saint Cash has put a respectable team on the court, but it's never set the world on fire. This year we're going to burn hell out of it."

He pivoted and resumed his seat to an ovation that shook the walls.

By the time the band in Moon's head had swung through "Tuxedo Junction," the ceremony was over. Outside, the student body stood about in huddles, gulping fresh air with relief.

"Jesus," one veteran complained, "for that bunch of bullshit I had to come in today? That wasn't worth getting a baby-sitter."

"Yeah," said another, "the only good speech was that short one about basketball."

Moon shuffled away in a daze. In closeup on the screen of his mind still gleamed the moist red lips of his professor of biology.

Seven

"Father, I hate to tell you," Maureen said, "but it's given up the ghost."

At his desk, Knox lowered his *Daily Racing Form* and scowled up at his secretary. "What has?"

"My typewriter. Space bar's jammed, roller's out of whack, and for goodness sake, the typefaces are so worn you can't make out the letter E."

"Why didn't you tell me sooner. I'd have given it extreme unction. OK, I'll requisition a new one."

"Call Mr. Vastasi. Patty in the business office told me they just got in a whole truckload of Underwoods. Nice new machines left over from the war."

"So that's it, you scheming bitch. You want something new and shiny. That's why all of a sudden your old machine got the collywobbles."

"Father, you call me names one more time and I'll--- I'll take your smelly whiskey and pour it all over your chair cushion."

"You do and I'll make you sit in it. Maybe that would sweeten that Irish ass of yours."

It was the usual sort of repartee they started the day with. A contest they both enjoyed.

Maureen shot back, "This Irish ass should take a squat on your filthy mouth."

"Better watch it. This mouth can bite, you know. Not that your butt couldn't use reducing."

"Oh, it's hungry for meat you are, are you, you heathen cannibal? Listen to the dirt coming out of the mouth of a priest! To hear you talk is worse than smelling cowflops!"

"Yeah? A cowflop would smell a lot better than that cheap perfume you have on. Where did you get it? Woolworth's?"

"Lord forgive him," Maureen said, rolling her eyes toward Heaven. "It's Coty, four dollars and a half. I ought to go find a dog turd in the street and stuff your nose with it."

They both exploded in laughter.

"OK, OK, enough, you win," Knox said. "One of those typewriters has your name on it."

He gritted his teeth and dialed. "Vastasi? Knox. Understand you've got new typewriters up the grommet. How about sending over one for my secretary?"

Vastasi sounded grim. "Who told you that, Father? We don't have any typewriters."

"Is that a fact? I have it on good authority you just got in a load of Underwoods free from Uncle Sam. Or were they popcorn poppers?"

"I'll have to check into it, Father. Call you back. Oh, by the way, about those two box seats for Mr. Peruccese—"

"Forget about that. I'd like a typewriter and I'm not swapping you anything for it."

After he and Knox had bashed down their phones, Vastasi sat for a moment, seething. Then he stalked into the outer office to confront his receptionist.

"Patricia, did you blab to anybody about them new typewriters?"

The young woman looked crestfallen. "Why no, Mr. Vastasi. Unless—maybe I mentioned it to Maureen, Father Knox's secretary."

The point of one lizard-skin shoe slammed into the front panel of her desk with a deafening bang and left a top-to-bottom crack in it. The receptionist shrank back in consternation.

"Hell!" Vastasi roared. "Didn't I tell you never to tell nobody-—-nobody—about the stuff we get? This is confidential business, girlie. Word gets out we can get free stuff from the government, every piss-ass school superintendent in the country will be down in Washington with his hand out. And you had to spill it to that gossipy bitch in Knox's office! From now on, sister, you keep your lip buttoned or I'll make it good and fat for you."

Patty's eyes widened in terror. "Yessir. I'm so sorry."

Vastasi went back inside his office, slamming the door so hard he rattled the glass. There was only one way to get Knox off his back. He dialed the Impeccable Typewriter Company.

"Hey, Solly? Glauco Vastasi at Saint Cash. You know that load of typewriters we just sold you? I got to have one of them back. Little problem in bookkeeping. You were only supposed to get thirty-nine of 'em."

Sol Fine sounded incredulous. "Since when? Forty typewriters we paid for, forty we got. Glauco, what shit you giving me? Since when is a deal not a deal?"

"Solly, pal, I'm really sorry. Just deliver one of them Underwoods to the Saint Cash athletics office. I'll mail you a refund. Remember what a bargain you got on those machines? You want more bargains like that?"

"Nobody's cheaper than you, Glauco. But what a way to do business. You're an Indian seller, am I right? You sell me something, then you want it back."

"Listen, Solly, you're getting first dibs on the next load of adding machines. And if you want in on a great jeep deal—"

The merchant appeased, Vastasi sat back and let his breath out slow. Close call. This could have been a problem.

Maureen's phone jingled. "Hey, Maureen honey, Glauco Vastasi. Tell Father we found some stuff I didn't know about. Your brand new typewriter is on its way. You're welcome, baby. Think nothing of it. Just let me know anything else you need. Like a little expert loving."

"No thanks," she said. "All I need is a typewriter."

When she told Knox that Mr. Vastasi was sending the typewriter, he gave a disgusted snort. "Yeah? That's a switch. At first he didn't know anything about that load of machines. Or so he said."

Knox fell silent, thinking. This whole incident seemed suspicious. Why would Vastasi pretend he hadn't got those typewriters?

An hour later Maureen strode into the inner office, bearing a package wrapped in brown butcher paper. "Father, I think you'd better look at this. Somebody must have sent you some fish in the mail. It's starting to smell."

She went out, holding her nose. Knox inspected the package. It was the size of a brick, addressed in cut-out letters to FR. KNOX. No return address.

He unwrapped it carefully, half expecting it to blow up in his face. Inside lay the body of a small brown rabbit, throat slit, fur clotted with dark blood. Stuck to the rabbit's body with hardened blood was a sheet of paper. A new message had been spelled out in words clipped from a newspaper.

QUIT COACH JOB. THIS COULD BE YOU.

For a long time Knox sat there staring. Then he made the sign of the cross.

Eight

As five hundred veterans crowded into the chapel, life-sized statues looked down in agony: the thorn-crowned Savior, the sorrowful Virgin, and Saint Cassian of Imola, the pens of his students implanted in his breast as thick as quills on a porcupine.

Moon and Konny squeezed into the last remaining pew. They had to crane their necks to see around a steel pole propping the roof. A frail gray bald-headed man in a white jacket had planted himself at a lectern in front of the altar. Doctor of Veterinary Medicine Maximo Bopp. He kept glancing up at the roof as if expecting it to fall.

In a shrill thin voice Bopp began. Too bad, but the shortage of classrooms had compelled the class to meet in this holy place. Textbooks, too, were scarce. Naturally, when a million veterans suddenly went to school, the printing presses couldn't keep up. Only two copies of their United States history book had arrived. He would place one on reserve in the library, where they could take turns reading it.

"Can't hear you!" a student bawled.

"LOUDER!" called another.

"Hey Boppy boy, get up in the pulpit, why don't you?"

Goaded, Bopp mounted the steps to the pulpit as though he were climbing Mount Everest. At the top, panting, he beamed out over the crowd. "Obviously not all of you will be able to read the textbook, so I'll read you the first chapter myself."

The class stirred uneasily. Newspapers were unfolded. Four veterans sitting on the floor broke out cards and began a poker game. One joker had a tube of rubber cement. He squeezed it, shooting gobs of white sticky stuff at other students' flies. Konny tried to take notes, but the dim light of the only chandelier made it impossible.

Moon retreated into his dreams of leading a famous swing band. He was Benny Goodman doing "Stomping at the Savoy", clarinet running up and down the scales. Then he was Gene Krupa doing "Sing, Sing, Sing," taking an endless drum solo, stoked on reefers, knocking out rimshots while the crowd hollered, "Go, Moon! Don't stop now, Moon!" and stood on the tables and cheered.

While Bopp droned on, the class gradually shrank. Two or three at a time, students got up and walked out, letting the chapel door swing shut with a boom.

When the next hour began, Moon and his roommates sat in the gym's crowded auditorium waiting for religion class with Father Knox.

"Piss and little puppydogs," said the Sarge. "This ain't anything like how I figured college would be. No boolah boolah, rah rah, coon-skin coats, no Wiffenpoofs raising their beers on high, shit like that. Which is OK, who needs it. But I thought at least there'd be babes. Sweethearts of Sigma Chi."

"Well you should have gone to a co-ed school," Crews said.

"Don't think I didn't try. Put in to Rutgers, Drew, Montclair State, but they wouldn't accept my ass. Couldn't get in noplace but here."

"You're lucky."

"You think so? I only seen one good-looking broad on this campus. And she's a teacher."

"You mean Mrs. Vastasi," Crews said.

"Damn right. That babe is one loaded piece. Built like the frigging frigate Constitution."

Moon piped up proudly, "I've got her this afternoon."

"I could take her any time," the Sarge said.

"Women don't interest me," Crews said.

"What does?" Moon asked.

Crews rolled his eyes skyward. "Oh, I don't know. Maybe union with the Mystical Body of Christ."

"Yeah," Konny put in, "or with the b-b-body of some altar b-boy."

"Oh, you dirty—!" Crews said in a huff, swatting Konny with his printed list of where the classrooms were.

At last a lean, wiry priest strode down the aisle. All eyes were on him as he made an acrobatic leap to the stage.

"At ease," he barked. "I'm Knox. Father Knox to you. This is Religion One-oh-one. Any lost soul think he's in organic chemistry?"

Moon hadn't paid attention to Father Knox yesterday in the gym, but now he inspected the priest closely. Steel-blue eyes behind steel-rimmed glasses. Short black hair, sharp-featured face, nose and chin that might have been hewn with a hatchet.

Knox skipped the roll call and began to talk, using the caged lion technique, pacing from one side of the stage to the other. Pivoting on one heel and pacing back again. He flicked a lighter at a Gauloise, drew smoke, and blew.

"That No Smoking sign means you," he said. "I'm exempted. Now as maybe you know, this course is required for everybody. Catholics, Jews, Hindus, Protestants, atheists, even Republicans. If any of you non-Catholics can't stand it, let me know and instead you can write a ten-page paper about what you believe and I'll give you credit for the course. But if any of you slimy Catholics tries to pull that line on me, I'll flunk your ass. Got that?"

Knox traced the beginnings of the Church from the first Papacy. Christ told Peter, upon this rock I will build My church and the gates of Hell shall not prevail against it. "Talk about a license from on high. Any questions?"

One hand went up.

"Father, if the Church was founded on a rock, how come some of them later rocks were pebbles? You know, popes that slept around? Poisoned their enemies?"

"Good question," Knox said. "Mother Church has had to carry her message in some pretty frail vessels. Popes, of course, are sinners like you and me. Why do you think the Church has lasted two thousand years? She may be staffed with bums, but the Lord looks out for her."

Another hand shot up. "Father, what's all this stuff about papal infallibility?"

"OK, that applies just to faith and morals. That's all the pope can't be wrong about. If the pope tells you the Dodgers are going to win the World Series, you don't have to believe him."

"Well, say the pope goes nuts. Completely off his rocker. What if he tells all Catholics to commit suicide. Should we take him on faith, and shoot ourselfs?"

"Bull. That's never going to happen. Even if the pope did turn coo-coo you wouldn't be bound by that order. Suicide is immoral. The pope can't tell you to sin, and he's not going to. So don't give me this hypothetical crap, wise guy." A blast of smoke. "Who's next?"

"Father, I went to Saint Eustasia's grade school, and we had a nun used to tell stories."

"Clean ones, I hope."

"Well, she said that when Jesus was a kid making mud-pies he used to shape little birds out of mud, clap his hands, and they'd fly away. Do you believe it?"

"One of those sweet nunny yarns. Like if you whack off, your hand will grow a web like the foot of a duck. Next question."

Impulsively, Moon darted a glance at his right hand. No web.

A voice from the third row drawled, "Hey Father, get this. Say there's this babe been shacking up equally with two guys. They all die and go to Heaven. Which guy does she live with there?"

Knox studied the questioner coolly. "None of 'em sounds like Heaven material."

Chorus of laughter.

The question had come from a guy whose crop of blond hair hung down across his eyes. Shithead, Moon had heard him called.

"OK," Shithead persisted, "say it was strictly legal. Say she was married to the bastards. One at a time. What the fuck—excuse me, Father—do they do about it?"

Knox dropped his cigarette to the floor and stepped on it. "They don't do anything about it. There's no marriage in Heaven. Everybody there is sexless. Like the angels."

"Aw, naw, Father, say it ain't so. You mean when I go to Heaven I reach for my dingus and it won't be there?"

"Why do you want to reach for it? I hope you'd only want to take a leak."

Huge roar.

"Matter of fact, you won't even need to do that," Knox went on, enjoying this. "You'll have left your body behind, and all your physical needs. Nobody ever took their body to Heaven except Our Blessed Mother."

But Shithead wasn't giving up. "Aw, Father, I don't want to be gelded. I don't want to go there if I can't bring all of me."

"All right, then, go to Hell. You can probably take your body along, so you can feel torment. But I'm telling you, you'd better try for Heaven. You get there, you won't miss your dingus at all. One last question!"

From the last row. "Father, while we're on the subject of fucking—"

"Are we?"

"I know this married couple does it funny. They lick and suck and do the sixty-nine. I'm not talking about me and my wife, of course—"

"Of course not," Knox said sarcastically. "Just somebody you hear lapping away next door."

"Well Father, what I want to know is, is that all right? In the eyes of the Lord, I mean?"

"Sure it's all right. You're married, aren't you? You can express your love any way you want to, as long as the seed lands in the right hole. Class dismissed."

"Wow! Hey, thanks, Father!" said the questioner, grinning happily.

They stood at attention while Knox stalked out of the auditorium.

The chapel bell tolled noon. Everybody headed for The Pit, a wooden shed that had been thrown up next to the gym. Each hungry man fought his way up to a plywood counter where a sign said HOT DOGS, COFFEE, COKE.

"Is that all there is?" Moon shouted to an overworked black woman.

"Yass."

"Gimme two hotdogs and a coffee."

The room didn't have seats. Moon and Konny stood on the packed dirt floor, fighting for elbow space, their coffees balanced on a counter of raw pine board. A jukebox blared tunes—"Don't Fence Me In," "Rum and Coca Cola," "Caledonia, Caledonia, What Makes Your Big Head So Hard?"

"Two bits for coffee," said Moon. "Steep price for a dump like this."

Konny stuffed half a dog past his buckteeth. "Why not? They've got a f-f-f-frigging m-m-m-monopoly."

Moon gulped down his lunch and sprinted off for his opening class in biology. To his surprise, Temporary Shelter Five, another Quonset hut, had fluorescent light and brand new chairs. He was the first to arrive. Determined to make an impression, he took a seat squarely in front of his instructor's desk and waited impatiently while half an hour slowly ticked by.

She came in like the dawn. Bright yellow blouse, matching yellow shawl, short white skirt, long auburn hair, a gold-beaded handbag on one arm and an infant in a pink blanket on the other. Moon's heart leaped. Yes, she was the same stunning apparition who had fascinated him in the gym. She was beautiful and she knew it. Large luminous green eyes with a gleam of mischief, lips moist and lush, lipstick applied carelessly, small upward-tilting nose, bra-free breasts straining her blouse's capacity. Gold sandals with high heels, from which bright red toenails glimmered through black net stockings. Her toes held Moon's stare. They were so long and slim that he guessed she could play the piano with them.

One veteran had leaned back, taking a nap, feet propped on a nearby chair. Aisling lit into him. "Get your big clod- hoppers off that chair, soldier! Can't you see this is nice new furniture? You don't deserve any better than the baby Jesus —you ought to sleep in a barn."

The culprit brought his feet down with a thud.

Her voice was rich and low, even when she delivered a tongue-lashing. It reminded Moon of some sweet, smooth substance being poured. Hershey's chocolate syrup.

She turned to Moon. "Here, hold my baby a minute while I get organized."

Moon was terror-stricken. "I—I've never held a baby before."

"Give her here," said a man in the front row. "Got three myself."

Aisling surrendered her charge. All eyes on her, she planted herself in the middle of the desk, crossed her legs, kicked her sandals off, and squirmed her stockinged toes. Her short skirt was tugged tight, the inside of one white thigh not thirty inches from Moon's lips.

"OK," she said, "this is Biology One A. I'm Professor Vastasi. I used to be a second lieutenant in the WAVES, so don't think you can get away with any happy horseshit."

"Wouldn't dream of it, honey," a student murmured.

"Don't get wise. You," she said to Moon, pushing a stack of mimeographed sheets into his hands, "maybe at least you know how to pass out things? This is the plan for the course, term paper, and a list of reading for extra credit. I'd advise you yardbirds to read a lot. You look as if you can use all the extra credit you can get."

Aisling called the roll and when Moon answered she looked at him searchingly and said, "James Gogarty. We met at registration, didn't we?"

He was thunderstruck. She had remembered!

When she came to the name of S. T. Pohl, a lean young black man sat up, unfolding his six-foot-eight frame. He had a thin mustache and a face full of confidence. Moon recognized him at once from his newspaper pictures. The star freshman basketball player. Moon stared at Pohl's hands. The size of giant flapjacks.

Aisling studied him up and down. "What does the S. T. stand for?"

"Ma'am, if you please, I just go by S. T. You don't need to know the rest."

"As you wish."

Aisling began to talk about one-celled animals. She could have talked about anything, Moon thought, and still held her audience spellbound. Her baby slept in the arms of the family man, but in the middle of the lecture, the tiny girl woke up with a plaintive cry. Aisling scooped up the baby, turned her back, liberated a breast, then spun around to face the class again, her long shawl draped over the guzzling child. Without missing a word about the euglena and the paramecium.

Moon was entranced. Slowly and deliberately, he revolved his thumb, drawing an unseen halo around her face.

Nine

Moon's schedule was insane. On Tuesday, Thursday, and Saturday, his philosophy class, Science of Being, met in a boiler room at eight in the morning. Its instructor, a timid young dropout from the seminary, seemed terrified to face the roomful of ex-GIs until one morning he staggered in giggling, having found courage in drink. On those same days at ten in the evening, Moon had French in a decommissioned men's room, urinals still in its walls. The teacher, Monsieur Pigout, was said to be a fugitive from the Foreign Legion. "Pee-GOO!" he would shrill. "That ees how you say my name!"

On those spaced-out days, Moon felt adrift. How to fill all the hours between dawn and dark? At least his awful schedule had its compensations. Sometimes he would take the bus in to Newark, get off at Broad and Market, and rush to the Adams Theater. If he got there before noon, fifty cents would buy admission to see a famous swing band on stage. He would come for the band's first show, endure the B-movie, then watch the live show over again. One morning Woody Herman kept clinging for support to his standing microphone. "Sorry I'm not with it," he confided to the twelve-person audience. "Been up all night counting my jewels."

Some days he'd catch a nap in the Little, a thirty-seat movie house that had shown nothing but Hedy Lamarr in *Ecstasy* for the past seven years. And some days he'd splurge on a matinee at the Empire Burlesk, where a tinny four-piece combo would play "Harlem Nocturne" while awkward dancers did bumps and grinds for an audience of bums jerking off. Only one girl, a smoothly moving black teenager, appeared to be enjoying herself. Every time he beheld her, Moon would rotate his thumb in an invisible circle around her face. Usually he would lunch at busy Hung Dong Café, a third-floor walk-up where the waiters kept yanking the metal cover off his egg foo yong, and seeing the dish still half full, bang the cover back down again angrily.

But none of these pastimes distracted him from his thoughts of Aisling Vastasi. O God, why wasn't it a Monday, Wednesday, or Friday? Throughout his spaced-out days, her braless bosom swayed before him, like a vision of succulent pears on a bough.

One morning two weeks into the semester, Konny noticed his sleepwalking state. "M-M-M-M-Moon! S-s-snap out of it! You're t-t-trying to eat your oatmeal with your f-f-fork."

"Our apprentice mortician is in love," said Crews. "Smitten with his biology teacher."

Moon started turning red. "Where do you get that stuff?"

Crews snickered. "Oh, I saw you hiding in the bushes outside Shelter Five waiting for her to walk by. You were going to jump out and walk to class with her, weren't you, but you didn't have the nerve."

"You're off your rocker. She's my professor, that's all."

"And you want to make it with her? Even though she's married to a tough gangster type? Talk about suicide!"

In history class, while Dr. Bopp droned through his reading of the unobtainable textbook, Moon didn't sink into his normal reverie. No longer was he Glenn Miller or Tommy Dorsey leading a band, he was Gogarty the Great Lothario, sweeping Professor Vastasi off her sandaled feet, murmuring soft words as he tossed aside her baby, ripped open her blouse, and clamped lips on her nipples, one at a time. Instead of taking notes on Bopp's monologue, he filled page after page of his notebook inscribing her beautiful name in Old English Gothic characters.

Father Knox's noon religion class slipped by like a dream. Impatiently, Moon skipped lunch and hurried to Temporary Shelter Five to stake out his chair in the front row. He had left off his underpants that morning, letting his member swing free. Somehow it made him feel empowered.

As soon as she had taken roll call, Aisling had turned to him and said, "Gogarty, what are you staring at?"

Moon had been savoring her long white net-enmeshed legs. He didn't have time to think up a lie. "You," he said.

All the ex-soldiers guffawed. Aisling's laugh went up and down the scales. "I'm flattered. But listen, Gogarty, you'd better keep your mind on single-celled animals. Work up to women slowly. All right, people, today we're discussing simple plants." Under her breath, she shot at Moon, "See me after class."

He could hardly live until the lecture ended. Then, when the room had emptied out, he approached her desk, hope shining in his eyes.

Aisling flashed him a smile. "Gogarty, how would you like to come over to my house tonight—"

His heart shot up like a skyrocket.

"—And babysit for me?"

His heart dropped back to earth with a fizzled fuse.

"My husband and I have to go to the Monsignor's party. Kiki Sue will be asleep. She won't be much trouble. I'll leave plenty to eat in the kitchen. Come around seven. Number ten Professors Row."

Moon heard his voice reply, "Sure, Professor Vastasi, sure thing. There's nothing I wouldn't do for you."

He didn't know why, but as he left the room a disturbing mirage rose from his memory. Loretta Snow, stretched out on the table in the mortuary. Her face and arms unnaturally pink, her frilly blue prom dress pressed, but her forehead still pierced with the terrible hole that hadn't yet been patched. He swallowed hard and blinked until she disappeared.

Ten

Ricky Peru in a tailor-made tux and Tessie in a white mink stole let Manny the Monk help them down from their bulletproof Rolls.

"Hang around, Monk," Peru told the driver. "We'll be going home early."

Tessie let out a whine. "Well what if I'm having a good time and don't want to leave? Here we are going to a swell party at this monsignor's house and you want to rush me home. Jesus, my corns are killing me."

Peru frowned. The old bag was getting cranky. Maybe one of these days he'd have to trade her in. The good thing about being married to Tessie was she looked respectable. Anybody would take her for the pampered, overfed wife of a small-time car dealer.

They struggled up the steps of Feeley Mansion. At the door, the college vice-president greeted them warmly and a sweet-faced young nun holding a guest list checked off their names. They stepped inside and, puffing and wheezing, made their way up a broad marble staircase and down a long hall with velvet wallpaper. From the walls glowered portraits of noblemen with rifles and hunting dogs---ancestral portraits that Sir Terwilliger had bought in a junk shop in Edinburgh.

"Jeez, I never been in a place like this," Tessie said. "Hey, dearie, why don't *you* ever spend dough this way?"

Peru grunted. "You kidding? I gotta keep a low profile. Not like these bozos. They love to flash it around."

Still panting from their climb, they entered the grand ballroom with its massive chandelier, a ton of glass beads suspended on a chain. Tessie gaped upward and whistled. "Imagine dusting that sucker?"

"You imagine it," Peru said.

In the vast room, people in tuxes and evening gowns stood around sipping drinks, making pleasant faces. In the center of one group stood the college president, Monsignor Malachi O'Malley, splendid in his crimson cape and gleaming big gold cross. Grabbing Tessie by the arm, Peru steered her over and shoved her in through a gap in the crowd. He shouldered past a bystander and stuck out his hand. "Hey, Monsignor, how you making it?"

Monsignor O'Malley, interrupted in conversation with a lesser benefactor, blinked once, turned, and thrust out an answering hand. The president was a short, poker-spined roly-poly with a jutting chin, close-cropped hair, penetrating blue eyes.

"Ah, Mr. Peruccese, Mrs. Peruccese. Our guests of honor. This is a pleasure indeed."

Tessie made a curtsey that left her with a secret rip in the seat of her underpants. "Bee-yoo-tiful place you got here, your majesty."

"Oh, it's not quite mine," said the president with a smile. "It still belongs to the Feeleys—Sir Terwilliger and Dame Millicent. They've deeded the house to the college, you know, but they continue to live in one wing. I merely have my office in the other."

"You don't live here?" Peru said.

"No, for the time being I'm still in the house down the road, keeping my solitary quarters. Of course, on some future day when the Feeleys pass on-—-Lord grant them long life!—I might move here."

"Looks like there's plenty of bedrooms. They couldn't squeeze you in?"

The president grimaced. "Yes, but I prefer to give the Feeleys plenty of room. Between you and me, they're very elderly and not always quite clear in the head. Why, one time"—his voice sank low and confiding—"when I was their overnight guest, Dame Millicent summoned me at three in the morning. She wanted me to hear her confession."

Peru gave a short hard laugh. "Big sinner, huh? She couldn't wait till morning? What did she have to confess?"

"Ah, the seal is on my lips. But as I recall, it was little indeed."

A girl in a lace cap offered Peru and Tessie drinks from a silver tray. Under his breath Peru said, "Christ, what is this ladypiss? You got any Jack Daniels?" The girl shook her head. He grimaced and accepted a glass of pink fluid.

"Lovely punch," said Tessie, sipping.

Peru had to work to keep from spitting the stuff out on the rug. Monsignor O'Malley introduced them to some of the bystanders. Then he moved on, leaving them adrift in a sea of meaningless society. Peru was asked what he did. The export business. Oh, import-export? No, just export. Tessie met other women and rattled on and on about how nice it was to be there and how much everything must have cost.

Glauco Vastasi, his thick bulk trying to explode his tuxedo, came over and Peru drew him off into a corner. "So how you coming with them season tickets?"

"The bastard's giving me a hard time. Knox. Priest in charge of athletics."

"You don't need to tell me who he is. So what's with him, he won't let go of two lousy box seats?"

"Not when I asked him. But don't you worry, Uncle Ricky, I'll get the Monsignor to put the squeeze on him. Give me a couple of days, I'll lay those tickets right in your hand."

"Make it tomorrow. I'm tired of farting around. And what about them Browning rifles? Are the Haitians going to take the ones you didn't sell Trujillo?"

"It's in the bag, Uncle Ricky. Talked with their agent this morning. Right away we can start shipping the stuff down to Port-au-Prince. I already shipped eighty cases to Trujillo City."

"Trujillo named the fucking city after himself?"

"Yeah. It used to be San Domingo."

"You collect?"

"Check came yesterday. A hundred and sixty-five. How's that for a few old rifles nobody else wants?"

"I like that, Nephew. But them box seats better be in my hand inside twenty-four hours. This jock priest is a pain in the backside. The other day I stood in line next to him at the opening ceremonies, you know, so I introduced myself. Said how would he like new uniforms for the team. You know what the asshole said to me? Said he didn't need any dirty friends."

"To you, he said that? Sounds like he needs his head broke."

Peru shrugged. "Well don't send your fuck-ups after him again. Not yet, anyways. He's a big cheese around here. You waste him, people would notice. So he doesn't like me, so what do I care. Unless he starts messing with our business."

Vastasi jabbed a thumb toward the far side of the room. "There he is over there. You want to talk to him again? Make peace, maybe?"

Peru's first reaction was to say, in a pig's ass I will, but then he had a second thought. What if he could still win Knox over?

"OK, what the hell. I'll show him Ricco Peruccese don't hold a grudge."

Knox was huddled with the publisher of the *Star Ledger* when Peru and Vastasi sidled over. Peru screwed his face into a smile.

Vastasi butted in. "Father Knox, maybe you know Mr. Peruccese?"

Knox jerked his head around, snapped to his full five-ten. He gave Peru a cold stare through steel-rimmed glasses.

"Sure, I know him," Knox said. "Mr. Peru put up some money to fix the chapel and now he's come to collect his glory."

The forced smile dropped from Peru's face. "You got me all wrong, Father. I don't need no glory. I'm just a guy made a little dough in business. Want to give it away to the right places."

Knox's look drilled him. "Look, Peru, what are you up to? Yesterday I got a package in the mail that stank to high heaven. A rabbit with its throat cut and a threatening letter."

Peru looked startled. "Holy shit, Father. What are you telling me that for?"

"Don't say you don't know anything about it."

"Hell no, I don't know nothing about a thing like that. It sounds like old time Sicilian style. The way the boys in a certain brotherhood used to do. But that kind of thing went out with the Model T. That ain't *my* style, let me tell you. I want to warn somebody, I call him on the phone."

"And sometimes you send a couple of thugs to rough him up?"

Peru frowned. "So you had a little run-in with somebody. That don't have no connection with me."

"Yeah? Well soon after that, I caught one of your flunkies, Cosimo di Montecassino, nosing around our team. I didn't like him being there and I told him so."

Peru forced a laugh. "Cosimo? He's just a sports fan, Father. Who wouldn't want to see your new star nigra do his stuff? I wouldn't mind seeing him myself."

"Yeah? Then call the box office. Bleacher seats go for seven-fifty."

Peru was still holding his barely tasted pink punch. He flung it down and stepped on it, grinding glass into the rug. He said, "Fuck you, Father," turned on his heel and stalked off. Vastasi threw Knox a look of apology and followed.

Knox grinned. "Guess I rubbed him the wrong way."

The publisher looked worried. "Father, I wouldn't have done that if I were you. Ricky Peru is a bad man to cross."

"I don't intend to cross him. As long as he keeps his slimy mitts off our basketball team."

Trembling all over, clenching and unclenching his fists, Peru stood in a corner recovering his calm. This stuck-up priest was riding for a fall. All the same, Knox was blaming him for things he hadn't authorized. He lit a Cuban cigar and chomped on it hard.

He said to Vastasi, "Glauco, about that bastard priest got sent a rabbit. That your dumb idea?"

"Of course not, Uncle Ricky. It wasn't me."

"I believe you, Nephew. But here I'm getting blamed for what some fuck-head is doing. Giving me a bad name." He ground out his cigar in the Persian rug.

As he was shaping and discarding different plans to get back at Knox, a lovely distraction appeared. Aisling came bouncing over in a gown that showed two-thirds of her bosom. The sight made him feel better right away.

"Come on, Glauco," she said, "you going to introduce me?"

Vastasi had no choice. "Ricky, this is Aisling. The woman I told you about."

Peru bent over and kissed her outstretched hand. He flashed her a gold-toothed smile. "Pleased to meet you, honey. Yeah, I've heard a lot about you. You're the best-looking Navy loo-tenant I ever seen. How you doing, peaches? This nephew of mine been treating you right?"

Aisling beamed. "Not bad. But Glauco's a cheapskate. The other day he gave me a hard time just because the baby needed a new crib."

"My, my, that's terrible," Peru said. "And don't he buy you no jewelry?"

"The only jewels he gives me are the family ones. Practically every night."

"Yeah? That's all? But you got jewelry there, you got a wedding ring on."

"It's zircons. Didn't cost him more than thirty bucks. It's only to make people think we're married."

Peru liked her a lot. She talked straight. Obviously she'd make a great squeeze. They chatted, he peering into her cleavage, inhaling her violet-based perfume. When at last she turned away, saying she had to go to the powder room, he reached out and gave her an affectionate pat on the behind.

Alone, he withdrew into fresh deliberations. How would he get rid of Tessie's body? Poke her feet in a tub of cement, drop her in the Passaic? Naw, couldn't use the river anymore. It was getting stacked too high. And maybe he'd better hang on to the old lady. She disappeared, the grandkids would ask about her. Besides, she was Cosimo di Montecassino's sister. If he had Tessie wiped, Cosimo would resent it. Family stuff always complicated things. Anyway, this Aisling babe could be his side girl. That was it. He'd take her away from Vastasi.

In the ladies' room Aisling inspected her face in a gold-rimmed mirror, redid her lower lip where the punch glass had smeared it. God, this party disgusted her. Vastasi, involved with Peru, had cast her adrift, not squired her around and introduced her to people. She had looked forward to meeting a lot of big shots, but the only big shot she had met was that old iguana Ricky Peru. He had practically gassed her to death with his cigar breath and undressed her with his slimy eyes.

She went back out to the ballroom and contemplated the scene. Crap awful. All the men were gray-haired futzers with inner tubes of fat, towing their hideous wives. But wait. Maybe things weren't hopeless. In a nearby corner of the room Father Douglas Knox was standing by himself, looking unhappy too.

The man was like a magnet that attracted her. Smoldering eyes, sharp features, expression that said take me or leave me, here the hell I am. He was a lot older than she was—-forty, maybe—but so what? She could go for him.

Knox was eyeing the doorway. She hurried over before he could get away.

"Hello, Father," she said, extending a soft white hand, "I'm Aisling. I've heard a lot about you."

Knox accepted the hand. "Any of it good?"

"All of it. Hear you're the dynamo in back of sports around here. Recruited this hotshot Pohl for the hoop team. Got the new gym built, didn't you?"

Oh-oh. She wasn't letting go of his hand. She was standing closer than a woman should come to a priest. Looking up straight into his eyes. The top half of her gown looked tight as the skin on a peach.

He managed to get his hand back. "The gym? I didn't have anything to do with building it. It got flung together. A fast and shoddy job. Hey, I've seen you around. Saw you in the faculty parade at convocation. You were the best thing in it."

"Yeah? Nice of you to notice. Wasn't that parade awful? Had to spend an hour waiting, standing in line in high heels. Wanted to walk in barefoot, but they wouldn't let me."

"You're teaching biology. Tim Walsh told me about you."

"Father Tim's a sweetpuss. Yes, I'm teaching the ex-GIs about living things. Some of them are already checked out about reproduction, but there's a lot they don't know."

She talked in a low voice, standing up next to him, bosom nearly up against his chest, probing his eyes with hers. He found himself staring at a little gold medallion that hung on a chain between her breasts. Fascinated, he watched it swaying back and forth.

Sweet Jesus, he thought, she's coming on to me. Holy-Mary-mother-of-God deliver me from temptation. Get thee behind me, Satan. Lord, what do You think I'm made of? Stone?

Eleven

In the kitchen of the little house across the road from campus, Moon smeared four slices of Wonder Bread with peanut butter and mayonnaise. Tonight hadn't turned out the way he had hoped. Still, he had been able to behold his beautiful professor in a low-cut gown, a gold necklace with a medallion swinging in the cleft of her bosom.

Glauco Vastasi, crammed into a tux, had looked as if his tie were strangling him. "Step on it, for Chrissake," he had barked at her. Moon had felt a powerful yearning to punch him in the teeth.

Departing, Aisling had blown Moon a kiss. "We'll be back by midnight," she had told him. "If Kiki Sue wakes up, change her and walk her around. There's a bottle of formula in the fridge."

Alone now, sandwiches in hand, he sprawled in a chair and contemplated his good fortune. She had kissed him! Well, indirectly. A quiet excitement stole over him. After all, he was here—he had penetrated her inner sanctum. This would be a rare chance to snoop around the house, get to know her better.

The furniture in the room looked hastily acquired from a bargain sale. Already the new couch, upholstered in purple plastic, was beginning to show cracks in its seat cushions. A sixty-watt floor lamp had a blond maple stem that matched the wood of the rocking chair and the coffee table. The only decorations were a print on the wall over the couch showing two little girls with bowling-ball eyes. The indoor-outdoor carpet was turd-brown except for a white milky splat where Kiki Sue had thrown up on it.

Idly, he picked up a book from the coffeetable. *Mating Patterns of the Rhesus Monkey.* On its flyleaf the owner had scrawled *Aisling Esther Weinstein.* She had written last month's date in it: *August 1946.* Funny. Why hadn't she signed herself *Vastasi?*

Puzzled, still mulling, Moon went upstairs to check on Kiki Sue. Curled in her crib in a pink warmsuit, the child was breathing peacefully. The room held a double bed. He imagined himself in it, clasping Aisling in his arms. For a second, only a second, a twinge of guilt shot through him. *Thou shalt not covet thy neighbor's wife.* But what if your neighbor doesn't deserve her?

Holy crow!—he gave a whistle of surprise. Hanging from one bedpost was a pistol in a leather sling. Moon knew nothing about guns, but the weapon looked businesslike. Was Vastasi expecting burglars?

Almost afraid he might find some intruder hiding in the bedroom closet, Moon yanked open the closet door. A jumbled heap of dirty clothes spilled out. A bra. A woman's underpants. With difficulty he restrained himself from picking them up and savoring the aroma.

He went into the upstairs den and flopped down on a couch whose slipcover featured big blowsy roses. He found himself facing a TV console. Television was so new that he hadn't seen much of it. On top of the set a four-inch screen stared up at the ceiling. Behind it stood an upright mirror, reflecting the screen. The picture came in right-to-left instead of left-to-right, and the mirror flopped it. Moon pushed a button and the set hummed, but all it would receive was a snowstorm. Lately the Federal Communications Commission had changed the frequency of TV stations. Already the new set was an antique.

Moon fiddled with the dial. All he could bring in was WDED-FM, the college radio station. A student with a lisp was stumbling through the news bulletins.

Ten top-level Nazis, convicted by the Nuremberg tribunal as war criminals, today went to the gallows.

High time they went, Moon thought.

Prime Minister Nehru of India has called on the United States and the Soviet Union to enact nuclear disarmament.

Bet they won't do it.

Viet Namese leader Ho Chi Minh has demanded that French forces pull out of the capital city of Hanoi.

Ho Chi Minh, ho hum.

In Korea, sniper fire broke out along the 38 degree latitude between a Russian patrol in the North zone and Americans troops in the South.

Why should I give a rat's ass? That stuff over there won't ever matter to *me*.

Now the voice of Crews, imitating a sports announcer, was waxing enthusiastic about Saint Cash's hot new hoop star, S. T. Pohl.

"Oh, wait till you see this gorgeous black bundle of muscles," Crews enthused. "Believe me, sports fans, he's too much for words."

So are you, Moon thought. He glanced at his drugstore wristwatch, wishing the time would gallop by, yearning for another glimpse of his gorgeous professor.

At half-past midnight Aisling and Vastasi got home. Half-dozing on the couch in the den, Moon heard the front door open and, in the hallway below, the start of an argument.

Aisling was yammering. "Why didn't you stop him? Peru pats me on the ass, and you, you chump, you just stand there grinning at him!"

"Aaaah, hell, he didn't mean nothing."

"Oh he didn't? I know a hungry wolf when I see one. What are you anyway, his god damn pimp? I bet if he snapped his fingers, you'd just hand me over."

"Sister, that would be the luckiest break you ever had."

Moon strained to eavesdrop. Aisling sounded close to tears. "You bastard. You don't care a nickel for me and Kiki Sue. All we are is something you collect and trade, like stamps."

A sharp slap. "Shut your mouth," Vastasi told her. "What are you bitching for? I take you in, I feed you, buy you clothes, get you a job, give you a roof. I let you use my name—on campus, anyway."

Aisling was snuffling. "Bastard," she said again.

"Yeah? If there's any bastard around here, it's that kid of yours. You don't even know who the father was. Always crying, stinking up the place. For two cents I'd kick the two of you out."

"Not so loud, you idiot. You want the babysitter to hear?"

The babysitter had heard. Moon sat there stunned, his hopes beginning to rise. Maybe he had a chance to win his beautiful professor after all.

Twelve

Knox's morning went downhill rapidly, but at least it started well. At eight-thirty he was sitting on the coach's bench in the gym, spellbound, watching the Quills work out. This boy S.T. Pohl was one smooth ball-handler. Plenty of giants were clumsy, but Pohl's lean frame moved down the court in a crouch, like a jaguar going for its prey. He'd dribble, switch behind his back, light out in whichever direction a guard hadn't foreseen. He never missed a rebound, just cradled the ball in one huge hand, sank distance shots with his eyes shut and a grin that said hell, nothing to it.

Knox beckoned him over. Pohl didn't even look tired.

"Mr. Pohl, they teach you to shoot like that down in Mississippi?"

Pohl cracked open a smile full of white teeth. "Kind of picked it up on my own, Father. All us kids did. Didn't have nothing else to do but nail a barrel hoop to a tree, put a rubber ball through it. You like those moves?"

"Yeah. Don't get a swelled head, kid, but keep it up and you might go a long way."

"Thanks, Father." Pohl loped away to the showers.

Maureen stuck her freckled face into the gym. "Father, the Monsignor just called. Wants you to call him right back."

Knox went out and slowly climbed the stairs to his office. He gritted his teeth and gave the campus operator the Monsignor's private number.

"Douglas," the president began, "I've a small matter to discuss with you. I hear that you denied a request for box seats for Mr. and Mrs. Peruccese."

"That's right, Monsignor."

"Kindly explain."

"Peruccese is the guy I warned you about. His name— he's called Ricky Peru for short—keeps coming up in connection with organized crime."

"You've heard those rumors about him. So have I, but I do not take stock in them. Douglas, I would regard it as a personal favor if you'd reconsider this. As you know, Mr. Peruccese is a most generous benefactor of this college. In view of his gift to renovate Rose Chapel, I believe we must extend him every courtesy."

"Pardon me, Monsignor, but I think we ought to extend him the boot. Maybe those rumors have something in back of them. Last night at your party, Mort Henderson of the *Star Ledger* was telling me plenty. He says Peru is kingpin of the Newark Mafia."

"Poppycock. I am not convinced that there is any such thing as the Mafia. A legend concocted by the newspapers."

"Well, Henderson knows this area like the back of his hand. Says Peru runs a protection racket in Newark and the Oranges. Says he dabbles in stolen goods, oversees prostitution, small loans with big interest, the numbers."

"Now, now, Douglas, let's be reasonable. None of those reports has ever been substantiated. To the best of my knowledge, Mr. Peruccese has never been convicted of any crime."

"He must buy out the cops."

"On the contrary, I have it on good authority that he's a perfectly upright citizen. Pillar of his church. Faithful

Mass-goer. It's only that his business rivals have tried to blacken his name."

"And who may I ask is your authority? Glauco Vastasi?"

The Monsignor cleared his throat. "I trust Glauco implicitly. He frequently does business with Mr. Peruccese's firm. He ought to know."

"He ought to know better. Inviting Peru to get involved with this college, you might as well invite Old Nick and an army of imps besides."

The President's patience snapped. "Douglas, I've looked into this matter more than adequately. I regard myself as a fair judge of character. I hold Mr. Peruccese in high esteem. You will issue those two season tickets. Please make sure those seats have excellent views. And I'd appreciate it if you wouldn't spread these lurid stories about Mr. Peruccese. That kind of talk can only harm the interests of this college."

Knox saw red. He took a deep breath. "All right, Monsignor, whatever you say. You'll excuse me for thinking, but maybe it would be in the interests of this college to keep our noses clean."

"Don't overstep your authority, Father. You do your job and I'll do mine. Good day to you!"

Knox put his phone back down, picked up a heavy gold-plated trophy from his desk and holding it by the neck of the basketball player, flung it at the wall. A triangular chunk fell out of the plaster. Then he leaped to his feet and place-kicked his wastebasket. POW. The tarpaper receptacle soared out through the open window.

A grunt resounded from below.

Knox leaned out over the windowsill. Sprawled on the sidewalk, somebody was trying to remove the wastebasket from his head and shoulders. It took him a couple of tries. When his head emerged, the victim looked familiar. Knox recognized the bland round face of a student in his class.

"You OK?" Knox called down to him. "You walk into something?"

Moon Gogarty sat on the sidewalk rubbing the top of his head. "Oh, Father Knox! I was just on my way to see you."

"Well come on up, if you have to. And bring that wastebasket."

When Moon sat in the office, blinking from across the desk, Knox took a closer look at him. His ill-matched brown sweater and blue slacks were brand new. The kid must be fresh out of high school.

"What's your name again?"

"James Gogarty, Father. I'm in your religion class."

"So, Mr. Gogarty, what's on your mind? Besides wastebaskets?"

"It's about the student newspaper."

"*The Immolator*? That lousy rag? Nobody with any self respect would wipe his butt with that sheet. News is always six months old. Reads like it was written by a five-year-old and proofread by a drunken Eskimo."

"That was last year, Father. Now that I'm the editor, *The Immolator* is turning over a new leaf."

"You? You're the editor? You're nothing but a freshman."

"That's right, Father."

"How did you get the job?"

"Nobody else wanted it. The veterans—that's most students—don't want anything to do with student activities."

"Don't blame 'em. Clubs and the radio station and the newspaper, lot fiddledy-fuck. So what do you and your *Immolator* want out of me?"

"Father, the paper is in a bind. It has to get a faculty advisor or it can't publish."

"As if that would be any loss. I thought you already had an advisor. What's happened to Farceau?"

"Oh, Dr. Farceau has left the college. He's gone into business. Importing French wine."

"I hope he knows wine. He doesn't know much else. He's no doctor of anything, he's got a *docteur ès lettres*, one of those quick degrees the French give foreigners to get rid of them."

"Father, we really need you," Moon said. "You'd be good for the paper, I know you would. People around here look up to you. Maybe they'd start respecting *The Immolator* too, for a change."

Knox lit a Gauloise, blew smoke, contemplated Moon through narrowed eyes. "And if I take the job, just what will I have to do?"

"Nothing, Father. Nothing at all."

"OK then. On condition you won't bother me about any little chickenshit and won't print swear words and pictures of babes in bathing suits with their tits hanging out."

"Oh, Father! Thanks!"

"How about a printer. You have one?"

"The paper used to use Dr. Farceau's brother-in-law, the Olive Press, but I understand he was always late. We haven't signed on with anybody yet."

"Well, don't. Call the Book of Kells Printery in West Orange, Edison three three five nine. They do work for our Athletics Department. Ask for Kell Kelleher, tell him

I told you to call him. You won't get your job done any cheaper anyplace. Only you had better step up the press run. There's a lot more people on campus these days."

When the student editor had left, face shining with triumph, Knox went out to Maureen in the front office. "Honey, call the plasterer, will you? A piece fell out of my wall. And tell the janitor to bring me a new wastebasket. My old one wore a hole in it."

"All right, Father. And Father, there's a messenger here to see you."

Knox glanced up to see a thin white-haired man, wrinkled face, standing there trembling. Jacket frayed at the sleeves and red necktie, wearing a black cap that said WESTERN UNION.

"You want to talk to me?" Knox said. "Aren't you just going to hand me a telegram?"

"I have to sing it for you," the man said, with downcast eyes.

"A singing telegram? First one I ever got. Who's it from?"

"He didn't say."

Knox didn't know whether to laugh. "Oh, all right. Go ahead and sing."

Maureen was getting a case of the giggles. She fought to regain a straight face.

The messenger pulled out a pitch pipe, blew a note, rocked back on his heels, and in a high shrill voice chanted tunelessly:

Douglas Knox,
Resign as coach.
If you do not
You will be sorry.

This is your last
Warning.

Knox's right hand grabbed the man's necktie and twisted it around his throat until the messenger's eyeballs bulged.

"You damned well better tell me who put you up to this," Knox said.

He let go, and the man slumped gasping to the floor and sat there clutching his neck. "I—I told you—I don't know. I don't have a clue."

"You have a manager I can call?"

"Yeah. But he wouldn't take the message. Didn't want me to deliver it. But the guy gave me twenty bucks, and so I did."

"What kind of guy? What did he look like?"

"He wore a blue serge suit like a big shot. Except one funny thing. The top of his head wasn't normal. He had a haircut like it was a cross."

Thirteen

Peru's favorite meeting place was Slovak Sokol Hall. It had the quietest bar in Newark, a place the cops never bothered with. It never gave his bag man any trouble, paid its hundred a month dues to the Protection Society right on the dot.

This afternoon the barroom was practically empty, just him and Vastasi straddling barstools and a middle-aged Slovak couple sitting at a table. Husky guys, the man wearing a pork-pie hat, the woman in a dress printed with petunias. Forty-watt bulbs bounced orange light off the mahogany bar. A jukebox churned oompah music industriously.

Vastasi had laughed himself into tears. "He wanted me to know," he managed to say, "that that bunny with its throat cut didn't scare him. I think the Monsignor did. Told him to give you the goddamn box seats after all."

Peru fingered his season tickets, noted with a frown that he and Tessie would be sitting back in the third row.

"Very funny," he said with a scowl, jamming the tickets into an inside pocket.

Vastasi stopped laughing. "That rabbit. That *was* your idea, Uncle Ricky, wasn't it?"

Peru swung around on his barstool to look his nephew full face. "Hell no it wasn't. Like I told Knox, what do you think I am, some old-time Sicilian bandito, pulling a stunt like that? It was some stupid cocksucker."

"Who?"

"The hell do I know. What I don't like is we get blamed for it. Whoever sent Knox that little valentine was trying to make it look like it came from us. From the brother-hood. That's what Knox thinks. You heard him lace into me at the party."

"Yeah. At least the thing shook him plenty."

"So what good is it, it shook him up. Me, I think you don't send a guy a serious warning unless you fol-low through with it. No, somebody else is laying for our sports priest, going to make a move on him. And I don't like it."

"What the hell, Uncle Ricky, somebody does a number on Knox, you wouldn't like that?"

"Oh, don't get me wrong, Nephew. I got no love for the guy. Only dammit, I don't want to see him knocked off just yet. I got a big surprise planned for him. He'll get the shock of his life when Saint Cash plays Holy Sepulcher. And I'll be there, sitting in a box seat enjoying hell out of it."

"What's going to happen?"

"Saint Cash is going to lose. Lose bad. Look completely fucking miserable. Knox will be disgraced as a coach. Ha, there's no way we could make him hurt more. That's how I'm going to even the score with him."

Vastasi guffawed. "You're a smart one, Uncle Ricky."

"Don't I know it. So meantime, you say you got a guy following Knox around? Tell him anybody tries to kill the padre, he should step in. Later on I might just want to take care of Knox myself. But right now I want to see him stay alive. For a little longer."

Vastasi had a twinge of worry. The guy following Knox around was Harrigan. He wasn't good for much except running errands. "Uncle Ricky, if you want Knox protected good, maybe you better lend me one more man."

Peru thought. "All right. Nobody tails better than Willy the Wire. Knox won't even know he's around. The Wire is over in Brooklyn on loan to the Mangano family, but he's been there long enough. I'll bring him back, have him come see you tomorrow. You can tell him where Knox hangs out."

"This is rich, Uncle Ricky. You protecting Knox!"

"Just for the time being. And you know what, Knox hasn't stopped Cosimo from talking with some of the basketball players. This black boy Pohl is the one we need. I think a poor darky from Mississippi, never had no money in his life, will be glad to come over, all right. So where's the check for the life rafts?"

"Oh yeah." Vastasi fished out an envelope and Peru added it to his inside pocket without looking at it. "Cashier's check?"

"Naw. College check. Better than gold. Trujillo's embassy paid me, so I'm paying you."

"You didn't hold nothing out on me, nephew? No little commission for yourself?"

Vastasi tried to look shocked. "You know me better than that, Uncle Ricky. A hundred and sixty-five they paid, a hundred and sixty-five you get." His mouth took refuge in his beer. Damn. The shrewd old fox, he suspects.

Peru smiled, patted his pocket, sipped his glass of Dr. Pepper—too early in the day to drink—and contemplated the painting hung behind the bar. A buxom nude lay sprawled on a river bank, her snatch concealed by a bunch of daisies. The picture had a gold plate with its title. *Beautiful Bratislava.*

Peru said, "So how's that good-looking squeeze of yours?"

"All right," Vastasi said. "She's a juicy bitch. But she can be annoying as hell sometimes."

"Yeah? You know, nephew, I could do you a favor. Take her off your hands so you don't get tired of her."

Vastasi felt a surge of anger. His uncle's remark sounded offhand, casual, but maybe it was wasn't. When Peru wanted anything, he got it. Anybody stood in his way could end up kissing fish.

"I'll let you know," Vastasi said, forcing a smile. "When I get tired of her."

Peru rapped on the bar with a gold-ringed fist. "Hey, Tommy," he called, "gimme one of them Nibble-a-Nab-for-a-nickels, will you? A peanut butter."

The bartender frowned. "Oh, you don't want none of them, Mister Peruccese. They're stale."

"Then why you selling 'em?"

"I'm not. I don't sell none in over a year. You want I make you a sausage sandwich?"

"No thanks. Them things go through me like a goddam express train. You got any peanuts don't have worms in 'em?"

"I look out back."

"Something else has come up," Vastasi said. "That second-hand bookstore we protect down on Market Street? That has an old geezer owning it?"

"I know the bastard. Always smells like piss. Looks like he runs around a spiderweb."

"That's him. Well, all of a sudden he could be useful. Saint Cash's has a problem. They need thirty thousand more books in a hurry. The evaluators are coming in a few days and the school has to bring its library up to full count or lose their accreditation."

"Accreditation, shit, why should I care? What are you saying to me?"

"The college doesn't pass inspection, nobody will go to it. So we need to prop the place up. Listen, that old fart must have thirty thousand books easy. I could take his whole stock, give him ten grand, enough to retire on. So I been down there talking to him, but he don't want to sell. Says his books are his whole life, crap like that. So I was wondering. How about we get a couple of boys to talk him into it?"

Peru shrugged. "OK, I'll send Jimmy and the Monk in the morning. The old fart, he'll sell out if he don't want a couple of busted knees. And don't give him ten, give him five. He ain't about to starve. I happen to know he owns half of a race track in Monmouth County."

"Thanks, Uncle Ricky, big thanks. You're the best friend a Catholic college ever had."

The bartender came back and slapped six bags of salted peanuts down on the bar. "Here you are, Mr. Peruccese, Mr. Vastasi, gentlemen. On the house. You find a worm in these, I be surprised."

Peru smiled. His smile never reassured anybody. "Thanks, Tommy. I find a worm, you'll eat it. Cellophane bag and all."

He munched. "You know, Nephew, you could use a vacation from that Aisling dame. Maybe she'd like to come live at my place for a while. I'll ask her first thing in the morning. Won't do no harm to ask her, right?"

Alarm bells were jangling in Vastasi's head. Betraying no emotion, he said, "Sure, Uncle Ricky. Go ahead and ask."

Peru was getting greedy. Muscling in on his nephew's love life. Vastasi made a mental note. One more reason why one of these days Peru would need removing.

Fourteen

The big black Rolls with the vanity plate RIP for Ricco Ignatio Peruccesi made its way along the waterfront and pulled up in front of the brownstone apartment building. Aisling, clutching Kiki Sue in a pink wool blanket, let the driver, Manny the Monk, help her down. The street was lined with warehouses facing wharves. Piers with moored freighters. Dark water tossing, full of restless garbage. Wisps of fog drifting in. A lone tugboat passed, blowing a cry that came and went. Overhead, seagulls creaked like rusted pulleys.

"See, honey," Manny said, "this neighborhood is high class. A lot of streets in Hoboken got taverns elbow to elbow, but not this one. No taverns, only two bars."

Aisling wrinkled her nose. "Just the same, the neighborhood smells like a bar rag."

Manny shrugged. "Longshoremen, they got to have their suds. And get the view. New York looks better from here than it looks from frigging Park Avenue."

He waved a hand, gesturing across the harbor at the skyline of lower Manhattan. Skyscrapers were sharp-edged cut-outs in the morning light.

"Come on," he said. "Ricky's expecting you."

They mounted steps to a short brick porch with an iron railing. The uppermost doorbell had a nameplate LATIN AMERICAN TRADING CORP. Manny pushed a button. A speaking tube rasped, and he answered. "She's here."

A buzzer buzzed, the heavy door unlatched, and they stepped inside. Manny opened the cage of a narrow elevator, the motor whirred, and the cage hoisted them slowly to the seventh floor.

They stepped out. Aisling's feet sank ankle-deep into an Oriental rug woven with a picture of a mermaid kissing her own tail. The apartment was a museum of stuffed birds. A snowy owl clasped a thorn tree branch, three orioles posed on a lacquered table pecking gold seeds, a bald eagle perched on a mantel, looking as if it resented having been shooed off its government bond. Someone had stuck a cigar in its beak.

With surprise Aisling recognized an object whose picture she had seen in the papers. It was a curiosity that had drawn throngs to Newark's cathedral until sold to an anonymous buyer. Under a bell jar, lit by a little spotlight, lay the celebrated Pizza of Paramus. Its cheese had melted into the shape of a face. Pious souls had believed it to resemble the sorrowful Virgin. Curious, Aisling inspected it. The Virgin had a pepperoni mouth.

Seeing her look of amazement, Manny chuckled. "Yeah, that's it. Ricky bought the thing. Siddown, he'll be right out. I'll wait for you down in the car. Might go have me a beer." He was gone.

Aisling sat Kiki Sue next to her right side on the yellow pigskin couch. In the baby's pursed mouth, a cry was gathering.

A varnished oak door swung outward and Ricky Peru charged in like an advancing tank. His squat, frog-like body wore a black double-breasted suit with inch-wide stripes, white shirt with gold collar studs, a tie like a sheet of gold leaf. Thin hair was combed across his bald spot. He arrived all smiles, in a cloud of cologne.

"Don't get up, dear lady," he said. He bent low, grabbed her hand from her lap, drew it to his lips, planted a moist kiss, and let it fall back down again. He seated himself in the chair facing her, flashing his gold front tooth with the diamond in it.

Kiki Sue gave a short wail.

"Beautiful child you got there," Peru said. "So what'll you have, darling? Bristol Cream? Naw, that's for old ladies. Champagne? Fourteen-year-old Scotch?"

Aisling stared past Peru out through the wide picture window. She fixed her gaze on the Empire State Building. She half expected to see King Kong at its top, holding Fay Wray.

"No drinks, thanks," she said. "Unless you have any milk."

Peru snapped his fingers and a white-jacketed houseboy appeared. "Luiz, milk for the young lady. Tell me, honey, you need anything for the child?"

"She's nursing. I come equipped."

"Swell. You're the natural type. Hey, I bet you like to sunbathe. You know what, this apartment house has a roof garden where you can stretch out and nobody can see you. Tan your ass, tan yourself all over. I bet you'd enjoy the hell out of that."

The houseboy reappeared, milk in a cut-glass goblet for Aisling, two more glasses, and a bottle of Moet & Chandon in a bucket of ice.

He said, "Cosimo on the phone, boss. He say he got to talk to you right away."

Peru frowned. "Excuse me, honey, I'll be right back. Luiz, pour the lady some bubbles. And where the hell's them smoked calamaris?"

He strode off. Aisling sipped her milk. The houseboy poured her a glass of champagne and went out, leaving the door ajar. She could hear Peru in the next room bellowing on the phone.

Peru was conducting business. "Perlmutter again? That fat fart. That gut he looks out over, he ain't seen his little boy in years. We've had enough shit out of him. Stick him in one of them fifty-gallon drums. But Cosimo, remember the last time you dumped somebody in the Passaic, he was full of gas and the drum came back up again. This time cut his belly open."

Aisling heard. She hugged Kiki Sue close. She felt slightly nauseous.

Peru bounced back in. He reseated himself on the couch to her left. "Don't feel like champagne, huh? Don't mind if I have some myself."

He poured, took a slurp, got bubbles up his nose, sneezed, said "Horseshit!" and blew his nose on a monogrammed handkerchief.

Kiki Sue was starting to fuss. Gently, Aisling swung the child back and forth in her arms.

She said, "All right, Mr. Peruccese, you've practically kidnapped me. Manny pulls up in your car and orders me in. Why do you want to see me anyway?"

Peru placed his right hand lightly on one net-stockinged knee. His touch felt cold. "Didn't mean to surprise you, honey," he said. "I just want to get to know you better, is all."

"Is that all?"

"Sure. You're a looker, you know? And I can tell, you got class besides."

He craned his neck over Aisling's lap, and leered down on Kiki Sue.

"Yeah, that's one sweet child you got there. See, she likes me." He tickled the baby's chin with a gold-ringed finger. The little girl's eyes bulged and her lower lip trembled. Aisling clutched the baby, soothing her.

"So who's its father?" Peru wanted to know. "Not Glauco. You ain't been living with him that long a time."

"Somebody I knew in the Navy."

"What happened? You split?"

"You could put it that way."

"Jeez, that's rough. You had to go it alone. Till you met Glauco, right?"

"Glauco's been good to me."

"I thought you said at the party he didn't buy you nothing."

"Well, no big presents. But at least he set me up in housekeeping."

"And now that's over with."

"What do you mean?"

"Didn't Glauco tell you? He's cutting you loose. You're going to be my best girl from now on."

Aisling reeled as though from a slap. "No, he didn't tell me any such thing. I don't believe you. Why would Glauco want to get rid of me?"

Peru was enjoying this. He swished champagne around in his glass, lit a Havana cigar with a gold Dunhill lighter. "I don't want to go into your personal life, honey, but Glauco told me you and him don't always get along. So I said I'd do him a favor, take you over. Me, I'm a lot of fun to live with. You'll find out."

Aisling felt panic sweep over her. She hugged Kiki Sue tight. Already, this wizened gnome saw her as his plaything. She looked at him, not saying anything, green eyes wide.

"You'll be lucky to get unplugged from him," Peru went on. "You think he'd ever buy you anything like this?"

Like a magician whipping out a card, he drew a small leather jewelry box from his inside coat pocket. He flipped it open and held out a pretzel-shaped gold brooch studded with four sapphires.

"Take it," he said to her. "Just a get-acquainted present. There's more where that came from. Go on, have a look."

Aisling took the box and tilted the brooch back and forth. The gems threw a shimmer of light. She shook her head, set the box back down on the coffee table.

Peru chuckled. "Oh, they're real, all right. You take this piece of work in to any good jeweler's, ask what it's worth."

"I—I can't accept such a thing."

"What are you scared of, honey? This little doodad comes with no strings attached. It's just to show you I'm a guy knows how to spend."

"This is crazy. You just met me the other night. And you come on to me like this?"

Peru took a toothpick, stabbed a bowl, opened his mouth, and plopped in a piece of squid. "What do you want, sister? Moonlight and roses? You expect me to sing like Frankie boy? I don't do that mush stuff. I'm a direct guy. I see what I want, I get it. And I never don't get what I'm after."

"High time you started not getting it. You're not Jesus Christ, you know."

Peru's seamed face broke into a slow grin. "I like you, honey. You got balls. We're gonna make beautiful music together."

"I thought you've got a wife already."

"Sure I do. But Tessie, I don't see her much. She's always across the river shopping at Bloomingdale's. Anyway, she knows I step out on her. Nothing she can do about it. Tessie knows her place. She's too smart to cut loose from me."

"Now let me get this straight. You expect me to be your mistress? One of a harem, probably? You're telling me you and Glauco can pass me around as if I were"—she groped for words—"a goddamn football?"

"Now, now, honey, it ain't like that at all. What I'm offering you is a chance to be somebody. Get written up in all the columns. You step into a night club, flashbulbs gonna pop. You eat in the best spots in New York, see the best shows, sit in a front row seat, meet the stars afterwards. Mink furs, necklaces—you name it. You go around with me, you go top of the line."

Kiki Sue began to howl. Aisling undid her blouse and let the baby's lips plunge in.

Peru looked on approvingly. "That's nice. Mike Angelo, one of them old birds, should have painted the two of you. Tell me, how much you make teaching at Saint Cash?"

"That's *my* business."

"Whatever you make, that won't be two per cent of the lines of credit you'll have at all the stores."

Aisling fed the baby silently. Peru's hand stole back down to her stockinged knee. "So listen, sister. There's a nice little apartment empty on the floor below. You can move in tomorrow. You need a nursemaid for the kid? I'll get you one. You stick with me, kid gets a college education—Wellesley or some fucking place where they teach 'em to use the right fork. All you gotta do is live downstairs. I drop down and see you once in a while."

Aisling picked his hand up from her knee and flung it back at him. "Big deal. And what about my students at Saint Cassian's? I'm teaching four courses, you know."

"Screw 'em. Just bug out."

"Can Manny take me home?"

"Sure he can," Peru said. "Go pack your things and he'll bring you back here in the morning."

"That's not what I mean. I want to go home and stay there. As for your offer, I've never had such a cold, heartless proposition in my life."

Peru looked at her steadily with narrowed eyes, not grinning. "Got a mind of your own, don't you. All right, sister, go back to your house and think about it. I'll give you a couple of days. Just remember, when Glauco throws you out in the street like I'll tell him to, you'll have to land someplace, so why not here? What you gonna do, you and your baby, live on your teaching pay in some goddamn furnished room?"

"That might not be so bad. Better than whoring for a horny old grandpappy."

"OK, OK, so I'm not so young anymore. Can't always get it up, but shit, I can do it most of the time. I got a rubber bulb I squeeze, blow up like a balloon. You ought to be happy to get what's left of a first-class man. The dregs of me, they could make ten men out of. You know who I am? Number one guy in New Jersey. I whistle and college presidents kiss my ass, the fucking governor does a jitterbug dance."

"Well I'm not dancing. I'm going home."

Peru pushed the jewelry box at her. "Take the brooch with you. Get it appraised."

"I don't want the brooch. I just want out of here."

Peru snatched back his gift, snapped the box shut, and jammed it into his pocket. He raked her with a glare, but his words were smooth. "You're making a mistake, sister. You better think about this. You change your mind, let me know."

All the way back to campus while Manny drove silently, Aisling contemplated her life. At the moment it lay in a shambles. God, the nerve of Peru, the smug little weasel, thinking he could buy her, that she'd leap to his bidding. And she was about to lose Glauco, that was clear. He slavishly took orders from Peru. There was always Harrigan, the stupid clod. A decent stud, but she'd had enough of him.

Time for a fresh romance. There was another man to make a play for. Father Knox.

Fifteen

Every time he stepped out of a doorway these days, Knox looked left and right. This morning he had ducked into the chapel for a moment of prayer, just to stay in touch with Headquarters. Now as he went down the front steps of the chapel, he didn't see anybody lying in wait. Nobody on the quadrangle but a cluster of veterans having a smoke. Reassured, he took a deep breath of air with no incense in it.

The sun was struggling through gray clouds, an uneasy breeze blowing. Brown leaves crackled under Knox's feet as he headed down the walk toward the gym. As he passed the library, someone stepped out. Knox heard footfalls quickening, coming after him.

A deep voice hailed him. "Wait up, Knox. I want to talk with you."

Knox turned. The voice sounded familiar, but he couldn't place the guy. Ruddy face. Round button nose. Stocky build with a paunch. Double-breasted suit, jacket left unbuttoned. There was only one odd thing about him. As the man approached, bent slightly forward, Knox could see that he was tonsured. Head shaved bald except for short brown hair left in the shape of a cross.

Smiling, but not offering a hand, the guy caught up to Knox. "You don't scare easily," he said.

Knox stood there sizing the guy up. "How's that again?"

"Threats don't worry you?"

Oh oh, Knox thought. Guess we've met at last.

The stranger didn't look like a threat. If he made a move, Knox could block it. The guy kept smiling like a salesman trying to win over a prospect.

"So you're the one," Knox said. "You like to cut words out of newspapers. Send me dead rabbits. I guess I ought to thank you for that singing telegram, but the messenger had a lousy voice. So why are you bugging me? Who are you anyway?"

"Call me Cross. I thought we might renew our acquaintance."

Knox was puzzled. Had he met this guy before? He tried, but couldn't make any connection. "So tell me, Cross or whatever your name is, why should I quit coaching?"

The smile vanished. "Because you thwart the will of Jesus Christ."

All Knox could think of to say was, "Oh?"

Cross looked like a preacher getting ready to launch into a hellfire sermon. His lips worked, his eyes were flashing. "My church is not your church of Rome, that whore of Babylon. Mine is the Church of the One Right Path."

"Never heard of it," Knox said.

"Oh, don't look for our church in the phonebook. For the time being, we meet in secret, like the early Christians in their catacombs. But soon we will be known in every corner of the world."

"Good luck," Knox said.

Cross went on. "You represent your Christ as a meek sufferer. But ours is Christ militant, the wrathful Christ with punishing flail who drove out the moneychangers."

"No argument there. That's another side of Him. So what has your Christ got against me?"

"You shamelessly corrupt the truth," Cross said.

"How's that again?"

"You act as if athletics were Roman Catholic property."

"No fooling. Saint Cash and Holy Cross and Seton Hall are pretty good, all right, but Catholics don't own the game. We don't pretend to. And say I quit coaching, like you want me to, what difference would it make? That wouldn't change anything in the sports world."

Cross seemed to be striving to find more reasons. "What is worse, you allow members of inferior races to do their monkey tricks. Throwing balls through a silly metal hoop from far away. Oh, I've read the newspapers—you glorify these minstrels. You crow with pride over them."

"You mean S. T. Pohl? Nothing inferior about that boy. Faster on the court than ten white men put together."

Cross frowned. "Talking with you is useless."

"Yeah," Knox said, "I guess it is. You know, Cross, you're fuller of crap than a Christmas goose. You've got a lot of brass-assed crassness to come nosing around this campus. I think you better get lost."

They had been standing beside the library steps, where Cross had maneuvered him. Now, out of shadows under the steps, two more guys appeared. Each of their heads was tonsured too. One was a fat guy leaning on a cane. The other was just a kid, his lips curled back like a fox terrier ready to bite. They didn't worry Knox until the fat guy drew a long thin sword out of his cane. He gave it a practice swing. It whistled in the air.

Cross's smile had returned. "Do you want to pray, Father? Be quick about it!"

The fat man took a step forward, blade pointed, ready to drive at Knox's throat. His eyes were cold and aloof, like one-way glass.

Cross was inching nearer. Reaching his right hand into the inside pocket of his jacket. Maybe he too had a knife. And the mean-looking kid was stealing forward along with Cross.

Knox's mind raced. He could aim a kick, try to knock the sword out of the fat man's hand, but that would be risky. He might get cut. Worth taking a chance. Then he'd still have the other two to contend with. Quick decision. He'd go for the fat man. One problem at a time.

With an ear-splitting yell Knox launched a kick at the hand holding the sword. The fat man fell back a step and the kick went wild. Off balance, Knox fell backwards, sprawling on the walk.

"Stupid of you, priest," Cross said.

Knox stared up into the expressionless face of the fat man standing over him. Bringing the sword slowly down to Knox's chest. Pinning him there. Ready to drive the point into his heart.

"Drop it," somebody in back of the fat man said.

The fat man winced, feeling metal grind into his spine. Then the sword dropped and rattled on the bricks of the walk.

"Put your hands up," the new voice said.

The fat man did.

Knox sat up and stared at the newcomer. A tall lean guy with a tiny mustache, scar on his left cheek, black felt hat, sunglasses. Looked like one of the mob.

Cross was sidling toward the lean guy, the flat blade of a hunting knife glinting in one hand.

The lean guy brandished a .32 caliber automatic with a white bone grip. "Don't try it," he said. "I wouldn't mind shooting all three of you."

He turned to Knox. "You OK, Father?" Offering a hand to help Knox up.

Cross seized that unguarded moment to run. He whirled and sped off, the kid scampering at his side.

The lean guy shrugged as if he didn't give a damn. The fat man looked after them as if he'd like to escape too, but the lean guy dug the automatic into his back.

"Don't get any ideas," he said. "Pick up his sword, Father."

Knox retrieved the sword. He kicked the fat man's legs out from under him. The fat man toppled like a tree and Knox nudged his stomach with the sword.

Knox glanced at the lean man. "I owe you big time," he said.

The other gave a short hard laugh.

"So who are you?" Knox persisted. "How come you just happened by?"

"Lucky, I guess. I came to do business with the college."

"With Glauco Vastasi?"

"Yeah."

"You with some company?"

"Latin American Trading."

Knox blinked. "You work for Ricky Peru!"

The lean guy figured he'd said too much. "So long, Father. Maybe you can keep this bozo covered with his sword till the town cops get here. I'll give 'em a call."

And he pocketed his automatic and strode away.

Four students had come running up. Now they ringed Knox and his prisoner.

"Holy Mahoney, Father," the Sarge said. "Who's this mug you've got there?"

Under the sword's point, the fat man squirmed.

Knox lit a much-needed cigarette. "Don't know. That's what I want to find out."

"You will—learn—nothing," the fat man said through clenched teeth.

"Don't worry, Father," another vet said. "You can take it easy now. This bastard ain't going noplace. I'll hold him down for you."

He squatted on the fat man's belly. The man grunted.

Knox bent down to the prisoner. "You belong to the Church of the One Right Path?"

The fat man said nothing. Knox kept after him. "Where's your home base? Newark?"

"Newark is nowhere," the fat man said. "Our home is the world."

"What's your name, rank, and serial number?"

No answer.

"All right," Knox said. "I didn't want to know you any better anyway."

The siren of an approaching police car screamed.

Sixteen

When Manny the Monk dropped her back at the house, Aisling found Vastasi in the kitchen in his shirtsleeves, a plate of meat in front of him, a bottle of beer in hand. She deposited a sleeping Kiki Sue in the crib upstairs.

"Hell no," Vastasi said around a mouthful of mortadella, "taking you over was his own idea. The old bugger always thinks he can have anything. Even you."

Aisling said, "He told me you wanted to get rid of me."

"Yeah? That's news. Why would I want to do that?"

The more Vastasi thought about it, the madder he got. Brass-assed gall, his uncle had—trying to swipe his own nephew's wife. Well, almost wife. But he wouldn't let Peru see his resentment. In the organization, you didn't resent things your boss did. You had to play ball, swallow insults, act like you didn't give a damn.

He scowled at the sausage on his plate. "This pig is stale. Haven't I told you always go to Taormino's for it?"

"That's way down in Newark. I should make a ten-mile pilgrimage every time you want cold cuts? I notice you're eating what I bought."

"Only because I'm starving. Jeez, this left-over pot roast tastes like an old shoe. You need cooking lessons."

"You need new tastebuds. So if you didn't want to hand me over to Peru, where did he get the idea?"

"Christ, ain't it obvious? He liked the looks of your ass. Them fat buns he patted the other night."

"Oh, you're impossible."

"I'm surprised you didn't take him up on it. You could have lived like a fucking queen, wearing sparklers, eating Russian fish eggs, shit like that."

"Well don't think it was your manly charms that made me turn him down. Thought he owned me. Thought all he had to do was snap his fingers and I'd drop my drawers."

Vastasi was washing down the rest of his lunch with another Ballantine. He glared. "Own yourself, do you?"

"Damn right I do. I just loan myself out once in a while."

"OK, as long as you don't loan to nobody but me. I ever find you dipping some other guy—"

"Guido, honey, don't you trust me? After almost a year we've been together? Sometimes I don't know why I keep living with you."

"Because you need me. Because you goddamn well like being Mrs. V."

"You stuck-up bastard. You think I couldn't be happy if I wasn't in this make-believe marriage? I'd be free as a bird."

"Careful, sister. I could cut you loose any time."

"And I could tell the Monsignor a few things about you. These deals you pull. And your uncle that you work for. I heard him talking on the phone. He's a cold-blooded murderer."

Vastasi lifted a beefy fist. "You wise-ass bitch. You ever blab to anybody—anybody—I'll open your throat from ear to ear."

"You'd love to do that, wouldn't you? Anyhow, don't worry, boss man, I'm keeping mum. As long as you keep paying the rent and behave. For a start, you could quit spitting in the ashtray. I keep dumping out cigar juice soup."

Still glaring at her, Vastasi flung on his jacket. At the door he turned around. "Don't look for me for supper tonight. I'm gonna go see my wife. Sleep with a sensible woman for a change."

The door slammed. The kitchen trembled.

Aisling saw clearly now. Vastasi was as bad as Peru. He regarded her as just another possession. Peru was going to order Vastasi to turn her loose, and whenever that order came from his uncle, the nephew would obey. Why hang around waiting to be thrown out? Time to get out under her own steam. Time to make her move on Father Knox.

She went upstairs to the bedroom and stripped. Naked, she studied herself in the full-length mirror. Not bad. A little too much blubber in the belly, maybe. Trouble was, weight always ran to her bottom half like sand in an hourglass. But her breasts were still terrific. She gave them an experimental shake, tweaked the nipples to make them rise. Tits were what men went for, every time. Did she need to shave her pussy? Lots of women did that these days. No, hell with it, she'd stay natural. Look like the real thing, not some touched-up French postcard. Slowly and carefully, she donned her see-through bra. Her fifty-dollar slip. If things got serious and she had to strip, she'd look like a bride.

She studied her wardrobe. Chose and rejected a couple of blouses before settling on the collarless white silk one with the plunging neckline. Leave one button unbuttoned, maybe two. Choosing the right skirt was still harder. Skirts had to be so damned long these days. She put one on and practiced in the glass, swinging from side to side.

Sandals, no stockings. At the bathroom sink, she applied eye shadow. Not too dark. Shouldn't look like some two-bit Egyptian whore. Just a touch. Another touch. Like that.

She'd need some pretext for coming to Knox's office. Father, I have to have your advice. Get up close to him, look him right in the eyes. Oh, he had the hots for her, she knew. The way he'd given her the once-over at the Monsignor's party. She had to fan him to a blaze. This encounter would be a challenge, all right. But she was ready for it.

Knox had spent an hour in a huddle with the Dedwood police, answering questions, doing paperwork. The cops had hauled away the captured member of the Church of the One Right Path. They didn't like it that Knox couldn't name the gun-packing stranger who had saved his life.

Sitting at his desk, recovering, Knox had put away a stiff one when Maureen told him he had a caller. He was about to say no callers this afternoon, but the door opened and in bounced Aisling, wafting before her the odor of violets.

He stared at her. Red lips parted in a smile. Her blouse didn't leave much to the imagination. Not waiting for an invitation, she parked herself in the chair directly facing him.

She hiked up her skirt a little, crossed well-made legs. "Surprised to see me, Father?"

"I am. How come I deserve this pleasure?"

"No reason. Just passing by. Thought I'd drop in and say hello."

"All right. Hello."

"I've just heard about those fanatics who attacked you. You're all right?"

"Never better."

"I'm glad they didn't kill you."

"Thanks."

"I thought we might go on with what we started. At the party."

"And what was that?"

"Our friendship."

Knox nodded, sat back in his chair. "All right by me. Where's your baby? I've seen you on campus, carrying her around with you."

"She's napping. She'll sleep for another hour. Sometimes having a child in my arms cramps my style. You understand, I'd like to know you better. Lots better."

"Okay, what do you want to find out? I'm forty-one, Scotch Calvinist extraction. Widower. Chaplain overseas in the Pacific. Favorite color's green. What's yours?"

"Pink, I guess. You like pink things? I usually wear pink panties. But I'm not wearing anything down there today."

Knox tried to sound stern. "What are you getting at?"

"Listen, Father, I don't have much time. I've got to teach a two-thirty class. The other night when we first met, I felt something happen between us. Call it fireworks going off. Didn't you feel it too?"

"I didn't hear any explosions. Figured we got along, was all."

"It was more than that."

She rose and softly shut the door to the outer office. Lord, she was coming toward him. She sidled around the desk and with a little cry dropped into his lap.

Soft white arms were twining his neck. Two spongy breasts were crushing against him. A warm tongue pressed his lips, trying to lick them open. Her breathing came shallow and hard. A powerful scent of violets swept over him. He watched one red-nailed hand probe south, stealing toward his fly.

No. He had to put a stop to this. Digging his legs in under him, he forced himself to his feet, Aisling in his arms, and unceremoniously dumped her to the floor.

He stood glowering down at her. "By rights I ought to tell Tim Walsh to fire you, if he wasn't so hard up. For teachers."

Stunned, she sat on the carpet, green eyes looking up at him, full of rage and pain. "Is that how you treat a lady? Who simply wanted to make friends with you?"

"Yeah? It felt like you were after more than just friendship, sister. I don't know what I did to encourage you, but kindly get discouraged right away."

Aisling sprang to her feet. "You son of a bitch!" she cried. Head down, she lunged straight at him, fists flailing the air. She landed a tattoo of blows on his chest. Her strength and fury took him by surprise. He grabbed her wrists and shoved her away. She launched a high-heeled kick at his crotch, but he sidestepped it and she toppled over backwards, landing on the carpet again, glaring up at him, spitting out a wandering strand of auburn hair, lips working but no words coming out. Then she rose, slowly and sullenly.

Knox said, "Let's forget this ever happened. Now clear out of here. Go say five Our Fathers and five Hail Marys and take a cold shower and quit reading *True Romances* magazine."

Keeping her voice low and level, Aisling said, "You bastard. You damned churchy bastard. I don't read trash like that. And I don't know any of your goddamn Catholic prayers."

The door banged after her.

———————

Trudging the black asphalt walk back toward the house on Professors Way, she felt as if a storm cloud hung over her. That visit to Knox had been a terrible blunder. Her interview with Peru and her quarrel with Vastasi had left her desperate, and she had recklessly moved too fast. It might have worked, if she had prepared him for it. Maybe she hadn't permanently ruined things between them, but this was a serious set-back. The coward, she knew he wanted her, but he was hiding behind his Roman collar. Sweet saints and Hebrew prophets, what was a healthy, red-blooded American woman to do for a little bit of love?

That kid, the babysitter. Her dumb doglike admirer. He always looked at her with helpless longing. She could get him with a snap of her fingers. He didn't look bad. Had an upturned button nose. Freckles that stood out when he blushed. His boyishness made her want to crush him to her bosom, poke a nipple in his mouth. Oh, he'd be awkward, green, inexperienced stuff. But he just might do until something better came along.

Seventeen

Moon was still reeling from shock. As usual in biology class, he had been sitting in the front row staring up Professor Vastasi's short skirt, trying to decide did she wear pants or not, and when all the ex-GIs had left, she had said to him, "You know, Gogarty, I'd like to talk with you. Really talk. Why don't you drop over to the house tonight? I could make marshmallow fudge."

His heart began to pound. "Will—won't your husband be there?"

"Not tonight. He'll be out of town. Kiki Sue goes to bed at seven, so come around seven-thirty, why don't you?"

His brain was still seething like a small pot of water brought to a boil. He didn't want to think about anything except the coming night. Yet here he was in the Quonset-hut office of *The Immolator*, supposed to interview S. T. Pohl.

Sprawled in Moon's swivel chair, long legs up on the desk, Pohl was washing down Fig Newtons with a quart of Hoffman's ginger ale. He said, "Moon, son, what's the matter with you? You look like you seen the Second Comin'. Snap out of it. You got me over here, ain't you going to ask me where I'm from, what's gonna happen this season, shit like that?"

"Oh. Yeah. Sorry. You're from Mississippi? But you talk Northern."

"Mississippi just a way-station on my development. Like till when I was thirteen. Then the war start heatin' up. My granma and old lady, they move to Motor City, get jobs stitchin' parachutes. They put me in the Christian Brothers School."

Dutifully, Moon scribbled notes. "So Detroit's where you got most of your education?"

"Brought me up fast. Learned about shopliftin', weed, gradeschool pussy. But I didn't do much weed. Interfere with my game. You get too high, poppin' a ball through a hoop seem piddly shit, like it's miles and miles beneath you, you know?"

"How come you came to St. Cash's?"

"Brother Merciful, the headmaster, he brought me here. Showed me off to Father Knox and zing, I'm in."

"I saw you work out this morning," Moon said. "You're fast. You've got the biggest hands I ever saw—you just wrap them around the ball. Is the team pinning their hopes on you?"

"On me and some other imports. Thad Kolowsky. Andy Crisp. Rob O'Malley. We all got full tuition scholarships. See, this place never had much of a team before. After all, what you gonna put together out of a few lily-white divinity students? Now they got all these four thousand five hundred ex-GIs, and the man, the Monsignor, he figure he gonna land us on the map. And there no way to do that quicker than have a famous team."

"What do you hope to get, yourself, out of college?"

"Sheet, what you want me to say? Catholic outlook? Make me a soldier of Jesus? Son, money is what I want to get."

"Getting an education—that doesn't count?"

"Just now, I'm not gettin' much. Got a voice and diction course with this Polack nobody can understand. Got a lit course, only the guy teaching it don't know nothin' 'bout Shakespeare, so he just talk about Catholic writers like Hillary Bollox and G. K. Chesterfield."

On the notepad, Moon's pencil slowed to a stop. "What do you think of Professor Vastasi?"

Pohl's face lit. "Grits and gravy. She yank that skirt up high like she do, make your old ding-dong stand up and walk. You see how Northern I am, son? Down in old Miss, a spook talk like that 'bout a white woman, next thing he danglin' from a tree."

"Money. That's the big thing for you, huh?"

Pohl emptied the Fig Newton package. "Matter of fact," he said, "it costin me to go here. I could turn pro if I wanted to. But I figure, get me a degree, gonna make more in the long run."

"So when you make all this money, what'll you do with it?"

Pohl's mouth tightened. "It ain't for me. I gotta close some unfinished business. Gotta go back to Mississippi, settle with a few people. Sister Agatha, she the first one saw anything in me, she running this little school need a new roof and a workin' toilet. Being Catholic in Mississippi, next worst thing to bein' a nig.

"Not just that." Pohl's voice sank low. "There's some rednecks I gotta fix. Know just where they live. Poke a few sticks of blow-up through they mail slots, like they done to my momma's Free Will Baptist church. Had to pick pieces of the preacher up off the cellar floor. Me, I'm no bomber, I'd need help. You can hire any kind of help you want, you got the bucks."

"Tell me, what does the S. T. in your name stand for?"

"You got to know?"

"If you don't mind."

"Son, I'll tell you, but you better not print it, or, so God is my judge, I'll ream your ass, you hear? First name's Scrotum. Like the sack your balls come in. The T was my own idea."

Moon stifled a laugh. "Scrotum Pohl! How did you ever get a name like that?"

"Momma so poor she delivered in a clinic. Didn't have no name in mind, so she let the med student write one on my papers. Sounded good to her. Well, so long, Moon. See you in pussy class."

He stuck out his right hand. Moon's disappeared in it.

After Pohl left, Moon sat trying to sort his jumbled impressions. All he really wanted to think about was the evening ahead of him.

The door of the hut banged open. In came the Sarge, out of breath. His gloved hand held a copy of the *Newark Evening News* folded open to the movie advertising. "Boy, have I got a story for you!"

"What's that?" Moon asked unenthusiastically.

"You know this Catholic action society I'm in, the DSSS? Dedicated Staunchers of the Sacred Side? Well we been down in Newark picketing this movie house has a show by that rotten commie Charlie Chaplin."

"Which movie is that?"

"Here it is advertised. Piece of doo called *City Lights*. We're putting the damn place out of business. Manager says our picket line turns away customers, so he can't make ends meet. Serves him right, the pinko bastard. He's even been showing Russian movies, *Battleship Pumpkin* and crap like that. But we fixed him. Nobody's going to show no red propaganda around here, not while us Staunchers are on the job."

"You've seen the movie?"

"Naw. What would I want to do that for? It's the lousiest movie I never seen."

"I saw it. Thought it was funny. Chaplin's a genius."

The Sarge grew livid. "Whose side you on, anyway? I don't give a shit if this Chaplin is Leonard di fucking Vinci. You gonna write this story or ain't you?"

Moon sighed. *The Immolator* needed filler. "All right."

"And while you're at it," the Sarge added, "say the Staunchers have started a ladies' auxiliary. The Vigilantes of Veronica's Veil. You got that?"

Cosimo di Montecassino swung his massive black Buick into the driveway that led to the rear of Feeley Mansion. He parked in a lot that said FACULTY. He consulted his watch. S. T. Pohl got out of class at noon, so he ought to be dropping by at any minute.

Cosimo stationed himself on the back steps. Maybe the kid had gone to lunch. Well, he'd wait for him. Couldn't get caught in the gym again, not after that run-in with Knox. Cosimo sucked on his Cuban cigar, watching it turn to a spear of ash that lengthened in midair and didn't break.

All of a sudden a tall black form blotted the sky. "Excuse me, man, I live here."

Cosimo sprang to his feet. "Mr. S. T. Pohl. Just the man I want to see. Mr. Pohl, I'm Cosimo di Montecassino. Big fan of yours."

Pohl just stood there looking him up and down. "Sharkskin shoes. Black shirt, white tie, diamond stuck in it. Got a cockeyed eye. You just like the type Fatha Knox say don't have nothin' to do with."

"Let me buy you a drink, Mr. Pohl. It might pay you to talk with me."

"You tryna bribe me, man? Don't never drink no booze. Make my shootin' hand wobble. But now, you know, a nice juicy steak, fries, few mushrooms on the side, that might be somethin' else."

"Steak! I know just the place! One-and-a-half pound tenderloin, best in Jersey, only five minutes away. My car's right here. All I want is a little talk with you."

"Can't do no harm just to talk," Pohl said. "Get your car runnin', I'll go leave these schoolbooks off inside."

Eighteen

It was hard to stay alert all the time. It was no fun keeping your guard up, expecting some bastard with a sword to jump out at you. Reluctantly, Knox had accepted an offer from Tim Walsh to accompany him when he had to go anywhere. But Walsh had classes to teach and the biology department to chair, and he couldn't be with Knox all the time.

At sundown this afternoon, Knox was alone. He stood at the door of the gym building, scanning the sidewalk that led to the library. All clear. He opened the door and set out. A sharp breeze had come up, there was a twinge of winter in the air. Maple leaves were spiraling down as Knox made his way to the library to see what the sports reporters were saying about S. T. Pohl. He had had a tough time getting the college librarian to subscribe to *Sporting News*. For years the periodical room had stocked nothing but the *Messenger of the Sacred Heart* and the weekly *Tablet*, the official newspaper of the diocese.

As he headed up the walk to the old brick library building, Knox got a surprise. All the lights in the basement were ablaze. First sign of life he'd ever seen down there. Voices floated up from open windows. What was going on? He descended the basement steps and went in.

In a musty cavern of a room, a dozen students hunched over long oak tables, scratching with pens. Piles of old books surrounded them, threatening to topple over. Father

Patrick Nolan, the librarian, satisfaction on his beef-red face, stood smoking his pipe, overseeing the bent backs of the scribes.

Knox had known Nolan for a long time, from before the man had developed a bottle problem. One day Nolan had toppled off the altar and spilled the wine and had had to be packed off to the priests' rest home. When he returned, the Monsignor hadn't known what to do with him, so he had made him college librarian. Must have figured it was a low-stress job that didn't matter.

Nolan looked up at Knox's approach. "Hello Doug. You want to know what we're doing here?"

"Sure, Pat. What?"

"Cataloguing a few books. These lads are writing the titles on cards, putting Dewey Decimal numbers on 'em."

"A few books? Looks like you bought out a second-hand store."

"As a matter of fact, that's exactly what we did. Glauco Vastasi found a guy in Newark who ran a used book store and he wanted to sell out and retire. It was a lucky break for us. Got to get the library large enough to satisfy the Middle States Association."

The librarian eyed a four-volume set of *The Decline and Fall of the Roman Empire,* yanked it out and set it aside. "Gibbon is on the Index. He needs to go in the cage under lock and key." For Knox's benefit, he added, "Where we keep Voltaire, Steinbeck, Freud—poisonous stuff like that."

At the nearest table, a delicate young non-veteran was toiling through a stack of books, earning fifty cents an hour.

"Working hard?" Knox asked.

Francis Percival Crews raised his head and smirked. "Terribly hard, Father. We've absolutely got to finish before the evaluation team gets here. But I really like doing this. Old books are sweet."

Knox sniffed. "You think so? These smell pretty sour to me."

Green mold had crept across the spines of many of the books, and some had lost their covers. Knox picked up a volume from the stack Crews was working on and blew a silverfish off it. *The Rompsey Girls, or, Jolly Days on Parsnip Farm.*

Crews turned to the kid seated next to him. "Hey, Konny, how do I classify this one?"

Konny inspected the book. *So You Want To Go Potty!* by Wee Wee Wisdom.

"C-call it l-l-life sciences," Konny stammered. "F-f-five s-seventy."

"How about this? *Secrets of Your Palm Revealed.* Do I throw it under medicine?"

Konny thought. "N-no," he said. "It's n-not about j-j-jerking off, it's about p-palm reading. Occult, I guess. A hundred th-th-thirty."

Knox glanced at more titles. *What a Girl Should Know When She Starts to Flow. Tom Swift and His Electric Runabout. Fascism, Hope of the Future. The Young Manhood of Warren G. Harding. 1904 Yearbook of the Milwaukee Bowling Association. Was Jesus a Kike?*

He whirled to the librarian. "Pat, aren't these books crap? What do you want to put them in the library for?"

"Because they count," Nolan said. "Numbers, that's all the evaluators care about. We need an additional thirty thousand volumes for a college of this size. We'll have everything catalogued and on the shelves by Monday or die trying."

"Don't you see anything wrong with this operation? Like you're trying to pull a fast one?"

Nolan coughed on his pipe smoke. "You think that didn't occur to me? Listen, Doug, I've thought all this through. It's perfectly all right to bring the library up to standard. Some of these books may be junk, but we can weed them out later. Right now all that matters is meeting requirements. Lord knows the college can't risk losing its accreditation."

"Why not? If we don't come up to standard, why not admit it? Then work on fixing where we fall short?"

"That's easy to say, Doug, but now we've got a duty to thousands of veterans. If the college doesn't get accredited, their degrees will be worthless. We owe them a first-class education."

"But are we doing that? Giving 'em the fucking *Rompsey Girls*?"

"Don't swear at me, Doug. The Monsignor has given explicit orders to go ahead with this. He's determined to get passing marks from the evaluation team. How we do it doesn't matter."

"The end justifies the means, huh? I thought it never did."

Knox turned and walked out, so mad he forgot to look at the *Sporting News*.

On the way back to the priests' house he met Tim Walsh, out of breath, hurrying up to him. "Sorry I'm late, Doug. Department meeting."

Knox told him about the fraud being perpetrated at the library. "I don't like it, Tim. A lot of what's going on around here. Fishy dealings. Like the other day the business office got in a load of surplus typewriters. Forty of 'em, even though in all the college offices we haven't got more than ten secretaries. Maureen needed one, and when I got Vastasi to send one over, you know who delivered it? The Impeccable Typewriter Company."

"What do you make of it?"

"Could be that Vastasi is selling those war surplus items to retailers. I called him about it, though, and he had an explanation. Told me those typewriters had been sitting in storage for years, so he sent them to Impeccable to tune 'em up. Wish to hell I knew if he was lying."

"Guess you'd better take his word. Unless you can prove otherwise."

"What really pisses me off is the Monsignor ordered me to give two box seats to that sonofabitch Ricky Peru. It's as if Peru has him in his vest pocket."

"Well, you know, Doug, The Monsignor is trying to do what's right by the college. He can't be too picky in choosing friends."

Knox paused on the sidewalk to light up. "Yeah? I think some of these new friends are worse than enemies. You know the saying, lie down with dogs and you get up with fleas. All we're doing is faking. Nobody cares whether or not we've got the genuine goods. Reminds me of one time I bought a Ronson lighter from a street vendor in Sasebo. It looked like a Ronson only it didn't work, and when I broke it open it was a piece of a Schlitz beer can. That's what we're doing, damn it. Running a fake excuse for a college."

"Doug, don't take it so hard. You can't reform this whole place single-handed. You been having any trouble today? Any more guys come after you?"

"Not since the last time. But I keep looking out for them."

"I still think you ought to ask for a transfer. Take a parish for a while in, say, South Dakota."

Knox frowned. "That's the worst idea I ever heard. Have they even got any Catholics in South Dakota? I thought all they had was presidents' heads made out of rock and a bunch of prairie dogs."

"Hold up, Doug." Walsh grabbed Knox by an arm and steered him in under an oak tree's shadow. "I just saw somebody. Not anybody that belongs here."

He pointed. Knox looked in time to see a bulky figure in a white raincoat standing, just standing on the walk on the far side of the central quadrangle, a hundred yards away. The figure turned around and moonlight reflected from his face.

Cross.

He shot the two priests a piercing look, turned, and disappeared into the dark.

Nineteen

Moon had never had a woman before, but he knew just what you did. He had studied his grandmother's copy of Marie Stokes's *Married Love*. Reeking with a men's cologne called Seduction, armed with six short-stemmed red roses and a pack of Trojans timidly purchased in the Dedwood Village drugstore, he counted the minutes to seven-thirty. Then, tense with anticipation, he headed for Professor Vastasi's.

The harvest moon hung overhead like a ripe peach ready to burst. Kiki Sue will be asleep, his beautiful professor had told him—just walk in, don't ring the bell. Mustering his courage, Moon squeezed the big brass handle, winced as the door creaked open, and bravely stepped into the front hallway, the bouquet held before him.

In the living room off to the left, she lay on the couch, dressed for a casual evening at home. Levi shorts, nothing across her bosom but a bright red scarf knotted behind her back. Shoeless, her long white legs in black net stockings, one foot tucked beneath her, dandling the other on the floor. In a pewter candelabra on the coffee table, five candles wriggled their flames like fingers beckoning.

She welcomed him with a smile, flashing white even teeth. She thrust aside her copy of *Biological Abstracts*. Slowly and deliberately she swung both red-nailed feet to the floor and motioned him down by her side. Luminous big green eyes searched his face. In a low, husky voice she said, "Want a piece of—"

Oh, my God, he thought.

"—fudge?"

"Oh. Sure. You bet."

"These for me?" Taking the roses from him. "You shouldn't have. But I'm glad you did."

She sprang up, bounced to the kitchen, ran water, plunged stems in a vase. Moon adjusted his glasses, following her every move with fascinated gaze. From behind, her shorts looked tight as the heads of a couple of drums.

Then she was back, holding a pan, knife, plates, paper napkins. She placed them on the coffee table and sat back down beside him in one smooth motion like a collapsing sand castle.

"Don't mind this dump," she said, waving a hand around the room. "Glauco bought all the furniture by just calling up the store and telling them to send over anything that was on sale."

"It—it's very nice."

"It's hideous. But who cares? You're here and I'm here and we're going to have a perfectly lovely evening, aren't we?"

With a conspiratorial smile, she handed him a napkin. Static electricity crackled. Moon winced, feeling a tiny shock.

"Isn't it crazy?" she said. "Must be the heat. Everything in the house is giving off sparks. Look at this!"

With an electric crackle, she peeled off one net stocking, revealing a long white leg, and flung the stocking at the wall. It stayed there, fastened like a vampire bat.

"See?" She jimmied loose a wedge of fudge, slid it to a plate, and handed it to him. Suddenly ravenous, he bit into the dark chocolate square. A dribble of marshmallow fell down his chin. She leaned soft bare shoulders against him, thrust out her tongue, and licked it off.

Moon gulped. "This is the best thing I ever tasted," he said.

"Did anybody ever tell you your nose is cute?" She touched its tip with her little finger. "Been shaving long?"

"Oh, sure. Ever since I was twelve."

"Early bloomer, huh? First time I laid eyes on you, I thought you'd just been hatched. Hey, how about another piece?"

"Yes. Please."

She plied the knife. "It's got Bushmill's whisky in it. Old family recipe of my Irish grandmother's. She had a sweet tooth. In fact, that was the only tooth she had in her head when she died."

"You aren't Italian?"

"Mother straight from Donegal, old man a Yid from the Upper East Side. I was born Weinstein. Still am, on my driver's license."

"But—you're Mrs. Vastasi."

"Only on campus. So I can live here with Glauco and it looks respectable. We've never been married. Glauco's got a wife and two kids over in Orange. Now keep this under your hat, you understand? You blab and you'll get me in trouble."

"Your secret is safe with me." Moon felt a surge of joy. She was free, she was up for grabs!

She gazed at him tenderly. "Here, have some more fudge. You stay all night, you're going to need fuel."

"I can stay—all night?"

"Sure. Glauco won't be home, he's seeing the wife."

She pressed a warm bare shoulder up against him. A strand of long red hair dangled across his mouth. His nostrils filled with the mingled aromas of fudge and violets. The scarf holding her breasts grazed his shirtfront. Static electricity crackled like frying butter.

"How old are you, sweet stuff?" she asked.

"Seventeen. In four more days."

"So what are you going to do in life?"

"I—I'll be a doctor." He drew himself up proudly. "Already I'm an apprentice mortician."

Aisling shuddered. "Don't tell me about it." The red-nailed foot without the stocking was massaging his left ankle. "Ever had it before?"

"It? Oh. You mean—well, no. Not exactly. But I've come close." Thinking of Loretta Snow that summer night on the banks of the Rockaway. "What about you, Professor? Were you ever married?"

"Once. To a son of a bitch ran a craps table in Vegas. I was out there dancing in a chorus for a while. Guy was a hunk, a Clark Gable, but he turned out to be the minister type. Used to give me lessons in how to brush my teeth. Squeeze the toothpaste from the bottom of the tube, roll it up, always put the cap back on. We didn't last."

"Then what did you do?"

"Came back East, lived in the Village on my alimony. Got a degree in nursing. Then the war started. What was I supposed to do, sit around ripping ration stamps out of a book, painting stockings on my legs out of a bottle? I got me a commission in Women Accepted for Volunteer Emergency Service."

"You travel?"

"South Pacific. I was a flight nurse, evacuating casualties."

"I thought WAVES didn't get sent overseas."

"Nurses did. We went anyplace there was fighting."

"Golly. That must have been tough."

"Sometimes. Once I was shot down, stranded on an atoll."

"All by yourself?"

"Oh, I had plenty of company."

"So after the war you met Mr. Vastasi and you had your baby?"

"The other way around. I got kicked out of service for getting pregnant. Went back to New York, picked up a master's at N.Y.U. And then Glauco came along."

Moon's brow furrowed in puzzlement. "How come you were attracted to a guy like that? Maybe I shouldn't say this, Professor, but Mr. Vastasi sort of looks like a thug."

"Yeah, doesn't he. He used to hang around my favorite Eighth Street bar. Couple of drinks one night and we were in the sack. Hell, I was broke, had this six-month-old baby, I was lonesome. Glauco said he'd take care of me. Always had a big roll of bills. I figured he was in some kind of racket, but it wasn't any of my business."

"I understand. You sacrificed your honor for your child!"

"Never thought of it that way. The nice thing about Glauco was he was a typical wop. Didn't mind bambinos at all." She reached over, removed his glasses, and parked them on the coffee table. "Enough history. Take your clothes off."

"Now?"

"When do you think, you ninny, next Christmas?"

She reached behind her back, undid the scarf and released her breasts, purple nipples erected. With a crackle of static she peeled off her other stocking and flung it behind the couch.

Through nearsighted eyes Moon beheld her, a beautiful blur, like a rainbow glimpsed through a waterfall. Faint sparks danced as he shucked off his shirt and pants. By candlelight, Aisling contemplated his flat bony chest and near-hairless body, massaging him with her gaze.

"Skin back your dick," she ordered. "Let's see if you can pass a short-arm inspection. Oh, never mind—I forgot, you're a virgin. C'mere. Gimme a hug."

Passionately, Moon hurled himself upon her, surrounded her with his arms. She drew his lips to her bosom, gave a small groan, and whispered, "Kiss, damn you, kiss."

He had arrived at the end of the rainbow. Within his grasp lay the longed-for pot of gold.

All of a sudden a foghorn voice interrupted them. "WHAT'S GOING ON?"

Hands on hips, Randy Harrigan stood planted in front of the couch, coldly staring down at them.

In shock, Moon sat bolt upright. The rainbow vanished with a pop, leaving fragments sifting downward through the air. He snatched up *Biological Abstracts* from the coffee table to cover his genitals.

"Sneaky bastard!" Aisling shrilled, one arm screening her breasts. "I told you never to come in here without an invitation!"

Harrigan squinted down in disbelief. "Moon Gogarty! I know this jerk. You're screwing with *him*? What's with you, baby, you desperate? You're scraping the bottom of the barrel."

Aisling glared. "Get out of here."

Harrigan didn't budge. "Jeez, I can't believe it. You expect me to take sloppy seconds after a twerp like this?"

"You're not getting anything," Aisling said. "Not any more."

Moon covered his privates with a sofa cushion. Should he launch himself at Harrigan's throat? He dismissed the idea. He wasn't really dressed for a fight.

Eyes flashing, Aisling leaped to her feet, breasts cavorting. "Why, you dumb mick Randy Harrigan, you think you own me? I'll entertain whoever I want. Now hit the road this minute or you're out of a job. All I have to do is say the word to Glauco and you're through."

Harrigan looked her up and down. "You're a slut, Aisling, you know it? There isn't anything in pants you wouldn't lay. Even this little piss-assed puddle of puke. You tell Vastasi to fire me and I'll tell him you been fucking with students behind his back. OK, I'm going. As for you, Gogarty, I ain't done with you."

He turned around and stomped out, slamming the front door.

Waaa! Waaaa! came a bawl from upstairs.

"That son of a bitch," Aisling said bitterly, "he woke Kiki Sue. Don't go away, kid—I'll be right back." She scampered away and bounded upstairs, bare feet slapping the steps.

Moon sat trembling, hugging the sofa cushion. The exchange between Harrigan and his professor had shaken him to the core. He couldn't believe it. Could she be promiscuous? Could she really sleep with a thug like Vastasi and a punk like Harrigan, then invite still another lover into her arms?

Twenty

In four minutes Aisling was back, carrying Kiki Sue in a stretch suit, cooing, patting, comforting. As Moon looked on, she settled in the rocking chair and began to rock, clasping the infant to one breast, crooning softly. By candlelight her face assumed a glow.

Moon felt the need to assert himself. He hauled out a pack of Orbit chewing gum, a gift from Konny, and said, "Mind if I chew?"

"Go ahead."

"Want one?"

"No thanks. I don't indulge."

"Does he—Harrigan—come here often?"

"He used to. When Glauco wasn't around."

"What did he want?"

"What in hell do you think?"

"I don't believe it, Professor—er—Weinstein. How could you—"

"Don't get puritanical with me, smartass. You know, there are people who keep their lives like hundred-dollar bills they don't want to break. What fun do they have? Not me. I'm the spending type. Hey, I think this child is falling asleep again. Yeah. Yeah. Come on, let's go upstairs."

Moon rummaged a pocket in his cast-off slacks and found the condoms. Clutching the package like an amulet, one last stick of Orbit gum in his other hand, he rose and followed into the hall. Watching her white cheeks and long white legs ascend the stairs ahead of him, he found himself getting back in the proper spirit. In his mind's ear, the Glenn Miller band was playing "In the Mood."

Aisling lowered the sleeping child into the crib. She waved Moon to the bed. The covers had been drawn back in readiness. She disappeared into the bathroom and shut the door. He waited nervously, trying to calm the drumbeat of his pulse. He unwrapped another stick of gum and chewed, carefully rolled the silver wrapper into a ball, and dropped it to the floor. The bathroom door reopened and the light went out. At last she lay beside him, warm and softly breathing, naked as the harvest moon.

Then she was on top of him, tonguing his chest, doing things of which Marie Stopes in *Married Love* had never dreamed. He wanted to cry out—started to—but she placed a finger to her lips. *"Don't wake Kiki Sue!"*

He whipped a Trojan out of the packet and ineptly drew it on. She adjusted it for him, rummaged a bedside drawer for a tube of lubricating jelly, and with practiced hand smeared goo on his upright shaft.

And then he was fingering the lips of her doorway. One of her hands was guiding him in. With a thrust he drove home. Was this possible? He was about to fulfill all his dreams!

Then, like a phantom stealing forth from the shadows, a pathetic figure loomed. Loretta Snow, naked, stretched out on the mortuary table. He could see the wound on her forehead, dark where the branch had pierced it, the small brown mole on her stomach, her undeveloped body lying just as he had glimpsed it, her breasts mere tentative buds. Her pale yellow hair hung to her waist in disarray, waiting to be combed. Her eyes opened and she looked at him, the way she had looked that summer night on the riverbank when she had told him, *Moon, Moon, I want it, but please, we'd better not do it, I'm scared,* and he had withdrawn his fumbling hands and they had fled, filled with alarm before a wave of feeling that had engulfed them and swamped them and nearly borne them all the way.

Now by the dim glow of a nightlight he stared. Inside the condom, his vital part had shriveled to an insignificant worm.

"For God's sake, what's the matter?" Aisling wanted to know. "Must be this rubber. Like shaking hands with gloves on. Off with it!"

She whipped the condom off him and flung it to the ceiling. It stayed pasted there.

"Try again, lover," she whispered. "We don't need anything between us. It's all right, the Lord protects nursing mothers."

She went down on him. She toiled and toiled. But his vision of Loretta had left him helpless, chilled, paralyzed. "Professor," he said at last, "it's no use. I—I just can't."

"You little puke. Harrigan was right. And me, like a fool—a good stud like him, I sent him away."

"I'm sorry. I really am. It's just—I can't explain."

"Scared, are you? Because it is your first time? Happens to lots of guys. Don't give up, chick, maybe there's hope for you."

From below came a sound like the crash of doomsday thunder. The sound of the front door opening, banging against the wall. The bump of an overnight bag hitting the floor.

"Oh no!" Aisling breathed. "It's Glauco! Quick, under the bed!"

Shoving him out onto the floor, she yanked the covers up around her. Moon, half expecting an angry God to sear him with a lightning bolt, slid on his belly in under the bed, hearing Glauco Vastasi's heavy shoes clumping up the stairs.

"Hi, hon," Moon heard Aisling call. "Back already? Thought you were staying over in Orange tonight."

And Vastasi's rasping answer, "Aaaah, the wife gave me a hard time. Just because I asked her to give me head. We had a blowup, so I left."

"Poor Glauco. Can't get along with either of his women. Welcome back, lover. Guess I'm the lesser of two hard times."

Then she was giggling. Looking out from under the bed, Moon could see Vastasi's legs standing there, up close. It sounded as though he was smooching her.

He let out a guffaw. "No nightgown on? You been expecting me?"

"It's a hot night. You hungry? Want some fudge?"

"Naaaa. I had a couple steaks and some beers. It's your ass I could use."

"Hurry up and get ready, hon. I really need you tonight."

Then Vastasi was in the bathroom brushing his teeth, spitting, making gargling noises. In a few minutes his enormous weight crushed down the mattress overhead. The box springs sagged and Moon's head and rump felt clamped in a vise. He wriggled on his belly over to Aisling's side of the bed. That helped.

He heard Aisling say, "Quick, lover. Sock it to me quick."

At once there was a furious creaking and jingling. Aisling was moaning, saying, "Yeah, good, that's the way," and Vastasi was snorting like a hog.

Moon could have wept. The humiliation! He, the deserving suitor, denied his longed-for consummation. And now Vastasi, the dumb thug, lay directly above him, violating the woman to whom only he, James Aloysius Gogarty, had a right. And the worst of it was that Moon couldn't protest, couldn't risk making a sound.

Overhead, Aisling gave a tiny scream of pleasure. The mattress slowed to a stop.

The quiet that followed seemed to last forever. Moon didn't move, hardly breathing. He passed the time by imagining he was Artie Shaw doing a broadcast from the Rainbow Room, opening with "Begin the Beguine."

At last, Vastasi was snoring. From over the edge of the mattress, Aisling's face appeared, upside down.

"You still there?" she whispered.

"Naturally."

"Scram. Fast. Never mind your clothes. Don't use the front door, the alarm would go off. Go out the bathroom window. You can slide down the roof and drop off."

Trying not to jiggle the mattress, Moon dug his elbows into the shag rug, tugged his hindquarters free, and, like a crab on its belly, crept over the floor. He made it to the bathroom. For a moment he glanced back at Aisling in the bed, motioning for him to hurry. He felt like Adam without even a fig leaf, casting a backward glance at Eden. Paradise Lost.

The late October night was still warm, and the bathroom window wide open. Moon stifled the urge to take a piss, knowing he didn't dare make any noise. Carefully, he unhooked the window screen and pushed it outward, removed it, and laid it on the downward slope of the roof. He poked one bare leg out of the window and then the other, leaning his head back so that his chest and buttocks would fit through. Sliding on his back, he got all the way outside onto the rough, asbestos-shingled roof and released his breath. So far so good. Vastasi kept on snoring.

Perched on a gable at the rear of the house, he squinted, trying to see, wishing he had his glasses. By the dazzling moonlight he could tell that the roof tilted sharply downward and ended in a copper rain gutter. It would be a jump of maybe ten feet from the gutter to the ground.

All right. He had to try. Inch by inch, he slid on his backside down the roof, suppressing an *ouch!* as shingles grated his bare bottom. Arrived at the edge, he fixed both feet against the gutter to halt his descent, and paused to calculate his next move.

WHANG!

The noise could have wakened the dead. With a shrill scream the gutter parted company from the rotted edge of the roof and crashed to the yard below. With nothing to stop his feet, Moon's body shot off into space. He landed in a clump of bushes, twigs jabbing his back, and fell in a heap to the ground.

In an instant Vastasi was peering out of the bathroom window, bellowing into the night. "Who's there, goddamn you? Talk up or I'll shoot!"

Moon kept still, not even daring to breathe.

BAM. BAM. Two streaks of fire ripped through the bushes, dug creases in the lawn, and chinked into a low brick wall.

BAM. A third bullet whined past Moon's ear. He didn't bother to think, he scrambled to his feet. The brick wall flung itself into his path, but he vaulted over it, and crouched down on the other side. Sweet Jesus, was this how he would die? Buck naked, shot by a jealous husband, a stiff lying on the undertaker's table just like poor pathetic Loretta, with his grandmother working on him? His bladder released its stream against the wall.

The pistol clicked on empty. Vastasi was cursing. "Out of ammo. Goddamn second-story man. But I scared him. He didn't get inside."

That's what you think, Moon said to himself. A tidal wave of relief swept over him. Yet for a long time he remained crouched down, motionless, staying invisible, huddled against the wall.

Waaa! Waaa! Waaaa! Kiki Sue wailed.

Twenty-One

Perched in their third row box seats looking down on the court, Peru and Tessie watched the Quills, St. Cassian's hoop squad, drub Seton Hall. Not that the game mattered, there wasn't any real money riding on it, but Peru wanted to see S. T. Pohl in action. See if the kid was the sensation he was cracked up to be.

Pohl didn't disappoint. He kept rocketing to the hoop, dodging and weaving, and at the rare times when he was stopped, snapping the strings with a fadeaway from the top of the key. He weaved his way around the Seton Hall stars, Bobby Wanzer and Pep Saul, who looked powerless against a superhuman force.

"God, that nigra kid can run," Tessie said, taking a pull of cognac from a silver flask.

"He can do anything," Peru said. He leaned close to her ear and added in an undertone, "Not only that, he's in my pocket."

"No fooling. You bought him?"

"Not so loud! You'll see. Just wait till the game with Holy Sepulcher. He's gonna mind me like a dog on a chain."

"And you'll be betting on the other side."

"How did you guess?"

"Ricky, you're just too smart."

"You can't be too smart in this world."

"Then how come we're sitting in the third row and not the first?"

Peru's face grew dark. "Be glad you're here. Glauco had a hell of a time with that sports priest, Knox. Getting any box seats out of him. But my good buddy the Monsignor put the squeeze on him. There's the bastard sitting down there on the bench."

"That the guy insulted you?"

"That's him. But I'll insult *him* one of these days."

"Ricky. You wouldn't do nothing to a priest?"

"No? Just because a man wears a Roman collar don't mean he can walk all over me. Gimme a pull out of that flask, will you? And keep your mouth shut about all this."

The cognac went down like fire. Probably give him indigestion. Before their eyes Pohl floated up in the air like a feather and banked in another basket.

Peru smiled expansively. "Lookit the size of this place. Biggest job Jericho Construction ever had. I brokered that deal, you know. Put a nice piece of change in our pocket."

"That's the way, hon."

"Did you know, doll, this gym got built in four months? That's a shorter time than it took the Romans to build the goddamn pyramids."

"Huh. Maybe that's why the back of my seat is coming loose."

———————————

Tim Walsh insisted on sitting next to Knox on the coach's bench.

"I want to keep a lookout for those creeps," Walsh said. "They could be here, in this crowd. That guy Cross."

Knox said, "Don't give me that crap, Tim. You just want a front seat for the game."

Walsh laughed. "Hell. You're wise to me."

Knox watched the game with mixed feelings. Most of the frosh still needed work, but they were shaping up. Pohl's performance filled him with glee, until he happened to glance up at the box seats. The two Perus. Tessie didn't understand the game and Peru was explaining it to her. Ah, sweet Lord, the power of money.

When the first half ended, the Quills were ahead by nineteen points. During halftime Bob Davies, the Seton Hall coach, nodded to Knox from his opposing bench, and jabbed a thumb toward Pohl. His lips formed one word. *Great.*

Knox found himself staring at the concrete wall across the court. A visible crack in its surface had appeared, jagged like a lightning bolt. Damned sloppy construction. Only the other day the janitor had found some ceiling plaster lying on the floor, a chunk the size of a wash basin. Be lucky if the building held together for another year. He had better call a structural engineer tomorrow, give the whole place a going over. Nothing had better happen when five thousand people were sitting there watching a game.

When the slaughter of Seton Hall was over, a middle-aged guy wearing a huge gold wristwatch and a new ST. CASSIAN sweatshirt got up from his seat next to Peru.

"What a game, what a game! That black boy was terrific, wasn't he?"

"Yeah," Peru said. "He's going to smash hell out of Holy Sepulcher. Better place your bet now, while you can still get good odds."

"Already did. A thousand bucks straight up says Saint Cash wins."

"Lay the points and bet Saint Cash to cover the spread. Your money is like it's in the bank."

"Yeah. Maybe I'll do that. Call my bookie in the morning."

They filed down cement steps and blended into the outgoing throng. Most of the crowd looked glad, but one Seton Hall fan grumbled, "It isn't fair they allow that Pohl to play. He's some kind of freak, he's not natural."

Rounding a bend in the corridor, Peru almost bumped into Douglas Knox coming out of the locker room. Trapped in the crowd, he and Knox had to inch along side by side.

Peru fixed Knox in a smile. "Well hullo, Father, nice seeing you. You in good health?"

Knox snapped, "Why wouldn't I be?"

"Heard you almost got knifed the other day. By some guy with a funny hairdo."

"Yeah. One of your boys told you about that? He came along just in time. When you see him, give him my thanks."

Peru chuckled. "That was Willy. Willy the Wire. You can thank me he was there."

Knox frowned. "What do you mean by that?"

"I was worried about you, Father. You getting that letter with the rabbit, and all. So I told Willy follow you around for a while, keep an eye on you."

Knox was doing a slow burn. "I guess you think I ought to be grateful? Well, I'm not. Listen, Peru, you don't need to worry about me. I can keep an eye out for myself. So don't send any more of your mugs nosing around this campus. If your man Willy wants to drop by my office sometime, though, I'll stand him to a drink."

Peru shrugged. "Then take your own lumps, Father, and good luck to you. By the way, thanks for the box seats."

"Wasn't my idea. You can thank the Monsignor."

"Jeez, I thought for once you was treating a friend of the college right."

Knox turned and looked at him full face. "Peru, maybe you have the Monsignor wrapped around your little finger, but you're *persona non grata* to me."

"Don't talk French to me, Padre. I know when I'm not welcome. Too bad we can't be friendly. I could do a lot for you."

"Lay off, Peru. We've been through this already."

"And another thing. I seen you at the Monsignor's party eyeing up the goodies on Vastasi's wife. Juicy piece of woman, ain't she? I guess we was both thinking the same thing. You still got a dick in your pants?"

Knox threw him a glare and shoved on by.

All the way out to the parking lot where Manny waited with the Rolls, Peru kept chortling. Tessie, climbing into the back seat, said, "What's so funny?"

Between chortles, Peru got his cigar going. "That priest thinks he shits vanilla ice cream. Wait till he sees what happens at the Holy Sepulcher game. I hope he lives that long."

Twenty-Two

Avoiding circles of light from the street lamps in front of Feeley Mansion, dodging behind bushes whenever a car went by, Moon slunk back to Temporary Shelter Thirteen. On his way he met no one but Professor Pigout, who was staggering home to Bachelor Faculty Quarters.

The beam of Pigout's flashlight played over Moon's bare body. *"Zut alors, Gogarty!* You were zee loser playing poker?"* Pigout belched and stumbled off into the night.

Late though it was, Konny, the Sarge, and Crews were still up when Moon arrived. They had been to the game. They looked at him and gaped.

"Holy Pete," said the Sarge, "what happened to your clothes?"

Moon stood there panting for breath. He hadn't thought to concoct an alibi. "Oh, well, it was like this. It was a stickup. That was it. Three guys jumped me and took everything."

Crews was tittering. Konny looked skeptical. "They even t-t-took your gl-gl-glasses?"

"Those guys were desperate." Moon slumped into a folding chair, wincing as his backside met cold steel, and modestly drew the *Star Ledger* over his crotch.

"M-M-M-Moon, b-b-buddy," said Konny, "we better n-n-notify the c-c-campus c-c-cops."

"No, no," Moon said quickly. "I don't want to bother them."

"Bother them, hell," said the Sarge, "it's their job. This happened on campus, didn't it? Whereabouts?"

"In front of the Mansion. As I was passing by."

"Where was you coming from?"

"The library."

"Yeah," Crews put in sarcastically. "The library closes at nine. And you smell like a dose of Seduction."

The Sarge grabbed the phone. After a long time the solitary campus cop, Callahan, roused from his sleep, said he'd come around and talk to Moon in the morning.

The next day was Purgatory. Callahan didn't show up till quarter to ten, so that Moon missed his morning oatmeal. Callahan pretended to take notes, but he did most of the talking, prolonging his interrogation with recollections of the war years ("The student body was just a handful of 4-Fs. Only twelve of 'em in 1943. The apostles, we called 'em"). He said there wasn't much he could do about the robbery now. In Dr. Bopp's history class, wearing shower clogs in place of shoes, Moon retreated into dreams. He became Raymond Scott in a CBS studio, leading his six-man quintet through his own compositions, "Powerhouse" and "Dinner Music for a Pack of Hungry Cannibals." Brilliant experimental stuff. Even the engineer at the control panel broke into applause.

Then, his heart pounding, Moon hurried to biology class and claimed his seat in the front row. Oh God, what was she going to say to him?

Aisling entered, looking grim, Kiki Sue in one arm, a brown-paper parcel under the other. She set down her burdens, not even glancing at Moon. He squinched his nearsighted eyes, trying to decipher her face. When she called the roll she spat out his name like a curse. Perched on the desk, she crossed her net-stockinged legs and lectured on phylum and species, but her customary enthusiasm wasn't there. Once, when Moon stuck up his hand to answer a question, she ignored him even though his was the only hand raised.

After class, he lingered expectantly. She glared at him and tossed him the package. His glasses, shoes, and clothes. "Gogarty," she said evenly, "you ever tell a soul about last night and so help me God I'll chew you up and spit you out in little pieces."

In his present dark mood, her offer sounded reasonable.

"That makes two people who want to kill me," he said. "You and Randy Harrigan."

"Lucky thing Glauco didn't go into the living room and see your clothes and stuff lying around. He'd have skinned me alive. From now on, Gogarty, this is strictly a teacher-student relationship. Unfortunately I'll have to look at your ugly face for the rest of this term, but then I never want to see any more of you."

"Believe me, Professor, I'm sorry about last night. I guess I was kind of a disappointment to you."

For a moment, Aisling looked at him with a flicker of sympathy. But then without another word she grabbed him by the shoulders, spun him about, gave him a high-heeled kick in the rump, and propelled him out the door.

Moon slouched back to his room and flung himself face down on his cot. For a long while he lay inert, his mind roiling. His thoughts shifted and rearranged like flakes in a kaleidoscope. His career as a Casanova had made a piss-poor start. Damn, why did Randy Harrigan have to barge in on their lovemaking? What right had that slob Vastasi to come back home and go to bed with his mistress? And Loretta Snow—why did she have to haunt him? Why didn't she just lie down in her grave and leave him alone? Was she going to sabotage his love life forever? If only he hadn't happened to behold her lying on the undertaker's table, mutilated, all exposed, last night might have been different. His mind busied itself with rewriting history. If only he'd never gone to Dover High, never come to Saint Cash's, never listened at the impressionable age of eight to that fake newscast by Orson Welles. If only he had never even been born. Maybe suicide was the answer. Some painless, dignified method that wouldn't leave marks. He imagined his body laid out in its Sunday suit, mouth packed with cotton, lips fixed in a gallant smile. He saw himself arranged in the mortuary's best silk-lined coffin, Aisling in black widow's weeds sobbing over him. The scene was profoundly satisfying.

After a while his stomach began to grumble. Reluctantly, he got up, put on his glasses, and headed for The Pit.

On the road in front of his Quonset hut, the Monsignor's big white Cadillac was waiting, Randy Harrigan at the wheel, wearing his chauffeur's flat hat.

The door on the passenger side flew open. "Get in, punk," Harrigan said.

"Why should I?"

"Because this gat says so."

The blue steel barrel of a revolver glinted in his hand.

Slowly, Moon hauled himself into the passenger seat. Harrigan eased the car into gear and cruised down the front driveway and turned left onto a service road. He parked behind a row of trees, next to an abandoned toolshed where nobody ever came. There was a field parked full of brand new Jeeps. No doubt war surplus consigned to the college.

Moon wondered what it was going to feel like, a bullet through the brain. At this point, he'd welcome it.

He strove to keep his voice from quavering. "What do you want with me?"

"Keep away from her."

"How can I? I'm in her biology class."

"Drop out."

"Too late. The deadline for dropping a course was two weeks ago."

"Then don't go to it anymore. Don't get smart with me, punk. She's *my* broad, see? You ever set foot in her house again, I'll fill you full of lead. And don't even give her any more of your little puppy looks or else it's curtains, unnerstand?"

The Mob, that word *curtains* was from. Moon had seen the picture too. Harrigan had even cultivated a sneer like Edward G. Robinson's.

Moon felt frustrated rage sweep over him. This would-be hood had scored with both Loretta and his professor, the two women in the world Moon had passionately desired. So what if Harrigan killed him? He had nothing to live for now.

He said, "Curtains, huh? Like the curtains you pulled down for Loretta Snow the night you drove her into a tree?"

"Why you little crud." Harrigan poked the revolver up against Moon's heart.

This is it, Moon thought. What was that prayer you were supposed to say—an Act of Contrition? He couldn't remember it. All he could think of was, "Now I lay me down to sleep..."

But Harrigan held his fire. "Shit," he said. He thrust the gun back into his jacket pocket.

Sir Terwilliger Feeley, out for a stroll, was approaching the parked car, waving his dog-headed walking stick. He came up to the open window on the driver's side.

"Indeed, if it isn't Mr. Harrigan," the old papal knight said cheerily. "Out for a ride, are you?"

"Hullo, Sir Terwilliger," Harrigan said. "We was just talking, my friend and me."

"Talk is cheap, they say, and yet certain conversations are golden. Ah, I recall such a conversation with Hilaire Belloc once, over high tea at the Savoy. He wanted to know how to increase the American sales for his *Bad Child's Book of Beasts*. Do you know that delightful work? No? What a pity, you must read it. I told him he needed to enforce its moral lessons, don't you know, tone down its untoward levity. Having little boys eaten by lions can hardly improve their characters, wouldn't you agree?"

"No. I mean yeah, Sir Terwilliger," Harrigan said.

"Indeed. Sometime I'll tell you all about it. Belloc was a force in Anglo-Catholicism, him and Chesterton and Cardinal Newman. Why do we not have their likes in this country? Well, I really must be off. Have to take my daily exercise, doctor's orders. Give my fondest regards to Monsignor O'Malley."

He tottered off, depending on his cane.

"Old fool. Now he seen us," Harrigan said.

He pulled out the revolver again and tapped Moon's forehead with its muzzle. "I'm warning you, Gogarty, and this is the last time. You ever go near Aisling again or you ever tell anybody else about that dead babe in Dover and your ass has had it."

His tongue clicked, imitating a trigger. He reached across Moon and flung open the passenger door.

"Get out, you little rat," he said in his best gangster snarl.

He landed a punch on Moon's jaw and gave him a vicious shove. Moon slid out of the seat and toppled with a crunch to the gravel drive. The car door slammed and the Caddy roared away, a shower of pebbles rattling after it.

Hearing the thump of a body, Sir Terwilliger turned and hobbled back, observed Moon sprawled on the ground nursing his jaw. His walking stick tapped Moon's chest.

"Fell out of the car, did you, young fellow? Careless, I must say. Better watch yourself. You could get hurt, you know. I must say, you young people today don't have the God-given reason of a flea."

Twenty-Three

Ever since the fat guy had pinned him down with a sword, Knox had been working out daily. Couldn't let himself get soft. He had fallen into a fixed routine, saying Mass, meeting his class, going to his office, coaching, talking to sports reporters, working out, staying on guard, feeling tight as a coiled spring.

This morning he was in the squash court brushing up on karate technique with Abner Lung. Lung was from Hong Kong, a short lean guy with a quick smile, sharp black eyes, slicked-down black hair. He'd been sent to America to learn accounting so he could take over his old man's business. Canned bird's nest soup.

The two of them faced each other on the mat, barefoot, in loose-fitting white exercise suits. "OK," Knox told him, "go for me."

Lung nodded, grinning. They circled each other, looking for openings. Lung threw a left punch at Knox's chest. Knox crouched, swept his left forearm in a half-circle, blocking Lung's fist. He exhaled hard, then with a sharp cry launched a punch with his right at Lung's midsection. Lung pivoted, dodging easily. He nodded. "That's all right, Father. If I'd stayed there, you would have had me."

Knox tried a horizontal kick, as if lifting his right leg over a table. Lung reacted as though he'd seen it coming.

He stepped back with trigger speed, letting Knox's foot fly past his head. Knox staggered, spun, then regained his balance. The two of them drew back, circled some more. Knox was breathing hard. This kid was good. Lung's grin spread out wide.

Knox threw another kick, this time with his left. He was fast, but Lung was faster. Lung reached out with his right hand like a man picking fruit from a tree, caught Knox's left foot in midair, held it for a second, then flung it high and sent Knox crashing backward.

Knox lay on the mat, stunned, blinking up at him. "What did I do wrong?"

"You advertised what you were going to do," Lung said. "When you looked at me your foot moved, getting ready for a kick. So I guessed where you'd try to land it."

"Hell," Knox said. "I get in a fight, I couldn't fool anybody."

"Oh, sure you could. Anybody that didn't know karate. Don't feel bad, Father. For an old man, you're pretty good."

In a rotten mood, Knox showered, went to his office and flipped through his morning mail, pitching every last letter begging for free tickets into the wastebasket. At least this morning there weren't any more dead rabbits.

He lit up and studied the smoke. There was that unexpected visit from Aisling, her throwing her body at him. What was the matter with the woman? Wasn't she happily married? Married to Vastasi, she probably wasn't. Wouldn't mind giving her what she's after. Oh-oh. Step on the brakes there. Virgin Mother, help me remember my vows.

Maureen's voice pierced through the intercom. Some caller said it was urgent. Knox picked up the phone.

The voice was familiar. Too familiar. "Do you know who this is?" Mister Cross said.

"Yeah. We've met before. I've been wondering where you've been lately."

"Oh, I'm like the divine spirit. Everywhere. One day you will turn a corner and I'll be there."

"And aren't you sticking your own neck out? Your man with the sword cane—what happened to him didn't teach you anything?"

"So I lost one soldier, but my war with you will go on. Until you are dead. Until athletics is delivered from the domination of your church, the Whore of Babylon."

Maureen brought in a sheaf of equipment orders. Knox grabbed a pad and scribbled TRACE THIS CALL. She nodded and hurried out to get on the other line.

Knox said, "Now just a minute. You've got a cockeyed take on everything. Since when is basketball church-related? I don't see the Knicks or the Celtics bending their knees at the altar. Killing me isn't going to un-dominate anything."

"Killing you will give me great satisfaction. Our first attempt failed. Our second attempt will not."

"Yeah? And just what do you have in mind?"

"You expect me to give you details? That would be foolish of me. But I'll tell you what is in store for you."

Got to keep this bird talking. "Go on," Knox said. "I'm all ears. Why are you warning me?"

"Because I want you to live in fear. To suffer, the way I suffered, to have nightmares instead of dreams. You escaped the knife a few days ago. Next time, it will go to your heart."

"So when will my execution take place?"

"Soon. When you least expect."

Knox sighed. "You going to give me a little time, get my affairs in order?"

"You gave *me* no such time. When you betrayed me." There was a sharp click as the caller broke off.

Betrayed him? What in hell had Cross been talking about?

"Maureen!" Knox bawled, throwing open the door to the outer office. "Where did that call come from?"

The secretary had the phone clamped to one ear. "I'm still working on the phone company. There's some supervisor on the line. She doesn't want to tell me anything. Says it would violate company policy."

"Let me talk to her."

"OK. Good luck."

"Hello, dammit," Knox bawled. "This is Father Knox at Saint Cassian of Imola's. For God's sake, this is a matter of life and death. Will you please let me know where that call I just took came from?"

"Are you a person in authority?"

"You bet your ass, sister. I can get you fired. Look, this is an emergency. Can't you get that through your thick dome?"

"Sir, you don't need to be offensive. Just a minute, I'll look into this."

The minute dragged on, became fifteen, as Knox clung to the phone, fuming. At last the supervisor came back on the line. The call had come from a pay phone in South Orange. She hoped that this information would be helpful.

In the lounge in Priests' House, Knox strode to the well-stocked mahogany bar and took down the quart of John Jameson with his name on it. He sloshed himself a good one and eased down into a wide leather chair next to the Right Reverend Jasper Fry.

"Hello, Jasp. How's your Children's Crusade doing? Keeping you busy these days?"

"Too busy. Going all the time."

In the chair facing Knox, Fry was nursing a glass of Bristol Cream sherry. He was thin and gaunt, hair starting to gray around the temples, deep-set eyes with dark bags under them. He was Knox's age, but the war had left him a lot older. He wore a yellowed undershirt, black slacks, no socks, loafers that looked as if he'd been kicking bricks.

Knox said, "What are we drinking to?"

Fry raised his glass. "To the innocence of childhood. Here's looking at you."

Knox thought that a peculiar toast. But he drank. "This Children's Crusade of yours—you do it all single-handed?"

"Just hired a girl to handle mail orders. Getting so many we have to truck them to the post office."

"I'm not surprised. Heard you on the radio last night. Quite a pitch you give 'em."

Fry shrugged. "Just a carnival barker, that's all I am. But it's starting to produce results."

"Any hot items?"

Fry gave a pained smile. "The water from Lourdes in a vial shaped like a teardrop. Can't keep the things in stock. And the combination crucifix-thermometer with the legend 'This is the weather to come unto Me'." His face fell. "It sickens me. Merchandizing all this schlock."

"Anyhow," Knox said, "your Children's Crusade doesn't depend just on sales, right? People send in donations?"

Fry nodded.

"And your radio talk about Saint Pelagia," Knox went on. "The saint that got cooked inside a brazen bull. I bet that really wowed 'em. Must take a virgin martyr to open their wallets."

Fry winced. "You might say so." His eyes took on a faraway look. "Next week I'm talking about Saint Mary Goretti. Died resisting rape. She must have been a hot little number."

The remark hit Knox as slightly disturbing. He shook out a Gauloise and lit up. Fry went and poured himself a fresh sherry and returned. "You understand, Douglas, I really don't like this huckstering. This radio program— Father Fry's Fireside Chats—it's getting to be too much for me."

"How's that?"

"Listeners think I'm their bosom friend. I get letters asking for all kinds of advice. 'Father, I've had a baby every year since we've been married, and now it's fourteen years. What shall I do, I can't stand another one.' Douglas, what can I tell these people? Your husband's a rooster, chop his head off?"

"You could tell them to practice Catholic birth control. The old calendar method."

"They write back that it doesn't work."

For a while the two priests sipped quietly. Then Fry tittered. Tittered, for Pete's sake. He said, "You know, what I like is the children. Do you know, I'm starting a swim club for the Dedwood Sentinels? That's the Children's Crusade's local organization."

"Sounds like fun."

"Douglas, might I reserve the pool in the gym for a couple of hours every Saturday? Going to give a few boys some swimming lessons. Used to be a water safety instructor."

"Sure. Nobody uses the pool on Saturday mornings. I'll tell Maureen to set up a time for you. You don't get any other fun these days? Aren't you doing any more photography?"

"Haven't had time."

"That's too bad, you used to do beautiful stuff. Those pictures of the jocks in action. I still have one of 'em framed, hanging in my office. You've kept your darkroom?"

Knox didn't know why, but Fry looked cagey. "It's still there. Although by now the chemicals must be useless."

"Tell me about your punchboards. How are they doing?"

"Quite well. At least around here. We don't distribute them in Newark. Someone else has punchboards there."

"Ricky Peru, I bet."

"So I'm told. But we've put our boards in every bar, drugstore, soda fountain, market, firehouse, public place in Dedwood and the Oranges. Wherever people will see them."

"I know. Can't miss the things. Sitting on the counter, picture of some pathetic kid looking at you. Kid deformed by the A-bomb. Gives me the willies. Those punchboards rake in the shekels, huh?"

Fry mused. "Two hundred punches on a board, fifty cents a chance on a five-pound box of candy. Average, a hundred punches before anybody wins a prize. Boards made in Japan cost us fifty cents apiece, candy costs us three dollars a box. You figure it out."

"Who chases around to all those drugstores?"

"I've been delivering to some of them. And all the parish priests and nuns have been bringing the boards in to the business people. A cleric making deliveries is very effective."

"Uh huh. Collar power."

"But I don't look forward to next month."

"Your annual campaign?"

"That. Means extra air time. And I've got to make about twenty talks to congregations."

"That's a lot. You must be raising a fortune."

"Would you believe it, Douglas? Two hundred seventy-five thousand last year in Northern New Jersey alone. And now the radio program is going out in Boston, Baltimore, St. Louis, Atlanta."

"Well, Jasp, I guess you're doing a lot of good. Raising that gravy. Where does it all go?"

Fry's recessed eyes looked feverish, intense. "Orphanages. Clinics for children. Oh, there isn't any shortage of need. Mostly I send the money to Japan, Poland, Eastern Europe—wherever children suffered during the war. Places where our bombers knocked things down. I—I feel a certain personal responsibility."

"That's great. But, look, Jasp, you can't do it all by yourself. You can't help every needy kid in the world."

"I know, I know. Sometimes I just want to sit in the tub and play with my swan."

For a moment, Knox had the chilling thought thought that Fry meant his penis. But Fry said, "My swan is my favorite toy. It floats in the tub. You squeeze it and it squeaks. A cute little girl in the Sentinels gave it to me."

Knox went and topped off his drink. He sat back down next to Fry. In a lowered voice, he said, "Jasp, I can't help worrying about you. You're working too hard. Ever think of taking a little vacation? Couple of weeks in the Bahamas?"

Fry's shoulders sagged. "I'll consider it, Douglas. But not right now. I've got to get through this coming campaign. Our Blessed Mother and my swan, they tell me to."

Twenty-Four

"It's time to dance," came the deep hearty voice of the announcer, "to the music of Moon Gogarty and His Celebrated Orchestra, featuring Helen Forrest and the Moonbeamers, coming to you from that Mecca of the bands, Frank Dailey's Meadowbrook on Route 23, Newark-Pompton Turnpike, in Cedar Grove, New Jersey. Don't despair, let your head save your hair, use Fitch Shampoo. Tell us, Moon, what great music do you have in store for us tonight?"

Moon stepped to the mike. "We've a whole bevy of hits lined up for you, listeners, designed to set your heart dreaming and your toes tapping in time."

He lifted his trombone and took a chorus of "Perfidia," sounding better on the instrument than Tommy Dorsey. Then the Moonbeamers, four bright-eyed teenagers in bulging sweaters, short skirts, bobby sox and saddle shoes, chimed together on "I'll Never Smile Again." Moon took another solo, to deafening applause.

Then an alien voice burst in. *"Mister Whatever Your Name Is!"*

Someone was shaking him. "Are you asleep? What's the matter with you?"

Roused, Moon found himself staring into the worn gray face of Professor Maximo Bopp. All the other students had already left the chapel.

"Oh. Sorry, sir," Moon said lamely. "I was just—thinking, I guess."

"Thinking. Well don't do that again. You looked like you were having an epileptic seizure."

In embarrassment, Moon collected his books and went out. He'd have to watch it. His dream world was taking over his life.

"To a Fundamentalist, Darwin's theory of evolution is a crock," Aisling told the class. "God tossed together the world in six days, put his feet up on Sunday. That doesn't leave much time for mammals to develop."

Thirty veterans and one recent high school grad followed her every word.

"You Catholics, now, and I take it that's most of you, you don't have any trouble with Darwin. You don't take the Bible literally, you have priests to tell you what it means. A day of creation? That could mean ten million years. So when evolution finally worked its way up to the human race, God stuck out a finger and, wham! one of those apes acquired a soul."

This was the most concise history of a complicated idea Moon had ever heard. He couldn't restrain himself. He started clapping.

Aisling smiled. "Thanks, Mr. Gogarty, but please don't applaud during my lectures. I don't want you to wear your hands out."

She had found it hard to stay mad at Gogarty. Like staying mad at your little dog for wetting on your rug. The spectacle of him pining away in the front row, drinking in her every word, was beginning to touch her heart.

Seeing him every other day, reading his labor-intensive midterm exam, Aisling felt herself softening. Maybe she hadn't needed to boot him in the ass. After all, that awful night had been his first experience. No doubt he'd been terrified. And when she pictured the poor kid cowering under the bed, pictured his skinny rump fleeing in a burst of gunfire, she couldn't help feeling sorry for him. His turned-up nose and soulful eyes still tempted her. His innocence struck a chord in her, his impotence challenged her seductive powers. Maybe she should give him another chance.

Today he lingered after class, looking downcast, as if hoping for some sign of forgiveness.

She picked up her briefcase and sleeping baby. "What's the matter, Mr. Gogarty? You look blue."

Moon lit up. She was talking to him!

"I'm always blue," he said, "thinking what a fool I made of myself that night. You remember?"

"How could I forget? That was a rough night for you, wasn't it. Hasn't life got any easier?"

"Not with being editor of *The Immolator*. It's more work than I ever expected."

He told her of his struggle to fill the paper with copy. Nobody else would write for it. And as for news, the College of St. Cassian of Imola wasn't a hot beat.

Aisling said, "Ah. I see. You want a news story?"

"Do I ever!"

"OK. I've got one for you. Did you know that the college receives all kinds of things from the government? Desks, chairs, typewriters? Why, this classroom was furnished with war surplus materials and it didn't cost the college a dime. Isn't that interesting? I'll bet nobody even knows about it."

"Wow! Tell me more."

"I'll do better than that. Let me show you something that will knock your eyes out. Right now I'd better take Kiki Sue home to finish her nap. But meet me in front of Rose Chapel in fifteen minutes."

At three-forty-five, as he was starting to abandon hope, Aisling came hustling down the brick walk in front of the chapel, a ring of keys jangling in her right hand.

"Come on," she said, "let's make this quick. Kiki Sue is asleep, but I don't know for how long."

She beckoned him around to the side of the crumbling chapel, down cement steps to a storm door into the basement. She tried keys till one of them worked. Moon followed her in. The place was thick with dust, strung with spiderwebs. He had to crouch so as not to hit his head.

Aisling groped, found a switch. Two weak bulbs came to life. "OK," she said, "what do you make of this?"

From one side to the other, the chapel basement was stacked with wooden crates marked U S ARMY PROPERTY. Aisling stepped to an open crate and hauled out an adding machine. "See this? Cost you seventy-five bucks in a store. The college got it for nothing."

Moon whistled. "Gosh, there must be hundreds of 'em here."

"Yes, and Glauco goes down to Washington all the time and puts in for more. You want to write your story, go talk to him."

They poked around, making footprints in the dusty floor. Cases of insecticide, fire extinguishers, pencil sharpeners.

"That's funny," Moon said. "Why does the college want gas masks?"

Aisling's laugh ran up and down the scales. "Maybe to protect the students from the lectures."

In the back of the basement sat a stack of crates stenciled with legends. 12 BROWNING AUTOMATIC RIFLES. 24 B.A.R. BIPODS. 20 GARRAND RIFLES. The crates reached to the ceiling. One of the crates sat on the floor, broken open as if someone had inspected the merchandise. Aisling reached into it, tugged loose one of the heavy rifles, and playfully aimed it at Moon. "Rat tat tat," she said.

Moon winced. "Don't point that thing at me."

"Don't worry. There's no ammo in it."

"How come these guns are here?"

"You tell me. I didn't know about this. Complete surprise. Didn't dream the college was collecting guns. What Glauco plans to do with 'em, I don't have any idea."

On the front page of his mind, Moon was starting to compose a headline. WAR WEAPONS STORED IN CONSECRATED CHAPEL. His brow wrinkled. He began to scribble notes on an imaginary pad. Rose Chapel, island of peace. Basement full of guns left over from the war. Why does a college need all this fire power?

He said, "Maybe I can catch your husband in his office. I'll ask him about these rifles. Professor, you've just given me the scoop of my life. I could kiss you!"

"Well," said Aisling, standing close to him, brushing a spiderweb from her chin and lifting full red lips, "why in hell don't you?"

Twenty-Five

Quarter to five. Glauco Vastasi was signing the last stack of purchase orders when Patricia's voice came over the intercom. "Mr. Vastasi, there's a young gent from the paper here. I told him you're about to go home. But do you want to see him?"

Vastasi sucked in his breath. "Who is he? What paper?"

"Says his name is Gogarty. From *The Immolator*."

Vastasi exhaled with relief. The campus rag. If a reporter from a real newspaper had come snooping around, that could have been bad. But who in hell ever read *The Immolator*?

"Oh, all right. Send him in."

Moon took the upright chair Vastasi waved him into. Vastasi glanced at this scrawny high school kid with glasses, turned up nose, yellow pad in hand, pencil behind his ear, trying to look professional. What a creep.

"Be with you in a minute," Vastasi said. He took his time signing the rest of the purchase orders, letting the kid sit there fidgeting. The kid took out a pack of gum, popped a stick in his mouth, rolled up the wrapper like a scroll and, not daring to park it in Vastasi's ashtray, put it in his pocket. Huh, Vastasi thought. The kid was so behind the times he still chewed Orbit. Didn't he know that Wrigley's Spearmint was back and the war was over?

Vastasi set down his big red Parker fountain pen and eased back in his swivel chair. "OK, kid, so what's on your mind?"

"I know you're a busy man, Mr. Vastasi," Moon said, "so I'll get right to the point. Why are there Army rifles down in the basement of Rose Chapel?"

Vastasi winced as if from an unexpected punch. Then he screwed his face into a smile. "Army rifles? What makes you think I know anything about that?"

"Because you're in charge of procurement. If anybody got those things for the college, it must have been you."

"Army rifles." Vastasi pretended to rummage his memory. "Oh, yeah. Them. Well, as you know, Mister—what was your name again?"

"James Gogarty."

"Yeah. Well, Mr. Gogarty, as you know, schools can get all kinds of things from the government these days. Stuff left over from the war, stuff the shitheads down in Washington don't know what to do with. So at Saint Cash's, we do our patriotic duty and take 'em off their hands. It's natural we accept anything useful. Useful in the education business, you might say."

"So how will St. Cash's use Garrand rifles? Browning automatics?"

Vastasi glowered. This kid was turning into a royal pain in the ass. Vastasi lit a Camel, taking a minute to think. "We're going to start a rifle club," he said at last.

Yeah. That was it. He warmed to his explanation. "Give the students a change to do some shooting. Like when they were GIs."

"Oh." The kid looked skeptical. But he scribbled on his yellow pad.

"So how in the hell do you happen to know about those rifles?"

"I went down in the chapel basement and looked."

Vastasi saw red. "And just who the hell let you in to that basement?"

Moon gulped. "I'm sorry, Mr. Vastasi. I'm not at liberty to say."

"Oh, clamming up, huh? Well, listen. Them guns are in storage only temporary. Till the rifle club gets going. We have a good educational use for them pieces, you got that? Is that all you want to know?"

"I guess so. Thanks, Mr. Vastasi."

When Moon had left, Vastasi smashed his fist down on his desk so hard the phone jumped out of its cradle. His receptionist came in, her coat already on, looking alarmed. "Why—is everything all right?"

Vastasi shrugged. "Sure. You can beat it now."

She wished him good night. Vastasi smoked thoughtfully. There was only one way the kid could have found out about the guns. Aisling. She must have taken the keys he kept on a nail in the kitchen and let the kid into the chapel basement.

He put on his coat and went out. He crossed the campus, walking into the blinding five o'clock sun. Blabbermouth cunt, she had betrayed him. Wait till she came home from teaching. He'd teach *her* a lesson. Leave some marks on her. She'd be lucky if he didn't break her jaw.

He unlocked the little house and kicked the front door open wide. The living room was strewn with laundry, mostly diapers. Christ, she kept house like a chicken keeps its coop. He hung up his coat and went out to the kitchen and poured himself a double Canadian Club with no ice. Drink in hand, he mounted the stairs to change out of his business suit.

As he entered the bedroom, his eyes took in an item he hadn't noticed before. A long white condom dangled from the ceiling, as if it had been flung up there wet and had dried and stuck fast. He didn't use white condoms, himself.

He stood there for a long time, swearing. He grabbed a fistful of toilet paper and yanked the thing down from the ceiling and flung it in the toilet and flushed, staring down at the swirling water in the bowl. Who the hell had she let into the house while he was gone? He made a tour of the bedroom, looking for more evidence. The night-stand, the dresser, under the bed, on the floor. On the rug next to the right side of the bed, he found it, dropped there and forgotten. A neatly rolled-up wrapper from a stick of Orbit gum.

Knox was ready to knock off work for the day, so he wasn't especially glad to see Moon Gogarty. Moon plunked himself into the chair in front of the desk and Knox glowered at him. "So what do you want? I thought you and your lousy rag weren't going to bother me."

Moon's lower lip trembled. "You still think *The Immolator* is lousy, Father? Haven't you read it lately?"

Knox relented a little. "Yeah. Read your last number. OK, maybe the thing's improved by two per cent. I used to think it wasn't good enough to wipe my ass with. Now it is."

"Wasn't there anything in it you liked?"

"That interview with Pohl wasn't bad. Didn't know about the bomber blowing up his grandmother's church. Didn't know he was so hot to make money. Got to have a chat with that boy, straighten him out."

Moon grinned. "I wrote that interview."

"Big deal. So why are you pestering me?"

"Father, I've got a front-page story. Only it might put the college in a slightly unfavorable light."

"Spit it out."

"Did you know that the college chapel is an ammunition depot?"

Knox's eyebrows shot up. "The hell you say."

"Honest. Down in the basement there are these cases of rifles. Rifles and shells. War surplus, you know, left-over stuff the college gets free from the government."

"What kind of rifles?"

"Browning Automatics, it says on the box. Garrands. Whatever they are."

"Service rifles. Combat troops packed 'em during the war. Semi-automatic jobs, gas operated. They pack one hell of a wallop. And Brownings—they're a portable machine gun with a magazine feed that could drill a hole through a shithouse door and out the other side. How much of this stuff is there?"

"Cases and cases. Maybe fifty, sixty of 'em."

Knox lit up, took a drag, and thought. "You talk with Vastasi about this?"

Moon nodded. "Just now. He said the college is going to start a rifle club."

Knox gave a snort. "Rifle club? Sounds as if there's enough heavy stuff in that basement to start an army."

"You don't believe Mr. Vastasi's story?"

"Sounds fishy to me. No college in its right mind would have any use for that kind of stuff. But somebody, all right, might have a use for it."

Moon unwrapped a stick of Orbit and started nervously jawing it. "What'll I do, Father? I mean, should I write this up for the paper? I can't call Mr. Vastasi a liar. That would be libel."

"That would be the God's honest truth. But you don't need to call him anything. Just write what he told you. Let people see what they make of it. *Nihil obstat. Imprimatur.*"

"Huh?"

"That means go ahead and print. I want to see what Vastasi does when this story comes out."

Moon's eyes lit up with enthusiasm. "Oh boy! Maybe I can get it into this week's paper. It's supposed to go to press tonight. But, gee, we'll have to rip out the front page. Mr. Kelleher down at Book of Kells Printery won't be happy."

"Tell him I said to do it. Kid, I'm beginning to think there might be hope for your lousy rag."

Twenty-Six

In the kitchen Vastasi was sitting in his shirtsleeves gulping Cribari wine, sour stuff, feeling like a volcano getting ready to wipe out a town. Parked in her infant seat at the far end of the table, Kiki Sue studied her booties, making her feet wave, while Aisling hustled about chopping garlic, grating cheese, starting water boiling.

Vastasi paged through the *Newark Evening News,* not saying anything. Ordinarily he liked to catch up on the nightly Uncle Wiggily bedtime story by Howard R. Garis about the canny rabbit gentleman who always kept one jump ahead of his enemies. But tonight Vastasi didn't give a shit if the bad Pipsisewah gobbled Uncle Wiggily and spat out the rabbit gentleman's bones. His mind was seething. Aisling had it coming. Right after they ate.

Aisling brought over two plates loaded with fettuccine and two plates of chopped tomatoes in oil. She poured him more wine. They ate in silence. Kiki Sue fussed and Aisling took a pacifier out of her apron pocket and plugged the little girl's mouth.

Vastasi set down his glass. "Kid named Gogarty came to see me today. You know him?"

"He's in my class, that's all."

"You know him a hell of a lot better than that."

"Since when?"

"Don't try to kid me. He's your little boyfriend. You lifted the key to the chapel basement and showed him them rifles. He knew all about them. What did you do, give him a goddam guided tour?"

"Glauco, how was I to know you were storing guns down there? The kid had the blues, I wanted to cheer him up. Thought I'd give him a story for his paper. I didn't know you were getting anything from the government except pencil sharpeners."

"I told you never stick your nose in my business. You stole that key."

"Borrowed it. Didn't think you'd care. Listen, honey, does it matter? I'm sorry if I did anything wrong."

Vastasi jumped to his feet, upsetting the wine jug. Kiki Sue spat out her pacifier and wailed.

"Wrong? Wrong? That kid is going to write a story in the paper about them guns. And that's not all, you two-timing whore, you been laying him behind my back!"

"You're not serious!"

"No? Then how to do you explain that rubber full of jism hanging off of the ceiling over our bed? That gum wrapper I found on the floor, the kid's special brand?"

Aisling sighed. There was no use pretending anymore. "That rubber wasn't full of anything. The kid couldn't come."

"So you admit it, bitch? I was dumb to have ever trusted you. What did I tell you I'd do, you let anybody else take a dip in you?"

"Glauco, honey, believe me. That was the one and only time, I swear!"

"Pack your things. I'm giving you an hour. You're still here then, so help me, I'll put these hands around your neck and strangle you."

Aisling looked shocked. "You can't mean this, honey. Have a heart. You're not going to turn me and this little baby out in the cold. After all you and I have meant to each other."

"Shit. What are you to me, anyway? A goddamn piece of ass I can't trust. And it's not *my* baby. No skin off my ass if I don't have to smell rotten diapers and listen to the damn thing bawling any more."

He tugged out his wallet, counted six fifty-dollar bills, flung them on the table. "Get yourself a furnished room. When this runs out, you can live on your college salary."

Aisling left the money lying, red wine on the table trickling into it.

Her tears welled. "Glauco, honey, you're making a bad mistake. I'll be good from now on. Cross my heart, I wouldn't dream of two-timing you again."

"The hell you wouldn't. Till the next stud with a hard-on comes along. Get moving. You got fifty-five minutes."

Aisling stood up, looked him in the eyes, slipped out of her apron, unbuttoned her blouse, let it fall to the floor. She stood bare-breasted before him. She came up close, laid her head against his chest, one hand undoing his shirt buttons.

"One more night," she said. "Just one more."

In bed they joined their bodies fiercely, bitterly, while at last the baby cried herself to sleep.

"How was that, honey?" Aisling whispered, massaging him. "You couldn't do without me, could you?"

Vastasi rolled over and turned his back on her. "That was nothing but one for the road," he said.

For three days Aisling and Kiki Sue survived in the Dedwood Motel, a cut-rate dump, but on the fourth day she found a furnished apartment in town, on the third floor over a Chinese laundry. The chairs were old and worn and the sofa had a spring coming out of it, but the place was cheap and clean. There was a cramped kitchen with a hotplate and a battered old Westinghouse fridge.

She asked her landlady, "Would you mind if I had visitors once in a while?"

"Missie, you pay you rent, what you do, I don't care."

"Your laundry do diapers?"

"Sure. You bring 'em down, we wash 'em nice for you."

Perfect. One of Moon's roommates, the Sarge, brought over his car and helped her move the crib and changing table. Before she left Vastasi's house, she squatted down in the middle of the living room and took a piss on the rug. Give the son of a bitch something to remember her by.

The day after she moved, her first visitor called. Kindly old Father Goodminton, white-haired, slightly stooped, wearing a shiny black suit, face full of benevolence.

She showed him in. "Sorry about these rickety chairs, Father. I don't have any better ones yet. Would you like a cup of tea? Maybe a shot of bourbon?"

"Oh, not a thing, thanks, Mrs. Vastasi. I don't mean to trouble you."

He sat, hands folded in his lap, and looked at her with compassion. "And how is your beautiful child? Is she well?"

"She's fine, thank you, Father. To what do I owe this pleasure?"

Goodminton blinked, as if remembering his script. "A report has reached my office—as you know, I'm coordinator of spiritual affairs—that you and Glauco Vastasi have separated."

"That's right."

"May I ask what caused this rift? Some little misunderstanding, possibly?"

"A big one. We couldn't agree on anything."

She was tempted to tell him that there wasn't any marriage to repair, that she and Glauco hadn't even been married. Hell, she'd better not. That might be cause to dismiss her from the faculty.

"You know, my dear," the old priest went on, "married couples can't expect to agree on everything. Sometimes it's a good idea to talk over one's differences in the presence of some neutral third party. Many times, obstacles that seem insurmountable will prove to be trivial after all."

She waited for the inevitable offer. It came. "I'd like to extend my counseling services to you and Glauco. If you'll make an appointment with my secretary, we can all get together some night and have a good heart-to-heart chat. I'm sure you will both be the happier."

Holy Moses. This nice old duffer didn't know the half of it.

"Thanks, Father, ever so much. I'll have to see whether Glauco feels like patching things up again."

In a pig's ass he will. No use calling him.

Late that afternoon, when the well-meaning old priest had left, another visitor arrived. A grinning S. T. Pohl, paper bag in hand, bringing take-out chicken, a pint of gin, a quart of quinine water, a fresh pack of Trojans and a tube of K-Y lubricating jelly.

With a shout of joy, she flung herself into his arms.

Twenty-Seven

Team practice had been a bummer. Oh, Pohl had been efficient as usual, catching rebounds in one huge hand, ducking and weaving and sinking shots like a greased machine. But all the other frosh looked terrible. They played as if their arms and legs belonged to somebody else.

For a long time after the squad loped off to the showers, Knox remained on his bench in the empty gym. What was he doing here? Once, a few years back, he'd been a curate, then a pastor, then the war had come along and freed him from the dreary round of baptisms and confirmations and marriage problems. Now, holding this cushy job, he felt a twinge of guilt. Most of the time he was actually having fun. Hard to believe he was helping anybody toward sainthood. And his own soul—would he make it to Heaven? He had his doubts. But suppose the freshmen didn't shape up and the team started losing, could you use basketball losses for your penance? Aw, crap. The pain of losing a game would be a piddling thing to offer up to Christ. Nothing like the agony on the cross. Not in the same league. Oh, he could resign as coach. That would be a real sacrifice. He could make a retreat, go into some monastery. But wouldn't that be admitting defeat, be just what Cross was after? He wished God would send him down some written orders, so he'd know what in hell was expected of him.

Tim Walsh had had to meet two classes this afternoon and couldn't be a bodyguard. Knox changed into his black suit, noticing that it needed a press, and working off his irritation, strode at a quick pace along the main road through campus. He'd drop by Priests' House, grab coffee. All but a few diehard leaves had dropped from their trees and a light cold rain was falling. This dismal afternoon fitted his mood. He'd have to schedule more hours of practice for those frosh. Dammit, the day didn't have enough hours in it. He wasn't wearing a hat and the rain was drenching his hair, starting to trickle down his brow. Fuckitty fuck everything.

About twenty yards ahead of him, a familiar gangling form was shuffling along the sidewalk, headed for the library. Moon Gogarty. The kid had done a fine job on that rifle story. It had drawn a rise out of Hoar and got Vastasi called on the carpet, so he'd heard. He'd catch up with the kid and give him a little praise.

Now somebody else had stopped Moon. A stranger holding a map, jabbing it with his finger, as if he wanted the kid to give him directions to a certain spot on it. The guy was heavy-set, balding, had a cauliflower ear, needed a shave. Reminded Knox of a pro wrestler.

Moon was holding the map, peering at it, when from behind them a dark blue Packard came roaring up the drive. While Knox stared in disbelief the big car veered off the road. Gunning its engine it climbed the curb and hurtled along the walk, aiming for Moon.

Knox sprinted forward. A shout tore loose from his throat—"Look out!"

The front grill of the car smacked into Moon, threw him flat on his back. The left front wheel rolled over his right leg. The car dropped back down to the street, its passenger door flung wide. The guy who'd been asking directions caught the map in midair, landed a kick on Moon's back, hauled himself into the Packard, slammed the door. The big car took off with a scream of tires.

Knox sprang to the fallen kid, dropped to the sidewalk, knelt, inspecting the damage. The kid lay on his side, unconscious, blood trickling from the right corner of his mouth. One pants leg was turning dark red where the wheel had passed. The stain was spreading. Damn! Had to get him to a doctor. Fast.

Knox heard footsteps behind him. Thank God, someone else had appeared. He glanced about. Legs stood nearby, a circle of shoes, people looking down at Moon's fallen body, a jumble of voices talking excitedly. Students— Knox recognized Crews—had arrived. But when Knox lifted his gaze he found himself looking into the grim, ruddy face of a fanatic. Cross.

Now, of all times, the bastard had had to show up, with four of his fellow worshippers. Knox leaped to his feet, ready to throw a karate chop. But Cross raised his right hand, palm outward. "Peace," he intoned.

"For the love of Mike," Knox cried, "can't you see this boy is hurt? Now is no time to—"

"Be calm, Priest," Cross said evenly. "Let there be a truce between us." He turned to a tonsured bruiser standing next to him. "Leo, radio for an ambulance." The bruiser galloped off to a long black van parked in the drive.

Cross turned back to Knox. "Help will be here shortly."

Knox felt stunned. Cross read his expression of disbelief. "Don't you know that we are Christians? That injured leg needs a tourniquet. You," he said to Crews, "give me your shirt."

Crews looked shocked. "But—but it's cold out!"

"Then give me your undershirt. At once!"

Crews gulped. He peeled off his shirt and then his undershirt and handed it over. Cross dropped to Moon's side, whipped out what looked like a hunting knife. He slashed through Moon's blood-soaked pants, bared the injured leg, wrapped the undershirt around it and tugged and made a knot. Dipping his finger in blood, he inscribed the time on Moon's forehead. 2:14. To know when to loosen the tourniquet.

Knox thought that Moon shouldn't be moved until the extent of his injuries was determined, but the kid's head was lying on the cold sidewalk. Knox searched his own coat pockets, found a loose leather glove. He knelt and said softly, "Gogarty, let's lift your head a little." He cradled Moon's head in his hands, raised it an inch, and stuck the glove in under it. The kid's eyes were closed, blood from his mouth trickling faster.

"I'm always glad to be a good Samaritan," Crews said loudly.

This was insane, Knox reflected. Moon battered by a hit-a-run, and then who shows up to rescue him? The Church of the One Right Path. Nothing made sense anymore.

Cross stood there in the rain, lightly rocking on his heels, not looking at Knox, occasionally glancing at his wristwatch. His man Leo came up again. He said, "The police ambulance has been called."

Moon was turning pale, as if the blood were draining from his face. To Knox's tremendous relief, the howl of a siren came from below the hill and in seconds a police car pulled up, followed by a bright red ambulance. Two attendants got out, bearing a stretcher. They lifted Moon gently and carried him to the ambulance and shoved the stretcher inside.

A state cop came up to Knox and Cross and said, "Don't worry, Fathers. He'll be in Dedwood General in three minutes' time. I'll give him an escort."

And he got back in his car, turned the siren on full blast, and shot off, leading the ambulance.

All but a couple of the students drifted away, figuring that the action was over. Knox let out a breath he'd been holding for too long. "I guess," he said to Cross, "I owe you one."

"You owe me nothing, Priest," Cross said. "But I have a debt to settle with you."

His hunting knife flashed. Sudden pain exploded in Knox's chest.

Crews, standing there staring, gave a long "Ooooh!" of surprise.

Knox took a step toward his attacker, trying to get into position to fight back. But Leo the bruiser had a hold on his arm from behind.

Knox staggered. A second pain exploded, this time in his shoulder. "You lousy bugger," he said through clenched teeeth.

His sight was blurring. He felt himself sinking to the walk. He tried to concentrate, stay awake, but his chest and shoulder throbbed. Cross was coming at him again. The sky was starting to whirl.

And then he couldn't see anything any more.

Twenty-Eight

Vastasi's red-white-and-blue phone jangled. Peru let out a blast. "So explain to me. Why did you send Manny and the Weasel to slam that kid?"

"Jeez, Uncle Ricky, wasn't it necessary?" Vastasi said. "Didn't you read the story in the paper about our rifle business?"

"Sure, but what I don't like is Knox must think that stunt was *my* idea. You couldn't have waited till that newspaper stink died down?"

"Not only that," Vastasi said. "The kid was dicking my wife."

"Which wife? Not Gemma, for Chrissake."

"Naw, Aisling. Doing it in my own bedroom, throwing rubbers up at the ceiling. Hell, one of 'em was still stuck fast."

Peru chuckled. "Whatta you care the kid was dicking her? You wasn't married. Anyhow, you just kicked her out of the house, am I right?"

Vastasi's voice fell low. "Nobody insults Glauco Vastasi twice."

Peru thought. "So all right, all right, Nephew. I like your spirit. So what's done is done. What's the real problem is that Knox is wise to our business. That story about the rifles must have told him what's going on. But we'll fix his hash at the Holy Sepulcher game. His goddam team is going to fall apart and he's going to look like the worst piece of crap ever was a coach. I want to see the look on his face and I want to sit there enjoying it. That's what

I'm waiting for. After that, it don't matter. Then we can whack him."

Vastasi said, "Maybe he don't need to be whacked. I just heard somebody else stuck a knife in him."

Peru said, "Holy shit. Find out what the fuck happened. I want a full report."

It had taken Vastasi four days to air out the house on Professors Square. Stale urine in the living room, the reek of messy diapers. Everywhere he looked, he had found reminders of Aisling and Kiki Sue. A lipstick. A pacifier. A dog-eared copy of *Biological Abstracts.* A black net stocking draped over the back of a chair.

Living alone in this empty house was giving him the willies, but it was better than going home to Gemma every night. Both their children were teenagers now, getting rebellious, and every time he went home his wife wanted him to give them a talking-to. Hell, he didn't know what to say to them. They reminded him of the way he had been himself.

Last time he was home Gemma had caught their daughter Veronica down in the basement giving her boyfriend oral sex. Holy Moe, his ears still hurt from his wife's screams. *Is that the way a good Catholic girl ought to behave? Is it? What kind of father are you anyway? What are you going to do about it?*

Vastasi had defended the kid. At least she wasn't a lesbian.

"Hell of an example you set for her, never going to Mass,"

Gemma had shot back. "Did you even make your Easter duty?"

"I get enough of a dose of priests at the college," Vastasi had told her. "Sunday, that's my day off."

"It's all your fault," his wife had flung at him. "You're never home. What am I, a single mother carrying the flag of God all by myself like Joan of Arc?"

"Tough shit," Vastasi had said. "You handle the kids, I'll handle the business."

When they were first married, Gemma had been a slim sixteen-year-old beauty. Now she had let herself run to fat, two hundred sixty pounds, and her double chin was giving birth to quintuplets. Her sweet girlish voice had turned to a foghorn rasp and she'd developed a buzz-saw snore. All that wouldn't have been so bad, but she didn't even pretend to like him anymore. Every time he came home all she wanted to talk about was some new domestic emergency. A leaking roof. A stopped toilet. A washing machine with a squeak in it.

Then there was his wife's mother, that miserable harpy. Always after him to make a novena, always bitching about her sciatica. Sciaticas and novenas. Those were her only subjects, and she never shut up from morning to night.

Tonight in the kitchen of his campus house, Vastasi was trying to fry himself a veal chop. Burning it. He threw it in the trash and made a cold pastrami sandwich. He poured himself a water-glass of Cribari red, went into the upstairs den, and snapped on the new TV. James Beard was doing his show "I Love To Eat," breaking eggs into a bowl. Cooking! Shit. Vastasia switched off the set. He was lonesome, that's what he was. He picked up the phone and dialed a number he knew by heart.

Inside of an hour the doorbell rang and a tall frizzy blonde holding a bulging handbag stood there, reporting for duty.

"I'm Pristeen?" she said. "From Confidential Assignations? You called?"

"What's your real name?"

"Greta."

"Come on in."

She sidled into the hallway, slung her cat-fur coat on a chair, and swept the living room with an admiring glance. "Oh boy," she said. "This is a nice place." She sniffed the air. "But it kind of stinks."

"Hold your nose. Want a drink?"

"Can't. Not allowed to drink on the job. It's twenty dollars an hour. Seventy-five for all night."

"OK. We got all night. And remember, you give me the company discount. Confidential Ass is run by my outfit."

They sat on the couch side by side. Vastasi sipped some Four Roses, eyeing her. She was a once-pretty woman the far side of forty, bleached blond with a squint. Hard lines around her mouth, purple dress with a zipper in front. Easy to climb out of.

"How soon you want it?" she asked.

"No hurry. I got a drink to finish."

"You want to talk first?"

"Why not. You ever get a call from a Catholic college before?"

"Oh, sure. I been here a couple of times. In fact, I was just here last Monday."

This was getting interesting. "No crap. Who was your customer?"

"Can't say. I'm not allowed to give out a client's name."

"Twenty bucks extra. In your hand."

"Yeah? OK, it was a priest."

Well what do you know. "What priest? His name by any chance Douglas Knox?"

"Naw, that wasn't it," Greta said. "I think his name was Fry. Skinny guy with eyes way sunk back in his head."

"I know him. Priest that runs the big-time charity."

"You tell me. All I know is he had funny tastes."

"Funny? Like what?"

"Well he didn't want to do anything. Just look. Not even touch. Had me put on a show for him."

"What kind of a show?"

"You know we can come dressed in any costume? He wanted me to look like a little girl. Sunsuit. Carrying a teddy bear. Wearing a hair-ribbon."

"And what did you do for him?"

"Tricks. Just tricks, you know? Squeeze it open and shut. Stick things up it. Wiggle my ass."

"So where did this little Radio City Music Hall take place? In the Priests' House? In his room?"

"No, it was in an office. With the blinds shut. At night, nobody around."

"You enjoy doing that?"

Greta gave a shiver. "Christ, no. He made me nervous."

"He pay you good?"

"Did he ever. Biggest tip I ever got in my life."

Vastasi was exulting. Fry, running his charity operation, had a lot of money passing through his hands. This information could be valuable.

In bed she performed mechanically. Then she leaped up and got dressed as soon as he was done. He missed Aisling. She was, he had to admit, one hell of a loss.

Twenty-Nine

Propped up with pillows in his hospital bed, his right leg suspended in midair, Moon spent most of his time day-dreaming. Often he'd be Artie Shaw on stage of the Paramount in Times Square, taking hot licks on his clarinet while Billie Holiday rendered "Any Old Time You Want Me, I'm Yours." Sometimes he'd watch the nurses passing by in the corridor outside his room. His critical standards were high, but once in a while he would draw an imaginary circle around a face.

Now he blinked in surprise at the visitor coming through the doorway. She carried an envelope in one hand and a package tied with a ribbon in the other.

"Professor Vastasi—er—Weinstein! I didn't expect to see you here!" He tugged himself higher in bed, wincing, gritting his teeth.

Aisling planted his brow with a kiss. "How are you feeling?"

"Lots better since you came in."

"Brought you this," Aisling said, handing him an envelope. The card inside had been signed by every veteran in his biology class. Some had scribbled messages. KEEP YOUR ASSHOLE WORKING. GET WELL YOU LITTLE FART.

"And this is from me"—handing him the package. He tore off its ribbon and wrap. A Whitman Sampler box had been filled with something homemade. Marshmallow fudge.

"Aw. You shouldn't have."

She eased herself down into the bedside chair. "How long are you in for?"

"I don't know yet. That car that hit me broke my kneecap to pieces. Busted two ribs. Concussion. Bruises. Could have been a lot worse, the doctors say."

"Any idea who mowed you down?"

"A couple of guys I never saw before. But I guess what happened to me was light, compared with what happened to Father Knox. You heard about it? Somebody tried to run him through with a knife."

"Poor Father Knox. I ought to go see him too. But I kind of hate to. We had a. A sort of a. You might call it a misunderstanding."

She dangled a sandal from enameled toes. The violet odor of her perfume banished the smell of hospital disinfectant.

"I'm just wondering," she said, "if the story you wrote about the rifles wasn't why they went for you."

"I've been thinking that."

"Maybe Glauco was behind it. You know, he was hopping mad at me for letting you into the chapel."

"You don't suppose—he couldn't have found out that I—I spent part of the night in bed with you?"

"And part of it under. Yes, he took a while, but he did figure that out. That's why he kicked me out of the house."

"I'm sorry."

"Don't be. I was glad to go."

"Do you know for a fact—does Vastasi belong to the mob?"

"Well he hangs out with some pretty scummy people. Like his Uncle Ricky Peru. Peru gives orders to kill people the way you'd tell a gas station attendant to fill it up."

Moon had a frightening thought. "Do you—do you think they'll come back to finish me off?"

"Nah. I think Glauco just wanted you slammed for being a pest. I'd bet you won't get bothered anymore. Unless, that is, you write more exposés for *The Immolator*."

"I think I'll just write about harmless stuff from now on. That article about the rifles didn't do any good. The Monsignor read it, I understand, but he didn't do anything about it."

"He likes things the way they are. Sometimes he acts like one more guy working for Peru. Like half the people in North Jersey. Except Father Knox."

Moon said, "You figure it was the mob that tried to kill him? The same people that went for me?"

"No, I hear that Father Knox has another outfit after him. Some religious nuts that like to wave swords."

They shared fudge. "How's your daughter?" Moon said.

"Fine, but she's got a cold. Keeps me up half the night. Well keep on resting, kid. When you're all the way better I'll show you my new apartment. And maybe everything that goes with it."

And she reached under the covers, under his hospital dickey, and gave him an intimate squeeze.

———

Visiting Knox, the Sarge was winding down his recollections. "So there we were, cut off from our outfit, kicking around Sorrento—beautiful town, ever been there?

And the fucking Eyetalians, supposed to be our enemies, was so glad to see us they started celebrating. Guy run a hotel, he opened up the bar, broke out the grappa. And the good-looking broads come in, sat in our laps, poured us drinks. I tell you, Father, we got waited on hand and foot. Just like you here in the hospital."

Knox shifted in bed, taking weight off his bandaged right shoulder.

He said, "Listen, Beckett, I never got around to thanking you. You hadn't come by when you did, that bastard would have finished me off."

"Yeah. He was trying. Had the point of that thing headed for your heart. But I swung like this"—swinging his mechanical hand—"and loused up his aim. I'm just sorry he stuck you like he did."

"Then what happened? Around that time, I started getting woozy."

"He went for me, but some more GIs come along, so he changed his mind and scrammed. Funny guy. Top of his head was barbered like a cross."

After the Sarge left, a vivid memory flashed through Knox's mind. That bad moment—Cross coming at him. The cruciform haircut. The gleam of the hunting knife. There was something disturbingly familiar about Cross, all right. This was baffling. The guy had to be somebody Knox had met before.

Knox's next callers that afternoon didn't cheer him any. The two of them came swaggering in, the woman bearing a massive vase full of red roses, the man lugging a five-pound box of Schrafft's chocolates. The woman plopped herself into the bedside chair and the man dragged up another chair and they both confronted Knox with oversized grins.

"How you making it, Father?" Ricky Peru said.

"All right," Knox said. "Till you came along."

Tessie gave a yuk of laughter. "Oh, Father, what a kidder you are. Hey, lookit these roses we brought. Real long-stem ones. Do you know, they cost ten dollars a dozen."

Peru said, "We was just passing through Dedwood and we heard about your accident."

"Yeah," Knox said. "I accidentially got butchered with a hunting knife."

Peru worked at looking sympathetic. "My, my, you mean some people don't like you? You know, Father, you wouldn't be here if my boy Willy had stuck around keeping an eye on you. You want I should put him back to work? Be your bodyguard?"

"No thanks," Knox said. "I don't need any mobsters protecting me."

Peru's grin dropped off. His mouth settled into a straight line. "You still got me wrong, Padre. You don't know beans about me and my company."

"Oh sure. You're just a straight-shooting businessman likes to give money to colleges. So who was it ran over James Gogarty with a car because he wrote that story about the rifles?"

"The hell should I know. I don't know nothing about them rifles."

"Well your pal Glauco Vastasi must know something. I guess he didn't like Gogarty blowing the whistle on him. Sounds to me as if he was selling that stuff on the sly."

"That's *his* business."

"And you don't know what he's doing? I thought you and him kept in touch. Real pals."

"That's right," Tessie piped up. "Glauco is Ricky's nephew. They always been closer than crackers and cheese."

Peru shot her a murderous look. He forced a wheedling note into his voice. "Come on, Father, you can't blame me for everything goes on around here. Anyhow, Gogarty getting hit by that car, that sounds to me like an accident."

Knox glared. "The kid was set up to be run over. I saw the whole thing. The mugs that hit him gave him a map to look at, so he didn't see what was coming."

"That right? He in this same hospital?"

"Just a few doors down the hall. Why don't you take him your flowers and candy. Maybe he'd appreciate them better than I do."

After Peru and Tessie and their gifts departed, Knox lay back trying to make sense of everything. The Sarge, that old vet, was one good egg. Have to give him an A in religion class. Saving a life ought to count more than exam questions. As for Peru, he keeps putting on a friendly mask, but he and Peru knew they hated each other's guts. What did it mean, these attacks happening on campus? Cross and his screwball church—they were worse than the mob. Well, all he could do was keep doing his job and stay on guard. O Lord, too bad You didn't patent the trademark of Your cross, keep some bastards from using it. Should he have accepted Peru's offer of a bodyguard? No, he was right to turn that down. Only, what had he done to deserve this? Here he was, right arm trapped in a rig so he couldn't move. Lord, are you trying to tell me something? Is all this doo a trial you're sending me, like Job's boils? Punishment for drinking too much and eyeing broads and forgetting to pray and acting proud? Dear Jesus, can't I work off my sins some other way? Thanks anyhow for sending Beckett in time to swat Cross. Thanks for not letting the car kill Gogarty. Make us both heal fast and get the hell out of here. The coffee tastes like tar. In the name of the Father and of the Son and of the Holy Ghost amen.

Knox had closed his eyes for a nap, but now he opened them to find a doctor in a white coat standing over him. The doctor turned to face his patient, a stainless steel hypodermic in his hand.

Knox stared up into the grim smiling red-cheeked face of Cross.

The needle swooped down, aiming for Knox's right arm. Knox felt a throb in his wounded shoulder as he tried to roll aside, but the rig on his arm held him fast. He let out a karate cry as his left arm, the free one, chopped down on the fake doctor's hand. The hypodermic rattled on the floor.

"Nurse!" Knox bellowed. "Help! Murder!"

Cross was kneeling, searching under the bed for the hypodermic. He found it, got to his feet. He was wearing a wig to hide his tonsure. He ground out, "Shut up, Priest. Shut up, I say."

A squawk box on the bedside table came alive. A nurse's calm voice asked, "Is anything the matter?"

"God, yes!" Knox shouted. "There's a killer in my room! He's trying to stab me! Get your ass in here! Fast!"

"I'll just be a minute," the squawk box said, and squawked off.

Cross scowled down at him. "You think yourself lucky, don't you. My knife merely injured you. But your luck can't last."

"You dippy bastard," Knox said, "you think you can come in here dressed like a doctor and kill me and walk out and get away with it? You said that I once betrayed you, but damned if I can remember. Who are you, anyhow?"

"You've forgotten? The old score I have to settle with you? It was back in—"

The nurse waddled in, a massive woman with purple bags under her eyes. Her mouth dropped open when she saw Cross. "Oh, Doctor, I didn't know you were here."

Knox had to admit, Cross looked pretty authentic. A stethoscope dangled down the front of his white shirt, his jacket said Dedwood Memorial, and his bland, cheerful expression looked professional.

"That's quite all right, nurse," he said. "This patient is out of his mind. I was just about to administer a sedative."

Knox exploded. "*Me?* Out of my mind? Nurse, this is the same guy that went for me with a knife. And he just tried to give me an injection and put me to sleep for keeps."

Cross smiled. He looked a lot worse that way. He said to the nurse, "There, you see? Delusions of this type are often a delayed shock reaction."

"In a rat's ass!" Knox cried. "You want to kill me, you son of a bitch! Nurse, this man isn't a doctor at all. He's only swiped some doctor's white jacket. Call the cops!"

"No need for alarm," said Cross smoothly. "I'm Doctor Church, consulting neurologist on this case. Now, nurse, if you will help me hold the patient down for a moment, I'll give him something to quiet his nerves."

Knox kicked off his covers. He wanted to leap out of bed, but the rig on his right arm held him fast.

"I don't need quieting!" he roared.

The nurse said under her breath, "Just a second, Doctor, I'll call the orderly. It's going to take two of us."

Cross hovered over Knox, hypodermic poised in mid-air. Knox tried to plant a kick in the middle of his chest, but couldn't get traction.

A tall white-mustached black man in hospital fatigues stepped into the room, looking solid as a grand piano. "What gives?" he said.

"They're both trying to kill me!" Knox shouted.

The nurse said to the orderly, "You get ahold of his left side and I'll get on his right. So Doctor Church can give him a shot."

Knox yelped, "Damn it, you're making a big mistake! This guy is no doctor! I'm a priest, I'm telling you the truth!"

The orderly said, "Yeah, yeah," reassuringly, and bent down and fixed his beefy arms on Knox's left side. "Okay," he said. "He ain't goin' noplace."

Knox's bare left arm, veins visible, lay ready to jab. Cross had a thumb on the push-button of the hypodermic.

WHACK.

A heavy object slammed into the side of Cross's head. He grunted, knocked off balance, staggering. The object swung down and slammed him again, with a clash of makeup cases and nail polish bottles.

Aisling, purse in hand, let out a shriek. She snatched the hypodermic from Cross's fingers and dashed it to the floor. "What's the matter with you people? Didn't you listen to Father Knox? Saying this guy is no doctor? I heard him all the way down the hall."

Cross drew himself erect, rubbing his right ear. He glared at Aisling through narrowed eyes. "What is your name, young woman?"

"Aisling Weinstein. What's it to you?"

"I intend to file charges against you for assault and battery. For interfering with a medical procedure."

"Screw you. I'm calling the police."

The orderly and the nurse had let go of Knox. Now they stood by in confusion, wondering who to believe. The patient, half out of his bed, was chortling. "Great work, baby! You and that purse are better than a battalion of Marines."

Aisling looked at Cross with contempt. "You claim you're a doctor?"

"He's Doctor Church," the nurse said.

"Then show us some ID," Aisling said.

Cross frowned. "Certainly. I'll bring it to you." He sidled toward the door.

"Grab him!" Knox bawled to the orderly. "Don't let him get away!"

The orderly wasn't accustomed to grabbing doctors. He stood making up his mind. And Cross was gone.

Aisling handed the nurse the hypodermic. "Be interesting to have your lab check this thing. I bet you it could kill an elephant."

The nurse's jaw worked. "You mean—he was an impostor?"

Knox let out a snort. "That's what I've been telling you."

"Why, how could he—why, there's never been anything like this in the history of this hospital."

"If you folks will excuse me," the orderly said, "I got to go punch out. Go get me a boilermaker."

Aisling slid into the bedside chair, clasped Knox's unsuspended hand. "You all right, Father?"

"Thanks to you. Hey, you want to try out for the boxing team?"

"The wrestling team, maybe. I was on my way to see you when you let out those godawful shouts."

Knox sighed. "That bird was the same one that put me here. Boss man of a nutty church. He was trying to finish the job."

"He doesn't give up easy."

"So why were you coming to see me? You wanted to make your confession?"

"I wanted to say I'm sorry about that time I jumped on you. I'd like to be friends again."

"Sure," Knox said, wincing as he straightened out in bed. "Why not. Anyhow, I never thought you weren't being friendly."

Aisling left a parting kiss on his lips. As she strolled away, Knox could hear her singing in the corridor:

Violate me in violet time
In the vilest way you know . . .

Thirty

After a few days, the pain had eased. Knox was grateful he'd been facing his attacker when the knife went into his chest. This way, he could change his own dressings.

"An inch to the right," the surgeon had told him, "and your heart would have got it. Going to have a nasty scar. Maybe you'll want a cosmetic transplant sometime. Take a piece of skin off your bum and relocate it."

"No good," Knox said. "I need all the bum I've got."

These nights he had to sleep on his back. Annoying, because he was a belly sleeper. His chest felt as if it had gone through a grater. They'd given him some pills to help the pain, but they made him drowsy, so he had quit them. Had to keep wide awake all the time, stay on guard.

As soon as they let him come back to campus, he fell back into his customary routine. Spending a lot of time watching the squad work out. This December morning a few flakes of snow were venturing down, and Tim Walsh was walking him over to the gym. Using a cane, Knox tapped his way across the central quad.

"So yesterday you went to see the Gogarty kid," Walsh said. "How's he coming along?"

"OK, but he's needs more mending. I guess they'll keep him in the hospital over Christmas."

"And your audience with the Monsignor?"

"Brief. I figure he just wanted to see if I was back in working condition. Still doesn't believe there's such a thing as a mob. But he admits there could be some religious nuts after me. Guy that stabbed me wasn't a dream."

"That's for sure. What's his take on these attacks on you and Gogarty?"

"He wants to sweep 'em under the mat, make believe they never happened. All he cares about is that nothing bad gets into the newspapers. He's hiring another campus cop to help Callahan. Bringing Kozlowsky out of retirement. Which is like calling Tweedledum to help Tweedledee. I guess we have to keep on being our own police force."

"You know, Doug, I'm glad to. But I worry about you when I'm not around. You're not exactly in shape to throw any karate kicks these days."

Alone now, sitting on the coach's bench waiting for the squad to arrive, Knox sent up a prayer of thanksgiving. For still being alive, back on the job. For Sarge Beckett, for making Cross's knife go wild. Mysterious ways You move in, Lord. Sometimes I wonder—are you really listening or do you let it go in one Ear and out the Other, like a shrink weary of people's crap? Prayer is OK but it's a one-way conversation. Oh, don't get me wrong, Lord. I trust You. You've always looked out for me. But You understand, I can't help feeling like a cat with nine lives, most of 'em scratched off already. Please keep those fanatic bastards from jumping me again. Unless you let me get hold of Cross and wring the son of a bitch's neck. In the name of the Father and of the Son and of the Holy Ghost amen.

As soon as the team came in, he was barking at them as loud as ever. He stomped around on his cane, giving orders, pointers, encouragement. The boys were trying hard to please him.

S. T. Pohl was a shot-sinking machine, traveling back and forth to the basket like a shuttle. Knox had a surge of joy. Holy Sepulcher was going to be a pushover.

For Moon it had been no fun spending Christmas in the hospital, but there had been good moments. On Christmas day his grandmother had taken the Lackawanna train in from Dover and surprised him with a portable record player and a stocking packed with Walnettos, chewing gum, and a Doc Savage pulp magazine. Father Knox had brought him Holy Communion and a book of cartoons by Charles Addams. His roommates had organized a trio to sing him off-key carols. And best of all, his gorgeous biology professor had brought him a fresh batch of marshmallow fudge. Oh, wow. Now he had hopes for the future.

Back on campus at last, Moon swung on crutches along the plowed walks, traveling between meals, class, and Temporary Shelter Thirteen, dodging the patches of ice. The faculty had been magnanimous about his missing five weeks of classes. His instructor in Thomistic philosophy hadn't even noticed he had been gone.

His leg still hurt. Getting around was exhausting. He spent hours in his bunk, taking refuge in dreams. His sessions on imaginary bandstands grew longer. Now he'd be Benny Goodman, hitting licks on his licorice-stick, now he'd be Artie Shaw doing "Frenesi" with Lana Turner and Ava Gardner swooning at his feet. Always in his mind's ear the roar of an enthusiastic crowd would surge in and drown out reality.

But reality kept intruding. The student newspaper. Another issue due, space to fill, an interview to write. With an effort Moon roused himself from his cot and left the Quonset hut to keep his morning appointment. Already the first snowfall of the year was looking cruddy. Where dogs had peed, the snowbanks were streaked with gold.

When the intercom on his desk spoke—"Father, Mr. Gogarty of *The Immolator* is here to see you"—the Right Reverend Jasper Fry hastily crammed three picture magazines back into the bottom drawer of his desk. *Hotsy Tots, Peachfuzz Pussies, Little Lickitty Splits.* He composed his face into that of Director General of the Children's Crusade.

Crutches parked, seated before the wide mahogany desk, Moon stared into Fry's sunken, cavernous eyes. The desk was bare except for the intercom, a stack of manila envelopes, and one other item. Swimming on the polished mahogany was a child's toy about eight inches high, a white rubber swan.

Moon opened his reporter's notebook and took a sharpened pencil from behind his ear. "Father Fry, sir, I really appreciate you seeing me, Father."

"Oh, you're quite welcome. I believe in the necessity of the press, Mister—?"

"Gogarty, Father."

"Gogarty. Even the student press."

"Yessir. I've just a few questions—"

Fry interrupted. "Perhaps I should tell you, Mr. Fogarty, that I've not much time to spare. Let me give you a press kit full of facts and figures about the Children's Crusade. I'm sure it will answer your questions."

"That'll be great. But Father, I'd like to ask you a little about yourself."

A shadow crossed Fry's gaunt face. "Oh? It's the Children's Crusade that matters. I myself am of no consequence."

"Some people don't think so. I looked you up in *Who's Who*, Father. You did your undergraduate work at Mortification College, where you were a Sorrowful Mysteries major. You've a doctorate in theology from the Louvain. You taught at St. Cash's before the war, then you were a chaplain in the South Pacific."

Fry sighed. "You seem to know everything about me already."

"Not everything. Would you mind telling me why you started the Children's Crusade? Did it have anything to do with your war experience?"

Fry swiveled away to stare out the window. His voice dropped so low that Moon had to strain to hear. "Indescribable. Kwajalein. The island covered with corpses. Marines scavenging for jewelry, yanking gold teeth out of the mouths of dead Japanese. Then Hiroshima. Those burn victims. Children. Sheets of skin that had slithered off . . ."

Moon said timidly, "You wanted to do something for those kids?"

Fry nodded. His swivel chair was creaking back and forth.

"Father, does the Children's Crusade take in much money?"

Fry snapped out of his revery. "I suppose it does. Is that all that interests you?"

"Oh no sir, I think what you're doing is wonderful. And I understand you've started a boys' swimming club here in Dedwood. But Dedwood isn't exactly a poor town. Are you trying to help rich children too?"

Fry's eyes narrowed. "The rich can be poor in certain respects. You see, Mr. Doherty—-"

"Gogarty."

"You see, I love children. All sorts of children. Their smooth skin...."

Fry's hands were beginning to twitch. His head jerked faintly from side to side. His fingers stole across the desk, circled the white rubber swan.

Moon jotted notes.

"The swim club has disbanded," Fry said.

"Not enough boys?"

"Too many—intrusions." Fry lifted the toy swan, pressed it to his lips. He was rocking to and fro in his chair now, his tic intensifying.

Moon sat rigid, an alarm going off inside his mind. Father Fry was behaving like a mental case.

With a sudden bang the office door burst open. Moon whirled. Ricky Peru and Cosimo di Montecassino came slouching in, followed by Fry's secretary shrilling, "You can't go in like this! You don't have an appointment!"

Peru beetled his brows at her. "Calm down, sister. I just made an appointment. Don't worry, Father Fry will want to see me, I bet."

He stuck out a hand heavy with rings. "Ricco Petruccese, Father. We met at the Monsignor's party. This is my man Cosimo."

Peru noticed Moon. "Hey, kid, you back, huh? You eat all them chocolates we brought you in the hospital?"

"Yes, thank you," Moon said.

Peru stabbed a thumb toward the door. "Beat it, kid. I got to talk to Father Fry personally."

Moon grabbed his crutches and hoisted himself to his feet. "I was just going. Oh, Father, did you want to give me that press kit?" Nervously, Fry tugged a manila envelope out of a stack on his desk.

When the student reporter had left, Peru eased his wide frame into the chair and shook ash from his cigar onto the rug. Cosimo, his cold fish eyes unblinking, stood motionless as an icon in a wall.

Fry fought to get himself under control. He manufactured a smile. "I remember you very well, Mr. Peru. You've been a good friend of the college, a most magnanimous benefactor. Is it about the Children's Crusade that you've come? May we hope to enlist your help in our work of mercy?"

Peru smiled back, flashing his diamond-studded tooth. "Absolutely, Father. The Children's Crusade is what I'm here about. You got a legitimate charity here, but in my opinion, you don't know how to milk it. You can use any help you can get with it, right?"

"What do you mean?"

"About them punchboards of yours. Think what a few hundred more of them would bring in. Pure gravy."

"I don't understand."

"Listen, I've been watching your operation. You distribute them boards in Dedwood and the Oranges, but you've never had 'em in Newark because Newark is already saturated with boards. Take a chance, win two tickets to the Yankees. Which happens to be one of my businesses. Newark is my territory."

"I see."

"Let's suppose you was to have your punchboards in every bar and restaurant and drugstore in Newark too. We take out ours, put in yours instead. You and me, we combine operations in Newark, Dedwood, the Oranges. Your boards have a better pull anyway. All them tear-jerking pictures of crippled kids. Must really wring the suckers' hearts. And my company, we're an experienced professional operation. We'll take care of the collecting for you."

"That's very generous."

"Oh, we can't do it for nothing, you understand. We got overhead, naturally. You and me, from now on we split seventy-five, twenty-five. The twenty-five is yours. Don't say Ricco Peruccese takes every last dime away from orphans."

Fry looked panic-stricken. "No, I can't agree to that. Your services sound overpriced. Should not the Children's Crusade receive the major share?"

"Under the circumstances, Father, I think you ought to be glad to get anything you can get."

"Circumstances?"

"You remember Saturday morning in the swimming pool? A young guy I know, Randy Harrigan, happened to be taking a nap in there. He woke up and heard you make the little boys drop their bathing suits. Made 'em promise not to tell their mommies and poppies. Then he watched you taking pictures of their weenies and asses and cute little balls. Told me all about it."

Fry's lips worked. No words came out.

Peru blew smoke. "I think," he said evenly, "maybe you don't want it to get out that a holy priest, the head of the Children's Crusade, has the hots for short eyes."

Fry's face looked like that of Michelangelo's sinner on the Sistine ceiling, appalled when he finds himself damned. "I—I—it's not true. Never. I have never in my life abused a child."

"Except how would all those mommas and poppas like it if the word got out you been taking scrapbook pictures of their darlings in the altogether? Your frigging Children's Crusade would be a roasted goose. I bet the Pope would rip your Roman collar off."

He settled back in his chair, enjoying this. Cosimo, standing beside him, wore a grim half-smile.

"And that ain't the best part," Peru went on. "I have it on good authority you rented a whore from Confidential Assignations. Put on a private peepshow for you, right here in your office. Had a little fun for yourself, did you? A little jerkoff session?"

Fry winced. "This is blackmail."

"You ain't whistling Dixie, Father. Sweetest piece of hush I ever heard."

Fry's head and shoulders were twitching again. He stared up at the ceiling where a tiny black spider was crawling. He fixed his eyes and contemplated it.

Peru ended his cigar, stamped it out on the rug. "There's a couple of details let's iron out. Your fund drive that's coming up. I seen the audit on last year's take. This year you ought to do even better. Suppose you and me, we share that pot. Say you guarantee me a flat hundred."

"A hundred dollars?" Fry's eyes tracked the spider. It was walking the ceiling in a slow spiral course.

"A hundred dollars? Shit, no—a hundred thousand. Anything over that much you can keep. Besides, we want seventy-five per cent of everything you make on that holy junk you sell over the radio. The same cut on any big-time donations that come in. Don't try to gyp us. We'll audit your books. Every month you can run them by Glauco Vastasi. And Father, don't try to start any secret bank accounts. I catch you doing that, you're over with."

"And if I don't agree to this—this extortion?"

"How you going to not agree? You know that radio station you broadcast on, WXXX? I happen to own it. And there's a guy works for me named Maxie Kline, has a news show. Ever listen to him?"

"An unprincipled snoop. A muck-raker."

"That's the guy. All I got to do is spill the beans to Maxie about you and the whore and the little boys. Believe me, he'd love it. You'd be the juiciest hunk of muck he ever raked."

Fry was swaying from side to side. His right hand had twisted the rubber swan out of shape. Its head protruded from the top of his clenched fist.

Peru leaned back in his chair. "So you see, Father, you don't have any choice. Cosimo here, he's my collector. Expect him every Thursday. Tomorrow we'll need your down payment on that hundred grand—say, fifty in unmarked twenty-dollar bills. And you can triple your order for punchboards right away."

Peru got up and walked out, Cosimo trailing him. The door slammed after them.

Fry's head slumped to his desk. From his throat came a high-pitched wail.

Thirty-One

Everything was going to hell this afternoon. Kiki Sue kept on crying like a banshee and wouldn't be comforted. What had happened, Aisling wondered, did my breast milk turn sour? At last the baby accepted a pacifier laced with Karo syrup and fell asleep. Aisling got down on her hands and knees and sponged up the pool of water that had leaked out of the fridge when she'd left it open. Then she seated herself at the kitchen table, donned her reading glasses, grabbed her fountain pen full of red ink and started working through a stack of quiz papers. The vets in her class, it seemed, hadn't understood anything. She had half a mind to cry.

Too late, she realized she ought to have latched the front door. Now it banged open and into her tiny living room barged Randy Harrigan.

He was holding a paper bag twisted shut around the neck of a bottle. He struck an open-armed pose like Gene Kelly about to go into a dance.

"Hey, how you like me, kiddo?" he said.

He was dressed completely new from head to foot. Gray felt hat, double-breasted blue serge suit, white shirt and red tie, shiny new patent leather shoes, silk socks with clocks in them.

Aisling removed her glasses and squinted at him. "What happened? You win the Irish sweepstakes?"

"Better than that. I ain't running around for the Monsignor anymore. I got a better job. Now I'm special aide to Mister Ricco Peruccese himself."

"That figures. Cruds of a feather flock together."

Harrigan looked disappointed. "Whatta you got against Mister Peru?"

"He's a big fat olive looking for an oil press. He fixes games, and he kills people."

"Nobody never proved nothing. Anyhow, what do I care. Peru's paying me good dough. He knows what I'm worth to him."

"Since when do dollar bills come in two-bit denominations?"

"Very funny. Hey, look, I brought us over a quart of Guinness so's we can celebrate."

"Can't drink. Got work to do."

"Oh. Mind if I have some?" He rummaged an opener out of a kitchen drawer, uncapped the bottle, sloshed foaming stout into a glass.

Aisling said, "All right, all right, I'll ask. What made Peru give you this promotion?"

"I gave him a tip turned out to be valuable. Told him something that's going to expand his territory."

"Yeah? You showed him a cigar butt lying in the street?"

"Shut up and listen." Harrigan took off his jacket and draped it over a chair. He loosened his tie. He sat down on the little couch next to her, made his voice low and confiding. "I got the goods on a priest that's been taking pictures of little boys."

"So what? Lots of people take pictures of little boys."

"In their birthday suits?"

"A priest did this? What priest?" A terrible thought crossed Aisling's mind. "Not Father Knox?"

"Knox? Naw. This guy, the one I caught, runs a big charity." He checked himself. "I can't tell you no more. Ricky made me swear I'd keep it under my hat."

"So that's why you bought a hat. That priest must have been Father Fry."

Harrington looked annoyed. "Don't tell nobody about this, or so help me I'll knock your teeth out. Had a slow day, see, so I was taking a nap on the pile of life preservers at the swimming pool. Woke up and Fry was running this swim class for boys. Only they didn't have nothing on. And he was down on his fucking knees, snapping pictures up next to their peters."

Aisling frowned. "That's awful. And he runs the Children's Crusade! Somebody ought to know about this. Somebody ought to relieve Fry of his job before something happens."

"Yeah, sure, sure. Ricky's going to tell the Monsignor one of these days," Harrigan lied.

"But meantime, I suppose he's blackmailing Father Fry?"

"Mmmmm. I think he's getting a few favors out of him."

"And you're going to work for this slime?"

"Damned right I am. Stick with me, kiddo, someday you'll be important too. I come over to tell you I'm not going to be around campus no more. Won't have no more free afternoons. But I've got practically every night to myself. So anytime you need servicing—"

Aisling looked at him with contempt. "When I need servicing I'll call Frigidaire. You think you're the only man in the world?"

"That Gogarty squirt. I don't want you seeing no more of him. I told him if he comes around you again I'll kill him. And if you start seeing him again, I'll take care of you too." He cocked his right hand and stuck his index finger up against her forehead and quietly went, *Pow Pow.*

Harrigan sat back on the couch as if proud of himself. "You saw what happened to Gogarty. A car ran over him."

"I know. Was that Peru's idea?"

"Naw, I think it was Glauco's."

She shivered, involuntarily. "You don't need to worry about Gogarty. He's going around on crutches. He's out of commission. But what's with you, Harrigan? You think you can say who I can sleep with and who I can't? Let me tell you something, buster, I don't take orders from you or anybody."

"Sure, sure, honey. But let's face it. Now that you busted up with Glauco, you need a new main man, and that's me. The thing is, you like me. Don't say you never did."

Harrigan kicked off his oversized new shoes with loud clumps. He bent close to her with a leer that he imagined to be a winning smile. The stout had left a moustache of foam along his upper lip.

Aisling glared. "All I ever liked about you was your cock. Too bad you had to be attached to it."

"You got to admit we've had some good times together. And right now can be another one."

"No it can't. I've got to grade biology papers."

"Come on, what's more fun, biology or fucking?"

"That depends. In your case, it's biology."

Harrigan took off his shirt and his undershirt together. "Come on, honey. Your baby is sleeping like a baby. Just a quick one."

Aisling flashed him a look of hate. "Put your goddamn clothes back on."

"You know," he said, standing up and stepping out of his pants, "all I got to do is tell the monsignor about you. You being a whore and all. Never even married to Glauco like you let everybody think. I say the word and your teaching job goes down the flusher."

"You wouldn't."

"Oh no? Suppose I did. Then how would you pay the rent? You'd be out on the street."

Slowly Aisling started unbuttoning her blouse. "This is nothing but rape," she said.

Thirty-Two

Moon let a day go by before he could muster enough ambition to look at the press kit from Father Fry. When at last he opened the manila envelope and dumped it out, he stared at its contents with shock. *Holy smoke.* Right away he headed over to the gym to see Knox.

With deepening frown, Knox flipped through the sheaf of glossy photographs. Shots of naked boys in swimming. One kid grabbing another kid's penis. Close-ups of body parts. Multiple shots of one kid in particular.

He glared across his cluttered desk at Moon. "Where did you get this crap?"

"Father Fry gave it to me. He must have made a mistake. Thought he was giving me a press kit for the Children's Crusade."

Knox leaned back in his chair, studying the ceiling. *Sweet Lord,* he thought to himself.

"Father Fry was in a hurry," Moon said. "He wanted to get rid of me. Because Mr. Peruccese and another guy came into his office like they owned the place."

Knox groaned. "Peru. Yeah, he'd naturally take an interest in the Children's Crusade. To give it money and be a big shot. Or else to muscle in on it."

Moon pointed to the photos. "You suppose Father Fry took these?"

"Well he's an expert photographer, all right. Has a darkroom. He could have made these prints. Not that these pictures mean anything. Hell, maybe they were taken for some respectable purpose. Naked athletes, that's old stuff. Ancient Greece, all the jocks in the Olympic games went bare-ass. The body beautiful and all that crap, you know."

"But—little boys? Close-ups of their peters?"

"I admit I don't like it. And I especially don't like it these were snapped in our swimming pool."

He depressed the switch on his intercom and said, "Maureen, honey, will you please call Father Fry. Tell him he can't hold his swim club in the pool again Saturday. Tell him we're cleaning it. That's not a lie, it's what the Jesuits call a mental reservation."

Maureen answered, "We don't need to call him, Father. He canceled that date two days ago. Said his swimming club had disbanded. Didn't say why."

Knox looked relieved. "OK, fine. But will you call him anyway? Tell him I need to talk with him. This afternoon. Will you do that, honey?"

He turned to Moon. "Good thing you showed me this stuff. Thanks, I guess."

"I figured you ought to know."

"Gogarty, when you interviewed Father Fry, did he ever say anything—do anything—strange?""

Moon rummaged his memory. "Come to think of it, he did. He started rocking back and forth as if he had the jitters. And he kept squeezing a toy rubber swan."

Knox winced as if struck. He lit a Gauloise and contemplated Moon through a spew of smoke.

"OK, Gogarty, listen. Keep this under your hat. Don't tell another soul what you've just told me. Nobody. And not a word about these pictures, understand?"

"Right, Father."

Knox leaned back and stared out through the window. "You see, Jasper Fry is an old friend of mine. We were both on Okinawa during the war. Went through a rotten time together. I want to talk with him about all this. Hear his side of the story."

"Sure, Father."

"Father Fry has been working too hard on his Children's Crusade. He's on the radio all the time, he runs a big operation. He's been under a lot of strain. To tell you the truth, I've been worried about him. And now it sounds like he's got Peru on his back besides."

The desktop buzzer buzzed twice and Knox picked up the phone. "Knox here. Oh, hello, Sid. Sure I remember you. You run the fancy market in West Orange that sells pomegranates. Saw you last month at the wrestling matches, didn't I? What's on your mind?"

As he listened Knox sat bolt upright. "You're sure it was him? In your warehouse?"

A torrent of excited squawks from the phone.

"Sid, what time did this happen? All right, don't let that truck get away. Tell the driver he's not to touch any of those cases. Absolutely not. Is the driver there? OK, put him on."

There was a pause and then a different voice squawked.

Knox said, "Shut up a minute and listen. No, you can't distribute that load as usual. Hell yes, it's made a difference. OK, Saint Cassian's College will buy your whole truckload. You can invoice the Athletics Department. Can you drive straight over here on the double? OK, come up the service road and park in back of the Prep. Meet you there in fifteen minutes. Thanks."

Knox hung up, turned to Moon, pain graven in his face. "Father Fry. He's flipped his lid. Held a one-man Mass in a warehouse. Consecrated a whole truckload of Ritz Crackers. Transformed every last one of the things into the Body of Christ."

Thirty-Three

Tim Walsh rushed over. He found Knox pacing up and down the office, doing his caged lion.

Walsh sat down heavily. "How do you know he did it?"

"He told the truck driver," Knox said. "Guy came to the warehouse, making his usual run. Said Fry's eyes were rolling in his head. Fry said something like, 'Drive with care, your truck is loaded with Christ.' Then he laughed like a banshee and ran off God knows where."

"Anyhow, Doug, he couldn't transform Ritz crackers, could he? I thought the Eucharist has to be unleavened bread. Nothing but flour and water."

"That's to make *lawful* wafers. But any kind of bread could be consecrated. It wouldn't be Kosher—I mean, according to canon law—and it couldn't be used in church, but there damned well could have been a transformation."

"You sure?"

Knox nodded wearily. "Pretty sure. One time I made a retreat in a far-out monastery where they baked the things using honey. Later on they found out it wasn't licit, but that didn't change the fact that for years all the monks had been eating Jesus. They had just been making Him too sweet."

"I think you'd better call Chancery. Ask 'em what ought to be done."

"Already did. Waiting for a call back now."

They had a stiff drink. The phone rang. Knox listened gravely, said, "OK, right, Monsignor. I'll get on top of it." He hung up and said to Walsh, "That was Cliff Bruno, the Archy's right-hand man. They're taking this seriously. Said that for safety's sake the things have to be consumed. To avoid the desecration of what may well be Hosts. At least we'll get some help—they're telling the Sem to take part of the truckload. So how's your appetite?"

———

That night Knox assembled them in the Prep School cafeteria, Tim Walsh and five other priests in their off-duty clothes, the seven wimpled nuns chattering with excitement—why had they been told to skip supper? Tersely, Knox explained that some demented priest had consecrated a truckload of crackers. He didn't name Fry.

"And we've got to dispose of them. Reverently. Darlington Seminary has agreed to take two cases off our hands, and the Convent of the Sacred Heart is taking eight. That leaves us only six cases to get through. Twenty-four boxes to a case."

He waved a hand at the pasteboard cartons stacked on a table. "You understand, this is urgent. We don't want to keep these consecrated Hosts sitting around, store them in the basement, am I right, Sister?"

Sister Dionysia, headmistress of St. Cassian's Prep, said quickly, "Oh no, we couldn't keep them down there. It's damp. They could molder. And there are mice."

"So we've got to act tonight," Knox said. "Not wolf 'em down, but thinking about what we're doing. But first we all have to be in a state of grace."

Walsh said, "So we're going over to the chapel? Make our confessions?"

Knox shook his head. "We'll confess right here. Priests, down at the far end of the room, hear each other. Sisters, I'll hear yours. You'll come out in the kitchen one at a time."

Knox went into the galley and stationed himself on the cook's stool. He drew an embroidered silk stole over his shoulders. The nuns took turns coming in and sitting on a bench to confess in whispers, looking embarrassed under the bright overhead lights.

He made short work of them. What was it some priest had said once? Hearing nuns' confessions was like a lot of popcorn trying to stone you to death.

"Bless me, Father, for I have sinned. The other day I had unkind thoughts about Sister Agatha."

Knox shrugged. "Quit thinking about her. If you're tempted again, pray. That'll be five Our Fathers and five Hail Marys and make an Act of Contrition. Next!"

"Bless me, Father, for I have sinned. When I was taking a shower this morning I laid a hand on my umpitty-ump."

"Your *what*?"

Sister Margaret Rose's smooth round face turned red. "You know. That thing down there."

"All right. Five Our Fathers and five Hail Marys, and from now on leave your umpitty-ump alone."

After all the nuns had been absolved, Knox himself sat down with Walsh. He began, in a low voice. "Pride. Bragging about the team, how I'm running things. Got half-soused yesterday. Took the name of Our Lord in vain. Six times, maybe. Oh yeah, felt a wet dream coming, and helped it along."

"You make a habit of it?"

"Naw, this wasn't routine. I was in the hospital and your woman bio prof, Aisling, came in and stopped Cross from killing me. Then she gave me a big French kiss. Got me hotter than a two-dollar pistol."

"You're only human, Doug. But watch it. And better watch that John Jamison. Why don't you lay off the sauce for a couple of weeks. Now make an act of contrition and take a trip around the Rosary and next time you run into Aisling Vastasi, look the other way."

When the last priest had been forgiven, Knox had them all take seats, priests on one side of the long table, nuns on the other. Crackers rattled out of packages onto cafeteria trays. Knox took a seat in the middle of the group.

"We look like the Last Supper," Walsh cracked.

Everybody laughed.

"I think those apostles had a better middle man," Knox said. "You're going to be more full of Him than you'll ever again be in your life. Sisters, the priests will lay Hosts on your tongues. As soon as you've got one Host down, open up for another. Priests, you can serve each other. Between nuns. This will be dry going. But the Archy—Archbishop Reagan——has given us a special dispensation. Your throat gets too dry, you can take a swallow of water."

"And shall we priests drink wine?" old Father Scully said hopefully.

"We drink wine all night, we'd get clobbered. Now remember, these Hosts are bigger than you usually get. Open wide, receive the thing whole. No biting, no munching. Let it dissolve part way, then swallow it. If anybody coughs, be careful you don't spray. No talk unless it's necessary. Any more questions?"

He glared around the table. Nobody had any questions except Sister Mary Immaculata. "Can I keep one of these empty packages?" she piped up. "There's a recipe on it for an apple pie you can make without apples."

"All right," Knox said, "but don't make your school kids eat it."

Father Scully wanted to know if they were going to work all night.

Knox glanced at his watch. "It's seven-thirty. We'll see how it goes. But don't figure on getting to bed early."

They began. Trays were emptied, refilled. Hours crept by without a sound but the rustle of packages opened, more crackers shaken out onto trays. Hard light beat down on them from the bare ceiling bulbs. Now and then, there was a strangled cough, the slosh of a glass of water.

At a quarter past midnight Sister Anastasia timidly raised a hand. "Father, this is a lot of crackers. Couldn't we have some jelly on them?"

Sister Ann flared. "Sister, what are you thinking of? That would be sacrilege. Surely you wouldn't smear jelly on the Body of Our Lord?"

Silently they went on eating. Knox had to take a break to go have a cigarette. Around one in the morning, Father Scully started nodding. Knox excused him and sent him off to bed.

An hour later, Sister Margaret Rose grew pale and said she was going to throw up. Knox had her lie down on a bench till her stomach quit churning.

In fact, Knox was starting to feel sick himself. Time and again, while he swallowed dry communion wafers, his mind kept racing over the same track. What had become of Fry after he'd left that warehouse? He must be hiding out somewhere. Lord, protect the poor guy. Don't let any harm come to him, not from others, not from his own hand. And for Christ's sake keep him from doing any more mischief, please. Tomorrow the Archy would suspend his priestly powers, but until then Fry could still cause trouble. What if he took a fancy to a boxcar full of Wonder Bread? Got to find him as soon as possible and bring him home.

Dawn was peeling apart the clouds when the final cracker on the last tray disappeared.

In his Hoboken apartment Ricky Peru was holding court. People wanting favors had been filing in to see him, some of them waiting hours for their turn. The last petitioner was Angelo Russo, whose son, a taxi driver, had been pulled over drunk after running a red light.

"He lose his licence," Russo whined, "he lose everything. Got a wife and three kids don't eat."

Peru nursed on his De Nobili twist cigar. "He should have thought of that. All right, Angelo. Your son gets another hearing. Have him in police court Monday morning a quarter to nine."

"Thank you, thank you, Mr. Peruccese!"

"But Angelo," he added, "make sure your boy shows up sober. And if I hear he's been beating his wife again, it will go hard with him."

He waved his hand. Russo backed out of the office, bowing as low as his belly would let him.

Cosimo had been waiting impatiently. Now he charged in. "He's gone," he blurted.

"Who?"

"Fry. Priest runs the Children's Crusade. Just now I went over to his office to collect that fifty grand. Secretary said he hasn't been in today. Yesterday neither."

"You look for him?"

"Nobody at the school knows where he went. It's like he's a ghost. He's disappeared."

Peru's fist tightened on his half-smoked cigar. It broke in half and the burning half fell on the table and left a scorch. He glared into Cosimo's right eye, the one that didn't roll toward the wall. "Goddammit, Coz. You'd think you could depend on a Roman collar, but you can't depend on nobody these days. Here we show him a way to keep his punchboards running, expand his territory for him, and he skips out on us."

"What you going to do?"

"Make him sorry. He'll show up someplace and when he does I want him wasted. You keep looking for him, you hear? I'll put out an order to the soldiers. Anybody finds him and does a number on him gets double pay and a week in Atlantic City."

Peru let his rage simmer down. He lit a fresh cigar.

"Anyway, we don't need him. We're taking over his punchboard operation right now. Anybody asks, you heard me and him make an agreement. Them boards are ours now, so you can start collecting on 'em. Hey, what about Knox? He been getting in the way lately?"

"Naw. Except the other day he did one screwy thing."

"What was that?"

"Well I was talking to Mario, the bookkeeper at Groaning Board, you know? Distributes to independent grocers. So he tells me last week he billed Saint Cash's

Athletics Department for a whole truckload of Ritz Crackers. What you make of it?"

"The fuck should I know. He must be feeding them to his basketball players, fatten up the skinny pukes. Knox buys 'em by the truckload, them crackers must be going too cheap. You better tell Mario to mark them up."

Thirty-Four

The physical therapist in Dedwood had worked wonders. Twice a week, Moon had reported for duty, straddled a stationary bike, kicked and stretched and limbered up his knee. Now he had cast aside his crutches and could get around under his own steam. But climbing the stairs up to Aisling's third-floor apartment seemed like climbing Mount Everest.

Laboring up each step, stopping to rest on each landing, he felt sustained by a growing excitement. She had invited him over to her new place tonight, just as she'd promised. Would she give him a second chance to prove his manhood? This time, was he going to succeed?

Halfway up the stairs he encountered S.T. Pohl coming down. All six-feet-eight of him. Moon's heart sank. "Pohl. What are you doing here?"

Pohl grinned, front teeth flashing. "Why, Moon, baby, you need to ask? Ain't we both come for a little after-school biology?"

"No. I can't believe this."

"You can't believe a beauteous white lady would get herself in a prone position with a jigaboo like me?"

"I—I didn't say that."

Pohl chuckled. "You was thinkin' it. Well, baby, you can think what you want. It's just like the preacher say.

On that great morn when we all stand naked as jaybirds before Our Maker, we gonna find out the indefinable, unscrew the inscrutable, and the truth it will all be revealed."

He loped on down the stairway, waved a huge hand, and tossed back, "Good luck, honey. Hope I didn't give you too hard a act to follow."

With heavy steps, Moon made it the rest of the way. He knocked and a low voice called "Come in." He twisted the doorknob and stepped into the tiny living room. Empty Ballantine bottles stood at attention on the coffee table. Sofa cushions lay on the floor, a pair of black panties had been flung in a heap.

Aisling came out of the bedroom in a long-sleeved pink coverup. Barefoot, hair mussed, lipstick smeared. She looked languid and radiant. Without a word Moon handed her the cluster of red carnations and a heart-shaped box of caramel chews.

She sniffed the odorless flowers and looked at him drowsily. "You're early," she said.

"Didn't you say seven o'clock?"

"Did I? Oh yeah. So you're here. It's OK, Kiki Sue's asleep, I can be your Valentine. Like a drink?"

"Maybe some root beer or Coke, if you please."

"Soda is for sissies. I'll get us something else."

Like a pink cloud Aisling billowed out to the kitchen and stuck the flowers in an empty mayonnaise jar. Then she came back carrying two glasses and a bottle of New York State champagne.

"Open this, will you?" she said, handing him a cap-lifter. "It's not very cold yet. Pohl just brought it. But let's celebrate. You're back on the job."

Moon flipped off the metal cap and the champagne fizzed. Half of it bubbled out on the floor. Aisling used the discarded panties to mop up the spill, then she made a casual attempt to pick up the living room. She tossed the cushions back onto the sofa and punched them into place. She floated to the bathroom and tossed the panties into a hamper.

At last she was sitting beside him on the sofa, project-ing the odor of violets. They sipped and Moon made a face. Not counting one quick sip he had had at a family wedding, he had never tasted champagne before. Kind of like sour ginger ale. He guessed it was all right once you got used to it.

"Professor," he said, "what was Scrotum Pohl doing here?"

"Just paying a social call. He brought Kiki Sue a stuffed toy octopus. Do you care?"

"Of course I care."

"You blame me for letting guys come have a drink?"

"No. But maybe—don't you think you ought to be more careful? About your reputation?"

She laughed up and down the scales. "James Gogarty, you're a Puritan. Of course I'm careful. I'm choosy as hell who I lay. Hey, my back has a crick in it. How about giving me a massage?"

"I don't—don't think I know how."

"Nothing to it. Anybody can massage. You just put some of this oil"—she handed him a tube—"on the skin and rub. Now sit down on the floor and I'll stretch out."

She rose and with a sweep of her arm the coverup fell aside. She sprawled face down on the sofa, long legs extending into space. Moon blinked with wonder at the hillocks of her bare behind. He knelt on the floor before her, like a worshipper at a shrine, obediently smeared her back with a blob of oil, and timidly gave it a rub.

"Ah, that's good," she said, emitting a purr. "Press harder. Get down lower, down where the spine starts."

"Professor Vas—Aisling," Moon said, "if I didn't know better, I'd think you were promiscuous."

She lifted her head and launched another gale of laughter. "Lover, let me tell you something. There aren't enough good men in this world to keep me supplied. Let me put it in Catholic terms for you. I'll never be satisfied, really satisfied to the hilt, until I've died and I'm face to face with the Beatific Vision. As long as I'm alive I've got to take a little bit here, a little bit there, wherever it's to be had."

He rubbed on, silently.

"And if I can possibly help it," she said, "I never go to bed with anybody I don't love. That's why Ricky Peru didn't get to first base with me."

Moon was touched. "You mean—you mean you love me?"

"Sure. You and Pohl."

"Aisling. You're one of a kind, you know? I've never known anyone like you. So open. I don't mean physically. So frank—"

She rolled over and sat up and faced him, magnificent breasts rising before his eyes like two full moons. She clapped a hand across his lips. "Don't talk. It's bedtime now, don't you know?"

Taking him by the hand, she led him into her narrow bedroom with its single twin-sized bed. Moon felt consumed by fever. He had never desired anything more fiercely in his life.

It began well. She helped him undress. At first he was hesitant, but Aisling helped him along. Fondling. Caresses. The warmth of her body next to his own made him forget the lingering pain of his injuries. She murmured his name over and over as he got up on his unbroken knee, ready for his ultimate onslaught.

Then to his horror the woman lying beside him wasn't Aisling at all. She was Loretta's naked little-girl corpse. And shrilling in his ears Moon heard the voice of his grandmother, complaining as she drew her comb down through the girl's flaxen hair, "Never saw so many snarls." Loretta's thin lips. The purple bruise in the middle of her forehead, spreading like a stain of ink. The thighs, not ample and wide and smooth, but shrunken and thin. Toenails that had never known a pedicure. The adolescent buds of her breasts. Her body was cold, and even as Moon clasped a living woman in his arms, the chill of the grave struck him like a blow from a shovel.

S. T. Pohl sped back to campus with long loping strides, hoping to slip into the gym without being seen. But rushing into the locker room to suit up for evening practice, he ran into his coach. Bumped smack into him.

Knox grunted, caught his breath, threw Pohl a corrosive glance. "Half an hour late, Mr. Pohl?"

"For once, Father. It won't happen again."

"Make sure it doesn't. Look, you birds still need a lot of work. We have to beat the pants off of Holy Sepulcher and it's going to take all the practice time we've got."

When Pohl suited up and hurried out onto the court, his teammates looked relieved. Whitey Bragg said, "Man, we were getting worried about you."

Pohl grabbed a ball and lobbed a few shots. Two of them missed. At any other time, he would have got mad at himself, but he was still coasting on the languor of his afternoon with Aisling. He felt sleepy. Shouldn't have drunk all that beer.

They mixed it up and the other players fed him balls and he drove to the hoop and sank all but three shots. The tempo stepped up, and soon he felt back in form. He did a fancy back-hand toss up over his head that swished right through. Knox whistled in admiration.

After a shower, dressed, he was heading back to the athletes' wing of the mansion when a figure in a trench coat stepped out at him. "Hey, Pohl, we gotta talk."

"What you layin' for me for, Cosimo? Thought we talked plenty already."

Cosimo's right eye looked straight at him. "Got to iron out a few details. Come sit in my car a minute. I'm parked just under them trees."

In the front seat of his Cad, Cosimo said, friendly like, "So how's practice going? You scoring?"

"Yeah," Pohl said. "I sure did score today."

"Lots of points?"

"We been playin' a real game tonight, I'd have dumped in seventy, seventy-five."

"Just keep it up. We want you to be the biggest star the game ever had. For the first part of the season, anyhow."

"You want everybody thinkin' I'm hot shit, can't do no wrong. And then you change the game plan, huh. When you want it to change?"

"Not till you play Holy Sepulcher. That's when the big dough will be on you. And the better you are, the bigger the upset."

"So then what happens? I break my neck? You break it for me?"

"Naw, nothing's going to happen to you. You just shave some points is all. Instead of your usual big number, say you score only ten. That'll be good enough to lose the game."

"We got to lose it? Not just shave down the spread?"

"That's right. Ricky wants to teach Padre Knox a lesson."

Pohl frowned. "Don't know as I like that part. Knox a good man. Been good to me."

"One loss won't hurt him. Just take him down a peg. So listen, suppose in the middle of the game you get a bum knee. You want to know how to limp, so it'll look right? I could show you a movie—"

"Cosimo, man, I don't need no picture show. I'm no actor. That look fishy as hell. Some jocks just have a off-night, you know? Try so hard to be great, they end up pissin' their shots away. That's what I'll do. I know how to get 'em in and I know how to rim 'em around and make 'em bounce out."

"OK, kid, do it your way. We don't care how, as long as it looks real."

"And listen Cosimo, don't hang around spyin' on me no more. We got us a deal, you don't need to worry 'bout it. Hey, when do I get paid?"

"Matter of fact," Cosimo said, reaching into his inside coat pocket and fishing out an envelope, "I brung you a little down-payment. Just to show you the color of what you're going to get. You'll get five times this much after Holy Sepulcher wipes the floor with you. "

Thirty-Five

After his second failure, the two of them still lying in Aisling's bed, Moon told her everything. Told her about his high-school crush on Loretta, about the shock of seeing the girl's naked body stretched out on the undertaker's table.

Aisling understood. "So you keep seeing that poor pathetic chick every time you're with another woman."

"Just when I'm with you. There aren't any other women."

"No?"

"Cross my heart and hope to die. I'm—I'm no Don Juan, exactly."

"That's for sure." Aisling wrapped an arm around him. "Lover, we need to straighten you out. You could use a good shrink. Must be one here in Dedwood."

The next morning, Moon phoned the office of Dr. Norbert Krugg, psychiatrist. For an initial consultation Dr. Krugg's fee would be two hundred dollars. Moon gulped. That would wipe out six months of his spending money. He said thanks, he'd think it over.

Damn. This wasn't the kind of problem you could spill to a priest in confession. It wasn't anything they could treat at the college clinic. That facility consisted of a room in the Prep where a kind old nun dispensed cough syrup.

Sister, I have this problem. Every time I get in bed with a beautiful sexy woman I keep thinking of this girl I knew's corpse.

Take two aspirins and a Bromo Seltzer, dear. You'll feel better in the morning.

Not likely that would help.

More and more of the time, he took refuge in dreams. His sessions on imaginary bandstands grew longer, made it harder to listen to Mr. Pigout or Dr. Bopp. Even Father Knox's lively religion lecture had become just a droning in his ears. Now he'd be Benny Goodman, hitting licks on his red-hot licorice-stick, now he'd be Bunny Berrigan, gravel voice singing "I Can't Get Started", launching into his trumpet solo, wowing the crowd.

One late afternoon the Sarge found him sitting alone in Temporary Shelter Thirteen, portable radio tuned to disk-jockey Martin Block's "Make Believe Ballroom" on WNEW, listening glumly to a song he didn't much care for, "Elmer's Tune."

"For Chrissake, Gogarty," the Sarge bawled, "if your face was any longer it would hit the fucking floor. I know what you need, partner. Come on, we'll go get us some drinks."

"I can't drink, Sarge. I'm only seventeen."

"Don't matter shit. Where we're going, they don't give a squat how old you are. Wrecker Rafferty's, the best damn saloon you ever smelled. Rafferty don't check ID cards. He don't have many customers younger than seventy-five."

The Sarge kept his Model A Ford in the parking lot next to the gym. He spent all his spare time proudly washing and waxing it, so that its black chassis gleamed like a spit-shined shoe. He fixed his good hand on the crank and twirled and let go before the crank kicked back. The engine coughed and sputtered into life. "Get on board!" he cried, leaping into the driver's seat and goosing the gas.

The Sarge steering with his mechanical claw, they headed for Newark. Moon glanced down through a hole in the floor and watched the road whipping past below.

"Damn it, Gogarty," the Sarge said, "today I feel like celebrating."

"What for?"

"Me and the Staunchers of the Sacred Side, we just closed a movie house in Orange was showing another piece of shit by that red rat Charlie Chaplin."

"*Monsieur Verdoux*?"

"Monsieur some fucking thing. About a guy kills women for a living. You imagine that? When we get done mopping up the movie business, there won't be anything you couldn't show to a two-year-old child."

They pulled into an alley and parked and the Sarge hustled them in through batwing doors. A powerful smell met Moon's nose, the smell of ancient floorboards drenched in ale and stout. At a dark oak bar that cried for varnish, two gray-heads stood in argument. Others just nursed beers. Four more were playing dominoes at a table in the corner next to a pot-bellied stove. Moon's sneakers scuffed through deep wet sawdust on the floor.

The Sarge hauled him up to the bar and slapped down a five-dollar bill. The bartender came over, tall guy with a lantern jaw, green shirt emblazoned with a map of County Kerry. "Sarge, you old bastard, what'll you have? And who's this you got with you?"

"Hullo, Jimmy. This here is my pal Moon Gogarty. He don't look very old, but he's a veteran. Give him whatever he likes."

"You paying? Then I don't care if he was hatched yesterday. What you drinking, kid?"

Moon remembered what Aisling had given him. It hadn't seemed bad. "Er—may I have a glass of champagne, if you please?"

A deadly silence fell. The two geezers at the bar had been watching them out of the corners of their eyes. Now they stopped talking and turned around to peer at Moon as if inspecting some alien bug. One of them spat loudly into a copper cuspidor.

Jimmy gave a snort, then a guffaw. "Champagne he wants! Champagne, for Chrissake! Listen, mister, you're in the wrong kind of place. We don't sell none of that lady piss here. We got beer, ale, stout, whiskey, gin, Irish Mist. Take your choice."

"He was only kidding, Jimmy," the Sarge put in quickly. "Give us a couple of boilermakers."

The bartender wiped two glasses on his shirt front, drew two Ballantines, and carved off foam. Then he poured two shot glasses full of Four Roses. The Sarge said under his breath, "Drink up, kid. Show these old cocksuckers you're all right."

Gingerly, Moon tasted the beer. It was the second beer he'd had in his life.

Two of the geezers returned to their argument. One, who squinted through a monocle like Erich von Stroheim's, was starting to totter on his feet. "Germany," he muttered. "Germany's better than Ireland any day."

"What?" said his companion. "You're taking the name of the Emerald Isle in vain?"

The other stood at attention on unsteady legs. "Emerald Isle my ass," he said thickly. "Somebody spat an oyster in the ocean."

One of the domino players, a red-faced Irishman, leaped up and made a stride toward the defamer, but not in time to punish him. With a sickly grin, the German closed his eyes, let go of the bar, and gently slid to the floor. The domino player picked him up and dragged him by the armpits and sat him in a chair in the corner.

"Sobering up's too good for him," he said. "Soon as he wakes up I'll beat the bejaysus out of him."

The Sarge grasped his shot with his mechanical hand, tossed it down, gulped beer, and let out a sigh. "Just what the doctor ordered. Hey, Jim, where's the Wrecker tonight?"

"Laid up with the gout. Been hitting the shellfish too hard. Guess he was trying to cut it with the Missus. But all them oysters threw him for a fall. Anyhow, they wasn't the kind somebody spat in the ocean, like the Kraut said."

"Wrecker Rafferty used to be a pro wrestler," the Sarge explained to Moon. "Got tossed out of the ring and broke his spine, so he went into the saloon business. Thank God he did. No better place on earth than right here."

Moon swallowed more beer, sniffed the whisky suspiciously. Tasted it, tried not to make a face. "This is a saloon, not a tavern? What's the difference?"

"All the difference in the world. A saloon, it's against the law for the bar to have seats. A man has too much, he just falls down on the floor. Like you just saw. Happens all the time."

A newcomer sidled up to them. He wore a white jacket like a doctor and brandished a pair of pliers. "Evening, gents. Got any teeth bothering you?"

The Sarge grunted. "Hullo, Dentist. You still yanking?"

"Fastest service in New Jersey. Keep me in mind, Sarge. I could save you a bundle."

A geezer at the bar piped up, "Mother of God, Dentist, I'm glad to see you. I got one in the back, right here." He pried his mouth wide and pointed. "This sucker's been killing me for days."

The Dentist squinted in past brown-stained front teeth. "Uh huh. Put your finger on it, Wally. Gotta get the right one. OK. OK, just hold still."

He fixed his pliers on the offending tooth, put his foot up against the bar to brace himself, and yanked. Wally gave a "Wugh!" and the Dentist waved the bloody tooth in midair. The patient took a mouthful of beer, swooshed, spat it out. Jimmy poured him a complimentary shot.

"That'll be two dollars," the Dentist said. "You want the tooth? For a souvenir?"

"Naw. Give it a pitch."

The Dentist winged the tooth the length of the bar and made a spittoon clang. After addressing the card-players and finding no more customers, he pocketed his pliers, said goodnight to the house, and went off to practice his art elsewhere.

The Sarge fell into animated conversation with some of the other regulars. How was his school going. The Sarge said all this studying was a bitch. Kept him tense all the time, needing ass.

Moon braved another sip of whisky. Tasted like boiler acid, but it warmed him. He swigged beer. He was feeling better and better. What the hell. Why not get drunk. Enjoy himself.

The batwing doors swung wide. In strode Cosimo di Montecassino, blue serge suit, hair combed up in a wave, a black leather briefcase in one hand. He made for the bar and said, "Hiya Jimmy. That time of the month again."

Without a word the bartender reached in back of the cash register, pulled out an envelope, and handed it to him. Cosimo squinted inside.

"OK," he said. "Sheltering Palms Protection Society. You made it out right this time." He tucked the check away in his briefcase. "And how about your Children's Crusade punchboard? Use another one?"

"Naw," Jimmy said. "Nobody ever looks at that frigging thing."

Cosimo reached across the bar and grabbed a handful of shirtfront. He drew the bartender's face down close to his.

He said, "Jimmy, you ain't talking up the punchboard like you ought to. You gotta remind the customers don't they want two tickets to see the Yanks. I come here next month, I want to see that fucking board empty. And in the meantime here's another one you can start."

He let Jimmy go. He was reaching into his briefcase for a fresh punchboard when a mechanical claw tapped him on the shoulder. He turned around to see the Sarge towering over him.

"What's with you, mister?" the Sarge said. "You giving Jimmy here a hard time?" He held his claw in front of Cosimo's face, working it open and shut. "I ought to pinch your nose off."

The geezers scurried away from the bar and gave the Sarge room. At the domino table, the players were listening intently. One held his double six suspended in the air.

"Never mind, Sarge," the bartender said hastily. "It's all right. Every month this guy comes in here collecting. He's from the Protection Society."

"Protection Society?" the Sarge echoed. "Ain't that a racket? How much you give this bozo?"

The bartender shrugged. "Hundred a month. I don't give a shit, it's the Wrecker's money."

Cosimo, left eye rolling toward the wall, the Sarge's belly pressing him against the bar, was striving to keep his dignity.

"Listen, cockroach," Sarge said to him, "you can scratch this place off of your fucking list. From now on you don't come in here no more. I catch you ever setting foot through them doors again, I'll beat the piss out of you."

He spun Cosimo around and, holding him by the back of his neck, marched him out into the street.

"You can't get away with this," Cosimo threw back. "The organization's going to hear about it. I'm coming back heavy next time." The Sarge flung him away and he reeled off into the night.

"I dunno, Sarge," the bartender said, pouring himself a stiff one. "Maybe you oughtn't to have messed with him. We don't want to get fire-bombed like the joint used to be across the street."

Calm returned. The Sarge took gulps of his boilermaker.

"What's with that priest?" he said. "The one that runs the Children's Crusade?"

"Father Fry? He's gone crazy. Completely off his rocker. Turned a truckload of crackers into Eucharists. They had the priests and nuns stay up all night, eating the things."

"No fooling. What will they do to him?"

"I don't know," Moon said. "I imagine there'll be trouble for him when he's caught. But nobody knows where he is. Father Knox is really worried. Afraid Father Fry might keep on trans—transubstantiating things."

The Sarge's eyes widened. "Is that a fact? I didn't know they were looking for him. I could have saved them a lot of fuss."

"What do you mean?"

"Listen, Moon, don't let this get around, but once in a while I got to get my ashes hauled, you know? Ain't no decent woman going to sleep with a man is part robot. So I been going over to this place in South Orange. That's where I seen Father Fry."

"You saw *him*? In a whorehouse? When?"

"Last night. He didn't have his priest suit on, but I'd know that face, all right. Black bags under his eyes. And they was set back in his head like he was looking out of a couple of Mammoth Caves. He's living right there where the action is. At Madame Diane's."

Thirty-Six

"Step on it, Sarge," Moon said. "Can't you go any faster?"

At the wheel of his Model A, the Sarge clenched his teeth. "Jesus, whattaya want? There ain't no speedometer on this crate, but we must be doing fifty." He shaved past a couple of terrified pedestrians.

Moon's head throbbed. Those boilermakers. The Sarge bore down on the gas, but when they got within sight of campus and the gabled roof of Feeley Mansion, the old Ford gave a groan and lurched to a stop, black smoke pouring from its hood.

The Sarge's shoulders drooped. "Shit. I think she's blown a gasket."

"See you later," Moon said. "I've got to find Father Knox. Tell him right away about Father Fry."

Moon eased himself down from the car and hurried off as fast as his mending leg would carry him. The sun was setting fast. From the tower of the campus radio station, a beam of light revolved through the early darkness. Snow was falling through the beam, making the sky look like a television screen where there wasn't any station. Along the long drive that led up to Feeley Mansion, Aisling was dragging a sled with a snowsuited Kiki Sue on it.

"Hi," Moon flung at her.

Suddenly he stumbled. He would have fallen flat on his face, but she caught him in her arms.

He glared at her. "You tripped me. You stuck your foot out."

"Don't I deserve more than a hi?" She sniffed. "My God, you smell something awful. Been hitting the booze?"

"No time to talk. Have to see Father Knox."

"What for?"

"Tell him—oh, if you must know, the Sarge has located Father Fry. Let me go!"

But Aisling held him fast. "I'm coming with you. I want to see how Father Knox reacts to this."

She picked up Kiki Sue, kicked the sled into the bushes, and holding the little girl aloft, sprinted ahead of Moon.

At Priests' House, they barged in past the RESIDENTS ONLY sign. The smell of dinner, corned beef and cabbage, weighted the air. In the lounge they found Knox playing nickel-ante poker with three other priests in their shirtsleeves, collars off, nursing highballs. He glanced up from his cards at Aisling and Kiki Sue and a red-faced, breathless Moon.

Knox set down his hand. "The hell you doing here?"

Moon stood catching his breath. "Father, I gotta talk to you."

"If it's about the *Immolator* it can wait," Knox said. "And you"— he said to Aisling—"being a woman, you're strictly off limits in here."

Moon blurted, "It's about Father Fry. We've located him."

Knox stood up as if a spring had triggered him. He handed his cards to the kibitzing Filipino houseboy. "Cezar, play this hand for me, will you? Play it good. There's thirty cents riding on it."

Out in the hall, Knox raked them both with a withering glare. "Now where is he? Shoot."

Moon said, "In South Orange. In a house of ass—assignation."

"The hell you say."

"It's true. He's been living there, hiding out."

"How do you know? You been there, saw him?"

"Not me. A guy I know that goes there all the time. Saw him and recognized him. There can't be two people with that face."

Knox grimaced, took his Roman collar out of his shirt pocket and buttoned it back on his shirt. "He must have completely flipped his lid. Probably doesn't know where he is, what he's doing. All right, we've got to go bring him home. Right away. Gogarty, you busy?"

"No, Father."

"Then you're coming with me. You don't look like a muscle man, but you're better than nothing. Might need help restraining him."

Aisling shot Knox a look of determination. "And I'm coming too."

"In a pig's—no you're not."

"Look, Father, I'm a trained nurse, WAVE lieutenant in the South Pacific. Believe me, I know how to handle a nut case. I've had experience galore."

Knox shook his head. "I wouldn't doubt that, sister, but nothing doing. This could be dangerous. And you're not taking that baby into a whorehouse."

"Why not? Plenty of babies get born there. For cripe's sake, Father, let's not stand around. You'll see, you'll be glad to have me along."

Knox sighed. The broad wasn't going to give an inch. He flung on his black jacket and grabbed his black felt hat.

"That nut case," he said, "has to be me."

In Knox's third-hand black 1937 Chevy with running boards perforated by rust, they headed down Old Short Hills Road. Moon sat hunched in the passenger seat, holding his breath while Knox swerved, dodged, ran red lights, going like a bat on fire.

In the back seat Aisling nursed Kiki Sue, humming a little song. "Hey, Father," she called, "you ever been to a brothel before?"

Knox grunted. "In Sasebo. Went in one out of curiosity. It didn't look like much fun. The war was just over. The women all looked starved. Hang on, we're turning this corner."

They went whipping onto South Orange Avenue. Knox tromped the accelerator and they shot past a truck and cut in front of a taxi, missing it by a hair, skidding in inch-deep snow. The driver honked and threw Knox an insulting hand signal.

Behind them all of a sudden, a red light blazed and a siren roared.

Knox muttered under his breath. He pulled over to the curb and cranked down his window. A burly cop approached, ticket pad in hand.

"Now get this," Knox said to his passengers. "He's going to ask me where's the fire."

The cop stuck his face up to the window. "So what's the big hurry, buddy? Somebody giving away free beer and pretzels?" Then he spied Knox's collar, studied his face for a moment in the half light. "Oh, excuse me, Father Knox. I didn't know it was you."

Knox said, "Hello, Branigan. How's the family?"

"In good health, thank you, Father. Some kind of emergency?"

"As a matter of fact it is," Knox said, making a mental reservation, "A fellow priest may be dying and I have to give him Extreme Unction."

"I got you, Father. Let me clear the way for you. Just follow me. Where we going?"

Knox told him the address and the cop gave him a look of disbelief. "I know where that is. You sure you want to go *there?*"

"Pretty high class location for a knock shop, huh? All right, Branigan, when we come to South Orange village turn your siren off, will you? This guy might be breathing his last. We don't want to scare him to death any sooner than necessary."

Thirty-Seven

The siren of the police car kept growling, bullying other cars out of the way, but Kiki Sue, sleeping in Aisling's arms, never stirred. In record time they reached South Orange and pulled into a street of fifteen-room houses with long uphill lawns. The largest house sat at the end of the street, a tall Victorian with a wrap-around porch surrounded by tall maples beginning to put out buds. Three or four cars clustered in front of it. Knox and the police car parked.

Branigan walked back to them and said, "Here we are, Father. What's with your dying priest? He have a heart attack getting off?"

"I don't know yet," Knox said. "I don't know what's happened to him."

"You want me to wait outside?"

"I want you to come in with us."

Branigan hesitated. "I don't know as I ought to, Father."

"Why not?"

"Kind of hate to be seen in a place like this. It might get back to the wife."

"She gives you a hard time, have her call me. I'll vouch for you. Listen, Branigan, we might need you. This man could have the strength of ten. I figure he's out of his mind."

"All right," the cop said reluctantly. "I've got my billy stick, I could bop him over the head, you want me to."

"We don't want to hurt him," Knox said quickly, "just make him come out of there. Mrs. Vastasi, we won't need you now. You and the kid better stay in the car."

Aisling clambered out of the back seat, clutching Kiki Sue. "Like hell you're leaving me out in the cold. I'm your medical support. Anyhow, I've always wanted to see the inside of a whorehouse."

Knox shrugged. They mounted creaking steps to the porch, Branigan lagging behind, his cap pulled down low over his face. Knox pushed a doorbell and a woman's voice came through a speaking tube, "Who's there?"

"Open up in the name of the law," Knox said.

The tube delivered a laugh. "Oh, the cops again? Always welcome." The door buzzed and unlatched and they stepped into a long narrow hall heavy with stale tobacco smoke. It led to a parlor that had three loveseats and two big mohair couches. Red velvet wallpaper, a painting of a nymph pursued by a satyr, and perched in the middle of a coffee table, a punchboard from the Children's Crusade.

A friz-haired blonde in an abbreviated purple dress occupied one of the loveseats with a patron, a plump sixtyish man in a striped business suit, dangling a gold watch chain, resting an affectionate hand on her nearer knee. They were sharing a drink out of a lipsticked glass. On a couch a kid Moon's age and a middle-aged man in a lumberjack shirt were sitting. The kid was scrawny with pipe-stem arms and legs and a cap that said CAPTAIN MARVEL. A young woman, wearing short shorts and a rabbit-fur vest that hung open over her breasts, stood leaning against a wall, smoking sullenly.

An imposing matron with prominent jowls, double chins, handsome once upon a time, in a gold evening gown and a necklace with a facsimile of the Star of India, cruised up to them and greeted the cop like a long lost brother.

"Why, Officer Branigan, where you been keeping yourself? Getting it at home for a change? Say, I've got you a new Latina named Dolores—"

Branigan's face turned a darker red. With a toss of his head he indicated Knox. "Listen, Diane," he said under his breath, "you don't know me. This is an official call."

"What you giving me?" the Madame shrilled. "I don't need any more official calls. I already gave to Sergeant Fitzroy for the Police Social Fund. Who's your friends?"

Moon stood gazing at the young woman against the wall. She looked sulky, resentful. His thumb revolved in his secret gesture of tribute, drawing an imaginary circle around her face.

Knox poked him with an elbow. "Don't get any ideas."

Looking at Aisling, the madam said to Knox, "My God, that's a beautiful woman you've got with you."

"Thanks," Aisling said. She turned on a winning smile.

"Suppose I wanted a job with you. What's the salary like?"

Madame Diane drew herself with pride up on her high heels. "Best pay scale you'll find in North Jersey, darling. Half of every trick, less forty a week for your room, eats, and laundry. But you'll have to get rid of that baby. We can't have babies here. They screw up the routine. When you want to start?"

"Let me think about it," Aisling said.

Snuggled in her arms, Kiki Sue was awake now, big blue eyes staring around the room. The henna-headed whore rose from between father and son and came over to Aisling, grinned down at Kiki Sue and chucked her under the chin. "Aww, what a sweetie! How old is she? Can I hold her?"

Aisling surrendered the child, who seemed happy to be trotted around the room while the other whores made a fuss over her.

To Branigan, the madam said out of the side of her mouth, "You know, sport, right now Dolores is available."

"Look, lady," Knox said, "we're none of us customers."

"OK, OK," said the madam, "you think I don't know you're a priest? I suppose you've come for the punchboard take."

"No. I want to see the guy you have staying here—"

A new face interrupted him. The Latina, a white rose in her hair, gown slit all the way up to her navel. She sidled up to him and cupped a hand over his fly.

"Say, meester, you look like you could use a little relax? Lucky you came in today, we got a two-for-one special, eesn't that right, Madame?"

Madame Diane brushed her away. "Beat it, Dolores, can't you see he's a gent of the cloth? That black hat and coat? That collar?"

"Sorry. I deedn't know. He look like he need it." She withdrew and started rubbing a hip against Branigan.

Knox said, "You have a guy rooming here, right?"

Madame Diane's jowls hardened. "I don't know what you're talking about."

"I think you do. Tall skinny guy, eyes far back in his face?"

"Maybe he's here, maybe he isn't. What's it to you?"

"Friend of mine. He's sick in the head."

Madame Diane abandoned all pretense. "Boy, don't I know it. He hasn't stirred out of his room in a week. We bring him his meals on a tray."

"Want us to take him off your hands?" Knox said.

"All right, maybe you could. I'm starting to get sick of him." She stepped close to Knox, her voice low and confiding. "He's staying in a peepshow room. All he does is sit there watching the action in the next bedroom through the one-way glass. So we're not making anything off him but his rent."

"Has he been doing—saying—anything crazy? You ever have to go in and calm him down?"

"Naw. He hasn't been much trouble that way."

"How did this guy—your roomer—find out about you?"

"Oh, him and me are old friends. Priest from Saint Cash's. Used to come in all the time, bringing punchboards for his children's charity. Always said he felt right at home here. So when he came to me and said he needed to hide out for a while, offered to pay good rent, I said okay. Isn't it like that poet Jack Frost says? Home is where when you got to go there they got to take you in."

Knox sighed. "Where's his room?"

"Come on, I'll show you." She led him down a hall.

Moon plunked himself on the couch across from the other kid, who kept darting nervous glances about. "You waiting for a piece?" Moon asked.

"Yeah."

"First time?"

"Yeah. My old man here, he's buying me a whore for my birthday."

From the other end of the couch, the middle-aged man flashed Moon a false-toothed grin. "That's right. Jackie here, he's just turned seventeen. High time he had himself a piece of tail. Jackie's shy. Now me, when I was fourteen I was dicking everything in sight."

"That's nice. The birthday present, I mean."

"Damn right it's nice. Nicest thing there is. He could of had one of them young broads, but I figure he ought to start on old Hilda. She knows how to break 'em in. So how about you? This your first piece too?"

"No," Moon said. "I mean, that's not why I'm here."

"Why else you here?"

Moon squirmed. "It's a church matter."

Down the inner hall, a door banged open and a fat man in his underwear staggered out, wheezing. "It's no use. Can't do it. Not right now."

"That's all right, honey," said a platinum blonde in a pink terrycloth robe, following him. "You just sit down in the parlor and rest a while."

"OK," said the fat man, slumping into a love seat alone. "But you understand, I'm not done yet. I paid my money. I want me a good old-fashioned blow job and a trip around the world."

Kiki Sue had been paraded into the kitchen and displayed to the cook. Now she was back in Aisling's arms and Aisling was nursing her. Passing whores oohed and ahhed. Branigan, drinking coffee, was telling the Latina a long involved joke and the woman was doing her best to laugh.

Hilda, a henna-haired veteran, came in, wearing a man's white dress shirt, stockings rolled down. She beckoned to the birthday boy. "OK, honey, I'm at your service. You got your token?"

The young man stood up, fumbled in his pockets, and fished out a round red plastic disk.

His old man said, "Hey, Jackie, want me to come in with you? Give you a few pointers?"

"Uh uh," Hilda told him. "Strictly not allowed. Anyway, don't he have to do it all by himself, if he's ever going to learn? Don't worry, Dad, he needs any pointers, I can give him plenty." She grasped the kid by the hand and led him down the hall to the room and slammed the door.

The father chuckled. "Hope he can pull it off. The first time, it's always lousy, ain't it? But what the hell, he needs to break the ice."

"What was that little red coin he gave the woman?" Moon wanted to know.

"They don't use no cash here. You pay the madam first, is how it works. She gives you a token and you give it to the whore. All the tokens she gets, she turns 'em in and gets paid."

Moon remembered the little red and blue coins that the government had issued during the war. Red ones were for meat rationing. Eight of them would get you a pound of hamburger.

Thirty-Eight

At the end of the inner hall the madam turned to Knox and said, "He might need to put some clothes on. He doesn't always wear any."

She tapped lightly on the door and called, "Father, there's a friend here to see you."

From inside the room Fry's muffled voice answered, "Go away. I don't have any friends."

Knox put his mouth up to the keyhole and said, "Jasper, it's Doug Knox. Open up."

Fry said, "Doug! Is it you? Just a minute."

There was a shuffling and a scuffling inside as if Fry were rummaging a dresser drawer. After a long while he unlatched the door and stood there in his underpants, blinking deep-set eyes. Looking sane.

Fry's lips worked, taking a while to get words out. "I guess I owe you an explanation."

"Later," Knox said. "Right now let's get you out of here."

"Why? I like this place. It's better than a monastery."

"Yeah," Knox said. "I guess you've been making a retreat, all right."

Fry stared off into the distance. "Nobody bothers me here. I'm safe. No gangsters threaten me. That's the only reason I came here, you know. To get away from that one called Peru."

Knox stepped into the narrow room, empty except for a cot, a small table with only a toy rubber swan on it, and a chair shoved close to a window in the wall about a foot wide. He felt uneasy, the way he had felt on Okinawa when one day he had gone out with a party of Marines to retrieve the bodies of two men needing burial. You knew that snipers were still lurking in trees. You couldn't see them, yet you knew they were there.

He inspected Fry more closely. The fugitive's chin was stubbled with a two-week growth. There were thin scars on his right wrist, as if he had started to slice it, then changed his mind. The room felt cold, even though a radiator was crackling.

"Jasper," Knox said, "you're coming home. Back to your old room in Priests' House. This time we'll post a guard, so the gangsters won't bother you. But tell me something. You remember changing that truckload of crackers into Eucharists?"

Fry winced as if struck. "I did what?"

"A team of priests and nuns had to stay up all night eating the damned things—excuse me, Lord—the Hosts."

"I never did anything like that. I wouldn't have."

"Believe me, Jasper. You didn't know what you were doing. Do you have any memory of doing anything else?"

Fry shook his head. "I—I—everything's a blank."

"Get your things together."

"There's nothing to pack. Didn't bring anything except the clothes I was wearing. And my swan."

Madame Diane gave Fry a grateful smile. She said to Fry, "Do like he says, Father. Your time is up." She turned and headed back to the waiting room.

Fry moved like a man in a trance. Knox had to open the clothes closet for him, help him button his shirt, tie his shoelaces for him. Swaying on his feet, clutching his rubber toy, Fry let Knox steer him down the hall.

In the parlor Madame Diane was talking with a short swarthy guy in a blue serge suit, his hair combed like a wave ready to break. Somebody Knox knew. Cosimo de Montecassino.

"I'm a little short on cash this month," the madam was saying. "You want to take it out in business?"

"No dice," Cosimo said. "Can't show the boss a piece of pussy."

The madam sighed. "Wait a minute. I'll write you a check."

"It better not bounce." Cosimo seated himself ceremoniously on a love seat and began a cigar. His face lit up when he caught sight of Knox.

"Well, hello, Father," he said, chortling. "You come here all the time?"

"Don't jump to any conclusions," Knox said. "I'm here on business and it isn't any of yours."

Cosimo, Knox reflected, must be high up in Peru's organization, and yet here he was, working as a bag man. Peru must trust him not to skim. Or not to skim too much.

Madame Diane reappeared, waving Cosimo's check in the air to dry. Cosimo snatched it out of her hand and stalked out, tossing back at Knox, "Enjoy yourself."

Branigan had finally got done telling the Latina his involved joke. His eyes bulged in amazement when he took in Fry. "Holy smoke, ain't this the Children's Crusader? He's the dying man? He looks pretty healthy to me."

Knox said, "This is a serious church matter, Branigan. Don't ever tell anybody you saw him here."

"OK, Father, I get it. Confidential, you want this kept. Anyhow, I should be getting back to patrol."

"We're all of us going now," Knox said. "Come on, Gogarty, stop eyeing the women. Come on, Mrs. Vastasi."

Aisling had been having an animated conversation with one of the whores, about Kierkegaard.

The madam said to Knox, "So long, Father. Thanks for taking the guy off my hands."

"His rent paid up?"

"For four more days," the madam said. "You want a refund?"

"Naw, keep the change. And you'll button your lip about all this, right?"

The Madame assumed a look of tremendous dignity. "You can rest easy, Father. The secrets of this house are sacred. Like the secrets of your confessional."

Knox walked Fry on down the hall, steadying him. The sullen young whore let them out. Opening the door for them, she gave Moon a parting goose.

"Come back tomorrow, cute guy," she said.

They regrouped in the street under the dim lamp light, Knox keeping a tight grip on Fry's right arm.

"Think nothing of it, Father," Branigan said. Always glad to help you out. You have any more trouble, you just call."

The patrol car took off and dwindled down the street.

"OK," Knox said, "let's get out of here. Mrs. Vastasi, can you drive? Gogarty can hold your baby. I think maybe he and I ought to sit in back, Father Fry between us so we can keep an eye on him."

Aisling nodded. "Sure thing, Father."

Knox let go of his grip on Fry, fishing for his car keys. That unguarded moment was a mistake. Fry let out a ringing scream, broke away, and dived headfirst into the street. A Buick was coming fast. Fry threw himself down on the pavement and rolled out in front of the big car's wheels.

"Look out!" Aisling yelled.

The driver heard. He swerved around the prone body and missed by inches. "You crazy bastard!" the driver shouted back, not slowing down at all.

Knox grabbed Fry by the legs and hauled him back, and the two of them sprawled in a heap next to the curb. "Gogarty," Knox barked, "get ahold of him." Between the two of them they managed to drag Fry up onto the sidewalk and stand him on his feet.

Fry looked changed, barely recognizable. His face was contorted to a devilish mask, eyes rolling. "Damn you Doug Knox, you shit-eating son of a bitch, you think you can stop me? I want to die!" He began laughing hysterically.

"Mrs. V," Knox said, "open the car trunk. There's a coil of rope in there."

Knox penknifed off two lengths of rope, wrapped one around Fry's wrists and the other around his ankles. "Sorry to do this to you, Jasper," he said.

Knox and Moon picked up Fry and slid him into the back seat. Then, with Moon on Fry's left and Knox on his right, Aisling eased the car into gear and and headed for Dedwood, holding Kiki Sue on her lap. The baby started to bawl.

In between Knox and Moon, Fry was thrashing and writhing. He had expanded his tide of abuse to include the Blessed Trinity. Knox made the sign of the cross on Fry's forehead. Then he made it on his breast. Fry snarled like a trapped animal.

"Dear Lord," Knox prayed aloud, "You who cast forth devils into swine, have mercy on this afflicted servant. Please rid him of whatever evil spirit has possessed him, in the name of the Father, the Son, and the Holy Ghost."

In his bonds Fry was struggling more violently, kicking the back of the front seat. His head snapped viciously to his left. Moon gave a cry of pain. "Father, he's trying to chew off my ear!"

Knox produced a pocket handkerchief and stuffed it into Fry's mouth.

"Gogarty," Knox said, "you know how to pray? Then say the Our Father and the Hail Mary and the Salve Regina together with me, will you? Mrs. Vastasi, can you join in?"

Aisling, weaving through traffic, said, "I don't know those prayers, Father. My Jewish old man wouldn't have 'em around the house."

"Then pray in Jewish, as hard as you can pray."

While Knox and Moon intoned, Fry quit struggling. His eyes closed. He was asleep.

Knox let out his breath. "This kind of case is beyond me. When we get back to campus I'm calling the exorcist. Maybe a couple of psychiatrists besides."

Thirty-Nine

In Priests' House, Dr. Norbert Krugg, psychiatrist, came out of Jasper Fry's room looking pale. Knox, waiting in the hallway with Tim Walsh, said, "Whatta you think, Doc?"

Krugg lit a Parliament and took a deep drag. "He's the most curious case I ever saw. Might call him a schizoid personality subject to manic depression. But that isn't the half of it."

"What else?"

"Well—this is really odd—I can't believe it, but for a moment I had the impression that his body was floating in the air."

"No fooling."

"Just now as I was winding up the session, he gave a hysterical laugh. Then it seemed as if he drifted up from his bed. Suspended a couple of inches in midair. I—I've never seen anything like it."

Tim Walsh said, "Uh huh," as if that had proved something. Knox didn't say anything.

"You understand, gentlemen," Krugg went on. "I'm a rational man. I believe in medical science, not deviltry. Now there must be a perfectly logical explanation for all this. But certain things, you know, science hasn't yet explained. Maybe your church can deal with Father Fry's problems. Sorry, but I don't think I can be of any help to you."

Knox saw the shaken psychiatrist out of the house, then phoned Chancery.

That afternoon the Right Reverend Ambrose Mollo, exorcist, reported for duty. Mollo was thin, white-haired, with a built-in look of cheer. He listened carefully to Knox's retelling of Dr. Krugg's story. Then he spent an hour in private with Fry.

When he came out he beckoned Knox into the lounge with him. Walsh stayed behind and posted himself as a sentinel, his chair propped against Fry's closed door.

"We have reason to go ahead," Mollo said gravely. "He exhibits some of the classic symptoms. You notice how the skin of his face has turned smooth, free from wrinkles? You feel a chill in his room even though the radiators are hissing? He won't want to look at pictures of our Lord. I held up a crucifix and he shrank from it."

"You think he's possessed?"

Mollo shrugged. "You never know for certain until the spirit talks. That may take a while. Usually at first the spirit pretends he isn't there. But we might as well try an exorcism. It never does any harm."

"You figure the shrink really saw some levitation?"

"Maybe he did, maybe he didn't. I always like to look first for some ordinary explanation. Hypnosis. Maybe the doctor was tired. Maybe Fry told him, 'Watch me, I'm going to rise into the air.' The power of suggestion."

"Can it happen? You ever see anybody levitate?"

"Once. An elderly nun possessed by seven spirits. Just before they were cast out, they hurled her body against the ceiling with terrific force. Broke her back, poor thing. But she lived."

"So when do we begin?"

"Early tomorrow morning. I'll come back and bring my assistant. You supply three Catholic laymen of good character, strong guys who can handle the victim if necessary. See you here tomorrow, seven-thirty."

Knox didn't want to risk any injuries to his basketball players. Where could he get three laymen who'd be dispensable? He phoned Moon at the *Immolator*. "You know three good church-going guys? To help in an exorcism. They gotta have some muscle. Unlike you."

"But, Father," Moon said, "I'd give anything to see an exorcism. I'm strong enough. You remember in the car? I helped you hold Father Fry."

"Yeah, you did. Maybe you'll do, if you can keep your ear away from his teeth. You know anybody else?"

"The Sarge. He's strong. My other roommate, Konny. He lifts weights. Only thing is he stutters."

"He won't need to talk. OK, the three of you show up at Priests' House tomorrow morning by seven-thirty."

Moon spent half the night sleepless with excitement. This could be the biggest news story in his life. At dawn under falling snow, he and Konny and the Sarge made their way to Priests' House, creating footprints on brick walks that still needed shoveling.

Father Mollo and his assistant, young Father Jason Murphy, exorcist-in-training, were waiting with Knox in the lounge.

Over coffee and doughnuts, Mollo briefed them.

"You can expect to take abuse. Verbal abuse, maybe physical. The spirit inhabiting Father Fry will probably attack you. Call you names. He may know secrets you don't want revealed. He will fling them at you, for everyone to hear. So before we begin, we should all make a good confession. Examine your consciences, tell everything. Go back and ask forgiveness again for any past sins you're particularly sorry for. I'll hear you, one at a time."

He sat in a far corner of the lounge and heard the confessions of Knox and the three students. After giving them absolution, he produced communion wafers and slipped them on their tongues. Then he made his confession to Knox, and so did Murphy. When all were shriven, he led the way upstairs to Fry's room where Tim Walsh was on guard. Walsh unlocked the door and let the six-man team go in.

The room had been stripped of furniture except for the bed where Fry lay, eyes drawn back in his head, staring sullenly. Every loose object that could be thrown had been removed. Mollo brought in a small table and placed on it a crucifix, a missal, and two candles. Fry struggled while Knox and Murphy held him and fastened him to his bed with a strap. Once the candles were lit, everybody took seats on folding chairs around the bed. Mollo began with the ritual of prayers and challenges to the invisible demon.

After three hours an unfamiliar voice came out of Fry's mouth. High-pitched, and jeering, it berated them, going through the exorcism team one at a time. The voice began with the Sarge. "You miserable sap, Roscoe Aloysius Beckett," it shrilled, "your claw really bugs you, doesn't it? You can't jerk off with it, you'd amputate your pecker. And when you go to the whorehouse every Friday night, some slut has to suck you till you get it up, is that not so?"

The Sarge sprang to his feet, looking flabbergasted. "How the hell did you—? You shut your trap, you hear?"

"Don't talk back," Mollo warned.

"And you, Konstantinos Odysseus Sarpopolis," the voice went on, "you drool over a girlie magazine while you beat your meat, prime your prong, twang your wang, whiz your weenie, flog your flute, jumpstart your joystick, don't you?"

Konny just sat there, gulping.

"Ah, Moon," the voice said, giggling, "moony Moon, James Percival Gogarty, show us your moon, you pitiful ass-kisser. When will you try to fuck that older woman again, that halfbreed Mick you hanker for? Couldn't come, could you? And that little dead whore you used to date. You didn't stop her from taking her last joyride, did you? So now she's roasting down in Hell, making goo-goo eyes up at you."

"No!" Moon burst out. "Loretta can't be in Hell! She's innocent!"

"Silence!" Mollo ordered. Moon fell back in his chair, trembling.

"And Holy Father Knox," the voice spoke, "you miserable lush, you think you're a saint, do you? You'd gladly screw that Aisling babe too, wouldn't you, you hypocritical piece of pigshit. Ha, you two-faced fart, don't deny it!"

Knox winced, shaken.

The voice went on, finding fault with Murphy, accusing the assistant exorcist of an attraction to a fellow young priest. At last the spirit turned its attention to the exorcist. It had more trouble finding fault with Mollo. It accused him of hitting the bottle and of getting a thrill out of his bowel movements. Through all of this, Fry's face remained fixed, like the face of some ventriloquist's dummy, only his jaw working, spilling a torrent of words.

At noon the kitchen sent up sandwiches and a pot of coffee. The team munched and sipped gratefully. Fry was given a sandwich, but he flung it against the wall.

"This is rough," the Sarge said. "I liked it better on Anzio."

Knox understood. He had had an easier day the day he and the Navy went in to Kwajalein and had begun the task of clearing away bodies. He looked at the inert form of Jasper Fry on the bed. He and Fry had lived through hell that day, facing the spectacle of mass slaughter, trying not to throw up. Now, he couldn't connect Fry's smooth mask with the familiar face of his old friend.

They set to work again, Mollo reciting prayers while Fry squirmed, trying not to hear. Murphy would take over the recitation for a time, then Mollo would go on again. They continued all day. The demon had fallen silent, except for an occasional oath. A few times it had seemed that Fry was talking aloud to himself, in languages Knox couldn't understand. A clock ticked. The hard steel chairs were starting to feel like graters.

Every once in a while one of the exorcism team had to go take a leak.

Fry, it seemed, never needed to.

At seven o'clock in the evening, Mollo said, "I think we'd better call it a day. Gentlemen, thank you. Go get some dinner and have a good sleep. But we still have to persuade this evil spirit to speak its name. We'll resume at the same time tomorrow morning."

Fry grinned at them with his smooth ventriloquist dummy's face.

Forty

Nobody saw Waxy and the Owl enter Priests' House at two in the morning and go up the back stairs to the room where Tim Walsh kept Fry under guard. Walsh had been spelled for a while, but now he was back, his chair propped against the door in case Fry tried to get out. He looked sleepy. When he turned his head for a moment the Owl sapped him, and caught him before he fell.

"Don't need to hurt him," the Owl said, easing Walsh's body down onto the floor. "Maybe he'll think the guy inside the room came out and slugged him, not even know we were here."

They lugged Walsh into an empty room across the hall, stretched him out on the bed, and shut the door. Then the Owl took out a penknife and unsnapped the simple lock on Fry's door.

Fry lay stark naked on the bed. He looked like a plucked white turkey. A dinner tray sat on his bedside table, salad uneaten, roll and butter untouched, coffee cup still clean.

Fry stared at them through cavernous eyes. "Who are you?" he said hollowly. "What do you mean coming in here?"

The Owl chuckled. "Where's your pants, Father? You having you a little jerk-off session?"

They weren't prepared for what happened. Fry leaped out of bed like a sprung jack-in-the-box and fixed both hands around the Owl's throat. The Owl gave a croak and staggered and fell on his back on the floor with Fry on top, strangling him. Waxy hurled himself on Fry from behind, wrapped an arm around his neck, and struggled to free the Owl. The Owl was kneeing Fry in the belly. The two of them pried Fry's hands loose and the Owl got up and stood on top of Fry, rubbing his neck and said hoarsely, "Jesus. The bastard is strong."

"You want I should plug him one?" Waxy said.

"No," the Owl said, "no gunshots. You want every priest in the place to come running?"

Waxy saw with shock that Fry's eyes glowed in their sockets like coals. The priest's lips worked. He spoke in the voice of a woman, in a language Waxy knew.

Waxy's jaw dropped. "Holy Mike," he said, "she—he's talking Sicilian."

The Owl was fighting to keep his foothold on top of Fry. "What's he saying?"

"She says we should be afraid of Satan's power. We'll go to Hell. We're going to be his slaves."

"Shit," the Owl said, "this bird is just doing fake voices."

"Nobody fakes Sicilian," Waxy said. "You gotta be born with it."

Fry's face seemed to writhe, jaw working, eyeballs rolling in their sockets. Now he spoke in a man's voice, in Italian, which they both could understand. He was the incarnation of Sathanas. Bow down and worship him.

Waxy looked worried. "Owl, I don't like this. I didn't sign on to deal with no evil spirits. I thought this was a ordinary hit."

"That's all it is, you dipstick," the Owl said. "Don't listen to him. You believe him? He's nuts."

"He looks like the goddam Devil to me. Looka that face. Them eyes. I never seen nothing like this. Owl, what if we killed the Devil? We don't want to do that, do we? Wouldn't that fuck up the world?"

The Owl gave a short, hard laugh. "We did that, for Chrissake, we'd be doing the world a favor. The Pope would make us saints, you and me."

He stared in fascination at Fry's contorted face. It seemed transformed, mouth twisted, teeth bared. A face more brutal than that of the man who had been lying on the bed. Staring, Waxy didn't realize that Fry's hands were stealing toward his throat. They shot out and wrapped him in a strangling grip. He started choking, tried to break Fry's grasp, but it was too strong. Then the Owl's sapper smashed down and Fry gave a grunt and pitched forward, his hands flailing the air.

"Hey, thanks," Waxy said. He cleared his throat and spat.

The Owl said, "Take him to the elevator. While he's still out cold."

Silently, they picked up the unconscious priest by his feet and shoulders and carried him down the hall. Nobody in sight. They shoved Fry into the freight elevator and got in and rode up to the fourth floor. Then, dragging the inert body, they stepped out onto the fire escape. A sharp wind was making swirls of snow.

The Owl kicked Fry in the scrotum. No response. "Throw him off," the Owl said.

They swung the naked body back and forth, then slung it into space. It plummeted like a limp doll onto a pile of bricks and landed with a thump and the sound of snapping bones.

"We better go down and see did that do it," the Owl said.

They rode the elevator down to the ground and stepped out the back door. Fry was sprawled on the brick pile, face up, blood seeping from one corner of his mouth.

"He's still breathing," Waxy said. "Want I should throttle him?"

"Won't do," the Owl said. "Peru wants it to look like suicide."

"Come on, Owl. It's cold out here. We don't need to stand around all night till he dies."

"We got to make sure," the Owl said. "We take him back up and throw him off again. Look out the blood don't get on your shoes."

Forty-One

Striding the brick walk to the college chapel, his flamboyant red cape and robes changed in favor of a plain black suit, Monsignor O'Malley scanned with displeasure the overflow crowd pressing to get inside. The funeral service for the Right Reverend Jasper Fry would be held this morning. The president had hoped to avoid attention to it, but word had got out and people had thronged to campus. The founder of the Children's Crusade had had a huge radio audience, and hundreds of the curious had come. The papers had reported that Fry had fled with millions in punchboard profits, and had been arrested in a brothel.

Although the official college press release had stated that Fry had died in an accidental fall, rumors had circulated that he had been murdered. The news reporters had favored the rumors. There had been signs of a scuffle in Fry's room, and two sets of footprints—one made by boots, one by patent-leather shoes—had surrounded the body where it was discovered in the soft mud of the courtyard. The president was annoyed to see two news photographers hoisting their Speed Graphics, shooting pictures of him as he approached, the flashes blinding his eyes.

Callahan, the red-faced old campus cop, cleared the way, and Monsignor O'Malley strode into the chapel, looking grim. To make matters worse, Douglas Knox had insisted on saying the Mass and preaching this morning, and his public appearances always drew a crowd. As Monsignor O'Malley advanced to his accustomed seat in the front pew, it seemed to him that the entire college was present, and half of Newark besides. Ricco Peruccese nodded to him gravely from the second row. Little boys, members of Fry's disbanded swim club, stood lining the chapel aisles.

Knox had mustered a choir of priests and nuns to sing the funeral hymns. The statue of Saint Cassian of Imola with his quill pens had been moved to the far side of the altar to make room for them. When it came time for the sermon, Knox ignored the pulpit, but stepped to the altar rail and faced the crowd.

"I suppose you've all heard about the troubles the late Father Jasper Fry has been having, troubles that ended in his death. I want to say that nobody knows the truth about what happened to him, but I want to make you a guess.

"Father Fry and I were close friends ever since the seminary, and we served together in the Navy chaplains' corps. When Jasper was in his right mind, I never knew a man who better exemplified the spirit of Jesus. He believed in the goodness of everybody, even when that goodness wasn't easy to find. He never knowingly did a thing in his life to harm another human soul. He loved everything the Lord has made. I remember in the seminary when he took in a broken-down old dog that he found sniffing around the garbage pails, a mutt all scabs and sores, and fed it and nursed it back to health. In the Navy he did the same for a lot of miserable guys who passed through his care. At one time I was becoming a lousy drunk, and he turned me around and pointed me the right way.

"You ought to know that Jasper Fry was the most sensitive guy in the world. He grew up on a farm in Iowa, converted when he was young, and started studying for the priesthood as soon as he could. So in his early years he never really had much contact with the rotten side of life. That's why when he was a chaplain attached to the cleanup of Kwajalein atoll in the South Pacific, it hit him hard.

"When the troops got done with Kwaj, it was nothing but dead bodies from end to end. Our bombardment had left hardly a tree still standing. Then the infantry had gone in and mopped up what was left of the enemy. The cleanup mission had to walk through, following bulldozers that turned up the earth and put the bodies under. But first, Jasper saw men––officers and enlisted men alike––going through the corpses, yanking out gold teeth with pliers, sometimes yanking off whole jaws, taking rings and watches and lockets, cramming the loot into bags. He couldn't believe that so many men could suddenly die, or that our guys could stoop to such swinishness. That scene struck him so hard that, if you ask me, he went into a kind of shock for the rest of his life.

"We'll never know for sure, of course, but I figure that the sight of the dead and those looters on Kwaj planted an obsession in Jasper. I think that explains why he wanted to look at naked little boys and naked women. He wanted to see some beautiful bodies to cancel the memory of all those mutilated corpses. Oh, he was out of his mind, sure, but his craziness had a reason behind it. I'm guessing, but maybe that's how it was for him.

"And why did he die? I believe he knew too much about certain undercover operations. Somebody wanted to shut him up. I'm not ready to make any accusations, but I'll bet you there's somebody sitting right here in this chapel this morning who could tell us exactly how that death came about. Anyway, I know Jasper Fry would have forgiven his killers. He'd say, 'Father, forgive them, for they know not what they do.' You know, 'The house of forgiveness is a holy place'—that's according to Saint Theresa of Avilar. And I bet you anything that just before he died Jasper was sane again, and in his last moments he made a perfect act of love, and died a saint."

The body of Fry lay in closed pine box on a wheeled dolly in front of the altar. Now Knox walked over to it, rested his right hand on the lid. "Jasper, you have made this chapel a holy place. Every morning of my life, I'm going to pray for you. And I'll keep trying to find your killers until they're in custody. I swear this to you." He turned to the pall-bearers. "Take him away."

Six black-suited priests slowly bore the coffin out of the chapel to the waiting hearse outside.

After the services, Knox stood Walsh, Moon, Konny, and the Sarge to drinks at Wrecker Rafferty's. They made the expedition to Newark in Knox's new second-hand Ford and Walsh's Jeep.

Moon was getting used to beer. He sipped with fresh confidence. "I'm still wondering, Father. When the exorcism was going on, was that the Devil talking? Through Father Fry?"

Knox took a drag on his Gauloise. "Maybe," he said. "Maybe not."

"B-b-but," Konny stammered, "wasn't F-F-Father Fry p-p-p-possessed?"

"Yeah," said the Sarge. "Otherwise how could he know that much about us?"

Knox said, "That wasn't the Devil telling him. Jasper had a pipeline to that information. Right, Tim?"

Walsh nodded. "When Father Knox and I went over his room looking for clues as to who killed him, we found something interesting. Next to his bed was an air shaft that picked up sounds from downstairs."

"It was like a radio," Knox said. "Father Walsh traced it and found where it came out. Over in one corner of the lounge. So he talked up through the vent, and sitting on Jasper's bed, I could hear every word."

Moon sucked in his breath. "That corner of the lounge—was that where you and Father Mollo heard confessions?"

"Yeah," Knox said. "So maybe it was Jasper Fry and not the devil listening in to our dirty little secrets."

Moon looked perplexed. "But how could he talk in all those different languages?"

"Oh, Jasper was a master linguist. Knew Chinese, French, German, Italian, and of course English and Latin. I think he even spoke Sicilian. Spent his vacations there when he was studying at the Louvain."

"So he wasn't possessed," the Sarge said. "He was just a normal crazy."

Knox shrugged. "You can think what you want. But you know what Martin D'Arcy said? In our time, the Devil has had one big success. He's persuaded most people that he doesn't exist."

Jimmy the bartender came over and said, "You gents look like you could use another round. Put your money away, Father. It's on the house."

Forty-Two

Streetlights were coming on when Knox tooled his third-hand black Chevy out of Dedwood and headed north for Secaucus. The town would be easy to find. You followed your nose while the smell of garbage dumps and pig farms grew stronger and stronger until you had to roll the windows all the way up and you were there.

In downtown Kearny, Knox glanced in his rear view mirror. A dark blue Cadillac was staying behind him. He speeded up, it speeded up. To be on the safe side, he made four right turns and rounded a block. But the Caddy clung to his tail.

Mother of God. He slowed down and made the Caddy pass him. Driver and passenger wore black felt hats. As they went by, the passenger, guy with a jutting lower lip, threw him a glance. Knox let the Caddy get a block ahead of him, then he swerved down an alley, roared in and out of a bus station, and parked in back of a hardware store. He waited five minutes. Nobody came after him.

Soon he entered Hudson County, crossing the bridge over the Hackensack River. By the time he got to Secaucus Plaza, center of town, the air was making him gag. Yet somebody lived here. Somebody had to patronize Marra's drugstore, Mueller's bakery, the Plaza movie house. Lord deliver them.

No sign of the car that had been trailing him. On First Street, a little way off the main drag, he located the meeting place. A joint with a neon sign that bent in the middle and wrapped around the corner. On it the silhouette of a nude and the outline of a champagne glass traced and retraced their shapes in winking lights. Out in front stood a tall young black man in a jacket stitched PROMINENT BAR & GRILL.

Knox rolled down the window. "Where do I park?"

"Step out, mister," the young man said. "I'll put it away for you. You want it again, you just tell the bartender have Dipso fetch it."

As Knox got out, the young man gave a whistle. "Hey, ain't you boss man of Saint Cash basketball? Saw your picture in that Harlem paper, the *Amsterdam News*."

"No fooling," Knox said. "I didn't know they printed pictures of honkies."

"Maybe it was 'cause you had your picture took with S. T. Pohl."

A blue Plymouth coupe, motor idling, was waiting for the valet to park it too. Kevin Burke's. The FBI man stood there, a manila folder under his arm. Tall Irishman, couple of chins, corduroy jacket, white shirt, no tie, build of a football player.

"Doug," he said, sticking out a hand. "It's been a while. You look like the sports racket agrees with you."

They pushed through glass doors and stepped into a thick tobacco haze. Right away it seemed to Knox an improvement in air quality. Behind the bar were statues of the Budweiser horses, a waterfall of amber light supposed to be Schlitz being poured, and a cardboard portrait of last month's Miss Rheingold. On a platform to the left of the bar, a bronze-skinned woman wearing only a sequined G-string was shaking blue-nippled tits, doing a solemn bump and grind. Nobody was watching. The patrons had their eyes riveted to a flickering black-and-white TV screen above the bar.

Burke grinned up at the dancer. "Hi, Rhondajune. What's the score?"

The dancer sounded bored. "Yanks, eight to one."

"You're throwing away your talent, honey. You're just a flower born to blush unseen and waste your sweetness on the desert air."

"Fuck, don't I know it. But I'm gettin' paid."

Knox and the FBI man took seats on the far side of the room at a wooden table grooved with carved initials. Their fellow patrons were heavyset guys in tee shirts, maybe truck drivers, all except for one guy's wife. She had made her husband sit with his back to the stripper while they tackled catcher's-mitt-sized hamburgers.

A grandmotherly waitress came over. "Evening, gents. Interest you in some pizza tonight?"

"Pizza?" Burke said. "What kind of guinea pastafazoo is that?"

"Something new. Cheese pie with tomato sauce. Lot of people like it. You know what you want?"

"Yeah, I want you to lie down on this table and take your panties off."

"You think you're man enough?"

"More than enough for you, toots. How about a crab-cake sandwich, lot of mayo, black coffee."

She turned to Knox. "And yours?"

"Whattaya got on draft?"

"Bud, Rheingold, Guinness, Marie Antoinette."

"Marie—huh?"

"The beer you got to cut the head off."

"Any Ballantine's Ale?"

"Bottle stuff. A quarter extra."

"All right. And a burger."

When the waitress had left, Burke settled back in his wooden armchair and fixed Knox in a wry smile. "Thanks for coming, Doug. Wonder why I picked this place?"

"Yeah, Kevin, why in hell did you?"

"I happen to love it. A dive with valet parking. And there's a German bakery in the neighborhood does crumb buns you wouldn't believe. Look, there at the bar, guy in the blue serge suit? That's Henry Krajewski, the rich pig farmer running for president. Calls himself the Poor Man's Party."

"For crumb buns and Henry, you ask me to come smell pigs?"

"I want to talk with you. About the mob. I think we might help each other. Here, nobody will recognize you. Who'd expect a priest to do his drinking in a dump like this?"

"Yeah," Knox said. Remembering how the parking attendant had seen though his layman's disguise—white turtleneck shirt, loafers, plaid jacket.

Burke looked serious. "Thing is, Doug, the mob has it in for you."

Knox shrugged. "The mob? Hell, they're the least of my worries. An outfit that call themselves the Church of the One Right Path have set their sights on me. Ever hear of them?"

"All I know is they're a bunch of religious fanatics. They're new on the scene. They been bothering you?"

"Three times now they've tried to get me, and once they pretty near did. Their leader stuck me with a knife and landed me in the hospital. Then he came by my sick bed dressed like a doctor and tried to stick me with a needle. I'm sick and tired of being stuck. Any suggestions?"

"Why don't you take a vacation, Doug? Get away from here. I know some hideouts where we send witnesses who need protection. They wouldn't find you in a million years."

"No dice, Kevin, I don't have time for a vacation. I've got a basketball season to finish. How about the FBI catching these bozos, taking them out of circulation?"

"Be glad to try. Tell me everything you know."

They talked, Burke scribbled notes. "OK, Doug, I'm glad you put me onto this. I'll look into this One Right Path. But meantime, I think the mob is a real threat to you. We have a source says they plan to knock you off. Right after your game in the Garden."

"That's all I need. How do you know this source of yours is reliable?"

"One of the best undercover men we have. He's worked his way up close to Ricco Peruccese."

"Also known as Ricky Peru. I've met the crud. He and I don't get along. Tell me more."

"Well, Peru has it in for you. He's been underboss for Longy Zwillman, the New Jersey Al Capone, but he's practically the big boss now. He's been getting more powerful since Zwillman's partner Willie Morretti started losing his marbles. Right now Peru runs a big protection racket. Collects dues from just about every business in Paterson, Newark, and the Oranges."

"So why don't you nail him?"

Burke shrugged. "In the past, he's stayed strictly local. You see, an operation has to cross state lines for the FBI to get involved. Sure, we've turned it over to the Jersey cops, but you know, a lot of them are on the take. Peru is well insulated. Surrounded with walls of money. He made tons of it during the war when the Zwillman family ran black markets in gas, meat, liquor, silk stockings, ration points. They even sold draft deferments. Oh, we've tried to nail them, but we never could get anybody to testify."

Burke's coffee and Knox's ale came. Burke sipped, made a face, and went on, "So Peru has had this nice North Jersey racket. But lately he's been getting greedy, trying to go national. Where the money is big and easy."

"Not the war surplus business?"

"How did you guess? What Peru does, he finds a front— some school or charity. Then the government gives the front leftover war materials for nothing, and he turns around and sells 'em for a good price."

"I'm starting to connect the dots," Knox said. "I think our college business manager sold some surplus Underwoods to a typewriter company lately. And we found out he had Garand rifles and Browning automatics stashed in the chapel basement."

"Typewriters, that's penny candy. But guns—they could be worth big bucks to South American dictators. Doug, you're in a position to keep an eye on Vastasi. Maybe you can help us get the goods on him."

"Don't you have agents to work on that?"

Burke sighed. "We're short-handed. Our boss, old man Hoover, doesn't take much interest in organized crime. We've got only three men in the New York office working on the mob, but a couple of hundred looking for communists. Anyhow, I'd like to zero in on Peru before he zeros in on you."

Forty-Three

A woman in a low-cut dress came staggering up to their table. Beautiful once, long ago. She stood there swaying on her feet, blowing down a hundred-proof breath. Her eyes shone bright as snowcrust under a full moon. "Evening gents," she greeted them. "Need an experienced piece of tail?"

"No thanks," Burke said.

Her face fell. "Big shots used to take me to the Astor," she muttered. "Used to buy me Salisbury steak. I'd light my little cheroot with a thousand dollar bill. Ah, would you believe it, every time I flicked an ash the bums used to fight over it."

Burke said, "OK, OK, don't give us the story of your life."

Peering at Knox now, she struggled to focus her eyes, her mind trying to break through its cloud cover. "You're that priest. You do something about basketball. I seen you on television."

Burke was losing his patience. "Come back another time, darling, all right?"

She drew herself erect, wrapped in her former glory. "Maybe next time you'll have to beg me for it." She turned and zigzagged off.

The FBI man opened his folder and tossed Knox a rogue's gallery photo. Shots from the front, back, and sides.

"This your pal the business manager?"

"Uh huh. Glauco Vastasi. What about him?"

"Picture was taken in Philadelphia. They picked him up in '43 on suspicion of murder."

Knox looked interested. Burke went on, "Truckload of furs got hijacked out in Montana and the goods started turning up in Philly. Then a shopkeeper got caught selling a stolen coat, so he decided to weasel on Vastasi, save himself some jail. Next day the cops came across an abandoned car. Found the guy with no back to his head and his mouth stuffed with a dead canary bird.

"So they grilled Vastasi, but they didn't get anyplace. It was a professional job. No witnesses and the car had no prints on it. But Vastasi must have figured Philly was getting too hot for him, so he came to Jersey as a lieutenant for his uncle, Ricky Peru."

A balding, sallow-faced cigar-smoker had come up to their table. Checkered pants and a yellow vest. "Hey, Kevin, man, where you been hiding? You don't come in here all the time like you used to."

"Things wrap up, I move on. Doc, this is Doug Knox. Doug, this is Doc McNulty, owns this place."

"Father Knox!" the proprietor said. "We're honored to have you here. See your picture all the time in the *Newark Evening News.*"

Knox sighed. "Guess I'm notorious."

"That tall boy of yours, Pohl," McNulty said. "I'm coming to see him play. Got tickets for your game in the Garden with Holy Sepulcher."

"Look me up when you come," Knox said. "I'll be on the bench. If you like, I'll introduce you to Pohl."

McNulty beamed. "Would I like? You bet I would. That kid's gonna be bigger than Joe DiMaggio. Say, what you think of my place?"

"It's all right," Knox said.

"It's a latrine. I'm selling out soon's I get the right offer."

"Listen, Doc," Burke said, "we could use a little information. You know a guy named Ricky Peru? Ricco Petruccese?"

The grin dropped from the proprietor's face. "I heard of him."

"How about Cosimo di Montecassino?"

"Him I know. Comes in here every month, I give him payments."

"For what?"

"For nobody tossing a brick through my plate glass window."

"You never complain? To the cops?"

"Who wants two busted kneecaps? I think the cops are part of the organization. So what can I do? It's the way things work. I pay my dues, they leave me run my business. You gentlemen got everything you need?"

"Still need a burger and a crabcake sandwich," Burke said. "Ordered 'em an hour ago."

McNulty frowned. "I'll go check on it. Kitchen's running slow tonight. Regular cook got the DT's. Started seeing hoptoads up and down the walls."

Burke said, "I would catch those little sons of bitches if I were you, Doc. Step on every last one of 'em."

Five minutes later their food arrived. Burke ate like a man starving. Knox still had four inches of ale when a uniformed cop came through the back door and blew a whistle blast. Two pickpockets working the bar whirled and sprinted out the front door.

The cop's voice filled the room. "Folks, can I have your attention. Anybody here used to own a black Chevy coupe, license plate W866?"

Knox stood up. "That's mine."

"Sorry to tell you, mister, but your car has got destroyed."

Knox felt as if kicked in the midsection. "What happened to it?"

"Somebody bombed it. Out in the parking lot."

"When?"

"Few minutes ago. The nigra parking cars must have stepped on the starter to move it—you know, pack the cars in tight—and when he did it blew up on him."

"He get hurt?"

"Hurt bad as you can get."

Knox got to his feet. "I'm a priest. Take me to him."

He and Burke started for the back door.

"Say," the cop said, peering at Knox, "I seen your picture someplace. Aren't you—?"

"Sure," Knox said. "I'm Cary Grant."

The cop's face broke into a grin as wide as from Dublin to Dingle. "Jesus, Mr. Grant, I didn't know you was a priest. Maybe this is a lousy time to ask, but my little girl sure would love to have your autograph."

Out in the parking lot Knox surveyed the remains of his Chevy. Its front doors dangled by their hinges and the paint had fallen away, leaving a twisted frame and a back seat full of smoldering upholstery. The police hearse had hauled away what was left of the parking attendant. Knox said silent prayers for him.

Flashbulbs went off. A police photographer took shots of the scene. Burke gave orders to the cop. The area around the car was to be roped off until a lab man could make plaster casts of any footprints. Burke found a few strips of paint from the door panels. "Going to send these to the lab. See if any prints survived. Come on, Doug, I'll drive you home."

Burke's small coupe had been parked next to Knox's car. Now a crack like a lightning bolt ran down its windshield. They got in and Burke headed out of town, past a garbage pile that almost reached the sky.

"The bastards," Burke said. "They must have expected you to step on the starter yourself."

"Guess they didn't know there was valet parking," Knox said. "That poor son of a bitch."

"They didn't do their homework. This job has amateur written all over it. It wasn't the mob. They would have done it right."

"You know their work, huh."

"We see it once in a while. They'd have used a charge powerful enough to blow a car to pieces and start a fire that wipes out all evidence. Joe Dominos, you heard of him? Used to be capo, head of the North Jersey mob. All they found was his upper plate and a couple of fingernails."

"And after that, Peru took over?"

"Right. That was a few years ago. Now they've got a new demolition man called Willie the Wire. No doubt he knows his stuff. So I would say he didn't do your Chevy."

"So everything points to the Church of the One Right Path. Bunch of fuck-ups. They keep trying, but they haven't nailed me yet."

Burke looked grim. "Don't get cocky, Doug. I wish I had more manpower, dammit. You know anybody who can ride shotgun for you?"

"Tim Walsh. Good man. He's already going around with me, backing me up. But you know, Kevin, I mean to keep looking out for myself. Anybody comes after me, I'll see him coming."

"Yeah? And did you see the guy that wired your car? You can't keep a three-hundred-sixty-degree lookout twenty-four hours a day all by yourself. Somebody could break into your office some night, fix your desk so that you open a drawer and you're gone."

"I won't look inside my desk anymore. Keep my whiskey out, next to the phone."

Burke sighed. "You have a permit to carry a gun? No? Get one. At least I can send a man to take a look around your office, your room, your classroom. Check for booby traps."

"OK, Kevin, I'd appreciate that. But you know, there's no preventing everything. You have to trust in the Big Guy. Stay in good with Him."

For a while they drove in silence. Then Burke said, "Well I hope He keeps an eye on you. But you ever hear that Russian proverb? When your boat starts sinking, pray to God, but row like hell for shore."

Cezar, the Filipino houseboy at Priests' House, met Knox when he stepped inside. "Father, some guy leave this for you." Handing him an envelope.

"What kind of guy?"

"Funny looking guy. All in black like priest. Hair on his head."

"Most guys have some of that."

"Not hair like him. Cut like a cross."

Knox went into the deserted lounge, poured himself a shot, dropped into an armchair, tore open the note. As usual, the message had been made of words and letters clipped from a newspaper.

A near miss. But your death is nearer.

Why didn't Cross give up?

Forty-Four

Aisling's look was quizzical as she faced Tim Walsh. "So what will I have to do?"

The two of them sat at close quarters in the office of the Biology Department, a closet that held two folding chairs and a card table piled with papers.

"Not much," Walsh said, trying not to rub knees with her. "Just open up the place once in a while. Anybody asks, you're Acting Chair. Any students come in to complain, you listen to 'em and don't do anything. Any textbook salesmen offering free samples, take 'em and say we'll consider 'em. I have an empty bookshelf to fill."

"I can do that," Aisling said.

"There might be a guy coming in for a job interview. If he does, see if he's worth hiring. I don't know anything about him, but we need warm bodies."

"That why you hired me? Because I'm a warm body?" She crossed black-stocking legs, letting her skirt ride high.

"Yeah," Walsh said, looking the other way. "Anyhow you'd been to grad school, so I figured you must know something."

"You want me to answer the mail?"

"Naw. Anything hot, save it for me. I'm hoping to get back pretty soon. But you understand, I have to hang out with Father Knox for a while. Ever since those crazies bombed his car, the FBI wants him to have steady back-up. OK, Professor, it's all yours."

Aisling looked around the cramped space. Where to begin? She picked up the crumpled papers that had missed the waste basket. Then she sat down at the card table to consider her new situation. In a way, it was a promotion, at least temporary. Good thing her landlady's teenage daughter could babysit. Walsh attracted her. He had a nice smile, a dimple, looked as though he worked out. She'd love to take off his shirt and run a hand over him. Too bad he was keeping himself so remote. But maybe a priest wouldn't be much good in bed. Except Knox. He'd been married before, ought to know something. Ever since she'd saved his life in the hospital, ever since the trip to the brothel to extricate Fry, his cold demeanor toward her seemed to have thawed. Maybe it wasn't too late to kindle a fire in him.

A visitor stood at the door. A thin, stoop-shouldered pre-medical student taking her advanced bio. Eyeing her up and down. He said hesitantly, "Professor Vastasi? What you doing here? I was looking for Father Walsh."

"Hello, Apicelli. I'm taking his place for a while. What's on your mind?"

Apicelli had a lean and hungry look. She knew what was on his mind. One of the things, anyway.

"Well, you know," he said, "I'm taking anatomy from Father Scully? And we're dissecting cats?"

"So I've heard. Your cat behaving?"

"It's gone. I need another one."

"What do you mean, gone? How can you lose a dead cat?"

"An old lady took it away from me. On the bus. I was sitting next to her with my cat in a paper bag, taking it home to do an assignment, when she saw the damn thing and let out a scream like the noon whistle. Not that I blame her. I had taken the front half of the skin off it and scraped the bones, but it still had its rear end on. She whipped it right out of my hands and threw it out the window. I was hoping you had a spare cat lying around, so I wouldn't have to tell Father Scully. He'd ream my ass."

"I think Father Scully keeps the keys to the cat locker. You'd better go see him and make a clean breast of this."

Basketball. Knox thanked God for it. Plunging into his coach's job, trying to shape up the frosh, he could forget about Jasper Fry and Ricky Peru, forget about the Cross gang blowing up his car. Watching Pohl dribble a ball around the court, he didn't think about Aisling anymore, didn't keep blaming himself for the weakness of his flesh. On the basketball court, life was plain. Focused on beating the pants off Holy Sepulcher.

From his coach's bench in the gym this afternoon, Knox was bawling instructions. Thad Kulowsky was practicing passes. His footwork was all wrong and he kept giving his moves advance advertising.

"For Pete's sake, Kulowsky," Knox told him, "don't look at Kelly before you pass to him. Anybody would know what you're going to do. Take a step toward where you're *not* going to go. That'll surprise 'em."

Kulowsky nodded, tried again.

Tim Walsh came in and sat down next to Knox. "Things going all right?"

Knox gave a nod. "Passable. So how's your acting chairwoman?"

"Aisling? She'll be great. She can charm the complaints right out of anybody. I think she kind of enjoys pinch-hitting for me. Likes having some authority, even if it's only holding court at a card table."

Moon Gogarty approached, holding a pad and pencil. Knox gave a mock groan and waved him to a seat on the bench.

Moon grinned. "Team looking good, Father?"

"Good enough."

"Can you give me a statement for the paper? On how the team is shaping up? How it's going to stack up against the Shrouds?"

"Listen, not now. You want to talk, wait till I get done here. Forty minutes, maybe. Then we can talk all you want."

"Okay." Moon got up and took a seat that had a back to it. He didn't mind watching the players, especially Pohl. The tall boy moved like lightning, slashing through the key, sinking shots every time. Moon couldn't help feeling a twinge of jealousy. It wasn't just that Pohl starred on the basketball court. Moon didn't doubt that Pohl had outperformed him in Aisling's bed.

Now Knox was waving to Larry Brunn, the janitor, motioning him over. "Brunn, how come the floor of this court wasn't swept this morning? There's flakes of plaster on it. You been goofing off?"

"Hell no, excuse me, Father, I swept it like I always do. Stuff has been dropping off the ceiling lately. Must have started again since the team came in."

"All right," Knox said, "I'm going to give 'em a little rest. See if you can get your broom working." His whistle shrilled. "Time out! Take ten!"

Basketballs slowed to a halt and the sweating players bounded to the sides and grabbed water bottles.

Moon wondered if he dared ask Knox to talk now, but just as he was plucking up his courage, a deafening BOOM shook the gym. The floor shuddered, walls buckled outward, and boards screamed as they broke.

Moon blinked through a cloud of powdery dust. A chunk of plaster the size of a grand piano had dropped out of the ceiling and landed in the middle of the court, missing the janitor by inches.

Knox was standing up, swearing. Lucky thing he had called a time-out. If there had been players out on the floor—

His whistle blew its heart out. "Outside!" he yelled. "Everybody out of the building! On the double!"

Players, janitor, and Moon streaked for the exits, tumbling over one another. Tim Walsh was in the middle of them, shouting, trying to calm them down. No sound but the thud of feet running, and a growing low rumble. Then a loud thunderclap followed by a crash as the platform holding the box seats broke loose and toppled to the floor.

Choking, half blinded by dust, Knox stumbled down a corridor and made it outside. The whole team stood clustered together, looking. Pohl was pointing up.

A dent perhaps ten feet deep had appeared in the center of the gym's peaked roof. Where the piano-sized piece had come from, Knox guessed. He noticed a wrinkle in the building's right side wall, as if some giant had given it a kick.

Walsh gave a low whistle. "Will you look at that. Damned wall must have been made out of paper."

Blub O'Malley, the center, had a gash on his forehead, blood trickling down into his eyes. Walsh sat him down on the ground, mopped him with a handkerchief.

Then he had another player walk O'Malley to the nuns' infirmary.

Knox's Maureen had sprinted outdoors and stood coughing and gasping. Knox went over to her. "You OK?"

"I think so. Lord, Father, what a noise that was. I thought the whole building was falling."

"See anybody else inside?"

"No."

"Thank God," Knox said. He swatted dust off his jacket. Thad Kolowsky came limping up. He had lost one shoe. "Father, is it all right if we go in and collect our clothes?"

"No," Knox said, "it wouldn't be. Nobody goes back in there. Never mind your clothes. You can go to class dressed like you are."

"It's kind of cold out."

"OK," Knox said, giving a sigh. "Go back to your room in the Mansion." He bawled to the collected group, "You day students, why don't you go over to the Prep cafeteria. We'll send out for some clothes for all of you."

"Thanks, Father," Kolowski said. "I take the biggest size."

"That's what you're all going to get. Now move!"

The two campus cops, hearing the uproar, had pulled up in their cruiser. They got out and stood like scarecrows, ogling the wrecked gym.

"You two," Knox shot at them, "better rope off this whole building. Put up some danger signs. Nobody is to go inside."

Callahan the cop said, "We don't have no signs, Father. I don't know as we have all that much rope, either."

"That's your problem. Call the town cops for help, why don't you."

Moon's heart leaped. The building's near-collapse was pretty terrible, but he couldn't help feeling a burst of joy. Another inside story for the *Immolator.*

Forty-Five

When he heard Knox trying to open the stuck door into the Athletics Department's cramped new quarters in Feeley Mansion, Vastasi popped out of his spacious office.

"Well, whattaya know, Father," he said with a grin. "So you and me are neighbors."

Knox scowled, giving the stubborn door a kick. "Sorry to say," he said.

"Too bad, Father, about your gym. They going to fix it up pretty soon for you?"

"Hell no," Knox said. "They'll have to tear it down and build another one."

"You don't mean it, Father! I thought the place was beautiful."

"It was put together with spit and glue. Now if you'll excuse me I have work to do."

"Sure, sure, Father. Anything you want from the business office, just let me know."

Laughing silently to himself, Vastasi slipped back inside.

Knox said a few things under his breath and managed to yank open the protesting door. There weren't any windows in the narrow room. A single light bulb in the ceiling cast a weak glow. Lord, they'd have to put some new lights in here. There was a fireplace, the only visible source of heat. The place had been given a quick dusting and two desks had been wedged in, but there hadn't been room for Knox's file cabinets. They stood out in the hall, looking like a row of lockers.

Maureen was already at her desk, facing Knox's desk two feet away. She was sorting the mail, squinting in the feeble light.

"Morning, Father," she said glumly. "I'm glad this is only temporary."

"It had better be," Knox said. "And I don't like being next door to Vastasi. Any threats in the mail today?"

"Not today."

"Get Bluestone Demolition on the phone, will you? I want to know how soon they're going to blow up the gym and clear away the rubble."

"Mr. Bluestone already called. He said to tell you they'll start next Friday."

By a swivel of his torso Knox managed to squeeze around his desk and sink into his chair. He fought down the urge to take out his bottle of Jamison and take the hard edge off the day.

He said, "You know, you poor Rosary Society debutante, I didn't want us to move into this strait jacket. Asked the Monsignor for bigger office space, but he said this was all there is. Maybe we ought to pitch a tent out on the lawn, soon as it gets warm enough."

"Ah, we'll manage, Father. Just suck in your gut a little."

"And you, you'd better suck in that roll of fat around your middle. You look like you're wearing an inner tube. Better lay off those chocolate cherries from Woolworth's."

Their usual morning repartee broke off when Tim Walsh tapped on the half-open door. "Anybody home?"

"Come in, Tim," Knox called, "if you can fit."

Walsh gave a low whistle as he took in the cramped quarters. "This the best they could do for you?"

"Yeah. You'd have thought sports would rate a better deal. At least we're open for business again."

Walsh said, "Hi, Maureen, you make the move all right?"

"I made it here, Father," she said, "although I couldn't bring my potted plant."

"She's potted enough," Knox observed. Maureen began pelting him with a rain of paper clips.

Walsh eased himself down onto a corner of Knox's desk. "What did the building inspector say about the gym? Any chance of fixing it up again?"

"I didn't call the building inspector. That bastard's more crooked than an Italian cigar. To ever have OKed that construction job. Bet you anything the contractor was slipping him payola. So we got some engineers from Pittsburgh. Honest guys, not locals. They've looked over the damage and say the building has to be condemned. Sub-standard concrete, not enough steel beams."

"How'd the Monsignor take that? Couldn't have liked the idea of building a whole new gym."

"Said there can't be any new construction until he has more money in hand. Lord knows when that will be."

"So how will you get by?"

"We're holding practice at the Prep. The gym there isn't big enough to hold a crowd. So all the rest of our games this season will be away. Which is all right. The Holy Sepulcher game will take place as planned. In Madison Square Garden."

"Great," Walsh said. "I can't wait to see that slaughter."

Sir Terwilliger Feeley had summoned Moon to his suite in the Mansion, poured the young reporter a glass of sherry, and plunked a thick leather-bound volume in his lap. *An Architectural History of Feeley Mansion.* While Moon sat politely trying to sip and not make a face, the papal knight was turning pages for him.

"See here!" Sir Terwilliger cried, jabbing the book with a finger. "This photograph shows Grover Cleveland when he stayed overnight in 1897. President Cleveland was a close friend of my father. So was his illegitimate daughter." The old man cackled. "Oh, Mr. Cleveland made a clean breast of her. Admitted to the world that he had sown one wild oat."

"Very interesting," Moon said, swallowing a yawn.

"Of course you remember Al Smith?"

"Who?"

"Al Smith, you ninny. Greatest man in America. Came to dinner here many times. Why, in 1928 he nearly became President, but bigots launched a whispering campaign. They said that if Al was in the White House the Pope would dictate orders to him."

Moon nodded gravely. The old man sighed. "That was poppycock, of course. Showed the virulent anti-Catholic sentiment in this benighted country. Ah, young man, we will never see the day when a Catholic is elected President. Now look closely at these drawings. This mansion has twenty-six Doric columns and eight Corinthians. Not to mention some secret passageways."

"Er—why are you showing me all this?"

"You must write a feature story for your paper. Ever since this old house became an office building and a dormitory for basketball players, people have forgetten its illustrious past. Now drink your wine and be on your way. You may borrow this book, but guard it with your life."

After supper Moon dropped by the *Immolator* office and slouched at his typewriter. He didn't feel at all like writing about Feeley Mansion. But Sir Terwilliger, he knew, would give him no rest until he wrote something.

Idly, he flipped through the musty *Architectural History*. Long detailed reports on how the mansion had been constructed. Marble friezes brought over from Pompeii. Who gave diddly-squat.

All of a sudden he stopped, struck by a photograph. It showed a fireplace, a hand pushing on a brick. Then the next picture showed a sliding panel in the back of the fireplace, opening.

Concealed passageways are numerous in Feeley Mansion, he read, *enabling servants at times to pass from room to room without disturbing the occupants.*

And there was a map of the mansion, floor by floor, room by room, indicating the passageways.

Holy smoke. An idea exploded in his head. Not for a boring feature story, but for something that could matter. Father Knox had better know about it.

Forty-Six

Monsignor Malachi O'Malley wanted to impress his special visitor this morning. When the visitor's limousine pulled up at the front door of Feeley Mansion, the president made it a point to be there to greet him, shake his hand, escort him up the steps and along the hall.

When they passed a door newly lettered ATHLETICS DEPARTMENT, Ricky Peru jabbed a thumb at it. "That where Father Knox holes up these days?" He chuckled. "Looks like a closet. Must be a come-down for him."

"Yes, Mr. Peruccese, I'm afraid it is," the monsignor said. "Since that problem with the gymnasium, we have all had to cope with straitened circumstances."

In the president's own enormous office, they seated themselves in red leather easy chairs side by side. Coffee appeared, and a tray of petits fours. Peru waved aside the food, dumped cream into his cup, and slurped.

"I suppose," he said, "you're wondering why I came to see you."

The Monsignor took a calculated sip. "I admit I am. Kindly enlighten me."

"I want to see what help I can be to you, Father. You know, I'm always looking out for you."

"Indeed, Mr. Peruccese, you have been a true friend of the college. I cannot thank you sufficiently."

"Think nothing of it. I want to know what you're going to do now. About the gym falling apart."

A wrinkle crossed the president's brow. "That presents us with a considerable challenge."

"I hear you got to tear down the old place."

"So I understand. A reliable firm of engineers has condemned it."

"And then what? You got to build another one?"

"It seems there is no other way. Soon we will begin a drive to raise funds. A new gymnasium will have to be built more carefully. And more expensively, I daresay."

"You blame Jericho Construction? The outfit built the old place?"

"We shall be taking them to court for faulty work and misrepresentation."

Peru had to laugh to himself. Let them see how far they get. They hadn't read the fine print in the contract. Anyhow, he had a couple of judges in his pocket.

The Monsignor's face registered strain. "Meanwhile," he said, "we face the cost of demolishing the old building and clearing the site. I fear it will take time to raise the amount necessary. Then there's the cost of new construction. I—I don't see a solution in the immediate future." He looked almost ready to cry.

Oh, man, Peru thought, you're playing into my hands. He reached out and patted the monsignor's right sleeve. "Aw, don't worry, Father. It'll all work out. Anyhow, don't the college have piles of money these days? All the tuitions you're collecting from the GI Bill? You ought to be rich as a fucking—rich as a Ford factory."

"Tuition doesn't begin to pay for our rather sudden expansion. And although we receive some aid from the diocese of Paterson, we are severely short of funds."

Time to play the trump. "Lucky thing, Father, you got friends."

The president's eyes lit with hope. "Yes! Generous friends like yourself! May I presume to think—might we turn to you with empty hands in our hour of need?"

Peru lit a cigar with his diamond-studded Ronson, blew a cloud of smoke. "Leave me be frank," he said. "I can't buy you no new buildings. I'm fixed pretty good, but I don't have that kind of dough."

"I would hardly expect—"

"But I know somebody that can bankroll you, all right." Peru leaned back in his chair and swung his feet up on a hassock. "How's about some heat in this java?"

The Monsignor clapped his hands and his Filipino valet whipped away the cooling coffee pot. "My apologies. You were saying? About someone you know?"

"Yeah. Guy that runs a country down in the Caribbean. General Trujillo, boss man of the Dominican Republic. Him and me, we're thick as thieves, you might say. I do business with him all the time. And he's a real good Catholic."

The president frowned. "Trujillo. Yes, I have heard of him. Is he not a dictator? With a rather unsavory reputation?"

"Dictator, smictator—who cares what he does down there. That's his show, it don't have nothing to do with the U.S. of A. Thing is, Father"—and Peru leaned forward confidingly—"Trujillo could make you a loan. At pretty reasonable interest. If I put in a good word for you. How would you like about ten million bucks?"

The Monsignor gave a start. "Ten. Million. You really believe—?"

"I know it for a fact. I already run the idea through Trujillo and he's all for it."

And all for giving me a twenty percent finder's fee, Peru said to himself.

"Now, Father," he went on, "you know you ain't gonna find no local bank's gonna float you that kind of a loan. You won't get nobody around here to underwrite you for that much in a million years. But down in his country Trujillo runs everything. Hell, he's got so much spare change he has to move it around in wheelbarrows."

In the president's mind a new building was taking shape, like a phoenix rising out of ashes. The valet rushed in with a new pot of coffee and fresh cups, and nervously poured.

Monsignor O'Malley leaned forward. "How soon can you go ahead with this?"

"Today," said Peru, taking a sip. "I'll tell him you've OKed the deal. Don't worry, Father. Trujillo will fix the interest at only twelve percent, but he don't want no payment yet. Not for the first year."

"That's most generous."

"Just one thing. I think it would be nice if you gave Trujillo one of them honorary degrees. Doctor of Something or Other. Wine him and dine him and drape a hood on him, like you do at graduations."

"I am sure that that can be arranged."

Peru cupped lips around his cigar, took a long drag. "And you know, Father, between you and me, I wouldn't mind getting one of them honorary degrees myself."

Forty-Seven

When Moon squeezed his way into the Athletics Office, he found Knox huddled with Maureen, drafting a letter to the season ticket holders. Knox was saying, as Maureen jotted in shorthand, "Tickets will be honored for admission to away games, but we cannot guarantee the best seats." He glanced up at Moon. "Well if it isn't Front Page. So what do *you* want now?"

"Good morning, Father. How did you like the *Immolator*? The story on the gym building?"

"I thought it stank."

Moon's face fell. "I mean, what did you think of it as journalism?"

Knox scowled. "Gogarty, you'd be happy to see the end of the world if you could write a story about it. Did you come here to crow about your scoop?" He spied the antique book under Moon's arm. "What's that hunk of junk?"

Moon laid the cumbersome volume down on Knox's desk "Father, this is valuable. *An Architectural History of Feeley Mansion*."

"Saints in heaven. Who could care less."

Moon opened to a page and jabbed a finger at a chart.

"See this, Father? The layout of your office here. And this"—he jabbed again—"is your secret door."

Maureen squinted at the page. "Really? Where?"

Balanced on one corner of the desk, Moon twisted around to look at them. "It must be in the back wall of your fireplace. And see here? It says you push on a brick. A door should open up into the next room. Into what's now the business office."

Knox looked skeptical. "Where'd you get this thing?"

"Sir Terwiliger lent it to me. It dates from 1926, but the layout of the mansion hasn't changed since then. If you want, you can go right into Mr. Vastasi's inner office."

"Why don't we?" Maureen piped up.

"Hell," Knox said. "Somebody pops out of Vastasi's fireplace, you think he'll appreciate it?"

"He isn't there today," Maureen said. "He's off on one of his trips to Washington. Patty that works for him told me. She's closed up the office to go shop for her Easter hat."

Knox was musing. "Good chance to snoop around, all right. If that brick really works."

"Let's see if it will," Moon said. He sidled around the desk, probed a hand down the front of the fireplace, pressing one brick at a time. Nothing happened. And then one brick, more soiled than the rest, budged inward. There was an ear-splitting creak as if a rusty gate had wrenched open. The back wall of the fireplace groaned and lifted, exposing a crawl space through which streamed dim light.

Moon gave a shout of triumph. "There you are! Go on in, Father!"

"Now just a damned minute," Knox said. "I'm not sneaking into Vastasi's office like some kind of weasel. Which wouldn't stop me from letting other weasels do it."

"OK," Moon said. "I wouldn't mind doing it."

Maureen said, "Neither would I."

"You understand," Knox said, "if I don't go in myself I can look the Monsignor in the eye and tell him I never set foot in there. But Kevin Burke of the FBI wants to get the goods on Vastasi. Maybe there's some kind of paperwork lying around. About his war surplus racket."

"Mr. Vastasi keeps a logbook," Maureen said. "Patty told me about it. Every time she goes in to see him he hides it quick. Throws it back into his desk drawer."

"Might be worth a look," Moon said.

"Then what are you waiting for?" Knox said. "Go on through that hole."

Moon went first. He had to crouch to fit the doorway. Then, head down, he waddled through. "I'm in!" he called.

Maureen followed. The pair found themselves standing next to Vastasi's big mahogany desk. Maureen switched on the lights.

Moon plunked himself down in Vastasi's swivel chair and tugged at the desk drawer. "Nuts," he said. "It's locked."

"But," Maureen said, gritting her teeth, "this desk is no different from one I used to have. I lost the key to the drawer, so I had to jimmy it open all the time."

She reached up and extracted a hairpin, stuck its end in the lock and gave a twist. The drawer popped open.

Moon was all admiration. "Maureen, you should be a safe-cracker."

"A hairpin never fails. OK, here it is." She pulled out a worn dimestore composition book and started flipping through its pages.

"What's it about?"

Maureen ran a finger down one page. "Seems to be a list of war surplus materials. Kept in real sloppy writing.

Not Miss Prouty's work, that's for sure. Items, each with a dollar amount."

"Any rifles?"

"Let's see. Forty Underwood typewriters. Eighty-two life rafts. Couple of Jeeps. OK, here we are. Twenty-nine cases of Garands. Seventy thousand dollars."

"Hey, Father," Moon called back to Knox, "Maureen found something. How much Vastasi gets for the rifles."

For a moment, Knox thrust his head through the hole. "Yeah? Keep looking. See what else you turn up." He drew back.

Maureen strode over to Miss Prouty's miniature desk, opened the account book to entries inscribed in a spidery hand.

"Nothing crooked here," she said. "Just a record of business expenses, nothing over a hundred dollars."

"What about that little file cabinet? Next to the desk?"

Maureen pulled open a file drawer. "Miss Prouty keeps everything. Looks like cancelled checks. Signed by Vastasi."

"Any made out to Ricco Peruccese?"

"Vastasi wouldn't write checks to Peru. That would be too obvious. Here's a check to the Jericho Construction Company."

"That's the outfit that built the gym."

"Uh huh. This stuff won't help us much. Or maybe— wait a minute." Maureen's horn-rimmed reading glasses shone as she bent over the file drawer. "This one is inter-esting. It's made out to Jericho, and it's been cashed, but it's endorsed *Pay to Latin American Trading Corporation.*"

"Peru's company! How much is it for?"

"Plenty," Maureen said, looking up with glee. "Nine hundred and seventy thousand dollars."

Moon gave a whoop of joy. "So the construction company was sharing their take with Peru."

"It's plain as the nose on your face."

Moon stuck his head and shoulders back into Knox's office. "Hey, Father, what do you think Maureen just found? Ricky Peru made big money off of the gym that fell down. How do you like that?"

Knox broke into a grin. "Like it? I love it. Nice work, spies. This ought to hang Peru's ass for good."

Forty-Eight

Glee on his face, Douglas Knox laid four canceled checks in a row on Monsignor O'Malley's desk. "You'll notice, your grace," he said, "that every one of these amounts was turned over to Ricky Peru's company."

The college president blinked. "I don't follow this. What do you make of these transactions?"

"I make it that Peru collected kickbacks from Jericho Construction. You paid them twenty percent more than you needed to, so that that crook could get his share. It was Peru who urged you to give them the contract to build the gym, wasn't it? So that you'd pay extra for a shoddy job that fell apart."

The monsignor swung his chair toward the wall and looked away. He passed a hand over his brow. "Douglas, I don't know about that. We had no control over the construction company. How they chose to spend their payments is none of our affair. If they wished to compensate Mr. Peruccese's company, that was their business. They may have had some good reason for doing so."

"Good reason my aching butt, your grace. Excuse me, but it's clear that Jericho was in cahoots with the mob."

Monsignor O'Malley turned to face Knox. He looked suddenly old.

"And what do you expect me to do?"

"Nothing, your grace. There's a friend of mine, Kevin Burke, special FBI agent, who's interested in all this. I'm taking him this evidence, together with proof that Peru's nephew Glauco Vastasi is using the college to deal in war surplus materials. You can leave it up to Burke to throw the book at them."

"Now just a minute, Douglas. We must be careful here. That Mr. Vastasi is a relative of Mr. Peruccese means nothing. I don't want to incriminate the college needlessly, nor Mr. Vastasi. And I certainly don't intend to issue any complaint about Mr. Peruccese without hearing his side of the story. He has been a loyal friend to this college."

"If you'd pardon me saying so, this college has been a better friend to Peru than he's ever been to us. He and Glauco have been poison."

The monsignor frowned. "If, and I say just if, any action on these charges is to be taken, it absolutely has to hold off for a little while. Douglas, may I ask you to keep this confidential. For the next two weeks. Until I can make my own investigation."

Until Peruccese obtains the loan to the college from General Trujillo, the monsignor thought. The FBI had to be held off, to allow time.

Peru and Vastasi were soaking in a hot tub on the main deck of Peru's yacht, the *Golden Dollar*, anchored in Barnegat Bay. On this first Sunday in May the air was still cool. The two men stayed submerged up to their necks, a bottle of malt scotch and two glasses on a tray nearby.

Vastasi blew his nose on a towel. "Christ," he said, "there's going to be lawsuits. People got hit by falling stuff. They'll sue the college and the college will sue Jericho."

Peru finned water with a lazy hand. "Don't I know that, nephew? All it is is another opportunity. I help Jericho out of a tight spot and they pay me plenty for it."

"No crap. How you gonna take the heat off them?"

Peru spat. "I got Moe Gomberg working on it. The way I see it, everybody—the engineers, the newspapers—they'll blame the company the goddam roof fell in. But we make out it was all Saint Cash's fault. The school wanted to shave costs. They insisted on a rush job. Jericho didn't have time to police the materials like usual, and some lousy cement slipped in."

"That'll sound pretty good. Blame the cement company. Sand Man Building Supplies. Shouldn't be hard. I know the old man runs that outfit. Pay him enough and he'll take the blame for everything. He can declare bankruptcy. What are they going to do, squeeze blood out of a turnip? Nobody will collect except the lawyers."

Peru said, "Jeez, I got to get out of here, my balls are melting." He hauled his dripping body out of the tub and swatted his loins with a towel. "And we got another opportunity. The college has to build another gym."

"You don't think they'll hire Jericho again, do you?"

"They ain't *that* dumb. But they need money. I been to see the monsignor. Offered to fix him up with a loan from Trujillo. He's hard up as a monkey, see. When I told him he'll get ten million bucks he jumped at it. And Trujillo's gonna give us a piece of the interest."

Vastasi grinned. "Beautiful, Uncle Ricky. I got to hand it to you."

"As long as we got the monsignor over a barrel, we might's well stick it to him. Where else is he going to find that size dough? The college is nothing but a busted gym, a few old buildings, a bunch of Quonset huts. They over-expanded like a fucking balloon. No bank would touch them with a ten foot pole. They ain't got shit for security."

Parked on a bench with a terry cloth robe around him, Peru pulled a Di Nobili twist cigar out of a pack. The world looked serene. He watched a seagull wheeling overhead. The breeze was trying to warm up. The yacht swayed gently on easy waves. Between puffs he said, "What about Holy Father Knox? How'd he like it his gym fell apart? He must be madder than a bird with buckshot up his ass. You keeping an eye on him?"

"Does an owl watch a mouse? He went around kicking stray cats and fire hydrants."

Peru chuckled. "I wish I seen that. That would of made my day. Anyhow, I'll get to see him at the Garden a week from Thursday night."

"The game Pohl throws?"

"Right. The kid fucks up in front of a big-time crowd. Cosimo has him paid not just to shave points, but to make Saint Cash lose bad. I want them Quills to look pathetic, end their season like a wet fart. Oh man, I been waiting a long time for this. Want to watch Knox squirm. He's going to need plenty of cats and fire hydrants."

Aisling finally responded to the pounding on the door of her apartment. Bathrobed, barefoot, hair in disar-ray, she opened the door a crack. Randy Harrigan stood clutching in each hand a bottle in a paper bag.

"Let me in, darling," he said. "I invented a hell of a new drink you gotta try."

"I've had enough of you and your drinks. Go away."
She started to shut the door.

But Harrigan intruded a foot. "Believe me, baby, this
is terrific. Two-thirds Guinness's stout, one third rum.
One slug knocks you higher than a cloud."

"Big deal. Pour it up your ass and have an enema. Get
out of here."

Harrigan adopted his best tone of menace. "You better
remember, baby—I've got the goods on you. You want me
to tell the Monsignor about your phony marriage? About
your kid you don't even know the father of?"

"Go ahead and tell. I should have told you to do it long
ago. How do you think Vastasi would like it, you spilling
the truth about him keeping two wives? I'm not about to
be fired. All of a sudden I'm too valuable. They have me
running the whole biology department."

Harrigan's face fell. "So anyway, let me in. We could
have us a sweet time."

"Listen, you ox-faced stupe, I'm done with you, you
hear? I was a fool to ever start."

"Yeah? How about we have one little drink together?
For old time's sake."

"Randy Harrigan, if you don't get out of here right
now, I'm calling the cops."

Harrigan took back his foot. "That's the way you want it?"

"That's the way."

Still clutching the bottles, he stomped back down the
stairs. "You're going to be sorry," he called back. "I'm getting Ricky Peru to see to you."

Aisling slammed the door. She turned and went back
to the bedroom, shedding her robe as she went. Scrotum
Pohl lay naked on the bed, his six-foot-eight body rippling

with muscle, skin shining with massage oil. His deep brown glow reminded her of Vastasi's mahogany desk.

She lay down beside him. His hands supplied her with a bra. "Who was it, Professor?"

"Only a bum looking for a handout. I got rid of him."

Pohl brought his body up against hers. "Aisling, you some woman, you know? You make a man forget . . ."

"You want to forget something?"

"A lot of things."

She rolled aside, fumbled for a cigarette. "I figured that. You haven't been yourself today. Kind of worried, thoughtful."

He didn't say anything.

She blew smoke and covered his privates with a cloud. "You want to tell mama anything? Get it off your mind?"

"Maybe," he said slowly, "it's the game tomorrow."

"The big game with Holy Sepulcher. You nervous?"

"Me? Nervous? Sheeeet, I ain't never nervous. It just don't seem like a game I want to play. Especially I don't know as I want to play it in Madison Square Garden."

"Listen, lover, I'll come watch you. Mabel Chen can babysit. I'll hitch a ride in with the team. I'll cheer for you."

He frowned. "No. That a no-good idea. You don't want to come to this game."

"Why not?"

"I—I ain't saying. But take my word for it, sweet buns, this is one game nobody ought to see. Not especially you."

She crushed out her cigarette. "I don't get it," she said. "You'll be playing in the Garden, on TV. Your chance to be a big-time star. This game—you're going to feel ashamed of it?"

Forty-Nine

In the Quonset hut office of *The Immolator*, Moon waved the tickets under Konny's nose.

"Look what Father Knox sent over. Two seats for the big finale of the season. Saint Cash versus Holy Sepulcher. Seven o'clock tonight in Madison Square Garden."

"Who's g-g-g-going to g-g-g-g-g-g-go?"

"That's a problem," Moon said. "Everybody on the staff has quit except you and me. You know anything about basketball?"

"Sure. Who d-d-d-doesn't?"

"Well I don't. Had to play it in gym class in high school, but nobody ever told us the rules. Never did figure out what it was all about."

"You're an in-t-t-ectual, M-Moon, is the tr-tr-trouble with you."

"Can you go to the Garden tonight, write the story?"

"I c-c-an't write worth b-b-beans. You know that. I'm the b-b-business m-manager. I c-can sell ads, that's all."

And not many of those, Moon thought. So far this year Konny had brought in only four small one-timers. Catwash Carwash, the Royal Procrustean Motor Inn, Garden State Screw and Die, and a reducing salon, The Shrine of Fatima.

Moon sighed. "All right. If you watch the game and tell me what's happening, I can take notes and write it up. We'll both go in to New York."

———

In the locker room at the Garden, Knox felt obliged to give a pep talk. He guessed the team expected it of him. He kept it brief. "So forget fifteen thousand people are watching. Forget the television cameras. Just play the way you always play. God bless you, you bastards. You'll do all right."

But he was puzzled. The squad wore a hangdog look. His best players moved as if in a trance, faces long, chins sunken, gazes cast down to the floor. Well, maybe the boys would shape up when they heard the cheers of the crowd.

Knox made his way over to Pohl. The freshman star was tugging on his jock strap and tussling into porcupine-emblemed shirt number 4.

Knox said, "How you feeling tonight?"

Pohl avoided his eyes. "Not too great, Father. The right arm feeling sore."

Knox gave an inward groan. "When did this start?"

"I dunno. Yesterday."

"Can you play? You want me to call the doc?"

Pohl thought. He had to play, play like he was hurting. He'd be expected to earn his money. "Naw, it ain't that bad. Just don't mind if sometimes I got to rest my shooting arm a bit."

As soon as Knox went away Thad Kolowsky came over to Pohl and said in an undertone, "You know we can't win this. We don't dare."

Pohl blinked. "Oh oh. You been talking with Cosimo too?"

"Not only talking. He paid me off."

"Well then, sheet, that make two of us. That going to make it easier to throw this son of a bitch."

"You and me aren't the only ones."

"Who else?"

"Mastolino, Crisp, Schomberg, O'Malley. Half the team's going to be trying hard to get the piss kicked out of us."

Pohl frowned. "Got to hand it to Cosimo. He picked the best shooters. We none of us score much, getting whupped ought to be easy."

"Ought to be," Kolowski said. "But the hard part will be to make it look like we're *trying* to score, just not making it."

Pohl backed up to a bench and slumped down. "Don't like this, Thad. This motherfuckin play acting. Now I had to give Father Knox a line, about how my arm out of commission. This is one night I be glad when it's over."

"Me too. It stinks we got to be on national TV looking like a bunch of assholes. You and me, maybe we can get ourselves fouled out."

Humphrey Towne had been given this game for his first assignment, and the novice was determined to make good. He'd show Cross he could be trusted to do the job. Now in the seventh row of Garden, his handgun in a holster under his raincoat, he sat waiting for the game to start.

Towne had reserved a seat on either side of him. This way nobody would be sitting next to him when the moment came to strike. There would be time to place only one or two shots, and he wasn't going to miss. He had an unobstructed view of the coach's bench where Douglas Knox would be sitting. Personally, he had no grudge against Knox, but the priest had angered the prophet of the Church of the One Right Path. Towne did not question Cross's orders. The need for obedience had been drilled into him. He had had forty hours of target practice. He would wait for an exciting moment of the game, when the noise of the crowd would drown the sound of his gun. Then he would aim his first shot at the base of Knox's skull. Not likely that a second shot would be necessary.

Moon and Konny lost their way when they came out of the Hudson tube. They had expected to find Madison Square Garden on Madison Square, but at 23rd Street a woman sausage-seller put them straight. Not knowing how to take the subway, they sprinted twenty-seven blocks up Eighth Avenue and arrived three minutes before the game began. Breathless and panting, clutching a bagful of red hots, they sidled to their seats in the twenty-first row, dripping yellow mustard as they went.

"Watch out where you're leaking that slop, clown," said a fat man in the next seat. "You got me on the shoe."

"Excuse me, mister," Moon said. He whipped out his handkerchief. "Here, I'll wipe you off."

"Aaah, never mind. Going to take my shoes off anyway. You rooting for the Quills?"

"Not only rooting. We're official reporters. Covering the game for the Saint Cassian of Imola College newspaper."

"Is that a fact? I didn't know anybody at Saint Cash's could read. Hear the students are all ex-GIs never got past fourth grade."

Moon was gearing up to defend the reputation of his school when the whistle sounded for the teams to take their places. A cheer went up as five Quills slowly walked onto the court. The game began. The Quills' center mistimed his jump and the Shrouds took possession of the ball.

"Oh oh," Konny said. "Th-th-that's their tall man B-B-Buzz Fillmore g-g-going to shoot. How c-c-come nobody's g-g-g-guarding him?"

Fillmore halted directly under the basket and boosted the ball to the rim. It made a futile circle and dropped to the floor. Fillmore turned his back on it and it rolled out of bounds.

"The hell's going on," said the fat man with a scowl. "Those bozos asleep? Nobody lifted a finger to get that ball."

The referee's whistle blew and Thad Kolowski received. Thad passed the ball to Pohl. Pohl tried a weak layup that went far wide. Reluctantly, Fillmore picked up the rebound. At the other end of the court, he heaved a long shot that missed. He came back on defense just in time to meet the Quills' charging point guard, Andy Crisp. Fillmore stuck out a foot and tripped him. Crisp sprawled face-down on the paint and didn't rise.

The ref's whistle screamed. The game halted. Two medics rushed in. Knox beat them to the side of the fallen Crisp and stood jawing at the medics. Crisp was hoisted onto a stretcher and carried away.

"M-m-m-my God," said Konny. "What b-b-bum luck. And so early in the g-g-game."

"Fillmore did that on purpose," Moon said.

The Quills took two free-throws, Joe Mastolino doing
the honors. Both shots went wild. Boos and groans from
the crowd. The listless game dragged on.

"What's the matter with these guys?" Moon wanted to
know. "The scoreboard still says zero-zero."

"M-m-must all be s-sick," Konny said. "An
ep-ep-ep-epidemic."

"Craziest game I ever saw," the fat man said, spewing
smoke from a Kool. "The Shrouds ain't guarding that
hotshot Pohl. I thought they'd be all over him. You ask
me, we ought to get our money back. And me, like a fool,
I got fifty bucks riding on Saint Cash."

———

Sitting beside Knox on the coach's bench, Tim Walsh
felt a nagging unease. About Knox, crouched there in
plain view next to the court. He made a sitting target.
Walsh stood up and turned around, scanning the crowd.

Knox was chewing an unlit Gauloise, angrily. "What
you looking for, Tim?"

"Nothing, Doug. Just seeing who's here."

"I wish nobody was here," Knox said.

Walsh sat back down. "What do you make of this? Our
boys have stage fright?"

"It's not that. They're pulling their punches. Too many
missed shots, rebounds fumbled, too many passes six
inches too high. Pohl told me his right arm was sore, but
he's not doing anything with his left arm either. I hate
to say this, Tim, but I think Peru's man Cosimo and his
checkbook must have got to them after all."

"You believe that?"

"I don't want to," Knox said. "I trusted Pohl. And Kolowsky, and the rest. You know, I'd have trusted those boys with my life."

"Folks," the TV announcer syruped, "it's a do-or-die struggle here in Madison Square Garden tonight. Two great teams are evenly matched. Eight minutes into the game and they're deadlocked four to four."

"Deadlocked, hell," said the Sarge. "Both of 'em are dead on their feet." He took a long swig of his Krueger and with the back of his hand wiped suds from his mouth.

On the stool beside him at the bar of the Dedwood Inn, Aisling studied the twist of lemon in her dry vermouth. She had quit looking at the ten-inch TV. She could see why Pohl was ashamed of this game. Why he didn't want her watching him tonight.

"You ask me," the Sarge said in disgust, "the game fixers worked on both teams. Two different game fixers."

Aisling said, "Our team took bribes? I thought they were good Catholic boys."

"Pohl's a Free Will Baptist," the Sarge said. "Anyhow they're all from poor neighborhoods where their mamma uses the bedsheet for a tablecloth. Never saw any real money in their life till some gambler flashed it to 'em." His left hand, the flesh-and-blood one, was crawling down to her black-stockinged right knee.

Aisling squirmed aside. "Not tonight, Sarge. I don't feel like anything."

"Some other night, you mean?"

"Who knows?"

Fifty

In his seat two rows behind the Quills' coach's bench, Ricky Peru was grinning from ear to ear.

"Look at him," he said to Cosimo. "Holy Coach Knox. You ever see anybody that red in the face? Been waiting months for this. Fucking priest looks ready to be tied."

"Uh huh."

Peru wet his lips from his silver flask. "Hey Coz, what's gives? You ain't enjoying this? Pohl's shaving points like you paid him to, right? He ain't scored all night."

"Yeah. Only the Shrouds ain't scoring neither."

Peru's grin vanished. "Hey. That's right. What the fuck's going on?"

"I think we got competition," Cosimo said. "The Shrouds are shaving down to the bone. Eel Garber had something to do with this."

"Garber? That game fixer down in Hartford?"

"Him. In Holy Sepulk's neighborhood. He got to them, same as we got to Saint Cash. You want the Quills to lose? They're having a hard time doing it. These goddam teams are busting their asses trying to throw the game. Both of 'em."

Knox called a timeout, pulled Kolowsky and sent in freshman Simp Fallowfield, who hadn't seen much playing

324

time all season. Fallowfield looked bewildered. Then, grabbing the ball, he made a nervous drive that fell apart.

"Damn it," Knox said to Walsh. "Coach ought to be allowed to talk to his team during a timeout. That's a rule needs to be changed."

On their next possession, center Blub O'Malley, the tallest Quill, drifted near the basket, looking half asleep. Fallowfield dribbled the length of the floor. Surprised to find no Shrouds challenging him, he launched himself at the basket. The ball would have toppled in, but O'Malley lazily arced up and swatted it away.

"He blocked it!" Knox howled. "Our own ball!"

The ref's whistle blew. "Penalty for goal-tending," he called.

Knox was on his feet, shouting. "Goal-tending, you call that? He screwed up! Blocked a basket for own team!"

"Don't matter whose he blocked," the ref returned.

After the Shrouds missed their free throw, Knox replaced O'Malley with Schwartzkopf. Another untried freshman, too short to play center, but all he had.

In his high seat overlooking the game, Humphrey Towne felt his nerves beginning to twitch. His handgun was still holstered beneath his raincoat, useless so far. When would he get his chance? This game was so slow the fans were starting to go home.

Towne knew that he needed the cover of crowd noise. If the sound of the shot drew attention to him, it might be hard to make his getaway. He'd just have to bide his time. This game had to come alive. He'd get his moment to strike. He had to concentrate. He stared straight down to the coach's bench, gaze fixed on the back of Knox's skull.

———

All the while he dribbled and passed, not using his right arm, Pohl kept thinking. Here he was, the best power forward the Quills had ever had—so the sports writers said—and he hadn't yet scored. It must look suspicious. Maybe he had better sink a couple, just for show.

He came alive. Eased down the lane to the basket and using his left arm dunked one in. For a brief moment the crowd went wild.

Pohl decided he'd done enough for the moment. He passed to Fallowfield, who looked surprised to be presented with the ball. Fallowfield made a layup shot that hesitated, rolled twice around the rim, and went in.

The Saint Cash fans erupted in a brief roar. Cosimo scowled. "What's with that black bastard? He's been scoring. And that was a perfect assist."

"Easy, Coz," Peru said. "He done right to do it. He got to make this game look real, don't he?"

The ball went out of bounds. Pohl faced Fillmore for a jump.

"What you doing?" Fillmore said under his breath. "You sell out or didn't you?"

"Just like you," Pohl said. "This game looking too phony. Better sink a few."

Fillmore took the hint. He sank a shot. Pohl lapsed back to doing nothing.

———

When the Shrouds' coach called a timeout, Fillmore stood facing the Quills. "Hey, porcupines," he bawled, "you can't play worth shit, you know that? You're nothing but dumb fucking swine."

Referee Jurgen McCleeve shrilled his whistle. "Unsportsmanlike trash talk," he barked. "Quills, two throws."

"Yeah?" Fillmore shot back. "Fuck you, McCleeve. Just because you got a whistle in your mouth, you can tell me what to say?"

"Two more fouls!" McCleeve yelled.

Fillmore had the ball in his hands. He hauled back his right foot and booted the ball straight into the nearest row of spectators. An elderly bespectacled nun caught it in the bosom. "Jeepers!" she cried.

The ref's whistle screamed. "Fillmore, you're through! Off the court!"

Fillmore's face broke into a grin. "Good call, McCleeve," he said.

Halftime. The Shrouds' coach Micky DeVito launched a furious harangue at his team. Knox decided he didn't want to do that.

Tim Walsh said, "Doug, aren't you going to talk to them? Tell 'em a thing or two?"

Knox lit a Gauloise and blew. "What good would it do? They've sold out, OK, they've sold out. What can I tell them now?"

The second half began, but change was in the air. The Quills appeared to be trying. They were shooting, grabbing rebounds, keeping the hoop busy.

The fat man next to Moon had switched from Kools to Camels. Moon had to wave away the smoke to see the court.

"It's a m-m-miracle," Konny stammered. "P-P-P-P-Pohl, I mean. All of a s-s-sudden h-h-he's h-his old s-self."

Pohl kept working both oversized hands. Charging the basket, sinking his shots every time. The rest of the Quills caught fire. Joe Mastolino, who had spent the game hanging back, drove in, swished one through. Even Fallowfield and Schwartzkopf were looking like stars.

"Konny," Moon begged, "for the love of Mike, what's going on? Keep talking, can't you? I've got to write some details."

"I'm f-f-f-following everything. B-b-but I just c-can't t-t-tell it t-t-t-too f-f-f-fast."

Humphrey Towne had his handgun out, trained on the back of Knox's head. Pohl scored again, and a cheer swept through the Garden. Towne was starting to squeeze the trigger when Knox jumped to his feet in excitement, urging the team on.

Damn. Hastily, Towne thrust the gun back under his coat. Luckily, the action on the court had drawn all eyes. No one in the nearby seats had noticed him. Now that the game had picked up speed, he'd soon have another chance. He tensed, fingers closed around the handle of the gun. Any second now, the crowd would give a good, long-lasting roar.

"Good Lord, Doug!" Tim Walsh said. "I thought Pohl had a sore right arm. He's using it like a whirlwind."

"Yeah," Knox said. "Ever since halftime. He must have taken a quick trip to Lourdes."

"They're going to win. Not big, but it's a win for sure."

"I'm wondering," Knox said. "Why they changed their minds all of a sudden and started playing ball."

Aisling got up from her stool at the bar and said, "Good night, Sarge. I can't take this game anymore. I'm going home and find me a little excitement. Like grading papers."

The Sarge jabbed a finger at the small flickering screen above the bar. "You ain't been watching this? Hang on a minute!"

"This is sensational, folks!" the TV announcer cried. "All of a sudden the Quills are steaming over the Shrouds. This is the S. T. Pohl we've been waiting all night to see. The human dynamo."

Pohl took a set shot from nearly midcourt. The ball made a perfect arc and swished through. All the patrons at the bar set up a howl.

"Look at them hands on him," the Sarge said. "Can grab anything with hands like that."

"I know," Aisling said. She sat back down, gaze riveted to the screen, face wreathed in a smile.

The Sarge's metal claw waved at the bartender. "Two more!" he yelled.

They drank, and the Sarge said, "You still don't want to do anything tonight?"

She gave him a lingering look. "Who knows?" she said. "When the game is over, maybe I just might."

———————

Kevin Burke and another FBI man, Gus Munzenrider, had seats down front, ninth row on the aisle. Burke kept scanning the spectators below. "Hey, Muntz," he said, "catch that bird two rows down. Guy in a black raincoat. What's he doing?"

Munzenrider squinted. "Jesus. He's aiming at the coach's bench."

"Taking pictures?"

"He's got a gun."

"Let's take him. Quick."

They bounded down the steps two at a time. Burke slid in past a couple on the aisle, grabbed Towne's extended arm and twisted. The gun clunked to the concrete floor. Burke slammed a fist into the man's jaw. Munzenrider, in the row behind him, got him in a hammerlock.

Burke said, "Any cuffs on you, Muntz?"

"Naaa. I thought we were off duty."

"Keep a grip on him. He was packing a Colt forty-five. Hey, look, his head is shaved like a cross."

Humphrey Towne's eyeballs were bugging halfway out of his head. Munzenrider eased up on him enough to let him talk. "All right, mister," Burke said, "you belong to the Church of the One Right Path?"

Towne gasped out, "That—that is none of your business."

Burke persisted. "Drawing a bead on Coach Knox, weren't you?"

"Don't know what you mean."

"I figure you do," Burke said.

"He's only a kid," Muntzenrider said. "Sixteen, seventeen."

All around them, spectators had turned around to stare. One of the Garden security cops came over. "What's the trouble here?"

Burke flashed his ID. "FBI. This guy's a would-be killer. Trying to shoot a coach. We nailed him and his piece."

The cop's jaw dropped an inch. "For Chrissake. Hang on to him."

"Get a gun," Burke suggested. "Something to make him behave."

Towne looked as though he had lost all his determination.

Peru, clutching his flask and his jacket with the ermine collar, went storming out of the arena, elbowing a path through the crowd. He shot back to Cosimo, "Fifty-two to eighteen, they won. Some businessman you are. Fucking priest looked happy as a pig in shit."

Cosimo shrugged. "Could I help it Holy Sepulk got paid off too?"

"It don't excuse that black doublecrosser. Thirty-four points, he made. He don't do that to me and get away with it. We got to teach him a lesson. For keeps."

Fifty-One

Sprawled in the one easy chair in Aisling's apartment, the Sarge wore a look of contentment. "That was some night," he said.

Aisling, fixing breakfast, sloshed boiling water into their cups of G. Washington coffee crystals. "The game, you mean?"

"No. Not the game."

She threw him a long slow smile. "You're a real stud, Sarge. One of the best."

"You been with enough studs to know?"

"Don't ask for a list. Another dumpling?" She ladled a small pointed sack of dough into his bowl, ladled hot broth over it.

"These things are the cat's ass," he said. "Shrimps in 'em. Where'd they come from?"

"China. By way of Mrs. Chong, my landlady. She's always making things and sending some up to me. How's school going?"

"Not so hot. Guess I been away from the books too long. Too many words in 'em. And that damn history book, it's nothing but names you got to remember."

"Why don't you drop out? Do something you're good at?"

"Been thinking about it. What I really like is cars. Pretty good at keeping an old heap running."

"Plenty of car dealers around here. They're always looking for a mechanic, I bet."

"I could try. But maybe they wouldn't go for this." He flexed his right hand, the bright steel claw.

"As long as you can hold a wrench, why should they care? You could always get another hand, you know. One that looks real."

"Naaa. I could have had one back in the V.A. hospital. But I don't want no part of me looks like a doll."

"They make better ones these days. Some even come with hair."

From her crib in the kitchen, Kiki Sue woke up and started to cry.

"My alarm clock," Aisling said. "She's late this morning, bless her heart. Excuse me, Sarge, she needs a feed and a change."

"I'll change her for you," the Sarge said.

"You mean it? You know how?"

For an answer, he lifted the child gently and set her down on the changing table, unpinned her diaper, and expertly mopped her bottom with a cotton swab. Kiki Sue looked at him wide-eyed. Not unhappy. Then he whisked a fresh diaper from a stack. Aisling undid her blouse. The Sarge handed her the child wrapped in a blanket. The sound of steady chomping filled the room.

"Well what do you know," Aisling said. "You handle the kid like a professional."

"I was a father once."

"Not anymore?"

The Sarge sat down heavily, studied his coffee. "Crib death, they called it. One day he was fine, and the next morning . . ."

"Aw. I'm really sorry."

"Happened a while back. Before the war."

"You're not married now?"

"We split. She couldn't stand this thing." Flexing his claw. "I didn't think you'd stand for it either."

"Oh, I've seen a lot of those," she said. "I was a nurse in the South Pacific, you know."

Kiki Sue relaxed her grip.

"Give her here," Sarge said. "I'll burp her."

Aisling passed him the baby. He rested the little girl's head on his shoulder and strolled the room, patting her on the back. In a minute she delivered a belch.

"It feels good," he said. "Holding a kid again."

"You're a nice guy, Sarge. Even if you *are* part robot."

"I don't mind. At least I'm glad I'm not S. T. Pohl. You know, when that boy came alive last night he was a shot-engine. But whoever tried to fix that game will be gunning for him. I think Pohl wrote himself a one-way ticket to the cemetery."

In the Grecian Spoon in Denwood center, S. T. Pohl forked a chunk of porterhouse steak. Talking around it, he said, "So how come you treating me to dinner, Father?"

Knox took a sip of his ale. "Tell me about the game last night. After you do away with that steak. Any good?"

"Pretty good, for a place in Dedwood. Look, Father, I know I fucked up last night, you excuse the expression."

"But in that second half you took over the court. What made you change your mind?"

"Couldn't stand it no more. Doing nothing, letting the ball go by. You knew the Shrouds were on the take, same as us?"

"That was plain to see."

"So it didn't matter who won the game. Figured it might as well be us, after all."

"Cosimo the one who paid you?"

"Him."

"He told you to keep down the spread?"

"He told us to lose."

"You think he liked it when you didn't follow orders?"

Pohl shrugged. "I don't give a shit what Cosimo think anymore. He want his money back, I'll give it to him."

Knox looked at him piercingly. "How come you took that bribe? I never thought you were that kind."

Pohl looked hurt. "Maybe I'm not. Don't want to be. Only you see, Father, I got to raise some money. Need a heap."

"But you're here on a full scholarship. Tuition, books, room, board, spending money. What do you need more for?"

"For back home. What's been going on in Miss. Sister Agatha that was my angel, her old school falling down around her. And my mamma, she need a new church, make up for the one got bombed."

Knox thought. "Maybe we can do something. There's a lot of money left over from the Children's Crusade."

Pohl's eyes lit up. "That be tremendous, Father. You want to know where to send it?"

"You can talk to Maureen in the morning. And, you know, you'll make plenty of dough when you finish school. You have talents some people would pay for. Honest people."

"Like pro teams, huh."

"Right. After you graduate, you can play pro ball. Basketball is booming, pulling in the crowds. Since last summer there's a new outfit that the teams belong to, the National Basketball Association. Matter of fact, I just had visits from a couple of scouts from the Celtics and the Royals."

"They see me play?"

"They did. They liked you."

"You gonna tell 'em I took a bribe to fix a game?"

"No. Because thanks to you, that game didn't get fixed."

"Father, I'm sorry about this fixing shit. I know you got enough to worry about. The gym falling down, them fools trying to kill you, and all."

"That guy called Cross," Knox said, "I've stopped thinking about him. Maybe he got discouraged and gave up. I would have thought he had a chance to drill me last night in the Garden. There I was down front on the bench in plain view. Cross had wanted to, he could have popped me easy, got away in the crowd."

Pohl looked at Knox with admiration. "Damn, Father. You were risking your life just sitting there watching that game."

Knox shrugged. "So nothing happened. But another thing that bothers me is the mob. Peru is like some octopus, tentacles spread around the state, putting the squeeze on everything. There's nothing he doesn't touch. Business. The cops. Radio stations. Sports. The governor. The college. He has our Monsignor under his thumb."

The juke box flooded the room with sound. The Ink Spots singing "I Don't Want to Set the World on Fire." Pohl opted for the Grecian Spoon's dessert of the day, chocolate pecan pie à la mode. Knox nursed a cup of black coffee.

At last Pohl wiped his mouth and sat back, looking serene. "I guess you just heard my confession, Father. I ain't no Catholic, but if you want to give me some prayers to say—"

"You're absolved. For your penance, you can sink thirty shots. Maybe the season's over, but don't lose your shooting arm. There's still next year."

Knox charged their meal to the Athletics Department, then they stepped outside. Street lights were coming on, trying to shove aside the night.

A blue Cadillac sedan that looked half a block long was stationed at the curb. As soon as they came near it, two men got out. Wearing dark felt hats, dark glasses. One flourished a handgun. "Get in the car, black boy," he said.

Pohl stood for a moment, wavering, looking at the gun. For a moment he considered making a run for it.

"Easy," Knox said. "These guys mean business." He took a step forward.

The other man said, "I wouldn't try anything, Father, I was you."

Knox peered at him. Lean guy, tiny mustache, left cheek creased with a scar. "You're Willy the Wire," Knox said. "Hey, I thought we were friends."

Willy grimaced. "Too bad you know me, Father. I'm sorry you're with this kid. I guess you both better get in the car and come along."

The hood holding the pistol flicked the air with it. Knox and Pohl slid into the back seat and the hood got in with them. Willy threw the car into gear and they roared away.

Fifty-Two

When Manny the Monk slouched into the business office, his black felt hat pulled low over his eyes, Miss Prowdy stared up in alarm. This man looked like a criminal. Surely he didn't belong on a respectable campus. But when the secretary sent in word that a Mr. Monk had arrived, Glauco Vastasi sprang out to welcome him.

"Don't disturb us," he ordered. "We got to talk business." He waved Manny inside and slammed the door.

Well, of all things! Miss Prowdy said to herself.

In the inner office, Manny helped himself to a chair. "So whattaya want with me?"

"Manny, you and me been friends a long time," Vastasi began.

"Couple of years. So?"

"So I think I can trust you. That right?"

Manny made a gesture with open hands.

"I don't want this to get around," Vastasi said. "It's just between you and me. You don't have any special love for Ricky, do you?"

"Special love? I work for him, that's all."

"There's a lot of dissatisfaction in the troops. With how everything gets handled. You know?"

"Some guys are never happy."

"For plenty of reasons. Listen, like you must have noticed, Ricky is getting old and past it. That construction company that built the Humpty-Dumpty gym—dealing with them was a bad mistake. That priest with the Children's Crusade that he tried to put the pressure on, and the guy went nuts—dumb move. And the war surplus racket I run for him. He's making a mint. But does he ever pass down the profits to the troops?"

Manny shrugged. "I ain't seen none of it."

"And you ain't going to, long as Ricky is in charge. So what do you think—it's time for a fresh general?"

Manny looked hard at Vastasi. "It might be."

"Damn right it is. Look, Manny, for a long time I been thinking. I got the experience. Got it up here, you know?" He tapped his forehead. "And I figure the time is right to make a move."

"Ricky ain't going to like this."

"Ricky don't have to know about it. He never has to know. He gets popped, and he don't know a thing anymore."

"What's this got to do with me?"

"Manny, you're the guy to do it. Peru knows you, you can walk right up to him, drill him easy as taking a crap."

"How you want it done?"

"Any damn way. Maybe in his digs. Or maybe when you're driving him someplace, you pull down some alley, turn around, and—POW."

"What's in it for me?"

"I take over, I promote you to captain. Capregimo. You'll be raking it in. One-twentieth cut of everything."

For a moment Manny sucked his lower lip. "You're on," he said.

Vastasi opened a desk drawer and pulled out a bundle of greenbacks. He tossed it into Manny's lap.

"Just a little bonus," he said. "To keep your mouth shut until you make your move. After you do him, you gonna get double that."

Hunched over the phone in his Hoboken apartment, Ricky Peru was winding up an exasperating conversation with Michael O. Spillane, Joyce Kilmer Professor of English.

"Christ, don't ask me what to say," he bellowed. "What am I paying you for? This is a commencement speech. You been to commencements, ain't you? Put in about democracy. About business and stuff. Use your head. Oh yeah, you can say it's a swell idea the college should give me a honorary degree. Just make sure the goddam speech lasts twenty minutes. And I want it by tomorrow." He hung up.

"Dumb bastard English teacher," he said to himself. "He better make me sound good, or he don't get his fifty."

He took off his heavy shell-framed reading glasses and looked up at a hooked nose and a jutting lower lip. Manny the Monk had silently appeared and stood there shifting from foot to foot, acting nervous.

"Where the hell you come from?" Peru said. "You didn't see I was having a private talk?"

"Tessie let me in," Manny said. "I got news for you. I think you ought to hear it right away."

"Hear what?"

"Your nephew Glauco Vastasi wants to knock you off. Figures he should step in and take over."

Peru gave a start. "You shitting me?"

Manny shook his head. "He tried to hire me to do the job. This morning. I says to him, 'Glauco, you don't mean you want to whack Ricky. He's your uncle, ain't he?' 'And he says, 'That old country stuff don't count anymore. The bastard's lived long enough. Put a slug through him.'"

Peru let out a breath. "Yeah. He's been resenting me lately. I could tell. So he has ambitions. I love my sister, but her boy Glauco is a two-timing son of a bitch."

He stood up, clapped Manny on the shoulder. "You're a straight guy, Manny, you come and tell me this. I won't forget you stayed loyal to me."

Manny dipped a hand into a pocket and produced a roll of bills. "This is what Glauco gave me. For a down payment on knocking you off. I don't do it, so maybe it's yours?"

"Keep it. As long as you don't earn it. Fuck, that's chicken feed. You gonna make more, sticking with me. I want Glauco caught and brought to me. I want to talk to him. Then you can give him a little windpipe treatment and I'll give you a couple of grand."

Manny sank into a Hepplewhite chair that swayed under his weight. "If it's all the same to you, boss," he said slowly, "I druther you got somebody else."

"What's the matter? You don't want the job?"

"I don't want to see Glauco again. Getting paid to bump you and not doing it—that's sort of, what you call it, unethical."

"Holy creeps, you going moral on me? All right, all right, I'll call Ryan and Skelly. They ain't fit to wipe your butt, but they ain't done me a job in a long time."

At home that night, Peru took a long time eating his lasagna and fried peppers. At last Tessie, across the table, couldn't stand his silence. "Honey lamb, what's with you tonight? You got nothing to say to me?"

"Sorry, toots. Got a lot on my mind." He waved a hand toward the wine decanter and the houseboy refilled his glass.

Peru was going over his past talks with Vastasi. He should have known this was coming, known it for a long time. At supper he drank too much, then fell asleep on the parlor couch. At eight-thirty he woke up to a phonecall from Cosimo.

"Just want to tell you," Cosimo said. "Willy and the Owl picked up that darky. Your pal Father Knox was with him, so they brought the two of them in to headquarters."

"They had to bring Knox?"

"He knew Willy on sight. He could talk. What you want we do with them?"

"Right now, nothing. Throw 'em someplace, let 'em sleep over. I'll come by in the morning. I want to watch the boys work on Pohl. I want to fix him so he never plays ball again."

"What about Knox?"

"He could be useful. Can you believe it, Coz—our nephew, the sneaking rat, tried to put out a contract on me. That's right. Glauco. I want to give him a Christian burial. A priest just might come in handy."

Fifty-Three

Kidney stew at the nuns' cafeteria hadn't filled them up, and so that night Moon and the Sarge hiked in to Dedwood center for further nourishment. They had arrived at the door of the Grecian Spoon in time to see Knox and Pohl step into the blue Caddy and be driven away.

"Holy Mahoney," the Sarge said. "That looked like a kidnapping."

"The mob," Moon said hollowly. "Come to even up the score with Pohl. And Father Knox. What'll we do?"

"Call the cops. Hey, Aisling Vastasi lives two doors down from here. Over Chong's laundry. Let's see if she's home, use her phone."

They raced upstairs to Aisling's door, and the Sarge thundered on it. Aisling in her bathrobe opened the door sleepily. She didn't invite them in. "Whattaya want?"

"It's the crooks," Moon blurted. "We just saw them kidnap Father Knox and S. T. Pohl."

Aisling was wide awake now. She threw the door open wide. Sitting on her sparse furniture, they spilled their story.

"No use," she said calmly. "No use calling the police. The Dedwood cops won't travel out of town and the State cops are all in Ricky Peru's pocket. I know where they've gone, those hoods. To Newark, to headquarters. And I know how to get there."

Moon digested this. "So what do we do?"

Aisling looked determined. "We go after them."

"You crazy?" said the Sarge. "Unarmed, we take on the mob?"

"Who says we're unarmed?" Aisling said. She raced into the bedroom, rattled open a dresser drawer, and came back brandishing a short-barreled pocket revolver.

"Mother of God," the Sarge said. "A .38 Smith and Wesson. Where did you get that piece?"

Aisling wore a grim smile. "Little souvenir I kept when I left Vastasi."

"OK," the Sarge said, musing, "that's one gun. One against a hundred, against guys that know how to shoot."

"I can shoot too," Aisling said. "And"—displaying long white legs—"I might be able to get us in there before they know we're armed."

The Sarge gave a low whistle. "You might. You got the stuff, all right. Well, what the hell, let's go give it a try."

It sounded to Moon like suicide. "But Sarge," he said, "how are we going to get there? Didn't your flivver give up the ghost?"

The Sarge looked glum. "Yeah, poor old thing just wore out. Best friend I ever had."

"Don't worry," Aisling said quickly. "I've got another souvenir." She took down a ring of keys from a nail on the wall. "We'll take Glauco's convertible. I kept these spare keys in case I'd ever need wheels. He parks at the house on Professors' Row. The car is probably sitting in the driveway. Let me just drop down and get Mabel Chong to babysit for me."

With Aisling at the wheel of the yellow Buick convertible, they charged down Wilson Avenue into the Ironbound section of Newark's East Ward, made two turns, and ended up on a dark street where the wind kept rolling empty bottles and beer cans back and forth. The Latin American Trading Corporation made believe it wasn't there. Its headquarters in an ancient brick warehouse took up half a block. A steel mesh fence surrounded it. No name out front. No windows except in the basement. Two steel-blue Ford pickup trucks stood in the driveway, no company name on them either, but Aisling knew the place on sight.

"I came here once with Glauco," she said, "but he didn't take me inside. We'd better not park in front. It's the kind of car they might notice."

She swung around the corner and pulled up beside a row of three-decker houses in need of paint. A derelict leaning against a streetlight was taking pulls out of a bottle in a paper bag. His rheumy eyes focused on the yellow convertible and he lifted his bottle in salute. A dog, nosing in an overturned trash can, stared at them for a moment, then went back to his meal. They scrambled out.

"You going to lock it?" the Sarge said.

"Yeah," Moon said. "I think that bum is looking for a place to sleep."

But Aisling was already charging off toward the warehouse. They caught up with her.

"You guys need weapons," she said. She stepped to a trash can, grabbed an empty wine bottle, and thrust it at the Sarge. "Take this. In case you want to brain somebody." She stopped, hiked up her skirt, rummaged the top of one black net stocking, and produced a penknife with a three-inch blade. "Here, James," she said.

Moon gulped, accepting the weapon. "I'm supposed to use this?"

"Go for the throat. OK, all ready?"

Walking in single file, they made their way back around the corner and into the driveway to the warehouse, the Sarge first in line, tense, keeping a lookout. In the shadow of the old brick building, Moon let out his breath. No hoods in sight. They rattled basement windows, trying latches one after another until at last a window tilted inward.

The Sarge said, "I'm going in." Feet first, he squirmed through the narrow opening. They heard a thud as he landed.

"OK so far," he called up. "Come on."

Moon wriggled through the window, dropped two yards, and hit a concrete floor. His eyes adjusted slowly to dim light. On every side, crates were stacked, labeled US ARMY PROPERTY. A dartboard nailed to a wooden wall had darts piled on a crate in front of it.

Moon gaped. In the center of the floor, two oblong concrete domes had raised up, each about six feet long and three feet wide. One of the domes had started to split open. A limp human hand was sticking out.

"My God, you guys," Moon cried, "don't step there!"

The Sarge looked down at his feet. "Don't step where?"

"On those bumps in the floor. See that hand? There's a couple of dead guys buried there. They couldn't have been embalmed right. They've puffed up with gas. They could explode."

He remembered his grandmother's account of Mrs. Spritzer, the corpse who blew off her mausoleum's iron door.

"Explode?" the Sarge said. "Shit, I don't believe it."

"I'm telling you, it could happen," Moon said. "I'm a licensed assistant mortician. I ought to know."

Aisling shivered. "Let's get out of here. The mildew in this place is growing whiskers. There's some stairs."

"Let me go ahead," the Sarge said. "Scout for us.'"

Aisling creased her brow. "All right, but let's stick together. Strength in numbers, you know."

Moon had stopped before a half-open door that gave onto a toilet. "Just a minute," he said. "I—I have to go to the bathroom."

The Sarge groaned. "Well, make it snappy."

Moon stepped inside and drew shut the door. The toilet seat was cracked, the bathroom hadn't been cleaned in human memory. The place was lit with a low-watt lightbulb. He seated himself with a sigh.

Seconds later, a strange voice thundered in the basement. "What are you guys doing here?"

And another voice, gruff, said, "Watch out. She's packing."

Moon heard a clunk as if some metal object had been dropped on the basement floor.

"Swatted it out of her hand," the first voice said. "A little lady's piece. Grab it, Rock."

The second man gave a grunt. Moon guessed that the Sarge had slammed him with the wine bottle.

"Drop that," the first man said, "or I'll give it to you."

And Aisling's voice, anxious: "Sarge, do what he says."

A crash as the bottle met the concrete floor.

"You OK, Rock?" The first voice.

"Uh huh."

"Come on, you two," the first voice said grimly. "You're going upstairs."

"Fine," Aisling said. "That's where we want to go."

Footsteps on wooden stairs. Then silence.

Moon wiped, washed his hands with a cake of laundry soap and a trickle from a faucet, and dried them on his shirt. Holy smoke. Aisling and the Sarge were prisoners. His loose bowels had saved him from discovery.

He waited a long time before reopening the door and craning his head outside. At last he stepped out into the deserted basement, trembling from the narrowness of his escape. He sat down heavily on the floor behind a packing crate. He glanced at his watch. Ten-thirty, his regular bedtime. But no, he didn't dare go to sleep. Where had the hoods taken Aisling and the Sarge?

Fifty-Four

Seven o'clock in the morning in Ricky Peru's apartment. Peru lay on his belly, a towel draped over his bottom, while the massage therapist worked on him. The therapist, a wart-faced woman of fifty, kneaded his spine and said, "Am I getting it?"

"A little lower, darling," Peru said. "Yeah. Yeah. That's right. But don't get friendly with me."

The therapist laughed. "Huh! You don't have much left to get friendly with."

"Don't remind me," Peru said. He raised himself up on his elbows. "OK, boys, you think you nailed the son of a bitch?"

Ryan and Skelly, in armchairs watching the therapist work, stood up and snapped to attention.

"We got him, all right," Skelly said. "He was sitting in his car just down the street from headquarters, so we just cruised by and plonked him good. Blew the top of his fucking head off. When we got done you couldn't tell who he was."

The therapist winced, kept working. In all the years she had been massaging Peru's weak back, she had heard things even worse.

Peru scowled. "Whoever you got, it wasn't Glauco."

Ryan said, "The hell. It was him, all right, sitting there in his car. Nobody else has a car like that. Yellow convertible."

"Then explain to me," Peru said, sitting up and riveting them with a glare, "how come Glauco was shacked up last night with Florida Hessi, girl works for Confidential Ass? And how come when she went home Glauco was still walking around?"

Ryan's jaw dropped. "He couldn't still be alive," Skelly said. "Not after what we done to him."

"You dickheads. It wasn't him, I'm telling you. Molly the dispatcher at Confidential called me an hour ago. I knew Glauco was a customer, so I asked her to keep tabs on him. What you got to say about that?"

"Maybe we made a mistake," Skelly said quickly. "Anyway we got his car."

"Yeah, real smart move," Peru said sarcastically. "The worst part is now you bungling bastards have tipped him off. He's gonna know we're after him. This is what I get for hiring a couple of dumb micks. You guys could fuck up a two-car funeral."

"Listen, chief," Ryan said, "we'll put things right. We'll check out his house, his other house, his office, every place. This time he won't get away."

"Yeah? I ought to send the two of you to Jersey City, work for the loan sharks, but I'll give you one more chance. Go find him. Report to me. I want him brought to headquarters. I want to talk to him."

The hoods left. Peru's private phone rang. Cosimo. "Ricky, I got news. That broad Aisling tried to crash headquarters last night, but the troops grabbed her. Her and an old GI was with her."

Peru gave a short laugh. "She must have figured she could beat you up."

"I think she thought she could get Knox and that double-crossing black boy out of there. She had a thirty-eight, but we took it away from her. What you want we should do with them?"

Peru thought. "Maybe it's time Willy took 'em for a ride. But you know, Coz, this is too bad. Because over in Dedwood she has a baby she's still giving titty."

"You want to get rid of the kid too?"

"Cosimo, what kind of a man are you? Throw away a good baby? Didn't you say your wife wants to adopt one?"

"A while ago, she did. But I don't know—"

"Here's your chance. The little kid is yours. Raise her. Give her all the stuff you never had."

Peru slammed the phone down on its hook, convulsed in a laugh. Imagining Cosimo changing diapers.

In his house on campus, Vastasi was having a deep sleep. When the bedside phone jangled, his first impulse was hell, let it ring. But it persisted. He roused himself enough to look at the alarm clock. Quarter to seven. The phone kept on ringing. Christ, who could be calling this early.

"Hullo," he said sleepily.

It was the campus operator. "Mr. Vastasi, I have a call for you from the Police. The man says it's urgent. Shall I put him through to your home number?"

Vastasi snapped awake. "OK, I'll take it."

A man's voice came on. "Mr. Vastasi, Lieutenant Kroll from Essex County Police. You own a 1941 Packard convertible, license plate G-L-A-U-C-O?"

"That's mine."

"We found it in Newark, parked on the street in the Ironbound section. Somebody shot it up. Blew out the window on the driver's side. They drilled some guy sitting in the driver's seat. We figure he was a vagrant known as Benny, happened to climb in the car and took a hit. There's blood all over the upholstery. Quarts of it."

"Aw, Christ."

"You want to come down here and look at it? We got it out in the lot, but we can't keep it here."

"Nah, I don't want to see it. That much blood on the upholstery, a car is finished. Have it towed down to Pete's Auto Parts. I'll tell the adjuster to go look at it."

After he'd hung up, Vastasi started getting cold shakes. A hit, the cop had called it. A hit that must have been intended for him. Peru must have figured things out. Maybe Manny pulled a double-cross and warned him. All of a sudden Vastasi felt himself at the bottom of a deep pit with its walls collapsing.

The phone rang again. It was his wife. She sounded hysterical. She said in Neopolitan Italian, "Glauco, two men from your outfit were just here looking for you. They rang the doorbell till I had to get up out of bed. The one called Ryan and another Irishman. I told them you'd be back tonight."

"The hell you tell them that for? I think they're gunning for me."

"What? I thought they was your friends. Glauco, you done something wrong? Are you in trouble with Ricky Peru?"

"Yeah. Big trouble. Listen, Gemma, I'm going to have to lay low for a few days. Those guys mean business. Maybe they're thinking of bombing the house tonight."

His wife gave a strangled scream.

He went on, "Maybe I'm worried for nothing. Maybe they won't do anything. But listen, just to be on the safe side, you better take the kids and go over to your Mother's for a while. Now don't get your ass in an uproar. Just do it. I'll be in touch."

"Glauco, I don't like this. I've never liked what you do. Can't you find some honest line of work? Hanging out with these killers. All right, I'll go over to Mother's. But if we stay more than two days she's going to want rent."

"So pay her, for Christ's sake. Bring her a nice check when you say hello. And tell her not to blab why you're there, either. Keep the kids inside and off the streets tonight."

His wife finally quieted down, agreeing to do what he'd said. She ended, "Glauco, take care of yourself." That was the most affection Gemma had demonstrated in years. No doubt she was afraid she'd lose a good meal ticket.

He sat on the bed, thoughts whirling. He had to get out in a hurry. But where to go? There was the Monastic House of Saint Joseph's. They took in men for retreats. He toyed with the idea of living in a monk's cell, getting up for Mass at six in the morning, eating food with no salt or sugar. Piss on it. Only thing to do was leave the country. All right, he'd done a lot of favors for the Dominican Republic, getting Trujillo all those guns. Now they could do him one.

He showered, made himself a bloody Mary, dialed Trujillo's embassy in Washington, talked with the purchasing agent. Let the guy think he was still working for Peru.

"Sure, señor," the agent said. "We get you a suite at the Trujillo City Hilton. Anything you want. We welcome you with open arms."

Ryan called Peru's private phone. "He ain't around," he said. "We been to his office, the house in Orange, the one at the college."

"So what did I tell you?" Peru roared. "Creaming his car told him you were after him. Get to the airport. He's gonna show up for a flight to Miami."

Fifty-Five

Rumpled and unshaven, Knox had lost his Roman collar. His shirt hung open at the neck. Willy the Wire escorted him into Peru's office at headquarters. Knox looked at Peru with smoldering eyes.

Peru was sitting at a walnut desk scorched with cigar burns. He sprang to his feet and came forward, hands extended. "Father!" he said, as if greeting a long lost friend. "You all right?"

Knox scowled. "All right as a man who's been kidnapped, kept prisoner, made to sleep in his clothes on an old cot that had bumps in it."

Peru pretended disbelief. "No, no, Father, you ain't a prisoner. The boys shouldn't have brought you here. This was a terrible mistake."

"I'll say it was. What have you done with Pohl?"

"You mean that black boy? The basketball player? Some of the staff just wanted to ask him a few questions. And you, you got to be hungry, Father. Willy, get him some breakfast too."

"Take me to Pohl."

Peru made a soothing gesture. "All in good time. Relax, Father, have some coffee. I'll see if I can find your pal for you."

"This way to the chow hall," Willy said.

Ryan and Skelly hauled a sullen and defeated Glauco Vastasi into Peru's office. On a little TV set with an antenna like a wire carpet-beater, a chef was showing how to make mock creamed chicken using tuna fish. The picture kept slipping, stopping, slipping again.

Leaning forward in his chair, Peru took a drag from his cigar and slowly let out the smoke in Vastasi's face.

"Like you figured," Ryan said. "He was making a run for it. We caught him in a yellow cab almost to Newark Airport. He was taking a lot of suitcases along."

Cosimo stood watching. Peru turned to him. "Cosimo, go through them bags. Never mind the underwear, take out any dough, jewelry, traveler's checks, securities. Glauco boy was going to live on his savings for a while."

"Rinse all the oil off the tuna," the TV chef said. "Mash those canned peas to a smooth, creamy paste."

Vastasi glared. "Sure I was trying to get away. What did you expect? I knew you wanted to whack me. Like you did to somebody sat in my car."

"Our guys goofed. Thought it was you at the wheel, only it was some other bum."

"Uncle Ricky, just let me explain—"

"Explain?" Peru's feet came down to the floor. He leaned forward and slammed his fist on the desk so hard the Varga girl calendar on the wall tilted off center. "Explain to me why you tried to put Manny up to knocking me off. Explain why you thought you had a right to take over."

Vastasi turned his gaze to Manny, slouched against the wall, and fired him a look of hate. Manny smiled with just the corners of his mouth.

"Believe me, Uncle Ricky," Vastasi said, "I went nuts for a minute, but all that's behind me now."

Peru said, "Everything's gonna be behind you now."

On TV, the chef was saying, "Can you believe this, viewers? A princely main dish for a family of four, and only fifty-six cents."

Vastasi was sweating. "Listen, Uncle Ricky, I'll take an oath of loyalty. You can't put me away. I'm family. You need me. Need me to run the war surplus business."

"You think so? I need you like I need another asshole. You disappoint me, nephew. I trusted you. I was going to promote you to underboss. What good is it you take an oath? You took an oath once, and it didn't mean nothing to you."

Vastasi's chin sagged. He looked ready to topple. Ryan kicked him from behind. "Stand up straight. Ricky ain't done with you."

Peru put his face up next to Vastasi's. "You busted your oath. The one you took in blood. You tried to get rid of me. Sorry, nephew, but family don't count no more. You don't count no more. I don't want to keep you around."

Knox hadn't had such rotten coffee since he had got out of the Navy. But sitting at a card table in a room cluttered with old comic books and Doc Savage pulps, he drank two cups of it with creamer powder and ate a stale Danish out of a box. On the other side of the table, Willy the Wire sat chain-smoking, silent, keeping an eye on him.

Knox said, "Will, you're a decent guy. What are you doing working for this bunch of scum?"

Willy spewed smoke. "It pays," he said.

"You know, if you turn yourself over to the FBI, I think they'd go easy on you. You could give them plenty of help."

Willy forced a laugh. "What would I want to do that for? I like it outside the pen."

"You saved my life one time. I know an FBI man, Burke, old friend of mine. I could put in a word for you."

"Forget it, Father," Willy said.

"By the way," Knox said, "you know what they've done with S. T. Pohl?"

"Nope."

"Peru promised to find him for me."

Willy's eyes narrowed. "Dead or alive?"

Peru strode in, Cosimo close behind him.

"Sorry to keep you waiting, Father," he said. "Had a little business to tend to. You get fed?"

"Where's Pohl?" Knox said.

"We've had to keep him for a little while. But just like you, he'll be leaving here soon."

"Peru, you harm one hair of that boy so help me, I'll—"

"Knock it off, Father. I got to ask you one small favor, though, before I turn you loose."

"What's that?"

"To do a little priest duty. You know how to give the last rites?"

"Sure. Somebody sick?"

"Somebody's dead."

"Peru, the last rites are for the sick and the dying. Not for the dead."

Peru shrugged. "So what can you do for a corpse? A relative of mine. I want to see he gets a Christian burial."

"Well, call a funeral home. They can arrange for a service."

Peru frowned. "I don't want nothing formal. This is just a little family affair. He's got to be buried right away. Quiet, like. Can't you do something?"

Knox considered. Maybe he'd go along with this, find out what had happened. "Sure," he said. "I could say Mass for the dead."

"That sounds good. Can you do it right here?"

"In this warehouse? How about bringing this corpse of yours to the college chapel?"

Peru shook his head no. "There ain't no time for that. Suppose you just say a few prayers before we bury him."

Knox sighed. "All right. I can do that."

Peru turned to Cosimo. "OK, Coz. Bring him in."

Cosimo went out and came back with Ryan and Skelly carrying a board with a large body on it. They set it down in the middle of the room.

The corpse wore a business suit, a black felt hat tugged down over the eyes. Its heavy bulk looked familiar.

Knox went over and whipped the hat off the corpse's head. A round red hole had pierced the forehead, the skin around it burned black. Blood had coagulated. A fragment of skull stuck to the lining of the hat.

Knox made the sign of the cross. He said, "This is Glauco Vastasi. Somebody put a bullet through his head."

Peru let out a snarl like an angry cat. "This ain't none of your business, Padre. Start praying."

Knox dropped to his knees beside the board. For five minutes he prayed silently. He couldn't grieve, but he prayed for Vastasi's soul. Prayed for a measure of forgiveness.

Peru glanced at Cosimo. "Take off your hat, goddammit. Act respectful."

At last Knox stood up again. "OK," he said, "there's your favor. Now you can let me and Pohl out of here."

"Sorry, Padre," Peru said. "Too bad you had to get curious. We can't let you go running around telling stories. You micks, tie him up. So he don't try no ju jitsu stuff."

Cosimo held Knox in a hammerlock while Ryan and Skelly bound his wrists and ankles with cord. Knox didn't say anything. Just looked at Peru with clenched jaw and furious eyes.

Peru inspected the binding job. "OK, take him some place so's he can simmer down. Till his ride is ready for him."

Cosimo said, "How about we throw him in the closet? With the broad?"

Peru thought that was hilarious. "Yeah! Throw him in with that sex pot and he's all tied up and can't do anything about it. That ought to drive him nuts. Well, so long, Father. Been nice knowing you. You got to excuse me, I got to go home and practice my speech. Which I'll be giving tomorrow at your school commencement. When I get me a honorary degree."

Fifty-Six

Moon spent the night in the basement, chilled to the bone, his back against a crate. Laying plans of action, discarding them, losing his courage every time he heard footsteps overhead.

When the light of dawn began to squeeze through a dirty window, two guys came down the stairs. Then Moon heard the clunk of a pick and shovel, pounding the basement floor.

"Hell of a place to be buried," one voice said.

The other guy snorted. "Don't matter. Not to anybody that's dead."

Thunk. Thunk.

"I don't like this," the first guy said. "My old lady didn't raise me to be no gravedigger. This place gives me the creeps."

"Well then hurry up. Hey, look at the Ciardi brothers. Them bumps in the floor. They're getting bigger. Blowing up like a couple of fucking balloons."

"Think we should tell Ricky?"

"He should care? He said make a new grave, that's all we gotta do."

Moon sneaked a look around the side of the packing crate. Two heavyset guys were crouched over a fresh crevice in the floor. One of them was swinging a pick, the other shoveling chunks of broken concrete into a barrel.

"That's deep enough."

"Yeah. That's as good as better."

"Good enough for a rat like Vastasi. You hear what he done? Tried to put out a contract on Ricky. But the Monk wouldn't cooperate."

"Dumb bastard. He might of known you can't fox Ricky Peru. OK, his space is ready for him. Let's go bring him down."

They dropped pick and shovel and stomped upstairs.

Moon let out his breath. Had he heard right? The hoods were digging a grave for Vastasi? He stepped out from behind the crate. Now a six-foot trench gaped open in the basement floor.

Lord, he had to get a move on. People needed rescuing. For a moment he felt a stab of self-doubt. His gaze searched the basement, took in a door in the far wall. He went over to it and stood listening. Couldn't hear anything. Gingerly, he twisted the knob.

Another flight of stairs, narrower, led upward. To where? Only one way to find out. Quietly placing one foot in front of the other, he climbed. It was dark and he couldn't see where he was going, but when there weren't any more stairs to climb, he came to another closed door. From beyond it he heard mumbling, somebody talking to himself.

A familiar voice said, "Muthafucka, we sure messed up."

Moon flung open the door. Scrotum Pohl was seated wrong way around on a wooden chair with clothesline binding him. Slumped on the chair next to him, also bound, was the Sarge.

Pohl stared in disbelief. "Moon, baby! That really you? You ain't a mirage?"

"It's me," Moon said with a grin. "Been tied up long?"

"All night. Leastwise, I think it's morning. You can't tell time in this place, it ain't got windows. They coming back for us, and what they fixing to do to us, I don't know."

"Get us loose, will you?" the Sarge said. "My fucking back is ready to snap."

"Right," Moon said. With the penknife Aisling had given him, he sliced through their ropes. Pohl stood up, working the kinks out of his cramped arms and legs. He gave Moon a hug. The Sarge stamped about to get his circulation going. He said, "Moon, man, for once you look good to me."

"Where's Aisling?" Moon asked. "And Father Knox?"

"They threw her in a closet," the Sarge said. "Father Knox—I don't know what they did with him. So where you been all this while? In the crapper?"

Moon filled them in. "Oh oh," he said. "What's that?"

Outside the room, footsteps were clumping down the corridor, drawing near.

Knox couldn't walk with his ankles tied, so Ryan and Skelly carried him out of the room like a sack of potatoes. They opened a closet door in the hall and tossed him inside and slammed the door. A key twisted in the lock.

Helpless, Knox staggered backward, lost his balance and landed on a soft body lying on the floor.

"Father!" Aisling cried. "Is it you?"

"You were expecting somebody else?" Knox said, rolling over and sitting up.

Weak light came from a tiny lightbulb overhead, crackling as if ready to expire. Knox did a double take. My God, the woman was naked as a jaybird.

Aisling crushed herself against him in a passionate hug. She clung to him, emitting sobs. "Oh, Father, Father, I'm glad to see you. I was afraid they'd murdered you! I'm scared. They're going to kill us. Hold me, Father, hold me tight."

"I can't," Knox said, "my hands are tied. What happened to your clothes?"

"It's roasting hot in here. I've been locked in this steam cabinet all night."

He tried not to look at her. "How did you get here? To headquarters?"

"Gogarty and the Sarge saw you kidnapped. So the two of them and me, we came to find you."

"And you found me. And a hell of a find I am. You seen anything of Pohl?"

"No."

"Gogarty and the Sarge. What happened to them?"

"I don't know. When the Sarge and I were caught, Gogarty had gone to the toilet."

"Then maybe he's still at large. Although if he's any good to us I'll be surprised. By the way, honey, I hate to tell you this, but you might as well know. You're a widow as of this morning."

"Glauco? They killed Glauco?"

"Peru had me say some prayers over his body. They shot him. Don't ask me why."

"Poor Glauco," Aisling said. "He was a mean son of a bitch. But he wasn't all bad, sometimes. Anyway, I'm not a widow. We weren't ever married."

"No fooling," Knox said in surprise. "What about your child?"

"A lovely souvenir from the war. Glauco had other kids with his real wife."

They fell silent. Knox started praying. He called on Saint Expeditus, patron of lost causes. Send help. Plenty of it, on the double. And for Christ's sake cool this place off so this woman will put her clothes back on. Damn, he was hurting. The cords on his ankles and wrists were chafing.

He said, "Listen, can you reach around and work your hand into my back pocket? Get my lighter out?"

"All right. Just a minute. OK, I've got the lighter. Oops. Dropped it."

"It bounced off of my shoe. It's on the floor."

She squirmed in the semi-dark, the nipples of her breasts inches from his face. "Here it is," she said at last.

"Flick it on, will you?"

Aisling got a tiny flame going. Knox blinked at her through the faint glow. God, what tits. "OK," he said, "burn through the cords on my wrists."

"I'll try. But it's hard to see in here."

She pressed the flame to the cords that bound his hands. Putrid smoke filled the closet.

"Don't set me on fire," Knox said. Flame licked his wrists. "A—little—more!" He tugged against the cords. Gritted his teeth and strained. Kept straining. With a faint snap, the cords gave.

"Did I burn you?" Aisling asked.

"Nothing serious." He rubbed his wrists. "Here, give me the lighter. I'll work on my ankles." In a moment, his feet were free.

"Now," he said, "somebody sometime has to open the door. When they do, I'll hold my hands behind my back like they're still tied. All we have to do is wait."

"Oh, Father," she said. "I love you."

"Let's not start that again."

Overhead, the dying light bulb gave one last sizzle. The closet went dark. Aisling clamped her body against him. Her hand stole down and slowly unbuttoned his fly.

"Hey, knock that off," Knox said, wriggling aside.

Holy Moe. She was reaching into his pants. Rummaging around for his member. Finding it. Making low purrings. He wanted to shove her away, dammit, wanted to keep himself chaste—

Then all of a sudden that wasn't what he wanted at all.

Down in the basement, Moon tugged Pohl and the Sarge in behind a stack of U.S. ARMY crates. "We can't stay here long," he said. "When they find you guys gone they'll be looking for us."

Pohl's eyes were wide. "Where you figure we can go to?"

"Maybe out through that basement window. Hold on—somebody's coming. Stay back!"

The two hoods were struggling down the staircase, bent over, carrying weight. A dead man on a board. The corpse's arms dangled at his sides, bumping against each step. They stepped out into the basement and dropped their burden to the floor. The head of the corpse turned to one side.

"My gosh," Moon whispered. "That's Mister Vastasi."

An electric space heater sat next to the Ciardi brothers' dome-like graves. A hood switched it on and its wires turned red. "That'll take the chill off. Throw him in and let's finish the job."

They flipped over the board and Vastasi's body rolled off into the freshly dug trench in the floor, landing face down. "Looka that," the second hood said. "He just fits."

"We got to cover him up. Start mixing cement," the first hood said.

"You get a pail of water. Mix it in that washtub. Make him a nice blanket."

"Jesus, Ryan, we shoulda been undertakers."

They worked in silence, mixing, stirring. Moon and Pohl crouched in back of the crates, hardly daring to breathe.

The first hood said, "You think we'll have to bury that priest? Bad luck to kill a priest, they say."

"Whatsa matter? You superstitious? Naw, I heard Ricky's planning another way to get rid of him. Willy's gonna take him and the broad for a car ride. The car catches fire and it looks like an accident."

"Gimme the board," said the first. "Smooth out that wet crap. Like icing a cake. Make him look like he's part of the floor."

At last they straightened up. "So long, Glauco," the first hood said. "Rest in fucking peace."

They clumped back upstairs.

Moon let out his breath. He sidled out from behind the crates. On an irresistible impulse, he stooped down to the fresh concrete of Vastasi's grave and with a finger drew his initials. *J. G.*

The Sarge glared at him. "Ain't you scared doing that, Moon? You want Vastasi to come back and haunt you?"

"Yeah," Pohl said. "He gonna show up in a bedsheet and ream your ass."

Moon was staring at the graves of the Ciardi brothers. He could swear that the two domes had bloated a few inches higher than they were an hour ago.

Fifty-Seven

Moon clapped his hands. "I've got it! We blow up the Ciardi brothers. Those two bumps in the floor."

"You smoking weed, man," Pohl said. "All they is is a couple of stiffs."

Moon shook his head. "Listen, there's a lot of force locked up in them. Believe me, I'm an apprentice mortician. Those domes are bombs ready to blow."

"No crap," the Sarge said. "You think so?"

Moon drew himself up with dignity. "I know it. Those bodies swelled up because they weren't embalmed. We'll detonate them. We'll distract the hoods and get some time to locate Aisling and Father Knox."

The Sarge looked skeptical. "Play fireworks? With dead bodies?"

"Yeah, that don't sound too good, man," Pohl said. "We gonna blow up ourselves?"

"No way," Moon said, putting on more confidence than he felt. "It'll be perfectly safe. We'll keep down behind these crates. Those domes will explode, all right. All we need is something to puncture them."

He scanned the basement, looking for an instrument. Trash everywhere. Empty beer bottles. Old magazines. A stack of loose bricks against the nearest wall.

"Pohl," Moon said, "you've got great aim. How about you grab one of those bricks and pitch it at that closer dome? Hard as you can, hit it dead center?"

Pohl shrugged. He picked up a brick. Took aim and launched a perfect shot. The brick landed, rolled, came to a stop. They crouched down behind the crates, Moon holding his ears. Moments went by. A full minute. No blast.

Moon was tempted to look. Just as he was about to poke his head up over the crates, there was an ear-wrenching crack and the roof of the dome split wide. The buried corpse erupted with a BOOM that trembled the basement walls.

The blast had broken open the second dome. There was another tremendous blast. Fragments of cement flew all over the basement. Moon could hear the snapping of wooden beams, window glass tinkling to the floor. He gave a shout of triumph. "It worked!"

The Sarge was gasping for breath. "Yeah, and I think that space heater fell over and started a fire."

The basement had filled with smoke and a stomach-turning stench.

Pohl said, "Damn. I can't see nothing."

Moon tugged him by the arm. "Over here. Up the staircase."

Blinded by smoke, his nostrils burning, he groped for a doorknob, closed fingers on it. The door had come off its hinges and he had to tug it open. He placed one foot on a step and found that the wooden staircase had tilted crazily.

The staircase groaned under their weight. Bracing themselves against narrow walls, they made it to the top and stepped out into the room where Pohl and the Sarge had been tied. Plaster was dropping from the ceiling. Floorboards sagged. Wisps of smoke filled the room. Outside in the corridor Moon could hear running feet, yells, torrents of excited Sicilian. The explosions had worked. Hoods were charging down to the basement. Then it was quiet, except for the crackle of flames.

They charged down the corridor, and as they passed a closet the Sarge stopped. "Hey," he said, "weren't they going to throw Aisling in a closet? We ought to look in every one of 'em."

He rattled the closet doorknob. Locked.

"Damn," he said. "There's funny noises coming out of there."

They listened. A woman's voice saying, "O Father—Father—-ather—ather—ahh-h-h-hther—-ahhh!"

"My God, that sounds like Aisling," the Sarge said.

"Yeah," Pohl said. "That's the kind of noise she do make."

"Hello in there!" Moon shouted. "The place is on fire! We've come to rescue you!"

"Just a minute," came the muffled voice of a man. "Don't rescue us yet."

Someone was scuffling around inside the closet, as if collecting clothes off the floor. The Sarge had brought along a weapon—a shovel left by the gravediggers. Now he inserted its blade between the door and its jamb and leaned on the handle. The lock snapped. The door sprang open and by light streaming into the closet they could make out two figures. Aisling wearing Knox's shirt, Knox wearing only his pants.

"Muthafucka," Pohl exclaimed. "Ain't no man alive she can't get."

Knox stepped out, barefoot, and confronted his rescuers with a scowl. "No wisecracks," he said.

"I didn't say nothing," Pohl said.

Aisling followed Knox out into the corridor, looking sleepy. She smiled wanly at her rescuers. "Don't believe what you're thinking," she said. "It was hot in there."

Moon gulped. "It's going to get a lot hotter. The building is burning like tinder. Come on, we've got to run!"

Another form shouldered through the smoke and a new voice barked, "You ain't going noplace. Don't move."

Harrigan. Brandishing a sawed-off shotgun.

"Randy Harrigan," Aisling said, "you can't keep us here. We're all going to die if we don't get out of this building."

Harrigan gestured with the shotgun, threatening. Smoke was seeping up through the floorboards, wrapping around him like a wreath. He said, "Don't move, I tell you. You're still prisoners. And I'm keeping you right here till we get this fire put out."

Out of the smoke swam the face of Willy the Wire. "Put that rod down," Willy said. "Let them pass. I'm taking charge of them." .

"Oh, yeah," Harrigan said. "You're going to see to them? Take 'em for a little car ride? I heard about that."

"That's right," Willy said. "Hand me that gun. I can use it to prod them out of here."

Harrigan surrendered his shotgun. "I'll go find Cosimo," he said. "Tell him what's going on."

"Don't bother," Willy said. "A piece of the roof fell in on him. Get out of here, save your skin. Nobody's putting out this fire. It's got too good a start."

All about them timbers were snapping, as if some hungry giant were popping corn.

Harrigan whirled, started to run down the corridor. A hole six feet wide had yawned in the floor. Blinded by smoke, Harrigan stepped into it. He gave a scream as he toppled into the basement holocaust. Lances of fire shot up from the hole. He was gone.

Knox crossed himself. "OK, Willy. Take us out of here."

"This way," Willy said with a wave of the shotgun.

Knox was calculating. Another kind of death that had been planned for them, and Willy was leading them to it. At the right moment he'd have to overcome Willy with a quick attack.

Willy urged them along the corridor. "Come on, step lively, all of you. And watch out for spaces in the floor."

Outside, fire sirens were screaming. One soldier was still posted by the door out to the parking lot.

"It's OK, Barney," Willy told the sentinel. "I got them. I'm taking them to that old Packard stationwagon."

"Right, Will. Gonna give 'em their last ride, huh? I'm leaving, myself. This heat is killing me. I see Cosimo, I'll tell him you followed orders."

"You do that," Willy said.

Four Newark fire engines had pulled into the parking lot and firemen were tugging out hoses and unfolding them. A colossal torch of flame soared through the warehouse roof. More torches were shooting from every basement window. Moon heard a fireman tell the chief, "Chief, we gotta have more engines. You know who this place belongs to? Ricky Peru."

"Don't matter," the Chief shouted back. "The place is a goner. There's no going in to it now."

Willy waved them into the stationwagon. Knox tensed, ready to throw a karate chop. But Willy was grinning. "Relax, Father," he said. "I'm on your side."

"Since when?" Knox wanted to know.

"Since all along. Been working for the FBI."

"Well I'll be damned," Knox said.

Willy eased into the driver's seat, turned around and grinned again. "Where to?" he said.

"Back to campus," Knox said. "We've got a commencement to go to in the morning. Unless this car blows up, that is."

"It won't," Willy said. I was supposed to rig it, but I never got around to it."

"Thanks," Knox said. "If you report back to Peru, he's not going to like you anymore."

"Who needs to report," Willy said. "I'm out of a job, starting now."

He threw the car into gear and they rolled out into the street past a gaggle of curious onlookers. The roar of the fire had grown deafening. Somehow it sounded to Moon like the roar of a crowd.

Fifty-Eight

It was a puny commencement, held early to get it over with. On this twenty-fourth of May, the class of 1947 consisted of twelve wartime draft-evaders and one veteran who had joined the army in his junior year. Folding chairs were ranged on the grass under the flowering pear trees in front of a foot-high wooden platform that held armchairs and a lectern with a microphone on it. A sparse crowd of relatives had assembled, togged in their Sunday best. The day was warm, and the men had taken off their neckties and undone their collars and some of the women had surreptitiously peeled their stockings off.

Federal agents Kevin Burke and Gus Munzenrider, gunbelts slung low under their jackets, took seats in the third row on the aisle. "Good spot," Burke said. "We can get up there quick when we need to grab him."

Munzenrider said, ""You think we'll have to do it in front of the people?"

"Let's see what happens," Burke said. "If we can take him on the quiet, all the better."

A pot-bellied man straddling a chair next to Burke tried to strike up a conversation. "You got a son graduating?"

"Can't say I do," Burke said. "I came to hear the speaker, Mr. Peruccese."

"Is that right. First time I ever heard of anybody coming to a commencement that didn't have to."

The Prep School band struck up a quavering "Pomp and Circumstance" and the short procession stepped off. First came senile old Archbishop Reagan in his white-and-gold robes and towering hat, using his crosier to help himself along. Monsignor O'Malley followed, his scarlet cape traded for an ermine-trimmed academic gown. The president helped the archbishop up onto the platform and sat him down, then strode to the lectern and stood beaming while the rest of the procession dawdled in. Next came two dignitaries slated to receive honorary degrees: short, stocky Generalissimo Rafael Leonidas Trujillo Molina, president of the Dominican Republic, looking stern, resplendent in his braided and bemedaled uniform, and Ricky Peru, his froglike body hidden under his gown, smiling complacently, having a hard time keeping his mortarboard from pitching off his head.

"Who are those two bozos with Trujillo?" Munzenrider wanted to know.

"Bodyguards," Burke said. "He won't show his face in public without 'em, so the college had to rig 'em up in gowns so they'll look academic."

Peru and Trujillo took seats. The bodyguards squeezed into armchairs flanking the dictator, their massive bulks dwarfing him, and glared out over the crowd, scanning for assassins. Then a small band of conscripted faculty filed into the first row, and the tiny graduating class sidled into the second.

With a gesture of majesty, President O'Malley shut off the band.

"Archbishop Reagan," he began, "colleagues, distinguished honorees, members of the class of 1947, ladies and gentlemen. I hereby declare the eighty-eighth commencement of the College of Saint Cassian of Imola to be open."

After asking the Almighty to bless the graduates and their families, the president exulted over the rapid expansion of the college. In one year, its student body had increased from thirteen souls to four thousand five hundred. Next year Saint Cassian's would become a university by incorporating Mortification College from nearby Kearny and St. Simeon Stylites School of Architecture from Jersey City.

Then he introduced that loyal friend of the college, the generous philanthropist Ricco Peruccese, son of humble immigrants, who by his virtues had risen to the helm of the Latin American Trading Corporation. Mr. Peruccese would deliver the commencement address.

"Dear God," Dame Millicent Feeley said in a shrill voice that carried far, "I hope he won't run on forever."

Peru took off his mortarboard, laid it on his chair and strode to the microphone, beaming from ear to ear. He clutched his speech, "The Role of Capitalist Democracy in the Western World," lowered the microphone to his mouth, and started to intone, stumbling over the longer words. Washington and Jefferson had been apostles of freedom, even though they owned slaves. They were the first American capitalists. America must stride forward on all four wheels, turning both her faces—friendly and competitive—to the world. The audience fanned themselves with their programs, shifting buttocks from side to side on the hard steel chairs.

"This guy is deadly," Munzenrider said under his breath. "Should we pinch him now and spare everybody the rest of this?"

"Not yet," Burke said. "Maybe when they're giving out diplomas."

At first, his gaze fastened on his script, Peru didn't notice five latecomers walk in. They didn't take seats, just stood before him in the center aisle. A priest. A gorgeous redhead. A grizzled veteran. A lanky kid. A tall black basketball player.

"To have a vi—viable democracy, a nation must have people," Peru told the microphone.

Knox's voice rang out, so loud it could be heard in the last row. "Can it, Peru. When it comes to democracy you don't know squat."

Peru looked up, his jaw working on his next long word. He stared at the five apparitions. His speech slipped from his fingers and fell to the platform. Loose pages scattered in the breeze.

Monsignor O'Malley sprang from his chair. "Father Knox," he boomed, "can you not respect these ceremonies?"

"Sorry, your grace," Knox said, "but I can't respect a murdering kidnapper."

Peru whirled toward the president. "Gimme that degree, goddammit. I'm not staying here to be insulted."

Now Kevin Burke was on his feet, hauling out his service revolver, holding it steady, trained on Peru. "Halt right there, Peruccese. You're under arrest on charges of conspiracy."

Things happened fast. In the dim minds of General Trujillo's two bodyguards, a single fact loomed. Someone was taking aim at the platform where their boss sat. In an instant they had whipped their Lugers from under their black gowns and were firing out into the audience. The first slug caught Burke in the right shoulder. He staggered back, his own gun flying from his hand. The second slug clanged into the folding chair next to him, dumping the pot-bellied parent onto the grass. Munzenrider dropped to a crouch, working his own gun. The first bodyguard toppled backward as if kicked, a flower of blood opening in one thigh.

The second bodyguard didn't have time to respond. Knox sprang to the platform, thrust arms beneath his armpits, drew the man to his feet, and flipped him head-first into the center aisle. The bodyguard thumped to the ground and lay stunned. Aisling and the Sarge flung themselves on the fallen man's back and tried to hold him, but he threw them off and scrambled back to his feet, his Luger drawn. From behind him S. T. Pohl swung a folding chair. The chair crunched down on the man's skull. He grunted and collapsed. Dame Millicent Feeley minced over to his inert form and began kicking him with a pointed shoe. "Nasty brute!" she cried.

On the platform, Generalissimo Trujillo, in high excitement, had grabbed the Luger from his first bodyguard. He got off a shot that went wild. The bullet skittered through the audience, creasing the grass like a snake. Women shrieked. Men swore. A little girl laughed in delight.

Knox was still standing on the platform. He swatted the gun from Trujillo's hand and decked the generalissimo with a quick rabbit-punch. Trujillo lay sprawled on his back, medals jingling on his chest.

All of a sudden Knox felt like slumping into in Trujillo's vacated armchair. Why not do it, he decided. And he did.

The graduating seniors had scattered like rats, some flinging themselves to the ground, one curled in a fetal position. Relatives were running for their lives. Women in long summer gowns and high heels stumbled away. On the platform Monsignor O'Malley stood as if paralyzed. Beside him, the old archbishop was on his feet, clapping his hands, bleating, "Stop! Highly improper! Stop this disturbance at once!" The bandleader told his Prep School musicians to play, damn it, play. Bravely, they struck up a chorus of "Holy God, We Praise Thy Name." Only one graduating senior was left still sitting. The army veteran. He lifted his voice over the shouts of the crowd—"So when do we get our degrees?"

Knox and Munzenrider were at Burke's side, Munzenrider pressing his torn-off shirt against Burke's bleeding shoulder.

Knox said, "Kevin, dammit, how bad did he nail you?"

"Just winged me," Burke said through gritted teeth. "How's Trujillo's bodyguard?"

"Alive, but out of commission. Walsh is phoning for an ambulance. And the coroner."

Gunsmoke drifted between pear trees in bloom. The pot-bellied parent was still sitting on the grass where the bullet had dumped him out of his chair. "Be damned," he observed to no one in particular. "My tenth kid to graduate from college and this is the first commencement I ever enjoyed."

In the confusion, Ricky Peru had slipped away.

Fifty-Nine

Nowadays the door to the president's office in Feeley Mansion stood open wide, as if to signify a new policy. In his expensive double-breasted suit, Borcellino Panama hat in place, Cross strode in. Maureen glanced up from her desk. The big portly guy looked like a banker.

"I must see the president," Cross said. "I'm an old friend of his. I want to congratulate him on becoming president of the college."

Maureen smiled. "You're in luck. He'll be off the phone in a minute. Who shall I say is calling?"

"Don't say. I want to surprise him."

When Cross entered the inner office, Knox blinked up at him and started reaching into his desk for his gun. But Cross pulled out a Webley service revolver.

"I wouldn't try that," he said. He whipped off his hat, showing his tonsure. "Don't you know who I am? It's time you recognized me."

The man's black hair had lost its dye and had turned blond. The round owlish glasses were gone. Knox stared. He remembered.

"Shawcross," Knox said. "Lieutenant junior grade. The one who got busted and sent to the brig. So it's you. You've gained weight. And what happened to that big beak you had? "

"Rhinoplasty. Prosthetic surgery."

"No wonder I didn't know you. But the last I heard, you were going to do seven years in Portsmouth Naval Prison. Nobody escapes from there."

"I never got there. Two men were escorting me, but they happened to die. You had me court-martialed. You ruined my naval career. You had no right to."

"Somebody had a right. You bought cocaine, opium, heroin in Tacloban when the cruiser Willy Bee went in for repairs. Back then in the Philippines, that stuff was cheap. You were going to make a mint. Only you couldn't resist selling it on board. To the gunnery officer who fired the six-inch guns just to hear the bang. To that poor coked-up kid who went for a swim at sea, dived off the fantail and was never found. And you resented me for blowing the whistle on you?"

"Oh, I had months to resent you, when I was a fugitive. Months to plan my revenge while I was hiding, living in flophouses, panhandling. Until I forged myself a new life."

"As Cross the new Messiah. How'd you ever pull it off?"

"Living on the Bowery, I met others ready to swallow my message. That I had the key to heaven. All they had to do was work for me and follow my commands."

"I see. So your Church of the One Right Path is just a way to get you money and power. Slave labor."

"Exactly. You see, I couldn't let on to my followers that I was after revenge. I had to give them idealistic reasons for wanting you out of the way."

Knox gave a low whistle. "Then all that garbage about hating basketball was just a line."

"That's right. But now, President Knox, you're at the end of the line yourself. On your feet!"

Slowly, Knox got up and stood facing his executioner. "I don't get it, Shawcross. Why let me know who you are?"

Shawcross raised the revolver. "Oh, I didn't want you to die without remembering. My revenge wouldn't have been complete."

With the muzzle of the gun aimed straight at him, Knox looked about desperately for some missile he could hurl. There wasn't any. He began to say a silent prayer. The finger on the trigger started to squeeze.

BLAM.

Gunfire rattled the windows.

BLAM.

Another shot, this time from Shawcross's gun. It missed Knox and tore a hole in the ceiling over his head.

Knox's jaw dropped in surprise. Shawcross had staggered, his face twisted. His knees caved under him. He fell. His revolver clunked to the floor.

Maureen stood in the office doorway, pale and trembling, tears streaking her face. She was holding a pocket revolver. A wisp of smoke drifted from its barrel.

Knox bent over the inert form on the carpet. It lay face down. The back of its skull had been shattered. Blood trickled down over one ear. Knox turned it over. Shawcross wasn't breathing anymore.

Maureen's lips quivered. "Is he—dead?"

Knox looked up at her with admiration. "Dead as they come. You got him, honey. With just one shot."

"I—I didn't want to do it, Father."

"He would have killed me. My God, your timing was perfect. If you hadn't come in just then—"

"I knew I had to. Good thing you turned on your intercom. I could hear everything."

"How come you're packing that weapon?"

"So I won't be raped. My neighborhood in Harrison has gone downhill. All sorts of characters hanging around. Can't a girl carry something to defend her?"

"All right by me," Knox said. "Hey, I think I want to sit down."

Maureen stared at the body on the carpet. "I'm going to call the police. They won't do anything to me, will they?"

"They ought to give you a medal," Knox said. "For catching an escaped prisoner and a murderer. Me, I'd give you a big wet kiss if you weren't such a nunny type."

In sunglasses, his belly spilling down over the waistband of his swimming trunks, Ricky Peru lay stretched out on a deck chair on the terrace of a suite at the Hilton in Ciudad Trujillo. A tall glass appeared at his elbow, pineapple and cherries floating in it. He stared at it coldly. "What the hell is this?"

"Ees the Trujillo City Special, señor," the waiter said. "Weeth compliments of the management."

"Take it away and bring me a real drink. You got any Jack Daniel's? No water and not too damn much ice." Peru turned to Tessie. "Hey, sweetheart, you want anything?"

Tessie, sprawling in the deck chair beside him, shifted her lumpy body. "Just bring me a Coke," she said, not raising her head. "Nothing in it. I need a stomach-settler." When the waiter had gone, she said, "Jaysus, I feel awful. I'm still sick from yesterday. That ricketty little plane you hired to fly us from Miami. The lousy thing kept rocking and bumping all the way."

"Well we got here, didn't we?"

In sullen quiet, they soaked up sun. Peru gazed out across the battlements of the giant prison next to the waterfront. Political prisoners, allowed their morning strolls, were pacing up and down along a catwalk on top of one high wall.

"Lousy room service," Peru said. "Why don't Italy have an island in the Caribbean? Hey, I had a visitor this morning. Trujillo's number one flunky. Brought us an invite to a reception next Wednesday at the Presidential Palace."

Tessie gave a strangled gasp. "And I don't have nothing to wear but the dress I came in!"

"Get the concierge to call you a dressmaker. Bring samples, take your measurements, do a rush job."

"Maybe I'll look in on that shop in the lobby," Tessie mused. "Only I don't think what they got is good enough."

Peru grunted. "Buy what you want. I got to get me a white tux."

"When I think of the things I had to leave behind— Christ, it makes me sick. My white mink coat! And my Hepplewhite chair and a original Norman Rockwell."

"Most of that crap you're better off without. Anyhow I don't know if we're staying in this country for keeps. Ought to look at Cuba. Or Colombia, check out the hash business. We got enough dough, we do what we want. You brought that satchel, didn't you?"

"What satchel?"

"What satchel? Jesus, woman! The one full of treasury bonds. You didn't leave that behind, did you?"

"I told you. I couldn't bring nothing."

Peru slapped her across her face. "You stupid cow. This means we're broke. We're selling your rings and necklaces in the morning."

Tessie was sobbing. "You bastard. You think you're so smart. You had to lug along your silly honorary degree."

"Damn right I did. That thing is the high point of my career."

He craned his neck and gazed back into the shaded hotel room, letting his eyes feast on the big framed diploma propped on the writing table. It was written in Latin, but he knew just what it said.

Know all men that because of his outstanding service to his community the College of Saint Cassian of Immola has conferred on Ricco Francis Peruccese the degree of Doctor of Moral Theology.

The buzzer sounded. Peru grunted. Laboriously he got to his feet and opened the door.

It wasn't the waiter. It was a mustached functionary in a military uniform with gold epaulets and a hat loaded with brass. He had two soldiers with him, carrying war surplus rifles. The three of them marched in.

"Hullo, Señor Flores," Peru said, beaming. "You come for an answer to that invite? Sure, Tessie and me, we'll be there."

Flores wore a deep scowl. "There is no invitation," he said.

"The hell you say. You just brought it this morning."

"The reception for you is no more. Generalissimo Trujillo returned from America an hour ago. He is not pleased."

"Go on. You're kidding. The General ought to be grateful to me, getting him an honorary degree and all."

"The General is not pleased," Flores said again. "You arrange he go to America and receive honor. He get humiliation."

"Oh, you mean when that priest hit him and knocked him down? He can't blame *me* for that."

"You arrange his trip. You arrange everything." He snapped his fingers and the two soldiers stepped forward. Each grabbed Peru by an arm.

"Now hold on a minute," Peru said to Flores. "Don't do nothing in a hurry. You like jewelry? Tessie's got stuff that'll knock your eye out. Hey, baby, show him your diamond ring."

Tessie frowned. "Oh no you don't, Ricco Perucese. You're not going to give anybody *my* jewelry. You think I won't need something to live on in my old age?"

Peru gave a strangled gasp. "For the love of Mike, baby, it's only a ring, for Chrissake. You realize what's going on? What could happen to me?"

"Sure," Tessie said, glaring. "Maybe I got to think what could happen to *me*, for a change."

Peru wore a look of disbelief. The soldiers began walking him out to the corridor. The first soldier asked Flores were they taking their captive to the firing squad. Flores said no, the generalissimo doesn't want to be so easy on him. He will work to death in the bauxite mine. Throw him on the truck to Barahona.

Sixty

Kiki Sue in her arms, Aisling stepped to the frosted door of the inner office, twisted the knob, and quietly stepped inside. The new president sat in his swivel chair, back toward them, facing away from his desk piled high with papers, staring out of the window at a pear tree shedding white blooms.

Aisling set the little girl down, tiptoed up behind him, and clapped both hands over his eyes.

"What the hell!" Knox said, sputtering. He broke loose and spun around, ready to deliver a karate chop. Then his face broke into a grin.

"Oh it's you. What are you doing sneaking up on a man like that?"

"Maureen had to go take a pee. We let ourselves in."

"Mother of God, this child is growing. Come over here, kid. How heavy are you?"

He stuck out his arms and Kiki Sue stumbled toward him, clumsy in new shoes. Knox picked her up and sat her in his lap. She happily sucked her thumb.

Aisling squashed down into a leather chair and beamed across the desk. "So you're the president."

"Until they find somebody better."

"They won't. And I hear they're making you a monsignor. Listen, Father, I had to see you. There's something we need to work out."

"If it's about your next year's contract, it's in the bag. You're promoted. Associate prof from now on. Few hundred more bucks."

"Oh. Thanks. But that wasn't what I meant."

Knox eased back in his chair, rocking the child, looking at Aisling intently. Then he deposited the little girl on the oriental rug. "You're my second visitor this morning," he said. "Pohl came to see me. Told me his summer plans."

"What's he doing?"

"Taking off for Mississippi. He had a big win in a crap game, and now he wants to see about those rednecks that bombed his grandmother's church. I tried to talk him out of it, but he's determined. At least he'll have plenty of support. He's taking Willie the Wire. Those rednecks had better watch out."

"How's your new job?"

"Work. But somebody's got to do it. Start building the new gym. Raise dough. Few other things."

"Now about this talk we have to have—"

Maureen's voice came through the intercom. "Call from Washington. The Undersecretary of State."

Knox picked up the phone. "Yes, this is Knox. Uh huh. The Dominicans complained, did they? General Trujillo? Insulted and manhandled, was he? He got what he deserved."

A squawk from the phone.

"You heard me," Knox said. "And you can tell the Dominicans that if that son of a bitch ever comes around here again we'll give him worse." He slammed down the phone.

"That's telling him, Father," Aisling said. "Now about what we need to talk about—"

Tim Walsh burst in. He nodded to Aisling and blurted out his problem. He was having a hard time returning some war surplus material. The government didn't know how to take it back.

Knox drummed fingers on his desk. "Well, you're the business manager. Do something. If Washington won't take it, give it to the poor."

"Eighty cases of ammunition?"

"Sure. Help 'em win the class struggle."

"What are you, Doug? A commie?"

"Red as the cardinal's hat. Why not call the National Guard Armory, see if they'd take the stuff."

Lynch went out. Knox looked at Aisling. "You were saying?"

"Let's not try to talk here. Come over to my place tonight. We can have a drink together."

"Can't. Got a banquet to go to. Come on, spill it. What have you got to say?"

"There's something between us now."

Knox ground out his Gaulois. "It's over."

"It doesn't have to be. You're under all this pressure. Maybe I could ease it for you."

"That's nice of you, honey. But I can't take you up on it."

"Why not? Who'd have to know? You can come to my place any time. And you won't have to father anything. I'll tie my tubes."

Knox flared. "You want another secret affair? Another phony arrangement like the one you had with Vastasi? No good, sister. There's been too much cover-up around here. People are looking to me to shoot straight now. It's a whole new season."

"And what about me? Don't I matter to you? God damn it, you dried-up Dominican, you're the best man I ever laid. I'm sitting here juicing my pants for you."

"Quit it."

"I can't. You're—you're cruel."

Knox turned away from her, looking out the window. "I don't want to hurt you," he said, "but that screw in the closet was a one-time thing. I'm still doing penance for it."

"So what am I supposed to do?"

He swiveled around and looked at her hard and long. "Find yourself a good man. Somebody not a crook, not a priest. Somebody you wouldn't mind living with, you and your child."

"We could have so much fun together."

"Not in this life. Now get your sweet ass out of here, Professor Weinstein, before I boot it out."

Tears stung her eyes. She raced around the desk, crushed a powerful kiss on Knox's mouth, scooped Kiki Sue into her arms, whirled, and ran.

Maureen came in with a sheaf of papers to find Knox wiping lipstick away. She gaped. "Why, Father."

Knox scowled up at her. "Not anything like what you might think," he said.

Moon's grandmother had thrown a send-off party for him in the back yard. She had grilled hamburgers and dished out re-baked Campbell's beans, a Jell-O and carrot salad, and upside-down cake. People had washed it all down with a keg of Pabst Blue Ribbon. Moon's Aunt Millie had offered to knit him a sweater. Never mind, he told her, the Navy would supply him with clothes. His Uncle Jake had dug him in the ribs and warned, "Boy, when you're in Norfolk stay away from East Main Street. Them scurvy bars like the Red Rooster. They got whores too old and smart for you."

The following morning, he had stopped in the college president's office to say goodbye.

"You'll excuse me for saying this," Knox told him, "but the first time I laid eyes on you I wrote you off as a jerk. But you're not. Not totally."

"Thanks, Father," Moon said.

"That story you wrote about the rifles. Helped bust the war surplus racket. And we wouldn't have got out of the warehouse if you hadn't exploded those corpses. You really need to drop out of school, huh?"

"Temporarily. I don't want my grandmother to put me through college. She can't afford it. After I get out of service in four years, the government will pay for me."

Knox nodded thoughtfully. "Yeah, it makes sense. I'd like to give you a scholarship, but after everything this place has been through, we're broke. Anyhow, the Navy just might season you. Don't bother to write. I'm no good at answering letters. But any time you're home, stop back and see me, OK?"

And the wiry guy came out from behind the big desk and surrounded him in a bear hug.

That afternoon Moon found himself standing in a hot upstairs room at 90 Church Street, lower Manhattan, under a portrait of Harry S. Truman. He and thirty-nine other recruits raised their right hands and swore. Then a balding chief boatswain's mate lined them up and filed them through a door out onto a platform to a bus marked NAVAL TRAINING CENTER BAINBRIDGE. A paperback copy of *Moby Dick* was the only thing Moon was taking along with him to boot camp from civilian life.

"No, Miss, you can't come in here," the chief was protesting.

"The hell I can't," shrilled a woman's voice that he knew.

Aisling had shoved her way out onto the bus platform. Long red hair liberated, crammed into a flimsy white summer dress with no trace of an underlying bra, she bounded to Moon and handed him a box of fudge. Moist full lips crushed his own and her body clamped tight against him, warm hips grinding into his pelvis.

From the recruits already on the bus came a chorus of catcalls, whistles, and screams. "Jeepers! They're dry fucking!"

Moon felt a powerful stirring in his loins. If circumstances had permitted, he could have consummated his love for her at last. Right there on the bus platform.

She drew back far enough to look into his eyes. "This is just so you remember me."

"As if I could forget you," Moon said. "Will you wait for me?"

"Don't be silly. See this?" She held up her left hand, displaying the glint of a small diamond. "I'm engaged," she said. "To the Sarge."

Moon was thunderstruck. "You'd marry *him*?"

"Why not? He's a great stud, and he'll make Kiki Sue a good father. Maybe he has some rough edges, but I'm working on him."

"All right. Go ahead and marry him. But I'll never love anyone else. I promise—"

She clamped a hand across his mouth. "No! No promises! Listen, James, find yourself some sweet babe your own age. Someone inexperienced, like you. And when you find her, you go for her."

At his elbow the chief rasped, "Come on, move it, sailor. Miss, dammit, will you kindly get out of here?"

Aisling crushed Moon in one last full-body-length kiss. Then the chief was grabbing him by the scruff of the neck and the seat of his pants and hoisting him onto the bus. With a hiss of steam the driver slammed shut the doors.

Tremendous cheers greeted Moon as he stumbled to the last empty seat.

"Hey, dude, what's your secret?"

"Where do you pick up stuff like that?"

Already the bus was moving, heading down a ramp, slipping out into the street. Moon stared out with half-seeing eyes. In the air before him, a vision floated out of the traffic of lower Manhattan. Loretta in her blue prom dress. Not wearing a look of terror anymore. She gazed at him softly, the way she had looked at him that night on the riverbank. Her lips moved as if forming his name, saying goodbye. Then the apparition dwindled, thinned, and was gone.

A whole era was ending, his era of loneliness and frustration. The era of big bands. He would give one final performance, he'd be Glenn Miller leading his civilian orchestra in his last show, at a nondescript theater in Union City. It would be just the way he had read about it. The musicians, their pain dulled with reefers and beers struggling to get through "Moonlight Serenade." Vocalist Marilyn Hutton breaking down and blubbering, having to scamper offstage in tears.

Moon was Miller, Benny Goodman, Tommy Dorsey, Artie Shaw, Duke Ellington, Harry James all rolled into one. He'd say farewell with his trumpet—that was it. He lifted his horn to take a tremulous solo, *Stardust*. The notes came out long and mellow and round, as though fashioned of gold.

In the dim imagined theater Moon gazed out over the heads of the cheering crowd. He held the final note for a long moment, letting it gradually die away. With all his strength he tore the trumpet from his lips and flung it into the air, watching it spin end over end, releasing one last gleam. Then it vanished into the shadowy mass of the audience forever.